For our fathers,
Sven J. Hamrin
And Nicholas Wasylowski
And the women who loved them,
Rose and Anna

Psalm 127:3-5

Children are a gift from the Lord; they are a reward
from him.
Children born to a young man are like arrows in a
warrior's hands.
How joyful is the man whose quiver is full of them!

Sons

&

Daughters

Darcy and Fitzwilliam

Book Two

Karen V. Wayslowski

This book is a work of fiction. Any resemblance to institutions or persons, living or dead, is purely coincidental.

Cover design by
Hot DAMN DESIGNS
www.hotdamndesigns.com

Prologue

1823
"The Fathers"

"I don't understand how you had eight children and I only three. It makes no sense." Darcy strummed his fingers on the arm of his chair, his narrowed gaze fixed on his cousin. He absolutely hated to lose any competition to this man. "You're no more virile than I. Quite the contrary, in fact."
Fitzwilliam gave a snort of derision. "Bah! I am virility personified. It oozes from my every pore."
"Oh, is that what that is?"
"My seed practically leapt into her womb, for heaven's sake."
"Rather like a virus."

'Darcy and Fitzwilliam'

Karen V. Wayslowski, 2011

Chapter One

It was early morning, September, 1823, and the breeze from the open doorway was as crisp and clean as freshly laundered linens. The day promised to be a beautiful one; just the sort of day Fitzwilliam Darcy loved – autumn at its finest. He inhaled deeply. *Bracing*, was his considered opinion, *that's what it is - energizing.*

Then he caught a whiff of the Thames River and wrinkled his nose, searched for his handkerchief and sneezed.

Ah well. No matter, it was still his beloved city. It was London.

He turned back to his butler. "Winters, I should be home early for dinner this evening. Just something simple mind you, soup or eggs, nothing too spicy; no need for Mrs. Hobbs to prepare anything elaborate."

"You always do have an uncertain stomach when Mrs. Darcy and the children are not accompanying you, sir. Cook understands and generally makes the necessary adjustments to her menus."

"Absolutely right, the woman's a gem. Well, Mrs. D and the chicks should be here by the end of the week. I'll warrant Cook is eager to begin baking her sweets for the little ones. She spoils them dreadfully."

"She tries her best to, sir, as we all do."

Smiling, Darcy shrugged into his great coat. "I've several arduous appointments before me today, Winters. Ghastly, horrid hours that very well may have me bald by morning."

His butler tilted his head. "I had no idea you were to see Lady Catherine today, sir. Shall I summon your coach?"

Darcy tried not to laugh outright. The man had correctly guessed that one of his appointments that day would, indeed, include his formidable aunt.

"No, thank you Winters, it's too lovely a day. It should be splendid a walk."

"As you wish, sir."

Bowing respectfully to his employer the butler stepped back inside then closed the imposing doors to Pemberley House, providing Darcy with a rare moment alone, to stand and simply admire his surroundings. His gaze swept first across its pediment gables, its heavy cornices, its towering white columns. He loved everything about this house, every brick — even that creaking and immense iron lamp that hung above the front door. Suspended from two stories overhead, it was always lit, day or night, whenever any Darcy family member was in residence; a tradition as old as the house itself. It was lit now and he smiled.

Tradition.

This home contained his family's history, from his great, great grandfather's original frame structure, innovative for its day, to his grandfather's brick and stone rebuild, expanding the original structure to nearly three times its size, then on to his father's addition of a second story with larger bedrooms, individual sitting rooms, and a second library. Now, an unheard of third story had been added, housing the new nursery and schoolroom of the modern age, in addition to the upgraded servants' quarters. His latest improvement to the back of the house was a completely redesigned and most modern kitchen. He loved to keep everything up to date and state of the art. Each family had added and improved upon the previous; each family's unique character was impressed within the stones. Darcy loved both his homes, the one here in London and the ancestral estate in Derbyshire; both represented cornerstones in his world – stability, elegance, dignity... *Pride.*

Settling his fashionable beaver hat securely upon his perfectly coifed head Darcy looked to the street as he began to pull on his gloves. Two women passing by whispered their admiration at the sight of him, his Marcella waistcoat worn with the poise of royalty, his snow white cravat, his buff colored pantaloons...

His *huge* garrick.

He was, simply put, the perfect picture of masculine sophistication. Framed there between the lofty columns of his front portico Fitzwilliam Darcy was truly a sight to behold. At six and thirty years he was at the very pinnacle of his good looks, an esteemed leader in his community; and, he was staggeringly wealthy. Unfortunately, for the two brazen women openly flirting with him he was also very happily married and completely uninterested.

To the outside world an aura of exception had surrounded Darcy, his form and life blessed by the gods. The truth was he thought little of his looks. He considered any physical beauty attributed to him the gift of a lovely mother and an exceedingly tall, debonair father. If the then resulting arrangement of features had turned out sound, well, *that* was a mere chance of birth, not a hard won accomplishment. To his way of thinking his younger sister, Georgiana, was much the better looking, and she played the pianoforte.

Be that as it may, all others agreed this grand personal good fortune of his – his physical appearance, his great wealth – would carry him blissfully into the future. After all, humanity naturally bowed to perfection. He had every right to feel proud, arrogant, and even superior.

Except for one small thing...

Darcy knew it was all fleeting. He had seen it happened to a dozen acquaintances, had heard of a hundred more. Good looks fade – *everyone's* – eventually. One's money could easily be lost to disaster or illness; misfortune could strike at you from nowhere, one's elevated position in society could be reversed in a moment.

Oh, he supposed at one time in his life he *had* been proud to a fault. He had existed only within his own small set of acquaintances, had numbed himself to outsiders.

Then he met Elizabeth Bennet.

Initially they had fought their attraction to each other but now he could not remember life before her or imagine life without her. Capturing and loving Elizabeth had been the first true miracle of his life.

And then, through the astounding physical joining of man and woman, he and Elizabeth had created their precious, dear children, his heart and soul, his gift to all future generations. This was what he considered to be the second true miracle.

He had become a father.

Chapter Two

Deciding that such a find day warranted taking the long way round to his Aunt Catherine's house (truthfully any day warranted that) Darcy headed south on St. James Street toward the square. The roads were not unduly crowded at ten in the morning, but there was some activity. Nursemaids strolled with their carriages, delivery carts rumbled by, and hansom cabs waited at curbs. Occasionally a particularly fine coach would cross his view, peaking his interest.

When he reached Mall Street he turned to his right, observed the usual morning bustle about Buckingham Palace in the distance, noted the vehicles entering and leaving, some familiar, some foreign. No appointments there today, thank goodness. Across St. James Park, along the River Thames, stood Westminster and Parliament. That would be his final destination this afternoon, meetings lasting a greater part of the day as he and his fellow Derbyshire landowners discussed the current Whig reform debate.

Possessing one of the borough's largest land holds his family's future welfare needed safeguarding. Of immediate concern to him were the so called Rotten Borough and Pocket Borough voting irregularities in the House of Commons.

Darcy and the others were unhappy with their borough's member of Commons, one William Cavendish, a cousin of the very powerful 5th Duke of Devonshire. It was a delicate situation in Derbyshire, a form of family squabble occurring in the midst of a national debate. Momentum was building in the House of Commons for reformation but the House of Lords was unsympathetic, and the general belief was that the Duke of Devonshire had long ago lost interest. He loved his dogs and his hunting above all else and would just as soon leave matters as they had been for generations.

Darcy's walking stick banged the cobbles a little harder on that thought, sending a surprisingly strong vibration up his arm. Darcy was a patient man, easily as proud as the Cavendish family and nearly as aristocratic, unaccustomed to having reasonable requests ignored. His tolerance was growing thin. Again, as if to emphasize its agreement with his anger, his walking stick took it upon itself to bash against a coach stand.

Half way around the park Darcy checked his pocket watch, assuring himself he was still early for his first meeting of the day, that with his aunt, Lady Catherine de Bourgh. It was always one of three things when he was summoned into her presence like this. Either she was: one, feeling poorly and submitting to imminent death, two, there was a problem with the accounts and she required someone to blame, or three, she had a grievance with her other nephew, Darcy's cousin, Richard Fitzwilliam, a man who had recently, and most reluctantly, become heir to the family title after the death of his older brother.

If it was the third he would soon find himself involved squarely in the middle of a *real* family squabble. He loved both his aunt and his cousin very much – just not together. Together the two often fought like cats in a sack; and he, Darcy, was usually caught in the middle. His cane suddenly crashed into something metallic and created a terrible racket. Apparently he had just whacked the bloody hell out of an iron fence.

Seeing as how his mood was far from improving, and fearing further damage to his grandfather's cane, he slipped the stick beneath his arm and continued on with his stroll. Lost in thought he contemplated his second meeting of the morning with that very cousin, Richard Fitzwilliam. *And good heavens wasn't that poor man's life suddenly a mess?*

Richard's father, considering his son a directionless young man, had years before purchased for him a commission in the army (one of the only respectable career paths open to the nobilities' second sons). Twelve years later, the wars with Napoleon finally over, Richard returned from the Battle of Waterloo a National Hero. His father was content, but Richard was not, feeling as if he was back where he started – without direction, without purpose and without money.

Everything changed, however, when he fell in love. It was his love of, and marriage to, an American widow that began the rift within that family. The father and son ceased speaking and the subsequent estrangement and loss of funds forced Richard to the unthinkable – employment to support his wife and child. No true aristocrat would ever consider working for a living. Richard had not only considered it, he was actually employed.

It was soon after that Richard's older brother, Regis, was killed in an accident. Richard was now his father's heir, the future Earl of Somerton. He was *furious* with his brother for dying like that and leaving the expectations of the entire Fitzwilliam family upon his shoulders. Richard's father was *furious* because his heir was dirtying his hands with manual labor, married to a common colonial.

Richard's Aunt Catherine was *furious* – well, just because she was Aunt Catherine. It was what *she* did for a living.

Darcy's stomach roiled. He was formulating lists already and his day hadn't even begun. In fact, such a wretched day lay before him that he briefly entertained the thought of turning round, walking briskly back to his home and crawling into bed.

Home. Soon Lizzy would arrive with the children. Darcy sighed and shook his head. There would be toys everywhere, much too much noise to properly concentrate, *'don't tease your sister'*, women's trinkets and gee gaws mixed somehow with his cuff links and stick pins, *'if your friend jumped from the roof, would you do that also'*, experimental foods forced upon him, tears, laughter, recrimination, *'I said 'no' child - that is the reason and the only reason you need'*, visits from family, bickering, *'Elizabeth, I don't need a physician's opinion - it's an earache'*; disagreements...

It all sounded absolutely lovely, like... *home.* His shoulders relaxed and Darcy smiled once again.

The final ten blocks passed by much too quickly and soon Darcy found himself standing before Rosings Place, the town house of his aunt. He knocked loudly. Jamison, his aunt's long suffering butler, had slowed from old age and was notoriously hard of hearing, especially when Aunt Catherine was addressing him. If the man was avoiding one of Aunt Catherine's bad moods any response could be a while coming. The door was opened to him after several long moments.

"Mr. Darcy." The elderly retainer betrayed none of his surprise, merely inclined his head then backed into the foyer to allow the esteemed visitor immediate access. "Forgive one's delay. One was not expecting visitors this morning."

"Jamison." The two had a very long and very fond history together – in fact there had never been a time when Darcy had not known of Jamison. As a child Darcy had secretly believed the man to be the very thing about which old London town had been constructed.

Darcy turned his back to one of the under butlers who relieved him of his coat then he handed Jamison his hat, gloves and cane. Jamison in turn passed those articles to another.

"How is one feeling today, Jamison?"

"Quite well, sir. Thank you. Apart from one's knees. And you, sir?" There was a faint light of humor in the old man's eyes.

"Knees still good, eyes dimming, ears failing. Soon sense of taste will be my only joy in life. Is my aunt in her sitting room?"

"Yes, Mr. Darcy. If one can speak freely..." At Darcy's nod, the man continued in a confidential tone. "She is again taking her 'daily medicinal' beverage, as are both Miss Anne *and* Mrs. Jenkinson."

"Damnation."

"Precisely, sir.'

That shocking information conveyed, Jamison continued on in his usual formal way. "Will you be going over the accounts today, sir? We were expecting you on your regular day of Wednesday; however, her man of business, Mr. Holt, has only just left. One is certain one could have your desk prepared for you."

"No. I was summoned here today for some other horror – excuse me – purpose; what, I haven't a clue.

You wouldn't happen to know, would you? No, I thought not. A good general never shows her hand, and my aunt is nothing short of a military genius at times. I will need to leave by one at the latest, however, so if you could pop in, remind me when that time comes around?"

"Of course, Mr. Darcy."

Stalling a bit Darcy shot his cuffs, smoothed down the front of his shirt and fussed with his cravat, then passed his hand through his hair. "Good. Well, that's it then, I had better see what she wants."

"That would be very wise, sir."

They both stood by the family parlor door, heads bowed in uneasy silence.

"Are you watering down her sherry as we discussed?"

"Medicinal beverage, sir."

"Are you watering down her medicinal beverage as we discussed?"

"Absolutely, sir. However, one does believe this maneuver merely provides her with the excuse to now have an additional, late afternoon, medicinal beverage, sir."

"My word – she's very devious isn't she?"

"That has always been one's opinion, sir."

"Mr. Jamison?"

"Yes, Mr. Darcy?"

"How *have* we both remained loyal to my aunt for so very long?"

The butler thought seriously about his answer before he spoke.

"One supposes it is that she truly does need us, Mr. Darcy."

Darcy smiled and nodded. "You are a giant amid midges, Mr. Jamison."

The butler softly rapped at the door and began to turn the knob at Lady Catherine's command. He inclined his head slightly to acknowledge the compliment. "That has always been one's belief, sir."

Chapter Three

"The children, they are well, Darcy?"

"Yes, Aunt Catherine. The children are very well, thank you." *Just as well as they were five minutes ago when you last asked.* He rolled his eyes as his aunt tossed back a second glass of 'medicinal liquid'. Darcy had for years consulted with the many doctors who attended her and after very careful consideration they had all come to the unanimous conclusion that excessive use of spirits in the treatment of her constant heart complaints was unwise.

His aunt had, in turn, found herself more accommodating doctors.

As her eyes drifted closed her nephew cleared his throat.

"Ah, Darcy, you're here at last." Surprised at finding her glass empty she motioned for a refill. "You *must* try my new medicine – I am feeling ever so relaxed, much more 'the thing' as the young people say. My, doesn't Anne look lovely in brown? Wake up, Anne, don't slouch. Brings a sort of pallor to her skin so abnormal in nature as to be appealing, is it not? No, don't smile Anne, never laugh nor grin; you will develop wrinkles, my dear. My skin is as smooth as it was when I was ten and seven and do you know why? That was a rhetorical question, Anne; no answer is wanted. Where was I? Oh yes, my delicate complexion. My porcelain-like facade is due solely to the fact that I have not really enjoyed myself in over forty years."

Patience, Darcy he inwardly groaned. Patience was the thing needed when dealing with parents, aunts or uncles as they grew older. *Aunt Catherine must be nearing six hundred years by that reckoning...* Accepting a glass of the brownish liquid from his aunt's hand he took a tiny sip to appease her. His eyes flew open as the liquid fire was swallowed. "Good god! What in bloody hell is in this drink?!" he began to reach frantically for water.

"Your language, sirrah!" Her nephew's sudden shout and gagging sound had brought the quizzing glass up to her eye. "This is *medicine*, young man, med-i-cine. It needs to be strong. This mixture is specially blended to fight off possible infections of the lung."

"It could fight off the Huns."

Catherine narrowed her gaze at this comment and a moment of silence was savored by all before her attention wandered.

"Darcy, I hear Elizabeth refused to return to the city with you. Why I wonder?" So much for benevolent silence. "Does she have too many *cicisbeos* attending her perhaps?" Darcy kept his lips firmly sealed and stared her down as long as possible.

He broke first.

"Why do you bedevil these topics every few months? Elizabeth is not with me at present because she remained behind in comfort to her sister, Jane, who has suffered a miscarriage. Meetings already scheduled in town forced me to leave Elizabeth and the children at Netherfield. I can assure you she will arrive here at any moment."

"It's nothing to me..."

"Yes, and I'm gratified to hear you acknowledge that. And, there are no *cicisbeos* in our home. Not one. Only children and dogs, a number of ferns and perhaps one or two cats."

Catherine was fast losing interest now and had begun fussing with her hair and fichu, resituating to her cheek a small black patch that had wandered perilously close to her lips. "Never mind about that — have you spoken with your cousin? Not this one, the other. No, don't tell me, I have sworn to neither speak *of* him nor *with* him ever again and I shall tell him so directly when he and his family come for dinner on Sunday. I should like you to come also, Darcy. I am at my wits end with Agatha. She never acknowledges me when I speak at her, merely stares at her hands; very rude. But, she *is* American."

"Amanda, Aunt Catherine."

"Pardon?"

"Her name is Amanda. If she did not reply to you that could very well be the reason."

"Well, who is Agatha then?"

"I have no idea."

"Are you certain of this, Darcy? She's a tallish woman, comely in a dark light, masses of unruly hair, large, wet, brown eyes like a spaniel. Dreadful accent."

"How many wives could he have, Aunt Catherine? Yes, she is one and the same."

"Oh, how very suspicious. I wonder what necessitated her change of name? It won't help her situation you know, she's still foreign. No one will recognize her and all the political capital that fool of a nephew of mine acquired at Waterloo is now laid to waste. He could have done great things in the House of Lords, momentous things. I always said he was more suited to the Earldom than that idiot brother of his, Regis! And, he is still very well regarded among a certain raffish segment you know. Richard I mean, not Regis. And my brother is so very like his son, Richard – stubborn, foolhardy! He cried tears of joy when Richard was elevated to Colonel on his own merit. Now they barely speak."

"There were steps being taken toward reconciliation, were there not?"

"There has been a start, *I* have seen to that; but, for some reason it is still strained between them. The problem of course always was, and always will be, that American wife of his. Richard's wife, that is, not his father's. His father's wife was Scottish. She's dead now, did you know? Resembled a Foo Dog when she was alive, more's the pity. Now that she's dead I have no idea what she resembles..."

"Aunt Catherine, you're drifting again."

"Don't be ridiculous, my mind is as sound as...something. What was I saying? Ah, yes; what's her name is certain to be a hindrance to him when he takes his father's place in the House of Lords, you mark my words. How in the world will she entertain? *Whom* will she entertain?" Catherine began to fan herself briskly, old aggravations rising. "If still unmarried he would be in a position now to wed a Countess or a Duchess if he so chose, a *Princess* as well! Of course it would have to have been a rather *peculiar* Princess, but still and all..."

"Aunt Catherine, he loves her. Amanda is a very good wife to him and an exemplary mother."

"I never said she wasn't an adequate human being, Darcy. I like her well enough; merely that she won't do as a political wife." She spoke each word slowly, as if Darcy had suddenly lost his reasoning powers. "She simply will not do! It's not her fault, of course I realize that. I am nothing if not the soul of egalitarianism but were you aware that she oftentimes does her own cooking?" Catherine studied her cuticles for a moment. "You see what I am saying of course. She bakes bread, Darcy. I suppose she butchers the pigs and grinds the flour as well..."

"Catherine, that is barefaced snobbery."

"What *is* your point?"

"You frighten her!"

"Well, that's very kind of you to say, Darcy, but I shan't be moved. I have made overtures you know. I am more than willing to train the gel, perhaps start with something rudimentary but necessary, say the proper method of eating *Sole Meuniere* when dining with members of the Royal Family. However, my mere suggestion of that very thing set Fitzwilliam off into gales of laughter! Ignorant pup! I worry for that magnificent daughter of theirs."

"You refer, of course, to the daughter named for you."

She narrowed her gaze at her nephew. "I refer, of course, to the only daughter they have. Don't be ill mannered." Catherine smoothed a few imaginary stray hairs from her wig, then again resituated the slippery cheek patch. "The fact that she resembles me so closely in beauty is purely coincidental. I was thinking of *her* prospects really, more than Amelia's..."

"...Amanda," corrected Darcy.

"Whomever. As I was saying, I worry for Katherine Marie. I wish you to speak with him for me about this. I can prepare her for the future. That precious girl will surely suffer for her parent's misalliance..."

"She wouldn't be here but for her parent's misalliance..."

"...and I worry how she will make a suitable match without the proper training; without the guidance of a true aristocrat in her midst. Heaven knows

Fitzwilliam goes to great lengths in repudiating his heritage, engaging in demeaning physical labor."

"He is a member of the Ordnance Board, an appointment by the Crown through letters patent. He is Surveyor General, aunt – hardly what I would consider demeaning physical labor!"

"I am admiring your waistcoat, Darcy, very smart." Evidently her attention had wandered off again and Darcy hadn't noticed. "Well, thank you for stopping in to visit with your elderly aunt – a very pleasant surprise, I might add. Do you have any appointments today?"

He opened his mouth to remind her that this visit was her idea, but thought better of it. "I am to luncheon with Fitzwilliam then I have a meeting at Parliament regarding our Derbyshire MP problem. Cavendish is dragging his feet."

When it came to politics Catherine's mind was always sharp as a razor. "Cavendish is a puppet for Devonshire, don't ever forget that. Do be careful of those people, Darcy, a power struggle can be so very undignified. If you feel you must replace him take your time, train your man well, and then strike at the next election. I don't foresee you having much difficulty; the Duke can be a bit feeble minded at the best of times and is much weaker than he was. I never did care for that family, and his wife! Scandalous woman. Georgiana Spencer was infamous for behaving in the most common sort of way. The greatest beauty of her day they claimed! Poppycock! You know, of course, I debuted a few years later than she, otherwise..."

With one eye on the hall clock Darcy settled back to listen to this familiar and long winded harangue.

Chapter Four

It seemed to Richard Fitzwilliam, Baron Somerton when not at home, that his morning would never end. He had been besieged by the Royal Surveyors just returned from India with their long winded suggestions for map refinements and was now drowning in the inevitable paperwork snag. Five years earlier he had accepted the position of Surveyor General, a political office that often changed with the government of the day, and was currently reporting to Arthur Wellesley, the Duke of Wellington. Wellington had been his mentor for years, his friend and his former general in the Peninsular Wars; and, Richard had made a great success of his current position he supposed, but not in the way he hoped. He had envisaged traveling the world with his beloved family in tow, overseeing the plotting of exotic locales.

Instead, he spent hours entertaining humorless diplomats from foreign countries or the ignorant nobility of his own. But – well, it paid the bills and he could feed and shelter his growing family (speaking of which he made a mental note to speak with Amanda once again about this Catholic obsession with children. After all, they had five already; surely that was more than enough to appease the church. It was

time he put his foot down, metaphorically speaking –
time he took command of his own bedroom.)

He noticed a shattered cup on the floor behind a
chair and remembered his father's visit of the day
before. Richard had thrown the cup at the wall after
his father's angry departure and felt keenly again the
disappointment he was to that man. They had fought
bitterly, the same argument they often had – both
swaggering, both insulting, the threats becoming more
personal as the fight heated. His father was the finest
man he knew but too proud by far and stubborn, as
was his son. He dismissed the memory quickly. No
good could come of traveling that irritating road
again.

"You wanted to see me, colonel?" Patrick O'Malley,
Fitzwilliam's longtime batman, entered the room. The
two men often liked to enliven their boring working
hours the way they had entertained themselves
during warfare, by attempting to aggravate each other
as much as possible, usually successfully.

"O'Malley, you're sacked. I've been calling for you
for hours."

"That's a bit harsh, sir. Wasn't gone but a few
minutes. Maybe more."

"Where have you been?"

"I was takin' a piss, sir, and may have got carried
away with the sheer adventure of the thing."

"Well, piss on your own time. I need you to run
these papers over to the Peer's secretary for me. You
can go have a bite to eat after that since I'll be off as
well, that is if my cousin ever arrives. I don't expect
I'll be returning to the office until late. I'm to meet
Bretton and Finch upstairs later..."

Just then the door opened and in walked
Fitzwilliam Darcy.

"Darcy! It's about time you arrived!"

"Wonderful to see you as well, Fitz." Darcy then turned to O'Malley. "Hello, Patrick. Good to see you, how is Mrs. O'Malley?"

"Grand, sir. Just grand, and, I thank you for askin'. She's got a proper cap to wear now she does, enjoys bossin' around her new maid."

Fitzwilliam slammed a cup down to kill a roach.

"Excellent news, and well deserved I might add. And the boys? Getting quite tall I'll warrant."

"Growin' like weeds, they are, another on the way and, again, so good of you to inquire." Patrick swept away the dead bug with his hand then wiped his hand on his trousers.

"My, aren't you two delightful? A regular Tristan and Isolde without all that lovely prose to distract the mind. Well, as much as I hate to break up this heartwarming tableau I'm famished and you're nearly a quarter hour late, Darcy."

"And you're in a foul mood. Has he been like this all day, Patrick?"

"Naw. Most times, he's worse." With his packet of papers tucked beneath his arm, Patrick then turned and left before he was sacked once again.

"Well, White's or Brook's today, Darcy?"

"White's of course."

"Damn it to hell! I wagered you'd say Brook's, entered it into the book only yesterday." Fitzwilliam shrugged on his old overcoat, pulling his gloves out of his ancient beaver hat. "Don't look at me like that. You always go to Brook's when they serve brown trout."

"I never eat trout. You eat trout you big fool."

"Oh, you're right. *Damn.* The posted odds were awfully good too; ah well. You just cost me five quid so the meal is on you today. By the way, what color gloves have you on... *Damn!* That's ten quid you owe me now." He began to button his coat. "Darcy, out of curiosity, what do you buy Lizzy when she's out of sorts with you? Amanda and I had a bit of a disagreement this morning, haven't a clue as to why, I am a perfectly amicable fellow. Perhaps it's her woman's time. Lord, don't ever tell her I said that. I'll buy her something, maybe a hat."

"I wouldn't if I were you. Women are particular about fashion – a concept which I know is foreign to you."

"Are we speaking of women being foreign to me now or fashion?"

"Take your pick."

"By the way, she wanted to know when Elizabeth and the children will be here. Poor darling sounded pretty desperate."

"I'd say this week, possibly by Friday, Saturday at the latest. I could not begrudge Elizabeth staying behind with her sister, they've always been close."

"Quite right. The ladies take these mishaps very badly." Fitzwilliam locked the door behind him and both men walked down the long hallway in silence, lost in personal memories, recalling difficult pregnancies their own wives had suffered over the past few years. As fathers and husbands their very nature was to protect the family – but childbirth! Childbirth was outside their realm, unpredictable, very often dangerous. The terror of harm to the infant or of infection and worse to the women they loved, unthinkable.

They made their way down the high steps leading from the Home Office Building, returning greetings shouted to them and stopping frequently to exchange pleasantries with acquaintances, but lapsing into their usual companionable silence once alone on the street. Both were consumed with their own problems. Each man had family responsibilities now, problems unique to their separate lives. At one time they had been careless and reckless companions but now each walked down diverse paths, each dealt with distinctive and private pitfalls.

The sun began to peek in and out of darkening clouds and the winds were picking up strength. "It will be a bitter winter this year I fear." Darcy pulled his hat down farther and hunched his shoulders against the sudden cold.

"Probably so, my bones are aching already. I feel every one of my eight and thirty years today, and then some. Why in hell didn't you bring your carriage?"

"It was beautiful earlier this morning and you are endlessly complaining about being shut up indoors all day, how you miss an active life. I thought this would please you." Darcy's mood was growing as sour as his cousin's. "Please, no need to gush your appreciation and you can pay for your own damn meal. My lord you are a true pain in the arse when you're like this."

They continued on in silence for another block. Fitzwilliam spoke first.

"Sorry if I'm a bit waspish." Fitzwilliam cleared his throat and squinted into the distance. "I saw my father yesterday. It was not a pleasant experience."

"Ah."

"What do you mean, 'Ah'! Explain yourself!"

"Don't you start with me..." Darcy began to shout back and then closed his eyes in frustration. "I take it you and my uncle are still at odds, then."

Fitzwilliam somehow snarled and laughed at once. "That would consign us to a more civilized relationship than the reality. Truth is we very nearly ended up brawling on the floor. He's insisting I resign my post, and then I'm to follow him around House of

Lords like some lackey. He believes this endeavor will somehow instill respect into my thick skull for both my current title and the one to come. Ha! A lot he knows – as if anything could penetrate my thick skull! Do you know where he sits in there? Directly before the Lords Spiritual! I'd go mad, Darcy, if I was forced to take that seat in the future."

"What do you mean 'if'? There is no 'if', only 'when' – there's been a Fitzwilliam in Lords for years, centuries. You have no choice."

"No choice! Really? There has always been a Cavendish in Commons representing Derbyshire, am I right? You are not minding that bit of insurrectionism."

"It is not anywhere near similar. The safety and security of my family, my estate, my tenants – damn it my entire borough – is being threatened by an incompetent MP and a self-serving Peer and why in bloody hell does everyone believe I want to replace Cavendish, why is everyone saying that? We merely need his support for Reform. Bah, you're not even listening to me. You're just avoiding the true problem between you and your father."

Fitzwilliam's jaw clenched. "And what problem is that?" All of London society knew the reason for this current rift between father and son, the *ton* spoke of it in whispers behind closed doors, but none dared face the hotheaded colonel and say it out loud.

"Your wife."

"Well of all the – I should call you out for that."

Darcy rolled his eyes. "Oh, do be quiet! Everyone knows... "

At that moment two very pretty young serving maids passed between the men. The girls giggled coquettishly as they walked, wriggling their bottoms just a bit more than necessary; both had lowered their lashes but not before braving a wink at one handsome gentleman and a finger waggle at the other. Darcy and Fitzwilliam watched the entire procession in mute appreciation.

Then the women finally turned the corner and were out of sight.

"What were you saying?"

"Haven't a clue."

The two men began walking once again. "My father also demands that I return to Somerton and begin preparing myself for the future. He wishes me to meet with all his managers and his secretaries, learn about estate procedures, establish myself with the tenants..."

"That all sounds perfectly reasonable to me."

Fitzwilliam stopped walking and stared unseeing over his cousin's shoulder. He was clearly attempting to compose himself enough to speak. "Here's the part you don't know though, cousin, the part no one is to be told. Amanda is not wanted in the main house. Surprised? She must live separately in the dower house during any visit. Can you imagine? I nearly lost my mind with that one, I really did. 'You can visit her when you find you have need of her,' he said to me. I swear the damn old bastard was sneering as he spoke. She is to absent herself from any village functions we attend, or any private or public events. She's my wife, Darcy. When he insults her like this he insults me as well. He and I parted very acrimoniously."

Darcy was stunned. "But why would he say such a thing, Fitz?"

"He simply hates Americans. He finds them loud, crude; he dislikes their accent – he is still fuming over their blasted Revolution of forty-odd years ago, still resents his friends and relatives having died there! I'm to keep her hidden away, sneak over there like she's some sort of mistress instead of a wife. The children are acceptable in the manor house – that was good of him – but not their mother. I won't have her treated like this, Darcy. He insists she not fit to represent the family."

Darcy could see the hurt and anguish in his cousin's eyes. "Well. I suspect that's why Aunt Catherine said what she did. You know she's attempting to 'fix' things again. She mentioned she could take Amanda under her wing, educate her, and, possibly bring Kathy into her home for a spell, teach her..."

Fitzwilliam's gaze was intense. "I have heard all of Catherine's proposals, listened to all of her stupid demands, and I reject them. They are not going to hurt my wife, nor will they take our daughter from her. Darcy, let us be honest. They want the impossible. They want Amanda to somehow not be American. Well, she *is* American, that will not change no matter how many elocution lessons or dancing classes she attends. What in hell do they imagine she will do that is so shameful? My wife is a lady raised in a gentleman's home. All right, he was an *American* gentleman, but a gentleman nonetheless. Her manners are impeccable. It is only their own ingrained prejudices that have turned them away from her."

"You know there *are* cultural differences between the two countries. Have you ever considered that Amanda would appreciate some assistance? She's going to be lost at court when that time comes, Fitz; confused, frightened. And, worse yet, she will be at the mercy of the *ton*. Elizabeth can only be so much help. She's familiarized her with some of these cultural discrepancies; but, well frankly, Lizzy has no training for court either. She herself is a country girl, unsophisticated in the fine distinctions required. Perhaps if you went home, if your father could spend just a little time with Amanda, his prejudices would surely evaporate into thin air. He would be certain to learn what a fine person she truly is and he *will* soften, eventually. Keeping this distance between them will only continue his misconceptions."

Fitzwilliam studied the sky for a while in thought. "You may be right, brat," he said resignedly. "I don't know anymore – you may be right. She is a bit frightened of our future life. I suppose I can speak with her, see how she feels about all this. Damn, I feel very strange, as if I've lost my appetite. That's never happened to me before."

Chapter Five

"There he is, Hart; Mr. Darcy, how wonderful to see you. My goodness, the last time we met you were a young pup leaving for Oxford and understandably very excited to be on your own at last." Darcy arrived a bit late for his final meeting of the day. The imposing Duke of Devonshire was approaching. His hand was extended in greeting, a warm paternal smile upon his face, confirming an unheard of condescension by a Duke for an untitled member of his borough. Several people stopped in their tracks and turned to watch, whispering their amazement. "And so we meet again. I greatly admired your father, Mr. George Darcy, you know. Splendid fellow – had a real understanding of Bassets. Hart come over here, please."

The Duke's son and heir, the Marquess of Hartline, strolled to his side.

"So you're the fellow giving us such troubles. I say, good show. Grand to meet you, Darcy." The Marquess sounded polite but did not extend his hand in greeting as his father had. The two younger men covertly took each other's measure.

"Your Grace, Lord Hartline... you gentlemen do me a great honor and it's wonderful to see you both – but, where are the others? I had thought to meet

Creighton, Bestorfield and Sir Arthur Paisley. *Our* meeting with you both was not for another two hours or so."

"We dismissed them, Mr. Darcy." The Duke's smile was one of a man accustomed to having his way. "Why muddy the waters?"

"Darcy, you look vaguely familiar. Have we met before?"

Darcy's mouth twitched. "I believe we did your lordship, once – years ago, during a football game at Harrow."

"But we would not have attended at the same time certainly, ain't as young as you, I'm afraid. Wait, I remember participating in football matches only one time. Yes, that's it! Current Harrovians against Old Harrovians." His amusement faded with the remembrance; his eyes narrowed. "You and that big blonde fellow took quite a few yards. He was a terror on that field, tremendous kicker though. Whatever happened to him – swinging outside Newgate window by now I suspect. Kirkpatrick I think was his name, or Fitzhugh; he was as strong as an ox and mean as they come."

"He's my dearest friend and also my cousin. Richard Fitzwilliam."

"Sorry, no offense meant."

"Hart, I believe that's the Fitzwilliam lad. You remember the papers made a huge play of him for a while."

"Pater – you know if it ain't about horse or hound I've no interest in the thing."

"He's now Baron Fitzwilliam, heir to the Earl of Somerton," Darcy added with relish.

"The devil you say! Well, we're all old friends then, same club as it were."

"Your Grace, your meeting room is ready for your use now." A liveried servant had approached and led the three men down the hall a short way then bowed before the open doors of a private and exquisitely appointed salon. The Duke requested sherry to be delivered as they settled into their chairs.

"Now, we can chat about our real reason for wanting to meet with you, Darcy. Hart and I have been discussing this entire...situation; and, well, perhaps a bit of change *is* wanted – my cousin is nearly ready to retire from Commons anyway. Tell me, have *you* ever considered entering politics?"

The clock in the dimly lit hallway chimed, verifying the hour as very late. Fitzwilliam slowly climbed the stairs to his tiny library. Yawning, he crossed to his desk and picked up the day's correspondence, shuffled through them one by one. Correspondence from his father's secretaries, demands upon his time from the War Department, more bills, snappish note cards from his aunt... Bah, nothing unusual from the prior day. Unfocused, uncomprehending, unseeing, and bone tired, Fitzwilliam rubbed his red rimmed eyes and absently undid his hated neck cloth. He was hungry but too weary to eat and to top it all off, he dreaded to repeat the entire experience on the morrow.

"Sir?"

"Hastings, why the devil are you still up? You can retire, man; I've no need for you this evening." Hastings, an old soldier who had lost an eye at Badajoz, continued to concentrate intently at the far wall above his employer's shoulder. In spite of a severe limp, limited eyesight and his advancing age, he really had taken to this position amazingly well.

"Will you be requiring a tray or some tea? Perhaps a glass of port, sir?"

"No, thank you." After a day wasted among fools and senseless meetings, Fitzwilliam felt suddenly and irrationally lonely. "Has my wife retired for the evening?"

"Oh, yes, sir."

After a moment of silence Fitzwilliam realized the man still stood at his elbow making no attempt to leave. "Is there something else?"

"If I might have a word with you, sir? There was a minor incident today with cook, sir, and Mrs. Fitzwilliam. Apparently she – Mrs. Fitzwilliam – desired to help with the baking and cook became very agitated. Cook then (*ahem*) shed much of her clothes, sir, retaining only her apron over her chemise. Yes, it was quite a nasty sight I can tell you. She then proceeded to lock herself in the pantry – the cook, sir, not Mrs. Fitzwilliam. While employing spoons she commenced a dreadful racket. She tried to apologize most profusely – Mrs. Fitzwilliam, sir, not cook – however cook remained locked within that pantry for several more hours, loudly muttering the most dire invectives. I'm afraid her spells are getting worse. Cook's, sir, not Mrs. Fitzwilliam."

"Bad day was it?"

"Dreadful. I believe cook is one pea short of a casserole if I may speak frankly, sir. In fact, for a brief moment today cook believed herself to be Michelangelo, and, for some odd reason, Mrs. Fitzwilliam Pope Julius II. Well, she *is* getting older, ancient really."

"I trust we're still speaking of cook, not Mrs. Fitzwilliam."

"Exactly right, sir."

"Damn me. All right, all right. I had already begun inquiries for a replacement, seeing as cook's behavior has become odder by the moment this past month;

she's a soldier's widow so I'll call in some favors through the War Office. She has no one left, does she? What am I saying? Of course not – Mrs. Fitzwilliam would never have employed her if cook had a home, or any skills at all for that matter. The silly woman couldn't boil water without instruction." Fitzwilliam's lip twitched. "Cook, I mean. Not Mrs. Fitzwilliam."

The butler smiled warmly. "Mrs. Fitzwilliam does have a tender heart, sir. One cannot fault her for her goodness."

"Quite right, certainly." A bit *too* tender hearted, Fitzwilliam mused. At times their house resembled a haven for the poor, or a retirement facility for maimed military and their families. "Well, perhaps the day maid can keep an eye on cook during her particularly odd moments, just until we sort this out. We do still have the day maid, don't we? Well, that's good." Fitzwilliam had rarely seen the girl, a backward country lass and the daughter of a former private shot for treason. "Good night, Hastings." He pulled the chair back from his desk then sat and picked up his quill to pen a response to a friend.

It was a brief moment before Fitzwilliam realized the man *still* stood by his elbow. Apparently he'd have to pull out each bit of news piece by piece. "Anything *else* to report, Hastings?"

"Well, (*ahem*) apparently Master Matthew lost a tooth during an altercation with his little sister – they were both attempting to slide down the staircase banister, at the same time."

"Good lord. Were either of them injured?"

"I would not know, sir. Mrs. Fitzwilliam was most adamant in her desire to tend to them herself, no doctor was requested and there was no undo blood loss. At least nothing near as calamitous as the last incident. I also am to relay to you an urgent request of

Master Mark's. He had me promise that you would wake him, no matter what time you arrived home."

Fitzwilliam dragged his hand through his already mussed hair. *Damn.* He should have been home hours earlier, instead of drinking with Wellington and those penny-pinching bureaucrats he loathed so. He had little time with his children as it was and their young lives were speeding by much too quickly, the boys constantly into mischief, his adorable Kathy learning her abysmal behavior from them and rapidly becoming a hoyden in her own right.

"I'll go up now and see them for myself. Good night, Hastings."

Fitzwilliam peered inside first and then entered his twin boys' room. Bootless, he was moving as silently as his large frame could manage and yet the old floorboards creaked beneath his weight. His gaze went to the bed on the left where Matthew slept then he looked toward the bed on the right for Mark. When they were born he and Amanda had relied on different colored clothing to tell the identical pair apart, Matthew always in blue and Mark in green. Now, at five years of age, the boys were as different as night and day.

First born of the twins, Matthew was outgoing and adventurous; first to speak, first to wake, first to eat, last to sleep. He was eager for fun and when he could not readily find it, he'd simply invent his own entertainment. Screaming "death to dictators" he would drop sacks of flour from the upper windows, or, with a smashed tomato on his chest he would stagger around the front of the house pretending he'd been shot. Often he would infuriate by hiding pinecones in his father's boots when the poor man was already late for work, or he would compete with Mark to see how many kidney beans they could stuff up their noses. Once, he had even drawn with charcoal on his mother's face while she slept and then allowed her to answer a summons to the door that way. Matt was an endless supply of sport for the other children.

Punishment was rarely effective. Of course, Fitzwilliam reasoned rightly, he probably should not laugh outright when he learned of the antics.

Mark on the other hand was somewhat shy, a calming and cheerful counterpart to his brother, his best friend, and his fiercest champion. They were inseparable. Mark and Matthew knew each other's thoughts, felt each other's pains and guarded each other's secrets without hesitation.

Fitzwilliam smiled when he saw the small tooth sitting in the center of a plate on the table between the two beds.

"Papa, is that you?" a sleepy little voice whispered in the dark. The boy yawned loudly and stretched out his arms and his legs, then rubbed his eyes.

"Yes, Mark, it's me, but you should be asleep son."

"I have been trying ever so hard to stay awake though, Papa, I had to speak with you. I found a puppy today." He scrubbed his hands through his hair and over his face, eager to come fully awake now that he enjoyed his father's undivided attention. "She was hiding under Mister Demkirck's back porch and she was very hungry."

Fitzwilliam listened intently as his son described the day's adventures, a little voice passing on a child's version of the day's events. "She's tan with white socks and I named her Buttons. She's all alone, Papa, and very small. Mama and I asked the neighbors but they didn't know where she came from. May I keep her? Please?"

When Fitzwilliam was a boy there were hunting dogs and all manner of pets at his family's ancestral estate in Somerton, but only one elderly dog, Flash, lived in this worn old home of theirs in the city. "Well, since you've named the little mongrel, and she's nowhere else to go, I hardly think we could turn her out, could we?"

"Splendid." The boy smiled, his eyes still so heavy with sleep that he could barely keep them open. "That's what Mama said too, but she thought I should ask you." It was then that Fitzwilliam observed a small black nose peak out from beneath the covers. He brought the puppy out and laughed when he received a proper licking for his trouble.

"Has Buttons visited outside to do her business — what's this? Oh, see here, excuse me young *Master* Buttons. I believe Buttons is a he, Mark, not a she."

"Oh yes, I forgot." The boy yawned. "Mama and I took him out several times tonight. Buttons won't mess the house ever again and we're ever so sorry about the rug in your library. I'll take care of her, I mean him, I promise I will. I shall feed him and walk him and..."

There was sudden movement in the bed to the left then a flurry of small knees and elbows attempting to escape their confinement. Finally freed, Matthew scrambled to the edge of the bed, very nearly wide awake already. "Papa, is that you? Did you hear I lost my tooth! My mouth was so bloody, a really brilliant red, just like tomatoes! Beefy and I were racing for the banister and she tripped me but I never fell and was up right away and then I grabbed her leg but she screamed and then we were rolling around and..."

"Matthew, calm yourself! Are you hurt anywhere? Was Kathy? Are you certain? Let me see your mouth. No pain, son? Good. Now, young man, you know you are never to fight with girls! I have told you this a dozen times!"

"It wasn't a girl, it was Beefy."

His father rolled his eyes. "It's chilly, Matthew, get back under the covers." Fitzwilliam lifted the counterpane and gestured for his son to snuggle back inside. "First of all, your sister's name is Katherine. Not Beefy." He lifted a hand to stay his son's future objections. "Nor Bovine Legs. Do you understand? Nor Ox Face. Nor Buffalo Head either for that matter. And believe it or not she *is* a girl. Boys do not strike girls."

"I never did! If she said I did she's telling tales again! I would never really strike Buffa...Kathy. Well, hardly ever; she'd throttle me if I did that! I just grabbed her leg a tad, really her foot, and besides she tripped me."

"Matthew, enough."

"She bit my shoe!"

"Matthew..."

"I don't think she's right in the head."

"Enough!"

"Perhaps she could replace cook," giggled Mark, setting off a squealing gale of laughter from both boys.

"She was so mad, Papa! When she tried to bite my ankle I moved my foot and put my boot in her mouth instead and she bit it! Then she began screaming and she spit! It was so funny!" The boys laughed noisily.

"Matthew, go to sleep, please. Good gracious how does your poor mother deal with this all day! We will speak tomorrow, all of us."

"Does that mean you'll be home when we awake? Excellent. We drew you a picture of Buttons. Mark can keep her can't he? Please. He really truly likes her; it would mean a great deal to him. Can we go to the park? Tomorrow I mean. I can ride soon – but, you told me I could! No, you did, Papa. You promised!

Georgie is already riding. You never let me ride! I am not allowed to do anything. How can I become a general if I never..."

Fitzwilliam cupped his hand over his son Matthew's mouth. "*Silence*. Go to sleep – you are wearing me out!"

It took several minutes more of stern discussions, sensible reasoning and threats of terrible consequences to settle the boys back under the covers. When Fitzwilliam closed the door, however, he heard the whispers begin anew. *Bloody hell...* He banged hard on the door. "I can still hear you two!" He shouted.

It was a moment before Matthew spoke. "You can leave now. We're sleeping."

Moving on to his daughter Kathy's room he found his little girl too near the edge of her bed for his liking. One roll and it would not be the first time she'd fallen out of bed sending up frightened cries in the night and waking everyone. He went quickly over and chuckled at the sight before him.

Her thumb was shoved into her mouth, the covers tossed as usual, this way and that, and her face bore the faint remnants of 'war paint'. Amanda must have been reading to the children from the new Fennimore Cooper book, 'The Pioneers', again. Chuckling he picked her up as gently as possible, repositioned her onto her back in the middle of the bed then covered her, tucking her in tightly.

There was no chance she would awaken; she never did. When deep in sleep like this it was as if she had passed out from drink rather than playful exhaustion, and she always slept straight through the night. *The sleep of the innocent,* he thought, or in Katherine's case, the sleep of the wickedly worn out.

"Good night, Beef." He smoothed back her wispy blonde hair and admired her baby soft skin, pink round cheeks now flushed with sleep, her impossibly long lashes, her pink, tulip mouth that suckled energetically on her thumb. How much longer would she follow him about with her arms raised, he wondered – demanding to be picked up, needing his attention? And then when he finally would pick her up she would cover his cheeks with kisses.

Tears nearly came to his eyes. She really was perfection. How in the world the twins had come up with the name Beefy for her was a mystery. Well, perhaps she was a little bit plump, but she was his baby, she had years to slim down, accept gentlemen callers, marry...his jaw tightened at the very thought. He bent to kiss her forehead.

Her only reaction was a long sigh then a reenergized attack upon her poor thumb.

His final stop was his stepson Harry's room. The lad was ten years old and as much a child of his as any of the others. Fitzwilliam's heart always swelled with paternal pride whenever he spoke of him. The handsome boy excelled in his studies, was a natural at all sports and was a born charmer; he also possessed the grace of a young aristocrat, a legacy from his late father, a baronet. Of more importance than all that, however, was the child's incredible nature, good and true. Not for the first time did Fitzwilliam grin over the fact that this most faultless of the Fitzwilliam offspring was not a Fitzwilliam at all, but a Penrod.

The three children actually sired by Fitzwilliam were a rowdy lot - *blood will tell,* he thought ruefully. Well, perhaps he was being a bit unfair. They were wild young pups yet, none older than five years, surrounded with unconditional love.   Whereas,

Harry's first five years had been difficult to say the least; that had to have left its mark, poor lad. Harry might not be a child of his by blood but he certainly was his child in heart. Fitzwilliam pulled the boy's covers up higher then lowered the window on the night chill.

How different this all was from when he was growing up in the family country estate of Somerton. There had been acres of land as a playground, dozens of servants, governesses, tutors. In fact, by Harry's age he had owned his own horses, a half dozen of them, plus he had begun fencing lessons at the hand of a hired master, and was traveling to Scotland, Germany, Italy and Paris regularly with his family. Was his stubborn pride and this rather hard scrabble path he'd chosen fair to them, depriving his children of their birthright? One word to his father and they could enter a world of privilege unimaginable to them now, a world he disliked intensely. But, after all, he *would* inherit one day, they *would* need to move in those circles eventually. What difference did a few years make? But Amanda would be so hurt if she knew what was truly going on; she had no idea of the hatred his father had for her...perhaps he would talk with her. Yes, they should talk. Bah. He couldn't think clearly at the moment, tired as he was.

Chapter Six

He saw them, wife and infant, both sleeping soundly in a chair near the window, both swaddled in blankets. The baby had drifted off as he nursed, a tiny hand still resting on Amanda's bare breast as her head was slumped to the side and a rhythmic snore could be heard loudly and clearly, even from across the room.

"Who's this little man then?" Fitzwilliam took the babe from her arms, rubbing the little ones back for only a moment before a sudden and energetic burp erupted. The child's eyes grew wide in amazement. "Didn't know you had it in you, did you, son?" he laughed out loud. "Excellently done, Luke – you keep that up and you'll not only be surpassing the twins for crudeness but also become an incredible humiliation to your mother." Despite this high praise sleep overwhelmed the infant once more and his wobbly head slowly drooped forward. Fitzwilliam laid him in his cradle, carefully wiping a small drop of mother's milk from the boy's lower lip.

"Husband? Is that you?"

"If you feel the need to ask, Amanda," he rested his hands on his hips, "it rather makes me wonder who else is entering our bedroom while I am off working my fingers to the bone." Always beautiful in his eyes,

Fitzwilliam especially loved to look at her in moments like this. Dazed, vulnerable, warm as a soft kitten — then of course there was that added feature of her breast being bared to his view. *Ah, my wife.*

"Richard, what am I to do with you? Why are you sleeping in your good trousers…" her voiced slowly trailed off, her head slumped forward and she began to snore once again.

"It's good to see you also."

There had been a time when the view of her breast bared as it was now would reduce him to a babbling idiot, a twitching, panting imbecile; but, after five years of marriage he had grown accustomed to such a lovely privilege. Smiling, he reached out to gently pull her wrapper closed.

"Amanda," he whispered. "Come to bed. You're going to be very sore tomorrow if you've been sleeping here for as long as I suspect."

"What?" Her eyelids began to blink slowly.

"Come to bed."

"What time is it?" Yawning, she placed her hand on his and attempted to focus.

"Nearly midnight."

"You're dressed, are you leaving for somewhere? Oh! Dear St. Timothy's bones, where is the baby! I've lost Luke! Don't step anywhere."

"I wondered when you'd notice. Luke is already in his cradle."

"Did I place him there?" She rubbed her eyes.

"No, you did not. I did. Whatever were you thinking, nursing him here by the window? You both could have caught a draft and why is that fire out?"

"I was watching for you and I suddenly grew very tired." As her mind cleared she looked deeper at her husband's face, his weary eyes. "Oh my stars, did you say midnight – and you're just coming home! Oh Richard, you must be exhausted. Have you eaten?"

"I had something with Darcy at the club earlier. Did he come by for supper with you and the children as I told him he should? No. That idiot; too proud by half."

"Why didn't you let me know – "

" – no time really."

"I feared perhaps you were still angry."

"What? Amanda, I distinctly remember that you were the one who was angry at me!"

"A likely story. You look very tired, Richard, they're working you too hard at –."

" – cease your harping on that subject! Did you take your stomach medicine, where are – "

"Now who's harping? Yes, of course I took them. I'm not as foolish as – just look at your waistcoat! How did you burn your pocket?"

They spoke in the half verbal, half memorized conversational battles that married couples develop over time; yet, as soon as he helped her to her feet their arms were about each other, the warmth and security of love healing all their wounds.

It was their union that sustained them both.

"Damn but it's good to be home," he mumbled into her neck and sighed. Her hair smelled clean and felt cool and soft pressed into his cheek. Cupping the back of her neck, he tilted her head back so he could search deep into her eyes. "Everyone all right? Did you stay out of trouble today?"

"Well, the children were a bit energetic I must admit. Matthew has a frog hidden in his satchel for you and Mark has found a puppy. We gave it a good bath and that was exhausting." She grinned as her gaze drank in the sight of him, openly admiring this big man with the soft heart. Kissing his chin, she pushed the hair back from his forehead before she continued. "Then Kathy threw Matthew's toy horse into the chamber pot and later the two of them fought over sliding down the banister. Oh, and then Harry told me he has changed his mind again regarding attending Harrow. His friend Jeremy is entering early but I refuse to even consider sending a child his age off on his own, I don't give a fig what his friend Jeremy does. Harry is hopeful you can change my mind. By the way, you cannot. Baby Luke is my only friend. I missed you, you fierce creature. I thought you'd forgotten us."

"As if I'd dare... " He rested his cheek against hers and sighed. "I toyed with the idea of escaping to Italy though."

"I don't blame you in the least, dear; but not tonight, your eyes are red rimmed. You need sleep."

Cupping her bottom with his hands he squeezed gently then waggled his eyebrows at her. "You think that's what I need, do you?" They kissed tenderly at first but the kiss soon intensified with each movement, each little moan. When they separated, both a little breathless, he pressed his forehead to hers, his eyes dark with desire. "I need something, lady wife, something you and you alone can provide me at the moment." His voice had become a silky whisper.

"Ham cakes and basted eggs."

"Lord, woman, I love you." He gave her a noisy smooch and then sat down to remove his boots. "Damn but I'm hungry, I don't suppose you made some scones today also."

The couple made their way down the steep wooden staircase, a cold draft as they passed the front windows making them huddle that much closer to each other and scurry that much quicker toward the smallish kitchen in the back. The house was an old one, usually tranquil, but rarely at peace when the wind blew as it did this night. The increasing storm outside seemed to threaten an early winter.

Fitzwilliam piled kindling into the fireplace as Amanda placed her candle on the table and entered her pantry. Soon the room began to warm. He opened the side door and waited for Flash to amble into the yard, finish his business and then return a much happier pet. Amanda tied an apron about her waist and began to hum, always at her most content when she could care for her husband and children. All was familiar and safe. She felt needed. He felt at home.

"Hastings told me you had another problem with cook today."

"He shouldn't have mentioned it to you; you've certainly more important things about which to worry. Did I tell you, dearest, that last week Patrick's wife sent us some mincemeat as a gift? Wasn't that sweet of Juanita? Well, it was more than enough for our family's needs so I sent two pies back to Patrick's house today. I do hate to waste and besides, they love my mincemeat pie."

"You're changing the subject, Amanda. I know your tricks." Fitzwilliam bit into an apple he had grabbed from a bowl in the cabinet. "I told Hastings we'll look for a replacement cook immediately." He pointed a finger at her when she turned to scowl. "Amanda, I am serious. The woman is not right in the head as our Matthew would say – she could be dangerous to you and the children. I can't be worrying about you when I'm away solving all the ills of British military reconnaissance. Or if I'm at Tattersalls."

"Oh, Richard! It was probably nothing really, something she ate."

"Is that a fact? The way I heard it she thought you were the leader of the Northumbrians come to lay siege to London. She's out, Amanda."

A pot banged on the stove. "We cannot dismiss her into the streets. She's all alone in the world the poor old thing. What will Janet do?"

"Who the hell is Janet?"

"Cook! That is her name – that's cook's name. Everyone has a name you know, she wasn't christened 'Cook'. She's very often completely sensible, or was until she ripped off her dress yesterday. And she'll be so sad if she can't cook."

"Amanda, she couldn't cook to begin with."

"It will break her heart, that's what it will do. She'll just sit outside all day and cry and smoke her pipe for hours." Amanda gave an involuntary shiver at the thought of the old woman sitting out in the cold, friendless and alone... without her dress...

"And I care about this, why?"

"I do hope she doesn't remove her dress again. Kathy thought it was a game and kept taking hers off as well. It really was my fault; she never has become accustomed to my hair color for some reason. Lately, when I nod my head at her, it just seems to set her off."

"Well, when *Janet* had her last episode I told Patrick to search out someone for us and he found a respectable Irish widow. She'll be here next week. I'll see what kind of arrangements I can make through the War Office for...um..."

"Janet!"

"Whomever. In the meanwhile we'll shackle her in the attic or something. I forbid her to be back in this kitchen, of course; a few too many sharp knives laying about for my comfort."

"Very well." Amanda's demeanor brightened a bit. "I suppose I'll have to do the cooking for a while then. Yes. I can make that beef barley soup you enjoy."

"Amanda, we've been over this. You should not be involved with the cooking, as you well know; you're the mistress of this house. I'll see that Patrick finds someone for the interim, until the new cook arrives."

"There is no necessity – I truly don't mind. Oh by the way, it seems Kathy was the one who placed that strange cat on the bed this morning. She said you looked lonely. Isn't she the sweetest child?"

"No, and stop changing the subject, wife. You have plenty to keep you occupied with those heathens of ours upstairs, besides it *is* a necessity to have a cook in a properly run English home."

"And so you've told me a dozen times." She suddenly began moving plates and utensils about with renewed vigor. "I dislike having people about everywhere, strangers paid to perform chores I am perfectly capable of doing myself!" After untying and then retying her apron for no apparent reason she turned to him and lifted her chin imperially. "It is ridiculous."

"You don't appear to mind the other walking wounded we currently employ."

"Well, since you force this upon me it can do no harm to assist those in need, can it? If you insist on having a butler and a cook and a maid – well, why not hire people who would not otherwise find work...?"

"...you do half the work for them."

"Besides, they don't demand very high wages, though I am certain we can ill afford even that. I'm certain we could even do with a few less servants if necessary."

Fitzwilliam fought back his rising irritation. Money was always a sore point between them. True, it was a bit scarce at times but they were far from destitute. He was proud that he alone was caring for his family without bowing to his father's demands or shaming himself before his bedeviling aunt.

He tried to calm himself as she spoke so he intently studied his pipe, moved the fruit bowl, and then righted the salt cellar. He knew *positively* that he had chosen the only path possible for himself six years earlier when he had married the love of his life, this woman, defying his family in the end. He had never looked back, never regretted that decision.

That reality, however, seldom stopped her from driving him insane.

"Damn it to hell, woman!" His fist pounded the table.

"Do not shout at me, husband! I'm no army private!"

"You drive me to it! And deliberately! We are well able to keep a cook and a maid, and a butler!"

"*And* your valet..." She spun away from him before he could see her grin.

"My valet!" Suddenly his lips twitched in amusement and he struggled against a moan. "You push me there, Amanda. Oh, you vexing little fox, how I let you trick me into taking that man on, I'll never know."

"Trick you? I never did! What a thing to say. Besides, it was your decision to employ retired soldiers, and a patriotic and humanitarian decision it was! I was only doing as you requested."

"Amanda Fitzwilliam, you knew perfectly well that when I told you to employ a former soldier I expected you to choose from a current war! The Peninsular War! Not the War for America's Independence! The man's older than dirt."

"Well, who else would hire the poor old dear? He's practically deaf."

When Amanda dared look over her shoulder she was relieved to see the grin on her husband's face and they both began to chuckle softly.

"Well, the damage is done and now we have this sorry excuse for staff. My God. Two ancient soldiers – a deaf valet and a half blind butler – and then there's that footman, I'd forgotten him. A former horse thief; hopefully former at any rate. Then we have a house maid I've never even seen, who screams and hides whenever I enter a room, and a cook who believes she was once a member of Napoleon's Imperial Guard. I would appreciate it Amanda if you would discuss the next household staff member with me before hiring."

"You are not thinking of replacing anyone else are you?"

"I would provide each one with sterling references."

"*Richard*. That would be lying and I then would fear for your immortal soul. I also would be forced to go to each house and tell them the truth." She began to baste his eggs as she continued. "Besides, you could never live with yourself if you put them on the street without reference."

"If I tried very hard I could."

"Richard!"

"No, I suppose not..."

"Well, of course you could not."

"... but only because you wouldn't let me. It is a moot point anyway. Who else could ever be desperate enough to hire such useless baggage?" The couple lapsed into a companionable quiet as Amanda hummed Amazing Grace and her husband puffed on his pipe. His thoughts were now drifting back to his talk with Darcy earlier. Finally his meal was ready and she reached for her large platter.

"Dearest, don't be such a stick; fetch two plates down for the table."

With a grunt he tapped out his pipe then walked to the modest pantry, stood staring at the chipped plates and cups. "Is this the best we have?"

"Out with it, Richard. What is really bothering you?" She brought the plate of food to the table and fetched utensils from a drawer.

"Don't be so fanciful, wife." How did she always seem to know when he had something on his mind? It was irritating in the extreme. He took two plates and brought them over. "I spoke with Darcy today."

"Yes, you told me. That's why you thought he'd be here for dinner tonight. Wash your hands please, Richard, and I could do without the glower, thank you. What did you discuss with William?"

He went to a sideboard where a pitcher and bowl rested, along with rough soap and towels. Being a doctor's daughter Amanda was fastidious about cleanliness. "He said he spoke with Aunt Catherine today." He wiped his hands on a towel and turned around. "She mentioned to him how she was willing to prepare you, if necessary, for later on...for when we inherit the titles." The room had grown very quiet. "In fact she would like to instruct both you and Kathy in court etiquette. Amanda, are you listening?"

"Yes. I heard you. Oh my. Is that what you want me to do? Is that what your father wants? I'd hoped we had a little more time."

"I am to inherit the title, Amanda. I *will be* the Earl. Or, if I die before my father, Matthew will be the Earl, and then Mark if Matthew dies without sons..."

"Don't say such things, please." She crossed herself quickly and then clasped her hands tightly in her lap. "Besides, your father seems in excellent health, doesn't he?"

"Rosy cheeked and full of bile as always." Fitzwilliam sat at the table and reached for the plate of eggs and ham cakes. "However, he's not immortal, dear; our house will not escape this. Whether we receive the rest of the estate is entirely up to him, but the title is mine and cannot be refused. And truthfully, it is my sons' heritage; I find myself surprisingly proud of that fact. I have a great deal to learn myself, was never prepared for this you know, an unfortunate oversight on my parent's part, but not irreversible; and, I won't make the same mistake with my children. We can't take their future for granted. We won't. I want them to be part of my family's history, of our country's history."

"When you put it that way I see no other option; although, I suppose I had hoped it would go away somehow. No, what you say is true, Richard – we must both work to ensure all the children's futures. Should I contact Lady Catherine?"

"I'll speak with her. Normally I would be the last person on earth to force Aunt Catherine upon anyone, let alone someone I love as dearly as I love you; however, she's all we have at hand, she's willing, and she has the children's best interest at heart, if not ours. You know, when the time arrives, when my father passes, I will be expected to enter the House of Lords almost immediately. Unfortunately, it shall also mean appearances at court and the scrutiny you will receive there as the wife of an Earl will be far greater than the attentions directed toward you when you were married to that imbecile Penrod – excuse me, when you were married to your dearly departed first husband."

Her man could still become jealous and Amanda felt a bizarre wifely pride in that fact. "Richard, don't be unkind." She poured him a cup of tea before she settled down to her own plate. "My stars. What a strange day this has become. Life changing, really."

"I know. Neither of us expected this would be our future, neither of us wanted it; yet, fate interceded and here we are. That isn't even the worst part. My father also would like us to travel to Somerton sometime soon so that I can begin training there as well." His appetite was fading fast. Folding his hands together, elbows on the table, he studied his wife's reaction. He knew she still hurt terribly from society's rejection of her when she arrived in London, the bride of a baronet, Augustus Penrod. The *ton* had treated her cruelly, had scorned her Boston origins and viciously ridiculed her accent and ways.

"He *wants* me at Somerton?" Her voice trembled slightly with hope that the long estrangement was nearing an end. "I really won't mind being at the Dower house, don't let that bother you. I'm merely a bit anxious at being on my own."

"*Never* alone. I will make that clear to my father and we will *all* stay at the Dower House." He took her hand in his. "I am so sorry, Amanda. It's the course neither of us wanted and yet here we are, in the thick of it, or soon will be. It's a dreadful feeling you know, inheriting a birthright because of death." He suddenly scrubbed his face with his hands. "Bloody hell. I hate routs and grand assemblies, court visits. I've never felt comfortable with all that ridiculous pomp and I will never forgive my brother for dying and putting us in this position."

Amanda patted his forearm. "We will do this for the children, for their future, not ours. I don't really foresee our moving within those great social circles, it's not our way, thank heaven. But, the children will; they do need to be prepared. They must have every opportunity to decide their own destinies. And heavens, Kathy and I will certainly have the grandest teacher of social graces."

He brought her hand to his mouth and kissed it. "I love you, my Amanda. All right, then. We will begin."

With only the slightest waver to her voice Amanda agreed with him. "Yes. We will begin."

Chapter Seven

Darcy was deep in thought, still reflecting on his meeting days earlier with the Duke of Devonshire. It had been pleasant and cordial but in the end the Duke and his son appeared neither interested nor willing to decide in favor of the smaller landowners. With cheerful politeness they had dismissed the tribulations of the mines, with the best of good will they laughed off the future of the locomotive, the lack of employment, the rising pollution.

In truth, Devonshire and his son had been much more determined to discuss a political career with Darcy than with any suggestions he had brought before them – those *bothersome complaints* of the district.

Being both brilliant and conscientious Darcy would make an ideal candidate they explained to him. (In private, later, the father and son discussed how he would also be a grand addition at dinner parties being as he was very handsome, extremely rich and his conversation was stimulating enough to enliven hunting weekends. He was aloof, which was always a plus as that was considered discernment, he was certainly charming and witty and, yes, he would fit into their circle very nicely. Of course his wife's family was problematic but Darcy's lineage put that minor infraction to the pale.)

Their meeting with Darcy at an end Devonshire had stood to make his pleasant good-byes when he played his final card. Seemingly having just thought of the idea he suggested proposing young Darcy for knighthood. Yes, that was a real possibility, and good preparation for his future. Would he not, therefore, seriously consider becoming a Member of Parliament for their district?

Yes, they had made it perfectly plain that they had plans for him, important plans, but for one small favor in return. If Darcy would only reconsider his progressive plans for the future of Derbyshire they could very likely make him an important political figure in England.

On his way home Darcy went over and over in his mind the ideas that Devonshire had instilled there, the power which they could provide him along with the added prestige of an alliance with that particular family. It quite astonished him how tempting it all was, how easily they had flattered his ego. He shook his head, gratified as anyone would be that certain individuals considered important by the world had singled him out, noticed him.

They had never mentioned the negatives, however. Such a change would effect not only him but his entire family, he would be separated from them for months at a time while Parliament was sitting; and, if the children did come into the city, why he would see little of them anyway. In the life they described to him politics would occupy all of his time. Could he do that; could he sacrifice his presence in their lives to chase power and fame?

In the end he knew where his loyalties would always lie – with his family and with Pemberley. He loved his family and his home above all else. To ensure their happiness he would surely forego power and fame.

Wouldn't he?

He had not heard the activity below stairs, the door fronting the portico being opened by his butler, the patter of tiny feet running throughout the many ground floor rooms, the chattering as little ones searched below for him. So absorbed was Darcy in his thoughts that he looked up only when the massive hall clock struck the hour. That was when he first noticed a flutter of white in his vision's periphery, a brief glimpse of a cloth doll slipping behind the curtain.

Then there was the giggle. *Ah. At last.* His pen stopped in mid stroke, his heartbeat quickened. Closing his eyes he inhaled that elusive scent that was hers and hers alone.

Soap and hot milk posset.

"Fee, fie, foe, fum, I smell the blood of an Englishman." He pulled back the curtain at the left end of the window. "Not there," he muttered. "Be he alive or be he dead, I'll grind his bones to make my bread." Darcy walked to the right side of the curtains and pulled that back. He grunted. "Not there either. It will go very badly for whomever this is if I am forced to search much farther. Very badly indeed. You *are* Jack from Jack and the Beanstalk, are you not?"

"No." Replied the middle curtain.

"No? Such insolence! Such disrespect! What do you mean – 'no'? No – *what!*"

"No, *Papa.*"

"I knew it!" Laughing, he pulled the middle curtains apart to be greeted by shrieks and squeals, his gorgeous little girl hopping in place from the sheer ecstasy of seeing him. He adored this little bundle of enchantment, the joy of his life. Dark haired and delicate, she was a replica of her mother in so many ways, yet he often saw his own mother there, in her shy manner, in her gentleness. He grabbed hold of Anne Marie and hugged her, spinning her around, showering her with a dozen kisses.

She kissed his cheek in return and then leaned back to have a good look at him. "Papa, you feel scratchy!"

Another figure came striding in then, tall and straight, a striking miniature of Darcy himself. He possessed fine, aristocratic features and was considered beautiful of face, even for a five year old. "*Papa! There you are!*" Bennet George Darcy beamed. "I've been looking everywhere for you! I drove a pony cart, Papa, and I fell off when it dipped into an enormous river but I didn't cry at all and I got back on immediately, just as you said I should, and it was ever so much fun. Uncle Charles and I went fishing nearly every day except for Sundays. Do you see how tall I am now?"

It astonished him how alike he and the boy looked, although the boy's nature was much more carefree than Darcy's had been at that age. Still holding his daughter in his arms, Darcy crouched down to his son's level and extended his other arm. The boy raced to him. "My heavens but that *was* an exciting visit for you all." He cupped the back of the small head, bringing his son's forehead closer for a kiss. Immediately, Georgie wrapped his arms around his father's neck and hugged him fiercely. "Auntie Jane cried so often at first, Papa, and so did Mama – but only once. She missed you very much. I tried to care for her."

Darcy's heart ached for his boy; he felt the child's tears on his cheek. "I missed you too son."

"Here I am, William. These two raced up to see you so quickly I barely kept up with them." The children had jabbered about their father for over three weeks and she herself had thought of little else, of how much she dearly missed her husband. The sight of them all together was breathtaking. *He* was breathtaking. As she entered the library she handed children's coats to the waiting butler. "Thank you, Winters. Will you see if the coachman can find my daughter's shoes also?" As she spoke she patted her hair back down, smoothed the sides flat and tried to tidy herself up as much as possible. "She removed them somewhere between here and Cambridge. I searched the carriage floor but to no avail, it was too dark; it was all rather hectic I'm afraid. Also, can you bring tea, please?"

Elizabeth reached her hands out to her husband and beamed. "You look well, William," she said finally. "Did you miss us?" Her eyes twinkled with anticipation; she laughed, almost blushed as he put his children down, rose, and began to move slowly toward her. At first they only held hands, their gazes each taking in the other. Then they swiftly enfolded themselves within each other's arms and for several moments the room was wrapped in silence. The children watched, mesmerized. Here was tangible proof of their security, of rock solid shelter, before them. The force of true love vibrated between them all.

Darcy inhaled the sweet scent of her hair, then her neck, her cheek. He kissed her eyes. His mouth hovered a whisper away from hers, prolonging the moment of contact. "You look so bloody beautiful," he whispered, "and, oh yes, I've missed you, wife."

Lizzy smiled, all dreamy eyed and warm. "And I, you, husband."

His mouth found hers then and they kissed slowly, thoroughly.

And the children cheered.

Darcy poured Lizzy a second glass of wine and then poured another one for himself. Still awake, they were savoring their second afterglow of the night. "I should have asked this first, but I was a bit distracted. How is your sister, Jane? Feeling a bit stronger I hope."

Lizzy nodded and sighed, snuggling deeper into his arms. "Poor Jane. She is so good, so sweet natured; you know she would not appear downcast before us for the world. She still cries though. Two babies lost to them, William. *Two.* My heart breaks for her and for those lost little souls." Tilting her head back she looked up at him. "I pray they are with our little one and that all are happy."

The sadness had never really left them, the loss of their own child early in their marriage. Darcy knew his wife, knew that deep within her soul she believed that child still wished to be born, believed it to be inevitable. He rested his chin atop her head and, closing his eyes, he awaited the inevitable quarrel.

"William?"

"No, Elizabeth."

She stiffened immediately, as he knew she would. "How can you deny me something before I've even asked? Really!"

"You want another baby, I know you. However, you conveniently forget that Dr. Milagros said it could be dangerous for you. I cannot risk losing you and I will *not* risk my children being motherless. It is out of the question."

"My mother had five daughters! Five!"

"Your mother was a..." He abruptly stopped speaking when her head tilted up toward him, her eyes narrowing in their challenge. He cleared his throat. "...an exceptional woman. *And* a very large woman. You, on the other hand, are rather small... will you stop glowering at me! Now why in the world does my saying that always anger you?"

"You speak of me as if I am in miniature, a sort of fairy creature. I come from sturdy, country people, William, you tend to forget that. It is only your very unwieldy size that makes me appear so diminutive. Among normal Englishwomen I am quite average."

"Among normal Englishwomen, if such a thing even exists, you are a goddess."

She could find no wifely argument to this statement so she smiled and kissed him.

"We have been apart for nearly a month, Lizzy. Can we not think of better diversions to pass our time than arguing?"

Chapter Eight

That October morning dawned simultaneously on two very different households, perhaps shining a little finer on the Darcy's lovely Pemberley House than on the Fitzwilliam's rather scruffy residence, Crossgate. Both homes appeared to reflect their individual masters unique personalities.

Darcy's beautiful town home looked splendid as always, benefiting from yet another refurbished landscape design and its yearly polish and brush up. The gleaming brass knockers on the front portal dazzled the eyes – blinded the eyes, actually – appearing bold and bright against massive ebony doors, a wood that was used throughout the house for its beauty, its strength and for added security. Even the ivy covering the brick seemed washed and pressed. The perfection of Pemberley's façade was equal to the distinguished master within.

A mere five blocks away stood the Fitzwilliam's home. Here too the homes were well-built but smaller, less grand, closer together but solid. His was a two story frame, painted white with green trim; in the corner of the yard, and downwind of the family, sat a compost heap which was tended to with great dedication. Like its master, less importance was placed upon appearance in this house, more upon stamina.

The area upwind was filled to bursting with flowers, trees and toys. Paint chipped windows overlooked a now fallow garden but those windows were sparkling clean and the laughter from within the home was heart felt.

As customary the two families, the Darcy's and the Fitzwilliam's, would spend a great deal of time together when both were in the city; and, it usually began as soon as possible, with breakfast on the first convenient day for both, so that the weeks to follow could be plotted out.

This morning breakfast would be at the Fitzwilliam's...

The Darcy's chattered and laughed as the little family wound its way through those five blocks, the children eager to see their city relations. The cousins were more like brothers and sisters and the excitement for the entire "Fitzwilliam Mob" gathering together once again was almost more than could be borne. Anne Marie beamed with her excitement, skipping and hopping high over cracks as she held both her mother's and her father's hands. Her brother Georgie was much harder to contain. He was dashing back and forth, searching around corners and scanning beneath porches until his father would grow annoyed or anxious and call him back. These neighborhoods were so unlike their own that it was positively exotic to the young boy.

Coming at last to the Fitzwilliam residence the little family walked up the narrow front path leading to the house then proceeded up the stairs. Lizzy called to her son. "George, what *are* you looking at over there? Come here, please."

"Yes, Mama. Papa, there's a livery not two doors away, did you know that? Do you suppose that's where Uncle Fitz keeps his pairs?"

"His pair, George, and yes, I suspect he does keep them there. How he can stand the smell and the mess so close is another question."

"William. Little ears...repeat everything."

"Quite right. Forget I said that children." He banged on the front door. "Wake up in there – you've a hungry family on your doorstep." Hearing an overhead window open Georgie and Anne Marie looked up and squealed, spun around then ran back down the steps.

"Matthew!" From somewhere within the house Darcy heard his cousin's distinctive roar. It was prior experience that saved the couple, the familiarity with Fitzwilliam's children's exploits alone had Darcy and Elizabeth automatically turn and run, moments before the bag of flour hit the exact spot where they had been standing.

"Matthew! Mark! Are you out on that window ledge again?"

"Have you come up with any reasonable story yet?" Hands in his pockets Fitzwilliam glared down at his sons.

Amanda shook her head in doubt. "Tell me again what sort of punishment this is meant to be." The two little fellows sat side by side on the bottom step of the front staircase, scratching elbows and knees, looking anywhere but at their father.

"Well, since neither will tell me which one dropped the flour bag I am making them sit here until they come up with any plausible explanation."

"I'm still a bit vague on this. How will that help you determine which one to punish?"

"They'll have to decide together. If they're able to come up with one convincing tale I'll accept it. But they cannot leave that step until they do agree on one."

"And you are certain this is the position you wish to take?"

"It is."

"I will never understand you."

"It was me, Papa." Mark winced when his brother's sharp elbow dug into his side. "Well, it was."

"No, Papa, it was me," countered Matthew.

"See, not good enough. You still don't agree. Now, give it another go." The little faces leaned toward each other.

"I'll share a secret with you both – if you tell me the truth the punishment will be less severe."

"It was me," whispered Matthew.

Mark nodded. "Yeah, it was him. But he's very young."

Fitzwilliam tried not to chuckle as he took a glum faced Matthew by the hand. The two walked silently into the library and when they reappeared a few moments later Matthew was rubbing his bottom, but evidently was not overly upset since he hopped up onto his chair and immediately began reaching for food.

"Before either of you eat, I want you to apologize to your cousins for that unprovoked attack at our front door." With the wives fussing over baby Luke elsewhere, and the Fitzwilliam day maid hiding in a cupboard, the two fathers were the only functioning adults in the room.

"But it was though, Papa – provoked, I mean. First, to be clear on this, what exactly does provoke mean?" Precise to his core and always good natured Mark was duty bound to explain the twins' abysmal behavior.

However, he was also a detail man and, as usual, becoming bogged down with them.

"It means you are nasty boys and it means that you are wicked." Kathy crowed, taunting with her little sing song voice, smiling cheerily at her older brothers because anytime they were in trouble was a cause for celebration. "It means you cannot have cake ever again and crows will peck out your eyes."

Anne Marie cheered at that, she even clapped.

"Anne Marie Darcy, do not encourage your cousins." Darcy reprimanded. "They seldom require it," he muttered as he brought his daughter's plate closer to her.

"Kathy, where do you learn such nonsense?" Fitzwilliam grasped her little cup of milk before it toppled from the table but failed to save her silverware.

"They'll peck *your* eyes out, Beef!" shouted Matthew and Georgie, retaliating as always in unison. "And eat your brains – if they can find any! Yeah they will!" Matthew expanded on their previous comment and stuck out his tongue.

"Enough. All of you. Anyone who is shorter than I will henceforth cease to speak." Darcy's commanding voice sounded severe as he cut into edible pieces the small ham slice that had been sitting, untouched, before his daughter for nearly twenty minutes. "Eat something, Anne Marie – anything. I beg of you. At least one bite. How does your mother succeed with this and I do not?"

"Mama sings to me."

"Yes, she sings to me also. How lucky we both are. Now eat at least the little bit that is on this fork. Please." He turned to Mark. "And, 'unprovoked', my charming young hooligan, means that there was no just cause for the attack, neither upon your Aunt Lillibet nor upon your uncle – old what's his name."

Mark Fitzwilliam laughed heartily at what Darcy had just said, as if Darcy were the wittiest man alive. Actually, hunger had overtaken his senses and he wanted done with all questions. He reached for his fork. Darcy's arched eyebrow stopped him cold.

"No, Mark, you must answer the question first. Explain why you are tossing flour from the windows."

"The salt is locked away."

There was momentary silence.

"Darcy, you're getting nowhere with this vague line of questioning. When it comes to my children you must attack with precision, leave nothing ambiguous. Watch carefully and learn. Matthew, what provocation – close your mouth, Mark – what *purpose* was there for your attack upon Uncle Wills and Auntie Lillibet?"

"It wasn't meant for Uncle Wills. We love him and Auntie Lillibet." Matthew reached for a jar of preserves but could not get them without unsettling the pitcher of milk; his father immediately righted the pitcher and brought the jar nearer. "Thank you, Papa. Put the strawberries on my scone?"

"Please...?" Prompted his father.

"I already said you could, Papa."

"No, no, no, that is not what I meant, son. You should say...never mind. Now, these are not strawberries, Matthew. These are raspberries. Do you understand me, boy?" Fitzwilliam placed a large dollop of the raspberry preserves onto his son's scone and then sliced the scone into several smaller pieces. He pushed the plate over to Mathew.

"Well, never mind then."

"Whatever is keeping your mother so long?" Fitzwilliam mumbled as he stretched to look over his shoulder.

"Matthew, although I am gratified to hear that we were not your primary target," the fork that Darcy held before his daughter was relentless in it's pursuit of her mouth. Finally, he was successful. His gratification was short lived when she spit the food into her napkin and wrinkled her nose.

"It's gone cold, Papa. Might I have porridge, please?"

"If you promise that you will eat porridge then you shall have porridge. Are you certain? Very good. Now, Matthew, Auntie Lillibet and I are the ones with flour dust on our shoes. If you did not mean the assault for us, then I would suspect you meant to attack your cousins here. What I am curious about is the why of it." Darcy walked over to the sideboard and filled a small bowl with the hot porridge for his little darling. He returned and placed it before her.

After a short interval of surprised silence among the children, Anne Marie announced to the world what was common knowledge to the children. "Oh Papa, didn't you know? Georgie smashed a spider dead and put it into Matt's food at his birthday party but didn't tell him until he had finished all his soup and then later George sat on his head. No porridge, thank you, Papa. I'm not hungry any longer."

Young Harry, now ten years old, suddenly burst into the room, returned from his morning riding lesson. "Uncle Wills, excellent to see you again, sir! Papa, the new mare is brilliant – oh no, is this all the food there is?"

The arrival of Harry set the children into a frenzy of mischievousness which lasted for several minutes. The idol of all the young ones, the desire to impress Harry was especially fanatical among the boys, sending them to poking each other, giggling, making hideous faces when the fathers weren't looking and the occasional rude mouth noises which they all found to be hilarious. In the end, Darcy and Fitzwilliam had to separate Matthew, Mark and George. Peace was restored.

"Thank you again, Papa, for that beautiful mare. Could you pass me the kippers please? Oh, she's wonderful, a real high stepper and so sweet natured. May I have the ham slices – one more, please, and I would not turn down another. Thank you. Mr. Abernathy says that I have a natural affinity for the saddle, said I'd make an excellent cavalry officer, he was one you know, he was wounded in the shoulder and he says even when I was a little boy and driving my pony cart that he could tell I'd be first rate, smack up to the mark. Pass over those scones to me would you, George? You're the best. Love that new pony cart of yours by the way. May as well pass the coddled eggs also; hate to see those beauties go cold. So, I've decided to join the army instead of going to Oxford when the time comes. Perhaps I should enter earlier because what if I wait too long and all the fighting is over and done with. I should be very angry if I'm not able to charge into battle. Matt, are there more biscuits?"

Fitzwilliam, his chin resting upon his palm, observed his son's eating with a weary eye. "I would advise you to keep talk about the army to yourself, Harry. Your mother would be less than pleased about a military career for you. Don't frown so! We'll discuss this later, you and I; after all, you've still a good deal of time until you need make a decision that life altering. You'll change your mind a dozen times, of course, before you attend University."

"No, Papa, I will never change my mind."

"Last month you wanted to join Georgiana's husband Ashcroft in the Navy, become a cabin boy. Just yesterday you were telling me you were eager to be off to school to study science so that you could become a physician like your grandfather. At your age I wanted to become a pirate. It's all perfectly normal."

"And you very nearly did become a kind of pirate, if I recall."

"Darcy, please be quiet."

"Yes, you were mere moments away from an adventurous life on the seas." Darcy smiled at his cousin's groan. "If I remember the tale correctly, you packed yourself a loaf of bread and a boiled chicken and had even talked Gilhooley's son into joining you, the only reason being you thought he would bring some of his mother's peach tarts."

The children were a rapt audience, always eager for the stories about their fathers' childhoods. Richard scowled at Darcy and beetled his brow, cleared his throat – all futile attempts to stop yet another disreputable account being told.

"Whatever happened?" asked a breathless Harry.

"Papa, you were at sea?"

"Uncle Fitz was a pirate? I knew it!"

"Your father fell asleep in the bushes down by the lake as he waited in vain for Tad Gilhooley to arrive. And that is exactly where your grandfather found him and administered swift retribution to the seat of his pants." The children moaned and groaned.

"How old were you pa? How old was he Uncle Wills?"

"I don't believe that's truly relevant..." Fitzwilliam reached over in an attempt to pinch Darcy's arm. Darcy laughed, shifting quickly in avoidance.

"He was nine years old and very skinny."

"He was younger than Harry is now." Matthew and Mark jabbered, all amazement.

"He was very brave." George stated, quite impressed.

"He was skinny?" Kathy was merely skeptical.

"Enough, all of you! Darcy, I shall have a word with you later! And, I don't want you little pack of barbarians to get any fanciful ideas. It was a very foolish thing to do." It was already too late. Their eyes glowed with pride and they babbled with excitement.

"Quiet down, quiet down; you're mother is just upstairs and she'll hear."

"How did grandfather know what had happened?" asked Mark. It was the details that bothered him, always details.

"My elder brother made certain to tell him. Your grandfather was furious with me, and rightly so I should add. I didn't sit for a whole day."

"He should not have told on you." Kathy's look was fierce and protective, positively thunderous at this betrayal of her father. "That was very wrong of him."

"Well, you're always telling on us, *you big ox!*"

"*You booby!*"

"Matthew! Katherine! Enough!"

"Papa, when can I ride a pony by myself?" Emboldened by the tale of his Uncle Fitz, and immune by now to the Fitzwilliam mob's loud battles, Georgie took advantage of the continuing shrieks and chaos, swiftly snatching a toast point from Kathy's dish when her head was turned.

"George, you are still much too inexperienced and young to ride on your own. When you're older we'll speak of it again. I say, who ate all the apple cobbler? There were six pieces here not five seconds ago!"

"But when, Papa? I'm older now than I was before and I've helped Beckman saddle the pony and I know how to ride and I'm almost as tall as Beckman's son and *he* rides a horse all on his own – a full grown horse."

"There is nothing to discuss, son. Besides, Beckman's boy is a full head taller than you and two years older. Now, don't look so downcast, you've years ahead of you for riding and hunting. You've your whole life before you; don't rush into it so fast. It will pass on its own more quickly than you can ever believe."

Darcy's attention was distracted by the wives returning to the room so he never saw the proud and determined look that had come across his son's face.

"There, surely you heard that. Luke's just said Lillibet"

Amanda reached for her baby boy. "No, that was an unsettled stomach. I'm certain of it."

"Amanda, how can you possibly confuse a stomach grumble for Lillibet? There were definitely several syllables involved and all of them sounding exactly like... why is everything so quiet in there?"

The laughing twosome stopped as soon as they entered the room, confounded by the chaotic sight of the breakfast table.

"Oh my stars." Amanda turned in a slow circle, her gaze surveying the floor, the buffet, the table.

"I see the Visigoths have been and gone." Elizabeth stared open mouthed at the spilled milk, half eaten plates of food, soiled clothes and messy little hands and faces. "But did they need to take the entire breakfast with them?"

Buttons, that tiny, homeless puppy, was now triple the size she was a week before; she crouched to pee before her mistress, grabbed the last piece of sausage from a serving platter and padded gaily into the other room.

Darcy cleared his throat. "I believe there's a good deal of porridge left," he offered. "Coffee anyone?"

Chapter Nine

"William, are you coming to bed?"

"I'll be along in a moment, Elizabeth."

Darcy sat alone at his dressing room table, reading once again the invitation received that morning from the Duke of Devonshire, an invitation inviting both him and Elizabeth to Chatsworth House, the Duke's magnificent and famous country estate. There would be daily hunts and gambling for the men and picnics, opera singers, painting masters, archery lessons, musicales, and of course dancing, to amuse the women. The Duke's annual party was quite celebrated, an invitation to it elusive except among the very highest of society. Icons of culture and leaders of industry would be in attendance along with deposed royalty from the great houses of Europe, many visiting for months, treating Chatsworth as a second home.

And, as if that weren't grand enough, several members of Britain's own royal family always made an appearance. An invitation to the Chatsworth Hunt was considered to be as great an accomplishment as a private audience with the King, and very often much more difficult to obtain.

None of that interested Darcy. He knew the real reason these 'hunt parties' were so popular – *Politics*.

The Hart and Hind Hunt Party was where the real decisions of the year were made, over after-dinner port, before boring operatic duets, or during a round of cards. What was of concerned to him was the reason for *his* invitation.

"Whatever is the matter, William? Are you feeling ill?" Her arms slipped about his neck and she began kissing his hair when she spied the coveted invitation in his hand. "Oh, my gracious."

"Yes. Oh my gracious, indeed."

"Is that what I think...?" Taking the card from him she settled into his lap and read – "You are invited to attend the Chatsworth House Michaelmas Celebration Hart and Hind Hunt..." After studying the rest in silence she handed him back the invitation. "I am astonished. Are you going to attend?"

"We are both invited Lizzy, and I hope we will both attend, if attending is our decision. Perhaps this is something we should discuss." Lizzy's father was a gentleman, she was a gentleman's daughter; however, she was not schooled for the Royal Court and had often made sport of those who were.

"I don't know, William. These people are at a station even above Aunt Catherine in importance, aren't they? I wouldn't know how to behave. What if I embarrass you, pick up the wrong fork, trip over a deer hide or momentarily forget how to address a Royal?"

"Nonsense. You have no idea how perfect you are or how proud of you I am. I have no qualms about your being at my side, Lizzy." He brought her palm up to kiss. "My unease concerns why we were included at all. It's true the Duke and I rubbed along well enough during our meeting, but this? For some reason I think there's something else at play." He proceeded to explain to her the details of his meetings with Devonshire.

"It would seem they want to influence your decision then. You are becoming an important figure, William, your influence going even beyond Derbyshire. His Grace must realize that. To paraphrase your own words to me, you have no idea how handsome you are or how brilliant. Your name will be very famous one day, I'm sure of it." Lizzy returned her husband's kiss. "I say he's lucky to have you involved with Derbyshire's interests, probably wants to reward you in some way. Perhaps you *will* be made a knight and then I can be Lady Lizzy."

He laughed out loud. "I never before took you for an ambitious wife."

"Not ambitious, just proud."

"Well, I suppose I really must attend, mustn't I? One doesn't turn down something like this; it's rather like a command performance."

He wrapped his arms around her waist and she snuggled further down. He settled his chin upon her head. "I attended this event once before, you know; many years ago with my father. It was shortly after our year of mourning following my mother's death. My father, being the kind of man that he was, brought me along, refusing to leave me home alone. I was the only child in attendance and such a dour looking lad I probably spoiled everyone's fun. From what little I remember, though, it really was a grand affair." Darcy turned the invitation over and over in his hands, his thoughts lost in the past. "I often wondered if he had been offended, or heaven forbid, hurt, by their subsequent exclusion of him afterward. Perhaps I see this invitation as a sort of vindication. Fanciful, I know."

Elizabeth rested her hand upon his chest. It was moments such as these that the tenderness he hid from all but her, hid from the world, touched her heart. "I have always wanted to see Chatsworth House. It is said to be exquisite and easily as large as Kensington Palace. They even say Lord Byron attends. Can you imagine? I could be meeting Byron. Perhaps he'll perform Don Juan..."

"All seventeen cantos? Good lord, then surely we won't go."

"...and I'll need new clothes for this, of course; gowns, riding habits, hats, boots..." Her eyes were twinkling with mischief.

"Elizabeth, have I ever mentioned to you that I'm not made of money?"

"Frequently. My only concern is that we've never both been separated from the children before; this will be very difficult on them."

"That had crossed my mind." Darcy knew Elizabeth's true hesitance would be leaving the children. "What say we ask Amanda and Fitzwilliam to watch them? The cousins will be deliriously happy to be together."

"For three weeks in that small house? Fitzwilliam will go mad."

"A relatively short trip for him." Darcy was laughing outright now. "Besides, it serves him right." He gave his wife a brief, gentle kiss, and then revisited for a much more thorough one.

"It would be lovely to be alone for a while, just the two of us," she sighed. "Thank heavens Amanda loves children as dearly as Fitzwilliam loves horses; she'd have a babe a year if it was up to her."

"Well, the fact that they don't is apparently not from lack of trying. Good Lord! Remember when we stayed over last month? Those walls at their house are bloody thin..."

Elizabeth laughed as she pressed her hand over her husband's mouth.

Chapter Ten

"You must kiss my dolly Anne Boleyn, Papa." Kathy shoved the battered and headless doll toward her father. "She's not feeling at all the thing."

"Very well but then go to sleep." Fitzwilliam first kissed his daughter's cheek then kissed the foot of the old dolly before tucking both under the covers for the night.

"What about Anne Marie, Papa? Don't forget to give her a kiss also. She is very lonely for her Mama and Papa – you know they've gone away and abandoned her. She's feeling so badly that she may want us both to have cake for breakfast."

Fitzwilliam glanced at Darcy's daughter sleeping soundly beside his own. "Needs cake does she? Well, I'll see what the new cook can scrape together."

"Anne Marie may not remember insisting upon cake in the morning so don't bother asking her. Also, I believe that she wants me to go riding with the boys in the park when you take them there tomorrow. She wants me to ride in front, on the saddle with you, and wishes me to hold the reins."

"Demanding little wench, isn't she?"

"Well, it's because her Mama and Papa have..."

"...abandoned her. Yes, I heard about that."

"It will lift her spirits considerably."

"If *you* go riding?"

"I mean a great deal to her."

"I see. The only trouble is I was not aware that I'd be taking the boys out riding tomorrow. This is the first I've heard of it."

"Mama is going to surprise you. I heard her speaking with Uncle Patrick O'Malley and they've gotten it all arranged between them. Please act surprised."

"I certainly will."

"And don't forget about the cake."

Within an hour the children were all asleep, the lamps were turned low, the growing pack of dogs were brought inside after tending to their business in the yard. The new cat, Bonaparte, was escorted outside. Finally, both mother and father Fitzwilliam were retiring to their own chambers for a well deserved rest.

As Amanda walked into their room she began to remove the pins from her hair. "Did I close the window in the boys' room? Yes, I did." she mumbled to herself. "It's so damp and cold, perhaps they need more blankets." Her husband came up behind her and slipped his strong arms about her waist.

"Are you as exhausted as I?" He snuffled his nose into her neck, his breath tickling her there. "By the way, you smell like tapioca." He pushed aside her hair and nibbled her earlobe.

"Scoundrel." Wriggling her bottom against him she smiled. "You most certainly are *not* exhausted." She turned to face him, to hold him in her arms. "Do you know now dearly I love you?"

"No more than I love you...*and for as long as we both shall live.* However much you beg me, though, there will be no frisky play this night. I've an early day tomorrow, a dozen meetings straight through the afternoon."

"I beg your pardon?" Amanda followed him into their bedroom, a worried look on her face. "You have meetings tomorrow? All day? Are you certain? Patrick was here and never said a word."

"Last minute." He undid his collar. "The meetings piled one upon another, all out of the blue, all with boring and long winded fellows too." He turned to admire her in her chemise and winked. "Perhaps I'll rethink that whole frisky business and have a shave before bed. What do you think of that idea?" He waggled his eyebrows at her and her heart raced. She even blushed.

"Well, if we absolutely must... Here, let me help you." She reached for a towel as he prepared a bowl of soapy water, then she retrieved the strop for him. Happy and content she leaned her back against the wall and tried not to grin. "You don't mind if I watch, do you?"

He took the strop from her hand. "Would you obey me if I said no?" He grunted at her narrow eyed look of offence. "All right, just promise to keep very quiet for a few moments. No speaking, no questions, no loud exclamations. I start at my throat and therefore need all my concentration in order to not slice off my head."

"We've had quite a lovely two days, haven't we?" she blurted suddenly.

"*Blast!*" he barked.

"Ooh, you silly person you've cut yourself. Try and be more careful, will you? The Darcy's children are so well behaved, especially compared to ours. Of course, that's not very difficult, is it...? In fact, I truly believe our children behave better when they are with them, don't you agree?" Without meeting her husband's eyes she went on quickly. "George and Anne Marie will be here such a short time and we won't see them again until Christmas. They are such sweet children, and demand so little. "

It was a moment before she became fully aware that Fitzwilliam was staring at her, one fist leaning on the table and the other on his hip. He was not smiling.

"Amanda, you're not with child again, are you?"

"No, of course not. Not that I'm aware. Yet. Perhaps. Don't you want more children?"

He stared at her long and hard then shrugged. "Oh lord, I suppose I do but that's beside the point." She had suffered two miscarriages already, their baby Luke was just a year old.

"I wish you'd explain the point then."

"A woman puts her life at risk each time – you know this. With each child the odds of your having difficulty increases, especially with your advancing age." When he saw her eyes narrow at that witless remark he cleared his throat and changed course. "What I mean to say is Luke is barely a year old, still on the breast. Dear, even you must admit that this counting of days method for preventing your becoming *enceinte* is not working very well for us. We need to think of the children we have now; most especially we need to protect you. I don't know, perhaps we should sleep separately, make things a bit less convenient..."

"Sleep away from each other?" Tears filled her eyes. "After that – well what would be next, Richard? A mistress? I thought you loved me."

"How in the world can you make that leap of logic? Of all the...I would never take a mistress; I promised you that from the beginning. It's just that, well, you won't allow me look after you properly because of your religion." This was an old and familiar disagreement, often volatile – one that threatened the very heart and privacy of their marriage. He refused to understand her religion and she refused to disobey it.

"Richard, we must leave all that up to God."

"God and Father Riley." He continued his shaving with a more agitated gusto. "Dammit, you are with child again, aren't you? I knew it! You've been extremely grumpy in the mornings."

"I really don't believe I am; with child I mean. And I am *not* grumpy." she said indignantly. "*You've* been ill tempered. How in heavens name did this argument start? Weren't we speaking of George and Anne Marie Darcy?"

He tried his best not to smile and wondered when she'd begin to hint at her 'surprise' for him. "Well, you are right about those two; they are wonderful children. You know, George reminds me so much of his father at that age, a bit more adventurous perhaps but with Darcy's infuriatingly decent character. He'll be a truly good man when he grows."

"You missed a whole area here on your cheek."

"*I've barely begun, Amanda!*"

She learned forward to kiss his neck. "Well, hurry then." She yawned behind her hand. "We're not getting any younger."

"Then be still for five minutes." He continued on with his shave and scraped the razor over his cheeks in silence until he was relatively whisker free. He then rested his forearms atop her shoulders, turning his cheek first left then right as she used the towel to wipe the remaining soap from his face.

"Am I now Adonis?"

Smiling impishly she nodded. "You are to me."

"Excellent. Now, is there anything else we need to discuss because I really do need to leave early tomorrow so if we could get things moving along here..." He began pulling off his shirt.

"Yes, we have something else to discuss!" She knew her husband and could tell he was being deliberately provoking.

"Ah, I see. Enough of this. Amanda, tell me what it is you really want me to do, or tell me what the children did or what they want to do. Better yet, just tell me how much the whole damn thing will cost me."

"Well, of all the... I don't know what you mean, Richard, I truly don't. By the way, the boys would like to go into the park tomorrow and ride their pony carts."

He tossed his rolled up shirt into the corner. "Absolutely not. Call me overprotective if you like but there is a great deal of activity in Hyde Park this time of year and the boys are all far too young to go riding there with only our groom, Toby."

"Here's a thought. You could take time tomorrow, it's just one day after all, let someone else meet with the long winded gentlemen, and supervise the expedition yourself. Patrick has spoken to the Darcy's groom and he promised he would be there, plus Harry can keep an eye on things as well."

"I said 'no', evidently you cannot hear."

"I hear, I've evidently chosen to ignore. Now it's your turn to tell me the truth; Kathy already informed you, didn't she – about you taking the boys riding? I see, so there really are no meetings tomorrow, none of this is news to you and the boys are already expecting to go. I rarely ask you for anything, do I? Be quiet. Patrick checked your schedule and the next two weeks will be impossible; this is your only time available. So, now, will you or will you not take them to the park?"

"I will." His mouth was twitching with humor. An exemplary wife, she really never did ask for much and besides, she looked so pretty all aggravated and flushed.

"Splendid." She kissed his cheek.

"Any other demands?"

"Yes. Finish shaving, if you please, before I forget what we were about to do."

Chapter Eleven

Darcy and Elizabeth arrived at the outskirts of the Duke of Devonshire's property shortly before four in the afternoon two days after their departure. Their coach turned onto the long private road but did not arrive at the mansion itself for nearly half an hour. Elizabeth gasped when the building came into view.

It was larger than Pemberley, more grand than Rosings, and very nearly as extravagant as Kensington Palace. As she continued to stare in slack jawed admiration she observed the head butler, the under butler, several footmen, and a few maids scurry down the great stone entranceway and across the courtyard, assembling like soldiers to assist them to their rooms.

"Amazing how you remember things being so much larger when you're a child..."

Elizabeth pressed her fingers to her mouth to keep from laughing. "Behave yourself."

The carriage soon stopped and the couple within were assisted down. The butler stepped forward and bowed. "Mr. Darcy, Mrs. Darcy, welcome to Chatsworth House. Your rooms have been prepared for you and your valet and maid await you within." He then turned to his second in command. "I shall show

Mr. and Mrs. Darcy to their rooms personally, Joseph."

The couple was led through a long portico and into the grand foyer. "His Grace desired to greet you himself but is now taking his mandated afternoon rest. Dinner shall be served at eight o'clock and the Duke wishes you and Mrs. Darcy to be his particular guests this evening. Of course, there will be a smaller, more private gathering before dinner in the red parlor at seven. If you like, I shall send a footman to your rooms to escort you to that. Very good. The dressing bell will be rung directly at six. My name is Henderson, Mr. Darcy, Mrs. Darcy. Should you require anything at all please call on me; I have been instructed to extend to you my personal attention."

"Elizabeth, aren't you ready yet? It's after seven and we don't want to be too late in arriving. Fashionably late is one thing, but if we're any longer I'll need to shave again."

Elizabeth was hidden from his view, her maid Cara applying finishing touches to her hair. When the maid stepped aside Elizabeth stood and turned. "Well? What do you think?"

He was speechless; stunned. He hardly recognized the sophisticated beauty before him – how she had changed over the years from the little country girl he had married! The woman who stood before him now was perfect; loveliness personified.

Elizabeth believed her gown to be very nice, a royal blue color that went well with her dark hair and pale skin. The material was satin and luxuriously soft, with both puffed sleeves and a form fitted bodice intricately embroidered with design of shimmering silver and golden threads, as was the short train of the dress. Her creamy white bosom began to expand and contract as her husband studied her intently.

"Oh, William! You don't like my dress, do you? I was afraid you wouldn't approve. It's a bit extravagant I know but Madame Riche insisted this was the height of fashion and I do love the color, and the fabric. Are you all right, dear? Please say something."

"You misunderstand my silence, Elizabeth. It's just, well, I've never seen anything or anyone more beautiful in my life."

Lizzy clasped her hands before her and beamed.

Still trying to recover his wits he motioned to dismiss Cara, who left smiling broadly. "I almost didn't recognize you, Lizzy."

"Ah, well." She laughed. "I don't know if I should be insulted by that or pleased."

"Hush. Good lord but you're pretty. I've completely forgotten what I was going to say."

Suddenly feeling giddy and young and desirable she pirouetted, batted her lashes, flirted outrageously with her own husband. "Then you don't think this décolletage is too low?"

He pulled her tightly into his arms. "Yes, of course I do. But you are mine and no other man's." He dipped his head to kiss the top swell of her breasts. "That makes these mine as well. You'll turn many a head tonight; I can see I'll have to keep a close eye on you."

As it happened, they were very late indeed for the Duke's private party.

The evening that followed was a glittering amalgam of silks, satins, jewels, the finest music, the richest food, the most illustrious people. Each time Darcy would search for his wife he would discover a new group of interesting people hovering about her; why, earlier he himself had received gardening tips from none other than a Russian Prince. It was as if he and Lizzy were the Duke's newest toys, the favored pets — *the* couple to know.

The conversations taking place around him now, however, were very disturbing...

"What's all this fuss over the so called 'Rotten Boroughs'?"

"Sticking their large, peasant noses where they don't belong. And the Corn laws! Lot of stuff and nonsense! Don't see any need for change really, hardly worth all this fuss."

"True Bertie, very true. A lot of to-do over nothing, I dare say. Same as with the so-called Catholic problem. I can't see wastin' our time over a mandate that comes to us from none other than Henry VIII himself, can you? They're all of no account — nothing but garlic eating idolaters if you ask me."

"Gad, I don't see any need for a rail system, do you? The canals that I lease out are perfectly serviceable — especially for my purse, *(haha)*!"

"... gas lighting? Whatever are you thinkin' of in Derby? Everyone'll be killed in their beds. There now Darcy, you don't really want all this change, do you?"

The senseless, reactionary comments went on an on, aristocratic Tory sentiments that never failed to set Darcy's teeth on edge. He wanted to be polite and gracious; however, he was a Whig down to his toes. He was unsure how much more gibberish he could listen to when he noticed two deposed royals from the continent hovering too closely around his wife.

"Excuse me, your Lordship. What were you say?"

"Whatever are you lookin' at, Darcy? Not your wife! Darcy, Darcy, it won't do to behave like a jealous farmer, not at all. And certainly not with those two. Those popinjays happen to be very important people — nobility, Darcy! Gentlemen. Certainly nothin' to work yourself up over, we're all above that sort of emotion, I should hope. Have another glass of port."

The Earl of Lancashire leaned back in his chair and blew smoke rings up to the ceiling. "I say, are we playing roulette tonight? I've about ten thousand in my pockets."

"Well damn me." Darcy whispered when he saw Elizabeth stiffen and then subtly remove a man's hand from her elbow. He turned to leave. "Excuse me, gentlemen."

"Steady on, old man, keep your head; not the thing at all to create a scene here you know." Hart, the Duke of Devonshire's son, stood at his arm. "She knows what she's about, making an important conquest there, and you should be as well. I say, come with me. If its female companionship you desire I'm certain we can arrange a few discreet diversions for you. This is not for common knowledge; however, I'll let you in on a little secret. There are a few delicious surprises planned for us younger chaps later in the week. What say we go and enjoy a preview?"

Darcy had thought himself to be inured to the *diversions* common within the court of George IV. He found suddenly he was not. Darcy brushed off the Marquis' hand. "No thank you, Hart. Now, if you'll please excuse me, I've a wife to see to."

Elizabeth had been quite impressed with the stellar company, up to a point. Many of the guests surrounding her were foreign gentlemen, well read and charming. They had impeccable manners, were mildly flirtatious and extremely solicitous. If she were a few years younger and unmarried she would have been very flattered.

However, she was not single – she was a happily married wife, a mother, and all she really felt was

homesick. As the men discussed great art and
literature she thought only of bedtime stories and
finger painting. Were her babies missing her? Had
George gotten to ride in the park already? Would
Kathy and Anne Marie attempt to dress the Mama cat
again? *Anne Marie was scratched the first time – I
should have said something to Amanda.* She felt
fingertips touch her elbow then begin their slow,
delicate slide upward. Smiling, she turned, expecting
to see her husband; instead she saw a stranger. "Sir?"
she inquired as she discreetly pulled away from the
man; but, he was determined. He reached for her once
again. Elizabeth pushed his hand away. "Sir, please
do not..."

That was all she managed to say before a familiar
voice interrupted. "Excuse me." Staring hard at the
forward nobleman Darcy reached out his hand to his
Elizabeth. "Would you be so good as to move aside? I
wish to dance with my wife." Highly offended the man
locked eyes with Darcy for several moments. In the
end, however, Darcy's fury was greater than the
gentleman's lust; the man backed away.

The couple moved onto the dance floor. "Another
moment and that idiot and I would have been facing
off with our fists." His jaw was still clenched at the
thought of another man desiring his wife. As usual,
though, he calmed the moment he looked into her
beloved face. "Or, I could have bored him into
submission with drainage measurements." They took
their position for a waltz. "Sorry that I've neglected
you so much this evening."

"Is this what you expected it to be like?" she
whispered.

The music began and Darcy and Elizabeth stepped
into the twirling movements of the dance. "These
people are arrogant, rude, self indulgent and

opinionated – very similar to Easter at Aunt Catherine's. Yes, I'm afraid it's pretty much as I expected. What about you?"

"I've met some very interesting people."

"So I gather. Interesting and interested."

"Don't split hairs with me, William. For the most part they've been very polite and gracious, if a bit dull – at least until that last gentleman. I can reveal to you that I am fully informed about winter in Denmark and spring in Holland. Once that was discussed, however, conversation tended to drag. Why are you smiling?"

He arched an eyebrow for her benefit. "I am proud that you are the most beautiful woman in the room, Elizabeth, as well as the youngest by about twenty years. I am not well pleased with these men who follow you about."

Her eyes sparkled. "I do believe you're jealous. That's very gratifying to a wife."

"Well, if another man stares at your breasts, you'll be pleased to know I may have to shoot him."

"Are you having a splendid time?"

"I am now."

They retired to their rooms as soon as possible, much earlier than most, staying only until the evening's guest of honor, Russian Princess Lowicka, the former Countess Johanna Grudna-Grudczinska, retired to her rooms. Cara had waited up for Elizabeth, ready to help her mistress prepare for bed, eager for news of the ball.

As the two women gossiped the beautiful satin gown was carefully removed and set side, the tiara boxed, the necklace, bracelets and earbobs all locked away. Cara helped Lizzy remove pins from her hair then brushed it to a high sheen, leaving it unbraided, free and flowing. Lizzy, sleepy now and relaxed, thanked her maid for waiting up, dismissed her and said good night.

She found him leaning a shoulder against the open window frame, staring into the black night. He looked so young and handsome in his long robe, his feet bare and his hair messy. She softly called his name then hurried to his arms when he reached out his hand out to her.

"You've left your hair free. I'm glad." For the first time all evening Lizzy felt truly blessed and happy, content. They gently kissed then both turned to look out over the quiet stream that fronted the great house.

"You look very pensive, William."

"I was just thinking about my life before we married, about Aunt Catherine actually. She often hosted events very similar to tonight's party with dozens of houseguests, royalty everywhere."

"Do you miss all of that?"

He rubbed his cheek against her hair. "I was dreadfully alone in those days, even in a huge ballroom filled with people. I felt as if I were just drifting through life." Darcy stared intently into the dark outside. "It all came back to me tonight, the emptiness and the pride and vanity of that existence. Do I miss those days? Not for a moment. My life began with you, Lizzy, don't you know that? I have two children I adore. I never imagined my heart could be so full."

"Well, I was going to tease you but I find I cannot. You bring tears to my eyes."

"Don't cry because I am so happy. I love you, Lizzy. I want to give you everything; I want to give you the world."

She stared at him several moments before she spoke.

"Give me one more child then, William. Please. That is world enough for me. You and our children are my life."

He lifted her chin with his finger and saw in her eyes the yearning there, the need. "This is truly what you want, isn't it? You don't fear another childbirth."

"Never. I don't know if I could explain it to you, but I know that a child of ours is still waiting to be born."

"I shall do my very best then, although it may take us weeks and weeks of trial and error." He smiled wickedly and dipped his head for another kiss. "Besides, I confess, I do so love the work."

Laughing softly, their arms around each other's waists, they went in to bed; and, by the morning, a new life had begun.

Chapter Twelve

Georgie Darcy stared at the ceiling and hummed. In the bed across from him were his very best friends, his cousins Matthew and Mark, but they were asleep now and he was wide awake, his only companion the old cat purring beside him. Usually the shadows behind the cupboard bothered him, or the creaky old floor boards, the suspicious darkness in the corners. But not this night; no, this night his mind had other things to occupy. Sighing he snuggled deeper into the bed. What a wondrous afternoon it had turned into.

There had been three pony carts and six horses and everyone saw them, one and all smiled and waved. Then Uncle Fitz placed him in front of himself on his saddle, handed him the reins, and George had led their little parade. It was so easy to ride that horse, what was all the fuss! He was a natural born horseman – Uncle Fitz said so right out loud.

It was too bad that there would be no more opportunity to ride here, with Uncle Fitz busy with work; if only he could practice a bit he was certain he could surprise his father by riding right up to him. He'd be so proud of him that he'd shake his hand and call him a capital fellow!

Harry's mare was being kept in the stable two doors down and she was sweet and gentle, she really liked

him and had let him feed her apple slices. If he could
figure out how to put a saddle on her then he could
practice in secret. No one would ever know. It would
be an adventure he'd remember the rest of his life.
Just like Uncle Fitz running off to become a pirate...

Since he couldn't sleep anyway – why not sneak
over to the stable now!

Georgie sat up slowly and silently pulled back his
covers.

"Who found him?" Fitzwilliam was running toward
the house, his footman following close in his wake.

"Jonathan, the stable master's assistant, sir. Saw
the lad as 'e was comin' in to muck out the stalls, early
mornin'. Carried the boy across 'ere straight away."

It was into the second week of the Darcy's visit to
Devonshire when George's nurse discovered his bed
empty, her screams immediately awakening
Fitzwilliam and Amanda. The entire household had
been out searching for the little boy for over an hour.

Richard tore across neighboring lawns and was into
the house within moments, his heart pounding in his
chest. He heard the commotion from above almost
immediately, it was a single mad wail accompanied by
running feet and his wife's crisp voice.

"Bring me blankets," Amanda called the order to
someone. "Warm some milk. Stop that wailing if you
please!" George's frantic nurse, standing in the corner
of the room, clamped her hands over her mouth.

By the time Richard had reached the top step he
saw the children hovering around the master bedroom
door, all holding hands, looking frightened and
anxious. He lifted a sobbing Kathy up into his arms
and hugged her tightly. "Calm yourself, Kate. Shush,
lass." Harry and the twins stood just inside the
doorway, their faces drained of all color. "Come here

lads. Give your mother a bit of room. Amanda, how is he?"

"He's drenched through, wet and freezing, poor lamb," she muttered. Removing the sodden clothes first she dried him quickly then wrapped a warm blanket around him. Holding the child in her arms she sat on the nearby rocker while more blankets were tucked around him. The boy's lips were nearly blue from cold and he was shivering. A servant ran in with the jug of warm milk, spiked with just a touch of brandy.

"What in the world were you thinking, going out into the streets alone?" Fitzwilliam's initial terror was suddenly manifesting itself into angry barks.

"Richard, not now; give the poor child a chance to calm himself and become warm again. That's right son, sip slowly."

"Someone else here must know something! Matthew? Mark? Explain to me what happened!'

"We don't know, Papa," Matthew trembled at the sight of his dear friend, so pale and weak. "We thought he was sleeping. We were all sleeping."

Looking very solemn, Mark nodded his head in agreement. "He must have sneaked out early in the morning, before the light even. Papa – don't be angry – he's been going out other mornings too. We teased him about it but he said it was a secret; he was preparing a surprise for Uncle Wills."

"You mean you knew he was leaving the house but never said a word!"

"We're sorry, Papa." Matthew whispered as he fought back his tears.

"Sorry, Papa," Mark said at the same time.

"I shall deal with you both later..."

Kathy lifted her tear streaked face from her father's shoulder. "Is he going to die, Papa?" she sobbed, her breath coming in tiny gulps. *"Oh, poor dead Georgie!"*

"Don't say that, Kathy!" He motioned to George's nurse standing mute in the corner. "Here, you, whatever your name is, take the children to their rooms and wait with them."

"I think I had better stay with Master Darcy." The nurse's voice quivered as she spoke; she began to inch forward toward Amanda.

"Where is his sister?"

"Still sleeping, sir. Nothing wakes the little miss. Let me just take the boy to his room, ma'am, and I'll see to him. I'm certain this is nothing more than a guilty conscious..."

Amanda twisted away from the nurse and held the child tighter; Richard was certain he heard a low growl. He half expected her to snap at the woman.

"Word of advice, nurse – never come between a mother bear and a sick cub. Now take my daughter, if you please."

As Fitzwilliam tried to pull Kathy's clutching fingers from his neck the child's wild howls grew louder. *"He's going to die! Georgie is going to die! So young!"*

"Katherine Marie Fitzwilliam, stop that wailing right this moment. Now, believe me, dearest, he is not going to die. I will not allow that in my house."

Finally he was able to untangle her tiny fingers and remove her hands from his neck. He handed her to the nurse, patted his daughter's face tenderly and kissed her cheek. "Katherine Marie, you dear, sweet, little angel, you bring tears to my eyes. Such devotion to your friend, such love for your cousin." He sniffed. "You make me proud, lass. Never fear. We will not allow anything bad to happen to your Georgie."

"Well..." Sighing raggedly, Kathy rubbed the tears from her eyes, "...if he does die, may I have his pony cart?"

"Out!" Fitzwilliam pointed to the door and the children were hurried from the room.

"But he won't be needing it anymore..." his daughter wailed anew.

"Out!"

When Georgie began to feel warm enough, and strong enough, he lifted his head to speak. "Uncle Fitz, I'm sorry. Please don't be mad at Matt and Mark, I made them promise not to tell." The little voice wavered and he nestled closer into his aunt's comforting embrace. "I thought Harry's mare liked me – she did last week. But she kept shying away this morning, she never would stand still. When I wanted to lift the saddle it was very heavy and I fell and hurt myself. I tried to walk back home but my leg hurt very badly so I sat down."

A shudder wracked his body and Amanda made him sip once again from the warming liquid. "It began to lightning and thunder. Is Harry's mare all right? Did she run off?"

"Yes, child, but not far; we found her sooner than we found you. She's been dried off, fed and put into her stall. Now, take more of the warm milk. That's a good boy." Amanda gently kissed his forehead to test for fever.

He was warm – too warm.

Fitzwilliam sat on the edge of the bed facing them. "You know that was wrong of you, don't you George? You did many bad things. You made the boys promise something that you should not have, you jeopardized your safety, you jeopardized Harry's horse, you left the house without us knowing, you frightened your aunt and your nurse half to death..." Harry turned his face away in shame and began to suck on his thumb.

"I believe you've made your point, Richard," Amanda said softly. "How often have you done this George, how many times have you gone to the corner stable?"

"Three times." His voice sounded so small.

"I'm utterly speechless," Fitzwilliam rubbed the back of his neck. "How could we not know? I feel I've let Darcy down, but I never thought to keep guard over the child or that I needed to lock the doors. It doesn't bear to think what might have happened to him." He realized he was shaking. "Why, George? Why did you do it?"

"I wanted to surprise Papa."

"You foolish, foolish child."

"Richard, enough."

"Well, the boy could have died out there! Darcy entrusted him to my care; how can I ever face the man again? Of course if we employed a decent butler and footman this would never have happened!" The husband and wife glared at each other. "It will be necessary to punish you George. This type of behavior is unacceptable." Tears threatened, moistening Richard's eyes, refuting his harsh words. "An inexcusable dereliction of duty." Whether he was speaking of the child or of himself, only Fitzwilliam knew.

"Go no further with this, Richard!" It was not often that his gentle wife could shock him into silence, but the tone of her voice and her frank stare assured him his tirade was at an end. "Never mind your uncle, George. He has just been very worried about you." Amanda hugged the boy closer. "We've all been very worried."

His face peeked at her from within the gathered blankets. "Don't tell Mama and Papa, Auntie Manda. Please."

"I'm afraid we must George, or you must. When one has done something very wrong one must accept consequences. If you were to tell your father yourself, however, that would be very brave. It would say to him that you have accepted responsibility for your deeds and that you see them as wrong – you do see your actions as wrong, do you not? Excellent. In fact, Richard, I think you should send a rider out immediately and inform William and Elizabeth of what has happened."

"I've already done that. I've also sent for Milagros." With those words Fitzwilliam reached over and gathered both the boy and the blankets into his own arms to hold tight.

Unfortunately, the fever grew worse as the day progressed. Remembering her physician father's dictums, Amanda settled George in their one little guest bedroom, isolating him from her other children and reluctantly handed over responsibility of her own infant to the nurse. This would be the first time any of her babies had been cared for by someone other than herself, but it must be done. She could not risk the children's health and she would not leave George's side. She was determined to stay in the room and care for him as long as he was ill.

Tension and fear took permanent residence in her heart as the child's fever continued to mount.

It was not until late afternoon that Dr. Anthony Milagros arrived, fresh from his rounds at his hospital for the poor. The door was answered by the Fitzwilliam's nearly blind butler, Hastings.

"May I help you, sir?"

"It is I, Hastings, Dr. Milagros." The family physician and close personal friend moved smoothly past the man and into the entrance hall. As he removed his hat and gloves he realized the butler hadn't turned but still stood staring out onto the small front doorstep. Anthony tapped his shoulder. "I'm inside already, man; must have passed by your bad eye. Do remind me before I leave to check that vision of yours again. Well, I believe I am expected. How is the child?"

"He threw up on Papa, Uncle Doctor Tony." Matthew and Mark spoke in unison, appearing at Anthony's side from seemingly nowhere, staring up at him with their ivory blond curls, identical blue eyes and angelic faces. *Appearances can be so very misleading...*

"Rather careless of him."

"That's what we thought, unless that was his plan; then it was awfully good. But, we're not certain yet," said Mark.

"Papa says you must have lead in your bum." Matthew faced him boldly, his hands shoved into his pockets, while his brother Mark resumed sucking on a thumb. Anthony reasoned that as long as he kept his medical case closed and the sharp knives in his breast pocket, no one could get hurt this visit.

"Do you want us to let them know you're here?"

He chuckled at those precious upturned faces. True they were imps, often getting into trouble, too frequently into mischief; however... "Yes, that would be very nice of you both. Why don't you run and tell them... "

Matthew and Mark turned and shrieked in unison at the top of their lungs, *"The leech is here!"*

As Anthony passed he whacked them both on the back of their heads.

After a lengthy examination of Georgie, Anthony motioned Fitz and Amanda away from the bed and over to the window. "His lungs really are quite inflamed," he stated softly without any preamble. "You've done well with him, Amanda, as I knew you would. His fever has not been allowed to gain in strength and that is very important, *querida*. However, I believe I should remain here tonight just to be on the safe side, then I can monitor the powders I will give to him, perhaps adjust the dosage. Other than that, all we can do is wait and see. Since I have come straight from hospital and have had no sustenance all day I fear I'll need to dine here, repulsive as that thought is to me."

"We have a new cook, Anthony." Amanda grinned at her old friend.

"Truly? What happened to the one who believed she was Napoleon?"

"She has gone into retirement. That Irish widow was next, but she's gone as well."

"Have they found the body?"

"Lord you truly are an annoying person." Fitzwilliam rubbed his tired eyes. "I don't want you to associate with this man ever again, Amanda."

"Your words are harsh but your eyes speak of love. Well, be off the two of you – do not forget to send up my food, however. At this point I am no longer particular about who prepares it; I only ask that whatever is served to me not have died of natural causes. Go. Shoo. Neither of you need remain. Why are you still here?"

"I'm not leaving, Anthony," Amanda huffed, determined to do whatever she felt necessary for her family's well being. "If Elizabeth cannot be here with her son I certainly will not leave his side; she would do no less for any of my children. However, Richard, you should go and have a rest." He had already walked to the doorway and returned, having yelled first for the elderly, blind butler and then for the screaming maid he'd never met. He heard a crash downstairs and shook his head.

"I've not grown suddenly enfeebled, woman. I'll have you know I lived for years during the war in conditions that would make your stomach toss. Oh for heaven's sake, where are these damn servants when you need them?" He stomped over to a bell pull – a bell pull he had never before realized was there. *How very odd ...* A thought stumbled around in the recesses of his mind, a certainty that there were only two functioning bell pulls in the entire house – one in the sitting room and the other in the dining parlor. Perhaps this one had become entangled on something in the walls like the other two. He had fixed those by just yanking on them very hard a few times. If that was the case, if this was just tangled, a good hard tug might be all that was needed...

He tugged.

A half filled bag of flour suspended over the bedroom door dumped onto the floor sending an exploding white cloud wafting up into the air. The flour settled very slowly, but surely, upon everything and anything near the entranceway.

Fortunately, no one was standing beneath it at the time.

Unfortunately, it was a very small room.

There was momentary silence.

"Oh, my stars," Amanda coughed then cleared her throat as a grinning Dr. Milagros stepped back and looked away.

"Your children are hooligans, madam, completely out of control...!" Fitzwilliam began to shout.

"*My* children?"

"Precisely! Now, I will bloody well find someone in this madhouse – anyone – capable of providing us with food and drink." He eyed the still swirling white dust. "And a bloody broom."

Going into the hallway he leaned over the stair rail and pointed. "You – there! Girl! I see you... Oh good heavens, now what have I done, she's screaming again! Amanda! Get out here and talk to her. Milagros – port or claret?"

Chapter Thirteen

As Cara was fixing Lizzy's hair for dinner Lizzy noticed her maid appeared to be uncharacteristically quiet, chewing nervously on her bottom lip.

"Cara, what is it? Are you feeling unwell? Now that I think on it you looked upset this morning also."

"Oh, I'm sorry, ma'am. It's just that..."

"What?"

"It's just that I thought I saw someone early in the day and when I asked about it I was told to mind my own business and not be a tale carrier; but, I did see him, I know I did! I don't care what that horrible butler says."

"Good heavens, Cara. Whom did you see?"

"Well, ma'am, I thought I saw Toby McHugh. You remember; the Fitzwilliam's footman. He and I sort of stepped out once so I know him special well. I swore I saw him in the back pantry, just for a second, just as the door was closing and when I went to try and look I was told it wasn't him and to mind my place and all. But it was him, ma'am, it was. At least I think it was. Anyway, I've been searching around all morning and haven't seen him again, so perhaps I was wrong."

Lizzy's heart began beating erratically. Her mother's instinct had been expecting something to happen; her common sense had dismissed her growing anxiety as a mother's constant companion – but, she'd still been uneasy for days, her discomfort worsening every moment. "Continue looking around, Cara. It may be nothing; however, if you do see or hear anything, anything at all, come and tell me or the master immediately – no one else. We'll be playing cards again this evening in that big blue parlor, just the women. The men will be meeting upstairs.

"That I will ma'am."

"I won't hear of it, Darcy. You simply must remain. The Prince of Wales will be arriving her next week with half dozen of his closest friends, and I do believe my daughter has arranged for a theatrical presentation. It is a rare honor to be counted within the Prince's private entertainments like this and he can be very generous with his friends. It will do wonders for your future."

"Your Grace, I truly appreciate the honor it would be to remain here for the Prince's visit; however, my wife and I had planned on being absent from our home only three weeks and it's already stretched to four. To remain any longer would inconvenience my cousin and his family. They are watching our children."

"Leave it to me. I'll send someone to collect your children – what have you, two, three? The problem's easily taken care of, I can assure you; easily remedied. We shall have them brought to your home and arrange for someone to stay with them there. I imagine they have nurses and maids and all that."

"Not at present. My cousin's home is rather small so only one nurse is presently with my children and I would not allow her to oversee them on her own. As to your generous offer, I must decline. I believe it would make my children uncomfortable, to be watched over by strangers."

"Stuff and nonsense. What difference if they are 'uncomfortable'? They're children, Darcy, they have no judgment; they do what we wish them to do. It is my opinion that children should be seen by parents only at scheduled times — keeps them from getting underfoot as it were, teaches them self reliance. And, of course, their day to day care should be left solely in the hands of professionals. I have several excellent attendants that'll do the job well enough for such a short duration; but, if you find you feel a bit puckish with that idea, you can always buy them some toys or what have you when you do see them. That never fails to win them back. You needn't worry."

Darcy felt the strangest urge to jump up and grab the old man by the throat. The past weeks had taken their toll with Darcy growing increasingly weary of these unkind and snobbish people, many of them hiding bullying ways behind bored facades. Now, he couldn't wait to be free of them, the sooner the better in his mind. "My wife promised the children we would be gone only a few weeks. This is the first she's been separated from them and, truthfully, she misses them a great deal."

The Duke stared blankly back at him, with no obvious comprehension; then he began to snicker. "Oh, that's right. I suppose, coming from her background..."

That was the last straw; Darcy stood, trying very hard not to lose his temper. No wonder the man's children lacked character — it was the only thing he couldn't buy for them. "I'm afraid that this subject is at an end, your Grace. I am sorry if it displeases you but I have never broken a promise to my children before and I certainly do not intend to now."

"You cannot be serious."

"I can assure you, sir, I am perfectly serious."

"We are speaking of the future King of England, man. You do not refuse the company of your future monarch. Of course you will remain; my heavens, there is no question of that. You are behaving as provincially as your father did, bringing a weeping child to the hunt! They are merely children. They shall have nurses and nannies and all manner of fuss and bother about them." The Duke was becoming more and more annoyed. "Honoring promises to children – ridiculous; never heard the like! It's like honoring a promise to your mistress. I am beginning to have second thoughts about placing you in Parliament. Yes, I am. I have plans for you, sir, but you'd better learn your place now, Darcy. It is within my power to make you a very rich and important man, but I never waste time on a fool."

Did this old man actually believe insults to his father could go unchallenged, or that Darcy would choose fame or a bit of power over his family? Why in the world was he wasting one more moment with these people? Their beliefs, their priorities, were completely foreign to him.

"It is fortunate for me then, *Your Grace*, that I already *am* a very rich and important man; your bad opinion of me is of no consequence. As to my father, I am proud beyond words to be compared with him. He was, and is, the finest man I have ever known." Just then the door burst open and Elizabeth stood there, her eyes brimming with tears.

"This is becoming worse than 'A Sicilian Romance'." Hart could not suppress his sarcasm a moment longer. "Now the silly wife stumbles in. What's next, the thwarted lover?" He threw down his napkin and turned to face Elizabeth standing in the doorway. He saw the anxious, worried look on her face but was unmoved. "This entire family is beyond the pale."

"Hart, I'll thank you to keep a civil tongue in your mouth!"

Hart turned his back to Elizabeth. "How dreadfully rude of me, Darcy; so sorry. I'd like more burgundy, here, please."

"I wish to speak with my husband – alone. William?"

"Excuse me gentlemen."

When Darcy reached her he saw the tears that glistened in her eyes. Cupping her elbow he led her to the outside hallway where Cara was standing beside a visibly angry Henderson. "Whatever is the matter, Elizabeth? Are you unwell?"

"It's Georgie, William. I think our son is not feeling well. In fact, I fear he's very ill."

"Why? What has happened?"

"Toby came all this way – you remember him, the Fitzwilliam's footman. Oh, William, he's been here since yesterday trying to get word to us. They attempted to send him off but he hid himself away until he caught Cara's attention. Evidently, Georgie snuck out in the early morning and was hurt. He was out in the rain, William, alone. Oh, my sweet baby is ill, I just know he is." Her face was pale and she trembled with fear.

"Where is Toby? I wish to speak with that footman immediately."

"I was under the impression that he had left the premises, Mr. Darcy."

"But he didn't, did he?" Cara was much smaller than Henderson but appeared primed to do battle nonetheless. "In spite of you! Poor lad's been hiding in the stables but they just found him. I heard him, yelling my name as I went outside to get some night air. He was being roughed up by this lot."

"Oh, he was not – watch your mouth girl!" snapped Henderson.

"Well, they were pulling at him. Two against one! I'd say that was pretty rough!"

"*Now* what is the hubbub about, Darcy?" Hart leaned against the open doorway, clearly exasperated. "Are you coming in for cards or not?"

"My cousin sent his footman here to inform me my son was ill and your butler prevented the man from seeing me! I demand to know why I was not immediately informed!"

"Because we were all having such a fine time – or I thought we were. I told Henderson get rid of the lad, of course! Foot*man*? That's a laugh. From what I was told he looked more like a foot*pad*. I instructed my servants to throw him out."

"How dare you! What right had you to keep this information from me? Is your arrogance so great?"

"Don't be overly dramatic, Darcy. Good God, I will never marry for these very reasons; women you can find anywhere and children are such an annoying nuisance..."

Hart lay stunned on the floor with Darcy's first punch.

Chapter Fourteen

Anthony turned from his perusal of the autumn sunshine, stretched his arms high above his head and yawned. He could relax finally. It was now two days later and in the early morning hours the child's fever had reached its zenith then passed – the crisis was over. Georgie had awoken fever free, and a little hungry.

"Do they always snore so loudly?" Touching the back of his hand to the boy's forehead he confirmed that the fever was over and smiled. The skin was cool to his touch. Anthony had been back and forth to the house often over the last two days, supervising the Fitzwilliam's constant care of George.

Georgie nodded, the pink and cream coloring returning to his cheeks. "When they visit Pemberley we can hear them all over the house, even as far up as the nursery floor. You can do *anything* to them when they're asleep like this and they never know. Mark, Matthew and I once tickled their noses until they sneezed and sometimes Kathy puts feathers atop of their lips and we try to catch them as they float around. The feathers I mean."

As if he were a little prince, George was propped up against large, soft pillows and was being served a cup of warm milk and honey by his nurse. A half eaten piece of toasted bread smeared with butter was in his hand.

Anthony shook his head. "Well, it's a lucky thing they found each other is it not? Who else could stand the racket?"

Amanda and Richard were indeed sound asleep and snoring to raise the roof. She in her rocking chair beside the bed and he in a corner of the room, his long legs tucked under the chair, his head back and his mouth hanging open.

"They'll be very pleased to see how much improved you are." Anthony pulled the covers back from the child's badly bruised legs to examine them, apply a healing ointment and bandages, and then replace the covers.

"How are you feeling, George?" Harry stood in the doorway. "How is he Uncle Tony?" Chattering little voices could be heard approaching from down the hall.

"Papa is snoring!" Kathy clapped excitedly and pushed her way passed Harry. "Shall I get the feathers?"

Next to her appeared an anxious, wide eyed, Anne Marie. "Is my brother going to be all right now?"

"Yes, my darling one." Anthony walked over to the little group and picked Anne Marie up in his arms. "Georgie will be well very soon. You all must help care for him. Do not allow him to catch chill or overtire himself; and, he has several very bad bruises on his legs that will need to be monitored for infection."

Matthew strode into the room. "I'll see to it that he feels better." Anthony fought hard not to laugh outright. Not only was the boy the image of his father, he was also as irrationally confident of his own abilities. "Georgie, get up. Let's go outside and play."

"You were right Harry. Papa does snore louder than Mama but she drools." Kathy took another bite of the cake she had ostensibly brought for Georgie. "You don't want any of this do you, George? Oh, sorry, I finished it already."

Darcy and Elizabeth were packed and away in their carriage within the hour. There had been more harsh words and empty threats to and from Hart's direction but cold indifference from the Duke.

As they settled into the soft leather squabs for the long ride home he took his wife's hand in his and squeezed. "Don't borrow trouble, Lizzy. Fitz and Amanda are excellent parents which is why we trusted them in the first place. George will have the best of care."

"My mind knows this, William, but my heart is breaking. I cannot be at ease until I see him."

"I know. I feel the same."

"Was the Duke very angry at our leaving?"

"Livid. Do you care?"

"No. Not in the least."

Darcy smiled, put his arm around her shoulders and brought her closer, into the comfort of his embrace. "And neither to do I."

Chapter Fifteen

"Hello? Anyone here?" Fitzwilliam returned home from another day of useless meetings at the War Office to what appeared to be an unusually quiet, empty house. No butler to greet him. No wife. No children. He took a quick look around. "Where in bloody hell is everyone? *Hoy! Amanda!*" The hallway was deserted...except for a disheveled looking older woman who sat on a chair in the entranceway corner, a pail at her feet, a mop in one hand, and a pipe in the other.

His pipe.

"Who are you?"

"I'm Maudie ain't I. You the Baron?"

"I am. Where is everyone?"

"'ere and there, I expect."

"What's your business here?"

"I'm yer new maid."

"Don't tell me that."

"Missus up and 'ired me. Just like that. No warnin'."

"The woman's a menace."

"She fed me good though, won't say a word against 'er for that, so don't you ask me to. Just had me some exceptional pie. But now she wants me to mop this 'ere floor for 'er."

"Where's the other maid?"

"Which 'un?"

"The one who screams every time I enter the room."

"Does she limp?"

"Yes."

"Looks kind of squinty-eyed and mousey."

"Yes."

"'as a great wart right next to her left eye?"

"She does."

"Never saw 'er. Wouldn't have any tobacco laying about for this 'ere pipe would ye?"

"That's my pipe."

"Didn't say it wasn't." She shoved the stem into her toothless mouth. "I suppose now ye want it back."

"Not anymore, no." He tossed her his tobacco pouch. "Keep that. Now, where's 'the Missus'?"

"She the one with the light 'air..."

"Oh, good heavens..."

A sudden racket on the street had Fitzwilliam turning to look out the still open front door. Relief flooded through him. The Darcy's had finally returned.

Elizabeth and William's carriage had driven straight through the previous night, only stopping to change horses. Toby sat on top beside the Darcy's coachman with a second carriage following that carried Cara, Darcy's valet and the luggage. The moment they reached the Fitzwilliam's home Darcy opened the door and looked anxiously to his waiting cousin.

"He's fit as a fiddle, Darcy." Fitzwilliam had already come down the front steps and held open the rusty garden gate for them. Inside the coach Elizabeth was in a panic, clumsily gathering her skirts, clutching for her reticule. Her husband turned to her and repeated Fitzwilliam's words but it was a half moment before

Elizabeth comprehended their meaning. A great sob of relief escaped her. "Oh, thank the Lord." Pressing a hand to her heart as Darcy assisted her down from the coach Elizabeth's face was pale with the fatigue of their journey, her eyes wide with anxiety.

"Richard," she took Fitzwilliam's hand the moment she came near. "Is he truly all right?"

"Yes, go on up. I'm certain you will find him among a great heap of boys – just follow the shouts. Kathy and Anne Marie are in the back dressing the poor cat again." His eyes sparkled and he nodded as he spoke, revealing the truth of his words, and she finally believed that her son would be all right. Whatever had happened to him, whatever the boy had done, no longer mattered as long as he would be fine. Her eyes overflowed with tears of joy and she hurried into the house.

After a long and joyous visit in private with his son, wife and daughter, followed by a rambunctious gathering of both families in the children's playroom, Darcy required fresh air, peace and quiet. He needed a place to sit alone and thrash about his ideas, sort them through, calm his nerves. God, he had never been so frightened in his life. He believed himself immune to public displays of emotion yet the sight of his five year old son's gashed legs had nearly broken him. No words of reprimand would be directed at the boy, later they would talk. There was time enough for discipline. For now the sight of a healing child was all that mattered. Besides he felt a certain amount of guilt for being gone, for careless promises, for a million and one things that were beyond his control but for which he still felt responsible. He just wanted a few moments to himself, where he could let loose his pent up emotions.

He actually wanted a good cry...

"Darcy, I need to speak with you. Damn that smell from the compost...!" Fitzwilliam had followed him outside, bringing with him a large bottle of port and two cigarillos. "Darcy! Where in hell are you?"

Darcy toyed with the idea of ducking behind a bush but that seemed rather inappropriate for a gentleman his age. "Over here, Fitz, and for goodness sake stop shouting."

Fitzwilliam found his cousin seated at the rear of the property beside a shed, the area to the right of them a large garden now fallow; the rotting compost heap was downwind and to their left. The men sat in silence for a time, lit their smokes and drank their port straight from the bottle.

Fitzwilliam inhaled deeply. "I don't know what to say to you Darcy, I really don't – how can you ever forgive me? I feel absolutely terrible; it's my fault, of course. I would gladly have sacrificed my own life for his, if anything would have happened to him."

"But...something did happen to him."

"I beg your pardon?"

"You just said you'd sacrifice your own life if anything had happened to him. Well something did happen, so be off with you, just don't frighten any of the children or upset the women."

"It was a figure of speech, Darcy."

"And don't make a mess for the servants. Yours would surely perish from work. Do you need a gun?"

"You're not making this easy for me are you?"

"You can lie down in front of my carriage if you like."

"Eat glass and die, Darcy."

"Never mind then. And, well, I suspect it was not entirely your fault, Fitz." Darcy was finally grinning, happy for the quiet night, the smells of cooking coming from the kitchens that overrode the compost aroma, the distant sound of children laughing – the misery of his cousin. He was relaxing at last. He puffed on his cheroot for a moment. "I kept on and on at him about his not being experienced enough to ride out alone, even in a pony cart, told him when he had practiced enough we would see. He wanted so badly to make me proud, little man that he is. Then I told him that idiotic story of your trying to run away to sea when you were not much older than he."

"I see that now. Yes. Yes, you're completely right, of course. It *was* your fault." Fitzwilliam settled back in his chair. "Well, I feel much better." He grabbed Darcy's cheroot, lit another for himself with it then returned the original to its owner. "What a scamp. Barely tall enough to reach the door handles, yet he goes off alone, thinking to master riding, just to impress you. Thank the lord this is a quiet area." He looked over his shoulder, afraid one of the wives might overhear, then he whispered loudly. "I wouldn't say this in front of the women – but – you have to admire him for that, you know. He's a bit like his old Uncle Fitz, isn't he?"

"More bollocks than brains?"

"Give me back my liquor."

Darcy laughed outright for the first time, then he too leaned forward to listen for the wives, and, satisfied that he and Fitz were still alone, sat back again. "Well, I admit I agree with you. Not about him being anything like you, God forbid; but, I am more than a little proud of the boy's gumption. He's growing up so quickly, as they all are."

"Ah, Darcy. What would it be like to be twenty ourselves again when this lot are twenty? Between my hell raisers and your little man in there... oh, well. We are doomed to be forever thirty years older and on our best behavior in front of them. By the way, how was your visit with Devonshire?"

"Useless. We played whist and listened to a bunch of old men compare estate sizes as if they were cocks. It took nearly two days for them to notify me of George's illness. The arrogance is appalling, the lack of common sense and unconcern for their fellow man, unspeakable. They could see no cause for alarm; decided my child's welfare too trivial to interrupt their 'entertainments'."

"My goodness. Who'd you knock down – Hart or the Duke?"

"Hart."

Fitzwilliam let out a hoot of laughter. "Excellent choice; never did like that over bred monkey."

Darcy took another pull from the bottle then handed it back to his cousin for a drink. "I've decided to find someone to unseat Cavendish for our district."

"It's about bloody time. Good luck with that, cousin."

"It will take some work, but nothing will improve for Derbyshire if someone doesn't take a stand."

"Why not take the seat yourself? I remember you and your father discussing that possibility years ago, you wanted it then. You're certainly more than qualified for Parliament."

"A life in politics is no longer for me, Fitz. No, I find I quite like the life I lead and I love my family." He smiled and puffed on his smoke. "And above all else, I love being a father."

1828
"The Children"

Dependent, Emotionally Attached to Parents
Seek Adult Approval
Unlimited Curiosity
Sexual Awareness

He will turn the hearts of the fathers to their children,
and the hearts of the children to their fathers;
or else I will come and strike the land with a curse

Malachi 4:6

Chapter Sixteen

Bennet George Darcy looked down upon the top of his mother's head and attempted to sound disappointed. "Such a shame; you see, they don't fit. Although I do think it's well past time all of my trousers were long, don't you agree, Mother?"

"Whenever did you grow another two inches?" Lizzy shook her head in wonder. "Perhaps we have extra in the hem to let down?" Kneeling before her son, Lizzy motioned for him to turn so she and her maid might view the back of his pants to also see how tight they were across his bottom. "Oh George, what have you done to these?"

"We were playing cricket a bit rough yesterday. Is it very bad? It's much too bad to repair, isn't it?"

"The center seam is torn. I suppose they were getting a bit snug, weren't they? Well I am amazed, nothing left to it but have more trousers made. Jem," Lizzy turned to a young servant who waited by the window, "run and tell Mr. Winters we'll need to have that seamstress, Miss Carlson, back here, tomorrow if possible; have her measure Master George again for another three pair – make that four pair – of pants." Lizzy gave one more tug at the hem resting directly at his kneecap. "And we'll have to tell her to allow for a good deal of growth." Gazing back up at her son she experienced no small amount of pride. "You'll be easily as tall as your father by the time you've finished growing. You're nearly my height already."

He smiled. "Not too difficult, that."

"George."

"I really think it's time I had long pants, don't you, Mother?"

"Yes, George, yes, I heard you, I've heard you each and every time. I suppose you want a front button fly and suspenders as well."

"And riding gaiters if I might, like father's?"

"Oh, all right." Lizzy chuckled at his triumphant expression. Oh, she was so very proud of him, this beautiful boy of hers. Good natured, already of exemplary character – he was the very image of his handsome father in so many ways. "For now why don't you go put on those woolen pants we patched yesterday and hurry downstairs, your cousins are due at any moment – oh wait, I can hear the crash of tables even as we speak. The Fitzwilliam's have already arrived." She laughed happily at her son's whoop of joy.

"Excellent, we're playing football today, boys against girls – we'll annihilate them. Mummy, can we all have tea soon also? I'm famished"

"You are always famished and yes, tea will be ready in a quarter hour. And keep your eye on your baby sister – I don't want her getting hurt..." She was speaking to an empty doorway however; he was off, already gone from the room and down the stairs within a moment.

Her son was growing quickly, suffering fewer and fewer ill effects of the frightening lung ailment from five years earlier. True, any illness he did experience lingered a bit longer than usual but they had grown less severe with each winter. She still felt a mother's guilt, though, for having been away at a useless house party when her son needed her most.

At least there had been one happy outcome of that ill fated visit to Devonshire. Nine months after their return Alice Anne had been born, the darling of her father and mother, the pampered pet of her brother and sister; the joy of their household. Elizabeth's family was complete.

"Ma'am, will you want to send a note along to Mrs. Carlson, tell her what fabric you want? Last time she brought that wool you didn't like."

"Very wise, Cara. And I'll jot down a few extras I want her to bring with her as well. Come back in five minutes if you will." Elizabeth rose and walked to the desk in search of paper when her attention was diverted by children's laughter, by shrieks coming from the back lawn of Pemberley House.

She couldn't help but giggle whenever she saw these cousins together, the boys were already rolling on the ground. Yes, the Fitzwilliam children had arrived – Matthew, Mark, Luke and Kathy; the deafening noise level attested to that.

Then Lizzy saw her daughter Anne Marie come around the corner with her cousin Kathy. Both the girls showed promise of becoming great beauties in the near future, but for now they remained little girls, intent on mischief – and carrying a tub of water between them. Lizzy soon realized what the girls had planned for that tub as they made their way to the wrestling heap of boys. There would be bedlam in a few moments and she was glad to see that Kathy and Anne Marie had positioned the two little ones far enough away to not be involved.

They exhaust me just to watch them, Lizzy thought. *Oh, to have half that energy again...*

George had darted sideways – a poor attempt at a serpentine maneuver – and was already stumbling when Matt and Mark Fitzwilliam reached him and dragged him down to the ground. The three cousins began wrestling with each other, tumbling here, rolling there, arms and legs and fists all flung far and wide. They had not seen each other for – how long was it? Oh, several hours at least; they were bursting with pent up energy.

"That's not cricket," shrieked Georgie, laughing. Matt had him in a neck hold as George began pulling the boot from Mark's foot. "Not fair! Mark, help me out here..."

"Let's drag him to the pond, Markie..."

"Markie, take my boot off and we'll bash Matty with it..." The shouting threesome tumbled over and over again as Matt grabbed his brother's shirt and George tried to pull down Matt's pants.

And, unbeknownst to them, Kathy and Anne Marie were approaching carrying a tub of water between them. "Be set to run, Anne."

"Quiet, Kathy, they'll hear you."

"Do be serious; they're much too busy trying to exterminate each other. Now, Alice dear heart, you stay back there with Luke and watch closely, but do stay to the side, all right? We should only be a few moments. Will you do that?"

Alice and Luke hopped up and down, clapping their hands. "Want to watch – do it now – do it now!"

The boys on the ground were oblivious to this conversation; each had a hold of some sort of body part or piece of clothing of another, unaware of the drenching to come.

Then...

The bucket overturned as the girls screamed, "*Surprise!*" Arms and legs tangled and scrambled, the boys began to gasp and shout all at once. All three were drenched to the skin. All three were furious.

"*Run, Anne, run!*"

Kathy sped quickly across the lawn and into the house, hoping to find a hiding place for herself in the kitchens downstairs, an area generally off limits to the children. After opening and closing a number of cabinets she found a bottom cupboard where clean aprons and napkins were stored, crawled inside and closed the door. Moments later she heard her cousin Georgie and her brother Matt charge into the room.

"I'll throttle her, I swear I will." Matt was somehow both furious and laughing at the same time, his wet shoes slipping and sliding on the highly polished wood floors.

"Don't do anything rash, Matt. She's just a girl. They're all daft, don't know any better. Besides, you're to be an Earl someday; can't have a scandal such as killing your sister in your past."

She was vaguely disappointed that they were dismissing her fiendishness so quickly, not bothering to even search for her. She was about to make a noise to attract them when Matt spoke.

"Don't say that, George." Her brother sounded very somber. "I hate it that I'm to be the Earl. I don't want it; I wish it was someone else, not any of us either, just some other family."

"You cannot be serious. Whatever could be wrong with being an Earl?" George was opening canisters as he talked, searching for food. Eventually he found something sweet with berries and chewed on a biscuit as he spoke. "Seems to me like it would be great fun. You get to be very important and wear those fancy robes and order people about – you're a natural, Matt;

even Kathy will have to bow to you then. Maybe we can find you a ring she'll be forced to kiss."

After a moment Matt spoke, his high voice breaking a bit at first. "Don't you understand? I can only be the Earl when my Da dies, George, like his Da died making him the Earl." Matt sniffed once and turned away, furious that he could still be such a baby. "That was a bad night, you know, when they came and told us; my Da sobbed. I never saw him cry before – and he and his Papa didn't even care for each other." He shook his head. "I can't imagine becoming the Earl. I'm sure I shall hate every minute of it."

Knowing his friend was embarrassed to be seen crying George lowered his gaze to the half eaten biscuit he now held, not knowing exactly what to say. "I never thought of that. I would hate for Uncle Fitz to..." He cleared his throat. "Well, that changes things. I hope you never become Earl. We'll join the army and go away, and then they can't make you Earl no matter what happens."

Kathy found she had tears in her eyes and they remained there long after the boys had left the pantry, their quest for revenge forgotten. *Her Papa was going to die someday?* Suddenly her chest hurt and she felt as if she was suffocating. That couldn't be possible but then everyone died, didn't they? Wasn't Aunt Catherine always saying she was 'on the brink'? Kathy curled up her legs and held them tightly, pressing her forehead to her knees. She thought about 'that night' when the two gentlemen had come to the house, the night their fates, and their lives, would change forever.

The gentlemen had called late in the evening, long after supper was finished and the parlor lights were dimmed. One was exceedingly elderly and sickly looking but the other was young and quite handsome; both were very elegantly dressed. Hearing the door knocker thump so late at night was a novelty and the older children – there were all together now seven Fitzwilliam offspring – had scrambled from their beds and pounded downstairs against their mother's shouted objections. Anything was preferable to sleep, no one was tired, and a late night visitor could mean anything.

Harry, Matt, Mark and Kathy stared in fascination as the butler finally reached the door and opened it.

"May I help you?"

"Is *this* Baron Fitzwilliam's residence?" Kathy saw that the older gentleman was greatly surprised. Both men were studying the butler, and the rather shabby interior, in an incredulous manner that made her feel ashamed.

"Yes, however the family's gone upstairs to bed already, it's quite late you know."

"It is imperative we speak with your master this night. He will understand."

"Well...I don't know...whom shall I say is calling?"

Before either man could answer Matthew walked boldly forward. "Are either of you gypsies? I've never seen one, you see – always hoped to. I know some excellent card tricks I could show you...I say, sir, you look horrible..." Harry quickly grabbed his brother by the arm and pulled him back, placing his hand over the boy's mouth.

Fitzwilliam, attired only in an old banyan robe, had by now reached the bottom landing and was approaching the door. His face grew suddenly very pale. "Wentworth, is that you? What the devil are you doing here in London, and at this time of night? Come in, quickly. Hastings, build a fire in the front parlor will you and I'll show Mr. Wentworth to a chair; bring him some brandy as well."

Once the elderly gentleman was settled before the fire the little strength he possessed seemed to escape him and his shoulders slumped forward. Just then Amanda entered the room carrying their twin two-year old daughters. Known simply as 'the Mary's' the one twin still sound asleep in her arms was Mary Margaret. The other twin, Mary Elizabeth, squirmed, cried and reached for her father so Amanda set her down on the floor. Immediately the child charged, head down like a battering ram, into her father and grabbed onto his clothing. He took her up into his arms before his robe came undone.

"Mr. Wentworth, I hope you are well."

Evidence of dried tears could now be seen on the old man's cheeks. "I have seen better days, sir. Pray, forgive me for sitting in your presence. Help me up, son." The elderly gentleman struggled to his feet with the help of the younger man, then bowed deeply before Fitzwilliam. "Our deepest condolences, your Lordship."

"No..." Fitzwilliam gasped. Hearing those words he knew with a certainty what had happened, that his father was dead; and, that he was now the Earl of Somerton. He closed his eyes against a rush of emotion; his jaw clenched back a sob.

"Papa, me," babbled Mary Elizabeth, disturbing the tense silence. She tried to get his attention, have him play with her, suddenly saying "boo" with her hands over her eyes. Fitzwilliam gently held her wrists and she found that amusing for some reason, so she rested her head on his shoulder and giggled.

"Silly Papa. Papa, no crying. Please, no crying. No!" Mary Elizabeth began to fuss when she saw his tears. In fact, everyone was uneasy, all watching in amazement as the bed rock of their lives became as human as the rest of them, and therefore suddenly vulnerable. Kathy's eyes burned and her heart ached.

Her secure world seemed no longer inviolate.

"When?" Her father asked after a moment, his voice raspy.

"Yesterday, sir, just after his tea. It was quite sudden; no one really expected this, not even his physicians. They were called immediately, of course. I hope you may take some consolation in the fact that it was swift, he did not suffer. We came here as soon as possible."

Her father sat down very slowly, all at once looking years older, still holding onto his pouting baby daughter as if he had forgotten she was there. "I never replied to his last note...nor even said farewell...and we were all *finally* going to make that trip, to Somerton, you know, the whole family, so I could begin my... education." He gave out a harsh laugh then a sob escaped. "Damn me. He never did escort me through the House of Lords; I thought we'd have more time..."

Kathy neither heard nor saw anything else as her mother took the still anxious baby from his arms and began shepherding the children, leading them from the room. "Upstairs, everyone. Now, please." Then suddenly his wife stopped, turned to her husband and cupped his cheek with her hand. "I'll put the children to bed and be down as quickly as possible. Will you be all right?"

He looked somewhat confused for a moment then nodded. She kissed him and hurried back to the children. "Everyone to bed now."

"What's wrong with Papa?" whispered Mark. He was badly shaken. "I saw tears on his cheeks. Is he going to be all right?"

"I should like to have a few minutes alone with those two down there; they made Papa cry!" Matthew paced alongside his bed, frustrated and fearful, fighting off his own tears. Chin lifted in defiance, he crossed his arms over his chest when their mother entered the bedroom. "I shan't go to bed, Mama, I don't care what you say. You can't make me."

"Get into bed, Matthew, please. For me, dearest. Thank you. Now, there is nothing with which you children need be concerned; your father has had rather a shock but he is in fine health, he is in no danger of harm. For now we must all be brave for his sake however, give him a moment of privacy."

"Is it his father?" Harry was leaning against the door frame. He held a tearful and visibly upset Kathy against his side, about to bring her to the bedroom she shared with the Mary's. Luke, thankfully, had slept through everything but was now sitting up in his small bed in the corner of the twins' room, his eyes still heavy with sleep. Amanda settled him back under the covers.

"Yes, dear. I believe that those gentlemen were aides to the Earl of Somerton. Perhaps they still are; I'm not certain. I don't understand these things. The older gentleman looked familiar though."

"Which grandpapa is dead?" A groggy Luke sat up again. "The one we never see?"

"We don't see either grandpapa, Lukey, and now they're both dead. Don't be so stupid."

"Don't call me stupid! You're stupid!"

"Boys, please, stop this instant! Tonight I ask for no quarreling. Tonight we must all try to be good, stay together, and help your Papa. He will need our love and support very much."

"Well, if those men are not gone in the morning I'm going to punch them in the nose for making Papa cry." Suddenly exhausted with the whole business Matthew yawned, turned his back on everyone and curled up into a tight ball, bringing the covers up to his shoulder.

After putting the other boys back into their beds Amanda kissed Harry good night and walked with Kathy into the girls' room. The Mary's were already tucked into their cribs and sleeping. Kathy was very concerned – however, not about her grandfather's recent death or her father's bereavement.

"Mama, if you're going downstairs shouldn't you put a cap on? It's not proper for you to see those gentlemen with your hair undone, is it?" It sounded to Amanda more as a statement than a question.

"Oh. Well, I was just brushing it out when they arrived, Kathy." Amanda struggled to pat down her wild, loose hair knowing Kathy was coming into the age where appearance was everything. "You're right, of course. I promise to put my cap on before I return downstairs."

Studying her mother intently, however, Kathy suspected the worst – that her mother always wore her hair loose at night and the child had only recently learned to disapprove of that. Also, her Mama and Papa slept in the same bed which she had also just learned was frowned upon among married couples of the upper classes, let alone the nobility.

She was beginning to suspect that perhaps her parents didn't know very much.

It must be because her mother was American, of course, and Americans were always confused about how to do things properly; and, after all, father was the most wonderful man in the world so it could never be his fault. He was...well...wonderful. Kathy decided she would discuss the entire thing with Aunt Catherine next time she saw her. Aunt Catherine was teaching her how to become a proper English lady and would know.

Amanda blew out the lantern by the bed, kissed each of her daughters on their foreheads and was about to leave the room.

"And bring Papa his slippers," Kathy abruptly whispered. "He was barefoot in front of those gentlemen, and he was wearing that horrid old robe of his."

Amanda hesitated, turned and nodded. "I promise, Katherine. I will wear my cap and bring your father his slippers. Now go to sleep, child."

"Also, have him wake me any time tonight if he needs to talk. Will you do that, Mama? He might need me, you know."

Chapter Seventeen

It was late spring now and several months had elapsed since Fitzwilliam had inherited his title along with the grand old ancestral home of the Fitzwilliam's – Somerton. Both the Darcy and Fitzwilliam families had descended upon the ancient Tudor manor house together and the children were having a grand time of it, simply grand.

There were portraits of dead relatives everywhere; a definitely eerie and nasty looking group of people, all strangely dressed, some evidently annoyed with having their portraits done. Oddly enough, quite of few of them possessed more than a passing resemblance to Aunt Catherine, even the ones with the mustaches.

There were also really fine suits of armor – some of it *dented,* which excited the children to no end, in addition to ancient armaments nailed to the walls. An enormous attic was the very best discovery of all, a place of mystery where the children found massive old furniture, trunks of dank smelling clothes and strange old toys and whatnots. Each morning, during the seemingly endless rainstorms, the children would venture up the back staircase, down the servant's hallway, and up the aged steps into their musty new wonderland.

"You two are in for it now." George shook his head and let out a low whistle, happy that for once he was uninvolved in a disaster. He was a mere spectator.

The usual agenda for the day – running up and down the narrow aisles, the jumping from furniture to boxes to trunks, exploring the shadows, pushing, shoving, taunting and teasing – had earlier in the morning given way to whoops of excitement. The boys had finally uncovered genuine treasures in the attic; authentic 'Objects of Interest'.

In opening the door to an old cupboard they had found several trunks, one filled to overflowing with military memorabilia, including a full set of old regimentals, a captain's short red coat, trousers, a white sash and a shako with a bedraggled red feather. The uniform was discovered at the bottom of the trunk, hidden beneath several rugs and a large tin box of sketched portraits. The precious uniform coat, discovered simultaneously by both Fitzwilliam brothers, had been fought over viciously until the sound of a seam rending stopped the boys cold.

"What have you done?" gasped Mark.

"What do you mean, what have *I* done? We both grabbed it together."

"Do you think perhaps the shoulder was already torn?" Mark swallowed hard, refusing to acknowledge that there had been a definite tearing sound moments before.

"That's it; yes, it must have been! It's very old." Matthew pulled the redcoat onto his lap for a closer examination.

"Do you think it's your father's?" George sat up suddenly, eying the jacket with great interest.

"Who else's would it be? Yes, see, here's his name embroidered on the inside pocket, "Captain Richard

Fitzwilliam'. Look here! This bit looks like a blood stain!"

"Or wine."

"Or *blood!*" Matt insisted, caught up in the drama of imagination. "I wager that tear was from the lethal blow of a sword!"

"You're an idiot," laughed George.

"Why!"

"Lethal blow? Uncle Fitz is still alive."

"Oh, yeah – you're right. Well, perhaps it was a musket round then! Was Da shot or was he stabbed? I can never remember."

"Ooh, look at this." Unable to keep away any longer George had delved into the box himself to retrieve a large envelope containing gold medals and ribbons. "How ever did Uncle Fitz stand with all these medals on his chest and that big hat of his on his head?" George selected the largest, gaudiest award and began to pin it to his own shirt.

"A good many of these medals were presented after the war was over, I should think." Matthew solemnly accepted the packet of trophies that George passed to him, selected two medals for himself and then passed the envelope on to Mark.

"Do you think Papa will be angry at us for taking all this out of storage, Matt? Perhaps we should put them back before he catches us."

"You worry too much." Matthew slipped his arms into his father's jacket and grinned contentedly. "The way I see it we're safe enough. He and Uncle Wills have ridden off to the village with Mr. Hamilton and they'll most likely stop at the White Horse for some ale before they return and Mama and Auntie Lilibet are having dresses made or something. No one will be around for ages. Ooh! Georgie, Markie, look at this!

It's an old letter, from Uncle Arthur when he was just a general and not a Duke."

"What does it say?"

"He calls father an..." Matthew scanned over the horrid writing until he found the passage that had caught his eye. "Here it is ... 'an outstanding officer but morally lax when it comes to playing chess or dealing with loose women.' What do you suppose that means?"

"You can't be that ignorant. It means Papa played chess badly with loose women."

"What are loose women?"

"I haven't the foggiest idea, perhaps they're fat."

"Ooh, here's his other hat, the bi-corn one. I love this hat! I haven't seen this for ages." The old battered treasure had lost all its braid and bravado but still looked magnificent to the boys. Georgie grabbed for it and placed it upon his head and they all laughed as it slid down onto his nose.

That was when Kathy and Anne Marie entered the attic storage room. Kathy looked immediately to her nemesis, George Darcy. "Aha! I knew you'd be up here again causing trouble." She grinned triumphantly, hoping they had caught them red handed, involved in mischief.

"You both have to leave." George stood to confront her, one hand resting loosely at his hips, very much in the manner of his proud father. The other hand was holding the military hat in place on his head. "No women are allowed up here, how many times must we tell you?"

"To Dover and back with you and your rules. Have they ever stopped me before?" Kathy tried to outstare him, defiance in her gaze; George could hardly restrain his grin. She blinked first.

"You're blushing."

"I am not!" Immediately she turned away. "What are you all doing with Papa's things?" Dragging out yet another box from the trunk the girls plopped tailor style on the floor and began to examine its contents. This box was filled with odds and ends, papers, books, and, most dangerous of all, a young soldier's most private memoirs. Kathy pulled out a faded miniature. "Ooh, look, here's one of those portraits of father as a baby. Rather chubby wasn't he?"

"How do you know its Da? Could be Uncle Wills." Mark kept a straight face for as long as possible before he and Matthew burst into raucous laughter. The portrait showed a plump little boy with wild blonde hair and equally wild looking eyes.

"Why do you two always call father Da now? Aunt Catherine says only common ruffians use that expression. Aunt Catherine says girls should always call their fathers Papa, but Aunt Catherine said you boys should call him Papa but only until you leave for University, then you must call him Pater."

"Aunt Catherine says this; Aunt Catherine says that..." Georgie mimicked her voice perfectly. "I swear if Aunt Catherine told you to stick a Maypole up your bum you'd be walking oddly for a month. You, Katherine Marie Fitzwilliam, are become a horrible snob. Yes you are! Ever since you began those dim-witted society lessons with Aunt Catherine you're no fun at all." His exaggerated sigh was actually more amused resignation. "You think you're better than everyone."

"And you are a vulgar, rude child, George Darcy. Aunt Catherine says that people who do not value the proper manner of doing things are just...well...vulgar and rude."

Matthew tossed a pillow at her, angering her further by hitting her square in the face. "What does

Aunt Catherine say about your eating enough food to feed a small village?" he taunted.

"I do not eat that much – oh! You're only jealous because I'm taller than you are, Matt Fitzwilliam, and I ride better than you! I ride better than any of you!"

Matt's temper flared quickly as always. "You're not taller, well maybe but not by much! And I can outride you any day of the week, Kathy! And another thing, for your information all the boys on tenant farms call their fathers Da! You wouldn't know that, would you, because you're only a girl and you can't go out to visit with the men. That is what *real men* call their Da's..."

"And you sound just like a baby – da,da,da,da...!"

"And you sound like an old lady, a great big pain in the arse!"

"I do not!"

"You do so!"

Growing increasingly uneasy with the argument erupting around him, George huffed and grunted and fidgeted with his medals. Kathy made him very mad sometimes and she could be annoying. But, sometimes she made him feel...different. She had been so much fun until this past year, until she began primping and prancing around in satin slippers with her hair done up all pretty in ribbons. She looked very girlish lately and it bothered him. The warm way he felt about her bothered him. Snatching something from the pile he began to wander aimlessly about, half listening to the angry words tossed between brother and sister. He hated it when Matt fought with Katherine. It always made him unsettled and surprisingly very defensive, but for which one he couldn't tell.

Finally lying down on a torn settee he held up an ancient watch with an odd looking inscription. "What does this say?" Hoping to deflect the argument he shoved the timepiece directly before Katherine.

"It says...it says..." Katherine squinted very hard at the writing. "It says, 'don't stick dirty old things in my face.' How should I know what it says, I don't read Gaelic."

"You're so grumpy all the time, Beef," he mumbled.

She shoved his shoulder. "I am not grumpy – how dare you say that I am grumpy! And don't call me Beef! I am not fat!"

He shoved her right back. "I don't understand you, *Beef*; you're..."

As usual Matthew ignored the heated exchange between his sister and his closest friend, confident at least that *he* had bested her. He reached down into the trunk sitting before her and pulled up several covered sketches from the bottom. Suddenly he yelped and sat bolt upright.

"Holy shite! Look at this!"

Mark scrambled over, followed by the others. They all stared intently at the drawing before them.

"That," Georgie pointed out firmly, and after but a moment or two of serious consideration, "...that is an almost naked lady, isn't it?"

"Well, really, what a stupid thing to say." Kathy flinched when he made a half hearted attempt to pinch her arm. "Ouch. You could have hurt me."

George rolled his eyes.

"Is it someone famous do you think?" asked Mark.

The sketch that had so drawn the children's attention was an old ink rendering of a rather busty young woman leaning forward; she was wearing nothing but a skimpy chemise. To add to the boys' absolute delight there was plenty of cleavage and an outline of nipples showing through the material. "That's brilliant, that is. I bet this is some sort of great art piece. Looks a little like your nurse Barlow, doesn't it, George?"

The boys hooted and laughed at George's blush and sheepish grin. "Georgie has no sense!" Kathy's eyes flashed with jealousy when she saw him then study the sketch more closely. "Barlow's not pretty at all! And she's old – at least thirty!"

But the boy paid her no heed, he was mesmerized.

"You don't suppose she could be someone's cook do you?" Kathy wrinkled her nose at the thought. In her experience cooks were a bit odd in the head and when she was younger she remembered one had even run around the kitchen without her clothes.

"Gad! Here's another one!" Mark was awestruck. "It's the same woman and she's with a gent."

"Oh, he's got his hand on her chest and he's hurting her, do you see? The poor lady looks like she's in pain. What if he had been picking his nose or something?" Anne Marie pulled the box to her side and searched deeper into the pile of sketches. "My heavens, there are lots more in here. You don't think these belong to your Papa do you?" She began to pull the pictures out.

Kathy felt she should come to his defense. "Actually, these others look quite boring, just a lot of heavy women leaning over. I wonder why Papa would be interested – oh, no! Look! The ones on the bottom are very naughty!" Her face was beginning to blush.

She had found two more pictures, the first of which was grabbed by the ever curious and always scientific Mark. He studied it carefully. "Oh, I know what this is. The grooms lead two of the horses into a special pen and then something like this happens. It's when father wants them to have babies. I peeked once – it was loud and both horses seemed angry with each other; the stallion even bit the mare's neck. It can't be a very agreeable experience. You know, I think the bulls do it as well – to the cows, not to the horses."

"Well, of course they do it, everyone knows that! They'd have to, wouldn't they? People do it too I shouldn't wonder," Matthew said hesitantly, nearly positive he was right.

Katherine became suddenly uneasy, feeling perhaps it wasn't proper for them to be looking at these pictures, especially in mixed company. What would Aunt Catherine say? "You cannot mean to imply my Mama and Papa do this?"

"Well, yes you idiot, and at least seven or eight times by my count, poor Mama and Papa probably had to do it twice to get both me and Mark and then twice for the Mary's."

"Give that to me." Kathy narrowed her eyes at the picture. "I would never do that, no matter what my husband said."

"You'd be lucky to even have a husband."

"Oh, do be quiet, Georgie! You can be quite vexing at times!"

George angered her further by mimicking her words while the others continued to stare in shared curiosity. "Do you think men's thingies really get that big?" Mark was suddenly very concerned regarding his own appendage, the apparently inadequate one that lurked within his breeches. "Da's isn't nearly that big. You remember Matthew, when we go swimming in the river, just the boys and Da. We're all naked and Da looks nothing like this."

Matthew nodded vigorously. "And look at her big bum sticking out, and her bubbies! No, certainly those can't be normal either, unless she is a wet nurse. Remember Mrs. Thomson?" After a secret glance between them Mark and Matthew began to giggle.

"Well, *this* is very confusing," Kathy's attention had been drawn now to the second picture and she turned it around for them all to see. "Look here. I don't understand this at all; I mean, how in the world will the baby ever get into her tummy?"

Mark considered it intently for a moment, reasoned the problem out logically, tilting his head this way and that as each of the others studied the drawing and pondered Katherine's question.

"Well, I should think that's rather obvious, isn't it?" he said finally. "She would have to swallow..."

"The rain has stopped you know. Why don't you children go outside to play?" The sound of their mother's voice sent the children into a flurry of confusion as they scrambled to their feet. "Heavens look at this place, such a mess. What in the world have you children been doing up here...oh, my stars."

"What ever possessed you to retain these pictures?"

"They're works of art, Darcy! Very valuable."

"Oh, yes, I can sense the influence of Botticelli here, what would he call this, Venus Reclining in Barracks?"

"Don't look so smug. You don't understand, you've never been to war, brat. Alone, dispirited, terrified, and forced to live in appalling deprivation..."

"Your mistress secured a villa for you both throughout much of the Portuguese Campaign and, when in France, you stayed at the Palace. Please spare me the – oh, good heavens. Is that his foot?"

"Give me those. Oh, I say, Darcy, I actually met this woman in Paris. She was very pleasant."

"I spoke with George, explained to him all about procreation. He was bored to tears but then inquired about the upcoming horse race that Tattersall's is sponsoring, said he needed other thoughts to distract him from the horrors he had witnessed in the attic. The child is becoming a first rate manipulator."

"Did it work? Are you taking him?"

"Yes, of course I am. Guilt is a wonderful incentive. Did you speak with your children?"

"Good gracious no! I'm certain the boys would do better learning the way we learned, behind the barns or peeking in windows..."

"You are pathetic."

"Never claimed to be otherwise. Sweet St. Timothy's shin bone, Darcy, did you see this one?"

"I have not the same prurient tastes as you...ooh, let me see that. Good God! Is that Barlow?"

Chapter Eighteen

The Darcy's stay at Somerton had begun in late spring and was now into the beginnings of summer. Darcy, along with the Earl's longtime secretary, Randolph Wentworth, spent a good deal of his time acclimating Fitzwilliam to the world of property ownership, estate matters and procedures. Also begun were renovations on the old manor house, a revised and updated agricultural drainage system and visits to all the tenant farmers.

Over and above those chores the visit had also been a wonderful chance for the two families to grow closer, enjoy visits to town or picnics by the lake and other family adventures together. No mention was made again of the discovery in the attic, no one returned there. The boys were still relatively uninterested in sex; of course, the rains had also stopped and they much preferred being outdoors. As for the girls, emotionally they were beginning to become curious about life but were still a bit baffled.

All, however, saw their parents in a new light.

It was early one summer's evening that two very important visitors entered the lives of the families, affecting the futures of both houses forever. They arrived independently of each other for a small dinner party arranged by the new Earl and Countess

Somerton, their first in the new residence, given to meet the higher ranking members of town.

"Mr. Robert Wentworth" announced Somerton's long standing butler, Bates. Most of the Fitzwilliam's former servants were still with them, occupying positions on the estate, the older ones pensioned off and living in their own modest little cottages. Hastings was the only retired servant remaining with the family in the manor house.

"Ah, Robert, splendid to see you again. You remember my wife, Lady Somerton?"

"Of course I do. Good to see you again, your ladyship." The handsome young man bowed before her.

Amanda smiled warmly. "Is your father resting at home this evening? I'm very glad. He's been working so hard here with Mr. Fitzwilliam and Mr. Darcy. I wish to especially thank *you*, Mr. Wentworth, for all of the help you've provided in London for my husband, smoothing the way for him as he prepares to begin his new life in the House of Lords. Your dispatches have been keenly appreciated."

"It has been my honor, madam."

"Have you met the Darcy's?"

Darcy approached, his hand extended. "I've heard nothing but wonderful things about you, Mr. Wentworth. It's good to finally meet you."

"I daresay you've been listening to my father for several weeks. Anything he has to say about me is bound to be prejudiced in my favor."

"As it should be, father to son. However, I'd heard of you from others before this, praise of your assistance to my uncle, the former Earl. They say not only have you exhibited the finest mind in any of the Parliamentary offices – not a tremendously difficult achievement, perhaps – but also that you're terribly wasted as a mere assistant."

"Darcy do not dare try and steal him from me, he's *my* man in London." Fitzwilliam had been speaking with two other gentlemen but approached quickly. "I don't care if Derbyshire bursts into flames; you will not poach my Parliamentary secretary. I need him – haven't a clue what I'm getting myself into come September, so leave him alone."

"You've a startlingly suspicious turn of mind, Fitz; twisted and distrustful. I merely wanted to bandy about a few ideas with this young man. Oh, did you hear that – off with you now, I believe that was the bell for your dinner. Go... run along. We'll be there in a moment."

This was the first time the older children had been allowed to attend a formal dinner and the three boys, George, Mark and Matthew, looked very uncomfortable in their new attire. Only Harry appeared perfectly at ease; and, best of all, he'd been seated beside the loveliest girl he'd ever seen. The daughter of the local vicar, Celeste Baddely was the perfect English rose, fair skinned, blue eyed and blonde, with a figure no fifteen year old girl should be allowed to possess.

"Will you look at my foolish brother?" Kathy whispered to Anne Marie. They were sitting across from each other and between them, at the very foot of the table, was the elderly town mayor who was half deaf and kept dozing off.

"Which one?" Murmured Anne Marie as her gaze drifted from one squirming boy to another.

"Harry. I believe he's smitten with the vicar's daughter. Can you imagine? Well, that won't do. She has no family of which to speak."

"She's lovely, though."

"There is that. You don't think George is attracted to her as well, do you?" Kathy cast a narrowed glance down the table to her cousin who had just that moment glanced up. She wrinkled her nose and looked away.

"I don't believe so. He's still more interested in perfecting his cricket bowling than pretty girls."

"I'm sure it's nothing to me, I don't care a fig about George Darcy. However, did you see John Wentworth look my way? I believe he's smitten with me, Anne. He's so very handsome. I love his hair. I'm going to let him kiss me if he wants."

"Kiss you?" Anne Marie's heart sank. She too had noticed the striking young man with the blue eyes but he was older, far beyond their reach. They were barely twelve years old, too young for an experienced man of twenty-two to notice, even though Kathy's figure was already budding, the onset of her courses occurring the month before. Anne Marie prayed her courses would begin soon – then she wouldn't look so skinny and small, and so very young.

"Kathy, I shouldn't do anything rash," Anne Marie cautioned. Her friend was so impetuous, so eager to *begin* her life as she would say. Besides, it would break Anne's skinny little heart if John Wentworth noticed Kathy. She loved him herself more than anything or anyone in the whole world – and she'd only just met him two hours before!

"Your lordship, will you be attending our local assembly this week? It's a fine occasion and the dancing and music are top rate. There'll be people arriving from all the surrounding villages – it's quite well received."

"Yes, Mr. Baddely, I recall the assemblies here from when I was a young pup. I daresay we can easily spare the time, can't we, Darcy? What's the matter cousin, something off with your food there?" Fitzwilliam's lips twitched behind his wineglass. Darcy absolutely detested village dances such as these, even though he had encountered his greatest treasure at one – his wife Elizabeth.

"No, the food is very adequate, *cousin*. About the assembly, however, I fear we may be leaving soon." The muscles at his jaw constricted as he spoke; he refused to even look at Fitzwilliam.

"Nonsense, only this morning you told me you'd be able to stay at least another month. When do you think to leave?"

"Oh...I couldn't say." Darcy wanted to bash Fitzwilliam on the head. "When is the assembly?" he answered through gritted teeth.

Throughout dinner Kathy attempted a subtle flirtation with John Wentworth in all the ways Lady Catherine had instructed were proper for daughters of the nobility. She stared directly at him looking demurely away when she caught his eye – she dropped a napkin behind her chair shooing off the servant who tried to retrieve it, nearly sticking a fork in the man's shin – she batted her lashes until a stray hair caused her to blink feverishly. Finally, she employed her fan, but was confused as to the various signals that could convey. She was almost certain that opening and closing the fan meant 'you have won my heart', or was that the signal for 'you are cruel'. She tapped her cheek with her fan, another signal; she fanned quickly, she fanned slowly, both signals.

"What in the world are you doing?" snarled her brother, Matt. "You look as if you're signaling ships into the harbor. Put that silly fan down before you poke my eye out."

Kathy glared back at him. She couldn't help herself; she was desperate to catch John's attention. Then, all at once, John was watching her and she realized his mouth was moving. Good heaven's what was he saying to her? "Pardon me?" she squeaked out.

"I was saying that this assembly will be open to the entire family – children will be most welcome there. You and your young cousin should plan to attend as well."

Oh merciful heavens. He thought her a child! This was horrible. She closed her eyes hearing both George Darcy's chuckle and her brother's quiet snort of derision.

Thank goodness John hadn't heard the snickering, having turned away to say something to her mother.

"Yes, your ladyship, I visited Boston two years ago, was there for several months securing trade documents for the late Lord Somerton. In fact, we set up a very advantageous alliance providing tea for tobacco."

"Really? Perhaps we know people in common, Mr. Wentworth. Did you meet any of the Whitman's or perhaps the Delano's? They were neighbors and patrons of my father's hospital."

"No, I am sorry to say I never met those great families. I stayed with a gentleman by the name of Frederic Lowell and his wife; spent most of my time in meetings with men of business. Oh, Boston is quite a wonderful city. Of course, the winters there can be very harsh I imagine." Robert continued. "I never saw such rain storms in my life."

"Mother says a Norwegian completely destroyed Boston Harbor when she was a girl." Kathy looked very solemn when she spoke, but felt triumphant, having thus added her informative bit to the adult conversation.

The table stilled as all eyes turned toward her.

"Well she did."

The first one to cover his grin was George. Amanda reached behind her son Mark and touched her daughter's arm. "No dearest. I believe I know to what you refer. I was speaking of a Nor'eastern, Katherine. Not a Norwegian. A Nor'eastern is a very bad storm."

Kathy's cheeks turned a crimson color even before her twin brothers began to laugh outright. She stomped her foot and arched an imperial eyebrow at them. "It was a simple enough mistake."

"Not really. Everyone knows Norwegians only attack in the summer, Kath."

Harry leaned over and covertly smacked Matthew on the back of his head for that comment, even as his own lips twitched with amusement.

Chapter Nineteen

It was a wonderful assembly, magnificent, Harry thought, and it might end up the most superb evening of his entire life. *She* was there. *Celeste.* They had met several times during the past week, always by accident, planned or otherwise. She had even allowed him to kiss her cheek one time and at another time she placed his hand on her knee. *Perhaps tonight...* his increasingly lustful thoughts were abruptly interrupted.

"Harry?"

"Yes, sprout?" Looking down at his darling little cousin, Alice Darcy, he smiled. He felt a special affinity for this little urchin, for her wit, her sparkle, her natural charisma; most especially he adored her blatant hero worship of him. She was part hoyden, part odd pixie creature, and all charm. "I say, Alice, you look awfully pretty this evening."

"I do?" Alice seemed truly shocked, and not a little dubious. Well into her sixth year Alice had already accepted her own shortcomings, reveled in her strengths. That she was a bit odd looking was common knowledge, and one that gave her not a moment's concern. She knew her mouth was too wide, her nose a bit too broad in the middle and she had ears that stuck out; and, then there were her huge eyes, thick eyebrows and cheeks like large apples in that tiny head of hers. Mustn't forget the hair, either – straight strands that often escaped from her braids, the auburn tresses proudly defying all her mother's attempts at containment.

"...must be standing in an exceptionally good light tonight..."

Harry laughed at that and again tucked a few strands behind her ears. "What is it my fairy princess?"

She loved it when he called her that. "Will you dance with me Harry? If you let me stand on your boots I'll be able to keep up and no one will know the difference."

"I'd be honored sweeting. Not this dance however," he cast a heated look in the direction of the delightful Celeste, who had been watching him steadily. She blushed and looked demurely away. "This dance has already been promised. Perhaps the next?"

"All right, Harry." Alice skipped off but turned again to watch once she had reached a plant to hide behind. He was twirling around that awful Celeste and gazing at her as if she were broiled chicken. It was as bad as she feared. Broiled chicken was Harry's favorite.

"Why do you look like that?" asked Luke.

"It's my face, can't do anything with it after it's washed."

"Not that."

She finally turned to look at Luke. "Like what then?"

"Like you just swallowed a grasshopper." Before she could answer he slumped down onto a wooden chair and groaned. "This is so bloody boring I want to throw up."

"Would you like to help me do something fun?"

"Not really, I'm not *that* bored yet."

"I haven't even told you what it is."

"You don't need to tell me, I know it's about Harry – it has to be, you're watching him again."

"Don't be silly." She looked so sincere that he briefly believed her.

"Then what is it?"

"Help me make a present for Harry."

"I knew it."

"Luke Fitzwilliam, I've never asked a favor from you before…"

"Of course you have! A dozen times, and I always get into some sort of trouble."

She smiled at him. "You know you'll give in to me eventually. I have a charismatic personality no one can resist."

He snorted derisively. "You'll need to do better than that."

"I'll give you all the money in my pencil jar at home."

"All right, what must I do?

"Miss Elizabeth, may I have this dance?" Darcy bowed before his wife.

"*Miss* Elizabeth," the confused woman beside her queried. "I had thought you were married."

"She is, madam; to me. Please excuse us"

With that Darcy led Lizzy onto the dance floor and they joined in the lines for an exuberant country dance. The moment the music began riotous claps and boot stomps shook the floorboards.

As they passed each other Lizzy loudly whispered in his ear, "I am very proud of you, William."

His stoic expression was unyielding. They passed each other again.

"I have danced with every unaccompanied female here..." he replied. They separated to dance with others, then passed each other once more, "...you have no idea how many of them..." They separated again, bowed, skipped with their neighbors then passed once more, "... are in want of a husband..." Now they were in a circle with other dancers hopping, twirling, clapping and laughing – that is, the other dancers were laughing, not Darcy, but few noticed. Finally, the couple began promenading together. "...and hope that I am either a bachelor or a brother to one. Will this evening ever end?"

Several of the women he had danced with were now gathering into groups, pointing, whispering, giggling. He feared they would begin to advance on him.

"You've made them all fall in love with you and more importantly you've been kind. You are a grand success."

"Well, why isn't Fitz bouncing around?"

"He wants to stay near Amanda. She's with child again – don't look over at them! No one is supposed to know. She's not feeling very well."

"I thought she just lost a child."

"That was last year. Pay attention to your dancing." Again the couple separated and could not continue their loud whispers until they were paired once more.

"You seem to be getting on very famously with Robert Wentworth."

"He's a good man and I believe he has a very bright future. Despite Fitzwilliam's public grousing he's as keen as I am to help the boy. We've decided to groom him for a future election."

"Well, don't neglect George. He's your son."

"Lizzy, whatever are you..." Darcy looked at her quizzically before they turned in different directions.

Kathy Fitzwilliam tapped her foot to the music, seemingly uninterested in her surroundings. The village children usually danced with each other at these assemblies and she had been asked several times but declined them all. There was really only one person with whom she wanted to dance. She was holding out for Robert Wentworth; however, he was very much in demand tonight, a fact that greatly annoyed her. Anne Marie suddenly came running up to her, out of breath and flushed.

"My goodness, isn't this fun?"

"Provincial entertainments are so very...provincial."

"Don't be such a stodge, Kathy. That O'Shay boy keeps trying to attract your attention; why not dance with him?"

"He's a blacksmith's son." Enough said, in Kathy's mind.

"He's also *handsome and very tall*. You realize you're the only one not dancing. George, Matt and Mark are even having an excellent time."

"Don't speak to me about the boys. Have you watched them? They've danced with everything except the butter churn. I think someone has spiked the punch as well, very common behavior, if you ask me." That was when she noticed Robert Wentworth approaching. "Oh, I knew it, I knew it. Anne Marie, don't look now but Robert Wentworth is making his way here; he's finally gotten his courage up to ask me to dance. Stand behind me a bit will you my dear, give him room. Farther back, please. Farther...why, hello Mr. Wentworth."

"Hello Lady Katherine, Miss Darcy. I hope you are both enjoying yourselves." His hair was adorably disheveled and his tie loosened just enough for propriety. "You're not dancing, Lady Kathy? I know Miss Darcy was, and quite well I might add."

"I *never* dance at these village gatherings. My mentor, Lady Catherine de Bourgh you know, frowns upon even attending; however, my parents insisted."

Robert turned to Anne Marie. "In that case, would you do me the honor Miss Darcy?"

It was a moment before Anne Marie could speak, she was so flustered. "Yes. Thank you," she said finally, and, to Kathy's everlasting regret, she watched her dearest friend dance off with the current man of her dreams. Kathy felt as if she might cry — however, Lady Catherine abhorred public demonstrations of emotion, feeling that nothing could warrant such a want of dignity. For a moment Kathy thought of kicking Lady Catherine in the shins.

Robert Wentworth noticed something was different the moment he took hold of Anne Marie's hand. She was only a child, of course, but he had to admit that with her hair pulled back and in her long gown she looked older. And she really was lovely, wasn't she? She would grow into a beautiful woman. He swallowed hard, his suddenly flustered thoughts confusing and disturbing him; the fact that she gazed up at him as if he hung the stars in the heavens did not escape his notice either. It was all heady stuff indeed... *And she is a child, Wentworth, get a grip on yourself. She'll be the toast of London one day soon and then some fortunate fellow's wife before her first season is over.* If only she had an older sister...if only *she* were older, he mused...

By the time Harry pulled back from yet another kiss with Celeste he knew without a doubt that he must be in love. She was passionate and beautiful and soft, she smelled wonderfully too and he could see a hint of cleavage. Oh, her bosom was magnificent and he blushed when she caught him staring there. "I see you're wearing my locket. That makes me very happy," he whispered. "Very happy." In all honesty, however, The Locket was not Harry's. The Locket had belonged to Elizabeth Darcy as a child but then had been involved in some sort of unpleasant disturbance within the Darcy household years later, thereby possessing not a few bad memories for her. It had been given to Harry's sisters for 'dress up' play and then Harry had found the locket abandoned in a box in the children's old playroom...and since he had forgotten to purchase a present for his beloved's birthday...and since the old thing was just lying there...

"I love this locket Harry; it shows me that you truly love me, and with a lock of your own baby hair within as well!" He looked at her quizzically. He wasn't even aware it opened. "How funny that your hair color as a baby was so much darker than it is now, though... Nevertheless, it's very thoughtful and I love that you bought this especially for me."

She kissed him then, her tongue darting across the seam of his lips, and his trousers bulged in reciprocity – most impressively too. He so enjoyed when she did that to him that he deepened his kiss and his tongue met hers in a slow, wet swirl that seemed to go on forever. After several very heated moments he pulled back, glassy eyed and very, very aroused. *However does she know so much?* It was as if she were teaching him! She must be very wise, he thought.

"Would you like to see the chemise that goes with this dress? The colors match."

"Pardon?" His mind was a foggy mess. "What colors?"

She smiled coyly. "My chemise matches my dress, silly. Would you like to see, Harry?"

"I would kill to see, Celeste."

"No need, I'm happy enough to oblige you," she whispered as she gave him a peek. She pressed her hand gently against his growing trouser bulge, her mouth forming a shocked, 'Oh!'

She did not remove her hand, however; on the contrary...

"Celeste, oh that feels bloody wonderful. Don't stop doing that. Oh my word – you make me wild. May I lower your neckline again, touch you again, dearest, please let me, let me hold your breast while you're rubbing me. Yes like that, undo my buttons... I know...*oh god*...I know what you like and we both like this so very much..." Harry had begun to pull up the hem of her gown, was sliding his hand across her knee, up her thigh...

A noise on the path startled them both and they jumped apart.

"Oh no, not again! I cannot believe this – here comes that drab." Celeste's eyes narrowed first at Harry and then at the child walking slowly toward them.

"Pull down your skirt," he hissed at her and quickly buttoned his trousers. "Put your top back up."

"No! Why should I? Let her see that she's interrupting 'adult' meetings and should know better."

"I don't want her seeing this, she's just a child." Harry immediately pulled Celeste's hem down and then stood to block the view. "Hello, Alice, why aren't you dancing?"

Alice had been searching everywhere for Harry when she heard the moans, saw the figures huddled together on the ground behind a tree. She hurried in that direction never doubting that Harry would want to see what she had created for him as soon as possible, he always appreciated her gifts. "Hi, Harry," she called out cheerily and then her steps faltered.

He was with Celeste; she should have known. Oh well, nothing for it now but to continue and ignore the mean old bully. Harry would be happy to see her and that's all that mattered.

"What a repulsive child, pity she's so ugly looking," Celeste said in a loud whisper, making certain her voice carried far enough for the girl approaching to hear. "It will take *all* of her father's reported wealth *and* the lure of Pemberley *and* her families' connections to make that creature a good match."

Harry was angered by her comments, hurt by their harsh coldness. Alice was very special, as dear to him as his own sisters. "I don't think she's odd looking in the least – she's only six years old for heaven's sake. I doubt even you were the beauty you are now at six years."

"Hello, Harry! Hello, Celeste." Alice said in two completely different intonations. "I've made you a present for your birthday, Harry."

Going down on his haunches he accepted the roughly sketched picture she had made for him, gently capturing her hand in his. He pulled her into a side embrace so they could both admire her artwork together. "Alice, this is wonderful."

"Do you really like it, Harry?"

"Yes, of course I do. Did you do this all by yourself?"

"No. Luke helped me because I draw so poorly but he wanted me to tell you it was all my work. He is very nice that way."

Celeste began to snicker. "I can well understand his distancing himself from that horror." Unknown to the adults within, the punch that had been snuck outside for the young people's enjoyment had been secretly and freely spiked with wine. After several glasses

Celeste's personality had altered greatly from her usual ladylike demeanor. "What is that supposed to be, little brown mouse? A barn? A tunnel? Two goats mating?"

Alice's eyes began to fill with tears.

"Celeste!" Harry snapped. He never allowed anyone to tease the younger children and most especially his little Alice, who was so sweet. "Enough!" He kissed Alice's cheek and hugged her tightly. "It's lovely, my darling. Is it Chancery?"

Alice's emotions had traveled from abject humiliation to joy, and only in a moment. "Yes! How clever you are to recognize him! Oh, Harry, do you really, really like it?"

"Yes, little Alice, I really, really like it."

As Harry studied the baffling combination sketch and fabric cut outs Alice wrinkled her nose at Celeste and stuck out her tongue, squinting her eyes in the 'so there' look children give each other. She was, however, smiling sweetly when Harry looked back at her from his appreciative perusal of the drawing.

"Let me see that..." Celeste bent down to study the picture. "That's my handkerchief! You've adhered pieces of my handkerchief to this! Why you dreadful little troll, that handkerchief cost a fortune! I'm going to go straight to your father and tell him what you've done!"

Alice began to tremble and cry. This beautiful gift she had created with her own hands – well, with Luke's own hands – for her beloved Harry was now evidently criminal evidence that would land her in hot soup. Oh, this was awful.

Seeing how upset both were becoming Harry stepped between and separated the two females. "Celeste, she meant no harm. It was only a handkerchief after all and you have dozens."

"That does not signify! She is a spoiled, willful child and should be punished. I am sick to death of seeing her wherever we go. Beating is too good for her."

"Oh really?" Alice's small fists clenched in anger; she pressed them hard into her waist, no longer feeling like crying but more like bashing. "Well, it was a very stupid looking handkerchief, anyway. It looks better where it is, on the back end of a horse."

"*Ugh*! You see! She's a little beastie; she's a menace. Go away you ugly little thing." With that Celeste pushed up against Harry's side and took possession of him, slipped her arm through his.

Alice was beyond infuriated. She never did appreciate the manner in which this girl giggled up at Harry, neither did she like the possessive way the old witch had grabbed his arm and she really, really did not like her yellow hair, nor her silly smile, nor anything else about her.

And she had called her ugly just one too many times.

Alice suddenly charged forward and kicked the lovely Celeste in her big, fat, bottom, very, very hard.

Chapter Twenty

He felt her sweet warm breath on his cheek first, then he felt a small jam covered finger poke at his jaw. "Are you still mad with me?"

Darcy scrubbed at his face feeling the sticky residue there and then stared at his fingers. *Blueberries.* He roughly pushed his chair back, removed a handkerchief to wipe his hands. He stared frostily back into those huge light gray eyes watching him.

She was so adorable.

"You understand I am working here, or attempting to do so at any rate."

She squinted in thought then shook her head. "Up, please."

"You are supposed to be in your room, evaluating your very bad conduct, assessing the proper punishment for your actions tonight."

"My feet are cold."

Grunting his annoyance he lifted her onto his lap, hugged her tightly against both his chest and his better judgment and then pressed his face into her cool soft hair. *So much for strict discipline and cold authority.* Cupping both her tiny feet into his hand he tried very hard not to laugh. "You're a menace, do you know that?"

Certain now of his ultimate forgiveness she wrapped her arms around his neck.

"I'm sorry, Papa. I will buy that mean old Celeste another handkerchief – could you lend me some money by the way? Just don't be mad with me anymore." Her heart had been breaking forever, unaccustomed as she was to any separation from her parents, most especially her adored father. It had nearly been one hour since they returned home from the assembly and he had sent her off to bed *without a kiss*. Unheard of. She missed him dreadfully, loved him more than life itself.

"We do not refer to young ladies as 'mean' or 'old' Alice. Besides, you kicked her and made her shriek. Don't you feel badly about that?"

"Not so much."

"Alice!"

"Well, I made the gift for Harry almost all by myself and then she made fun of it, and of me, right in front of him! I wanted to cry, Papa."

Darcy closed his eyes and sighed. "Is that what this is really about? Harry, again?"

"No. Maybe. Yes. I like Harry so much, Papa. He is beautiful and brave and very smart but he likes Celeste. *He loves Celeste.*" She rolled her eyes dramatically. "They kiss, Papa. They look like this." Alice sucked in her cheeks and her eyes rolled up into their sockets. She then pursed her lips and made a fish mouth accompanied by sucking noises. "They kiss like that when they think no one else is around." She confided those last scandalous facts in a whisper; all the while she nodded sagely at what that implied.

Whatever that might actually be however, she hadn't a clue.

"And I heard you tell Anne Marie that when girls are alone with boys and let boys kiss them they could be in serious trouble and have a baby. The girls I mean. Celeste may very well be with child."

"Oh, good heavens." Darcy smiled as he pressed her cheek against his chest. "So you like Harry, do you?" In fact, the whole family was aware of her fanatical devotion to the young man and thought it precocious.

"Oh, very much, Papa. He's so pretty and tall and he smells good all the time. He smiles at me whenever he sees me. He has nice teeth." As she played with her Papa's neck scarf she rubbed her thumb across a spot of jam that somehow had appeared there, a spot that was increasing in size with every attempt of hers to eradicate it. *Oh, oh.* She sucked the rest of the jam from her thumb but it was too late, the collar was already covered with it. She patted him there. Perhaps he'd never notice.

When he looked down at her she smiled over brightly back at him. She never noticed the wistful look in his eye. His baby daughter was no longer his baby; she was growing up.

"If I tell you a secret do you promise not to tell?"

Her father nodded.

"I want to marry him."

"Ah." It was like a knife to his heart. "Well, that *is* very serious."

"Remember, you promised not to tell anyone — maybe Mama, but no one else." Her eyes were huge with concern, but only for a moment. "Oh, and you could tell Uncle Fitz too, if you like. And Auntie Amanda, of course. I love Auntie Amanda's biscuits. Maybe cousin Matthew and cousin Mark would like to know too; Anne Marie and Kathy already know. But that's all. Perhaps we could tell George..."

"Let's say this. I promise no announcements will be made to the general public without your express approval, all right. I only pray he is worthy of you. I cannot imagine any man deserving you, but I do believe Harry would come closest." Then he cupped her face and kissed her. "And you have not diverted me from why you are being punished in the first place. You should not have kicked Celeste."

"She said I was ugly, Papa. Am I very ugly?"

He would have liked to have kicked the chit himself when he heard that, but he swallowed hard against the sudden lump in his throat. "Certainly not; you are beautiful, Alice, unique. It was not very good of her to fib like that."

Alice beamed at her father, content now because he was always right. "I kicked her bottom," she giggled.

"Alice, you cannot kick people on their bottoms. It is un-Christian to resort to physical retaliation over petty insults. You must allow small differences to resolve themselves."

"It wasn't so small," she explained seriously. "She has a *really* big bottom."

"*Alice!*"

1833
"The Adolescents"

Struggle with a sense of identity
Lowered opinion of parents
Rule and limit testing
Sexual awakening

"I wish either my father or my mother, or indeed
both of them, as they were in duty both equally bound
to it, had minded what they were about when they
begot me."

Laurence Sterne

Chapter Twenty-One

It was a lovely May morning and the flower beds were making their first appearances; the landscape was bursting with new life. Kathy Fitzwilliam stood at the window and saw none of it. Her thoughts were with her mother and the estrangement that had kept them apart for so many months. It had been Kathy's fault entirely, she realized that now, and could not for the life of her understand why she had been so angry for so long. She adored her mother, she really did, and if anything were to happen to her now, before she could tell her how much she meant to her, how much she loved her, how much she needed her... A cry of pain from her parent's bedroom made her turn and cross herself; tears began to burn her eyes once again.

Kathy's mother, Amanda, was the worst of all possible things a parent could be in the eyes of the very young — different. She was a foreigner, with a foreign accent and foreign ways. She also laughed freely, something Aunt Catherine had told her was simply not done, excessive smiling was even frowned upon; but, her mother was a naturally happy woman, could not contain her joy at times. She adored her many children and she loved her husband.

"No good can ever come of over stimulation or excessive elation," admonished Aunt Catherine. "My nephew, Fitzwilliam, should be ashamed to have sired so many children – it's a scandal I tell you. Restraint in such things must inevitably fall to the woman, of course, men being the naturally unwholesome beasts that they are. An aristocratic woman knows this, is never disposed to enjoy her husband's amorous attentions. No, no, no – marriage and children are duties in one's life, not pleasures. To think otherwise is very common."

It was comments such as these that fed Kathy's growing feelings of embarrassment for her mother; and, of course, she also craved the esteem of her new companions – young men and women interested in her now that she was 'Lady Katherine', the daughter of an Earl. It was her eagerness to be received by these people that set the course for her slow and deliberate rejection of the person she loved more than anyone else.

Her memories of what she had said and done the prior year now tormented her.

The current problem began several months earlier, in September, when the door knocker finally went up at the Darcy's London town home, Pemberley House. Within moments Kathy appeared there, a maid in tow. She greeted her godparents very properly, accepting their happy welcome with a haughty nod. "Uncle William, Aunt Elizabeth, it is very pleasant to see you again. I trust you are both well."

Lizzy had been about to throw her arms open wide for their customary hugs and kisses when she sensed the tense formality of the occasion. Darcy merely shook his head, his infamous eyebrow raised as he set his hands on his hips.

"You've forgotten your coronet," was his only comment.

"Are you feeling all right, Kathy?"

"Minor aches, Aunt Elizabeth...small discomforts...nothing of a nature that another lady of my stature and breeding could not endure. And, if it is not too great an inconvenience, I should rather be referred to by my proper name, Katherine Marie. Lady Catherine de Bourgh feels that familiar names are too...familiar...or something. I can't exactly remember what it was, but it was bad. Might I inquire if either Anne Marie or Alicia is home to callers this afternoon?"

"No, you may not."

"William, behave yourself. Yes, they are both upstairs. Shall I call them for you?"

"There is, of course, no need. I am quite well acquainted with your domicile. I shall acquit myself upward, if that is perfectly acceptable with you both that...I do that. It is perfectly fine with me to...do...to go..." Kathy was quickly becoming tripped up with her own propriety.

A squeal from upstairs caught her attention and a child's happy smile briefly made its appearance before being beaten back into submission. Lady Katherine's austere visage returned. "If you will excuse me..." She floated past the Darcy's and out the family sitting room door. Then, when out of sight of the amused couple, she hitched up her skirt and bounded up the staircase taking two steps at a time, straight into the waiting arms of her greatest friends in the world, Anne Marie and little Alice.

The two older girls locked themselves inside Alice's bedroom, eagerly indulging their newfound passion for grown up 'ladies' things – speaking about young men, fussing with their hair, discussing the latest fashion, speaking about young men, sharing their deepest secrets. Speaking about young men.

Alice sat before her dressing table the whole time half listening, content and reading a book of poetry in Latin. Her job was mainly to hand hairpins up to whichever girl was braiding or curling her thick hair at the moment. The older girls' constant obsession with boys and appearance was boring beyond belief but she loved them both dearly, felt privileged and honored that they included her in their 'adult' discussions. There was also the added bonus of a seemingly non-ending supply of treats that usually arrived with Kathy Fitzwilliam.

"I have had a note passed to me in secret from Sir John Bromley through his footman. He says he admires my eyes. Sir John does, not the footman."

"Katherine," Anne Marie stopped hair curling ministrations on her sister to stare disapprovingly at her cousin. "Sir John Bromley is, well, old. He must be at least forty if he's a day. Whatever would he want with someone as young as you? Never mind, don't say it out loud. Alice, sweetheart, would you like a little fringe over your forehead?"

"I don't care. However, I did promise Mama not to allow you anywhere near my hair with a pair of scissors again." Alice thought little about her appearance but she did recognize a bargaining chip when it reared its head.

"You may borrow my box of paints."

"And your sketch pad."

"Yes."

"And your copy of 'The Evil Duke of Castle Rackrent'?"

"Why you greedy little...oh, all right."

"All right, then you may cut a fringe, but nothing too short."

Kathy's attention had been miles away during the sisters' exchange. "Perhaps he wants a new wife. Perhaps he wants a *young* wife."

"Whom? Oh him. Don't be ridiculous. His other one's just died, and that was his third I believe. How indecorous would that appear – a bit cold hearted, even for a Marquis. You've not even made your debut, and besides that you are barely fifteen years. It all sounds rather unseemly and havey-cavey to me."

"Yes, and splendidly wicked. I do so admire older men, especially ones with titles hanging about their ears." She squinted at the impish and odd little face of Alice Darcy staring back up at her in the mirror. "I think you should cut her hair a little more on the left. Ooh, no, I meant her right, my left. Sorry." They all tilted their heads to the right to study the damage. "Perhaps more fringes will hide that slight mistake. Really, Anne, I don't like him *that* way. It's just exciting to think someone older, someone terribly important, has even noticed me. He's ever so rich and he is the nephew, on his mother's side, to a Russian prince."

"He'll be a dead nephew to a Russian prince if Uncle Fitz learns about this; he'll bash the poor old fellow's head in," Alice continued reading from her book as she spoke.

"There is that." Kathy leaned closer into the mirror, examined the results of the Anne Marie's coifing attempt and made a soft moue of distaste. "Well, it doesn't signify, I never answered. In fact, Aunt Catherine and I have set our sights on another. No offense, Anne Marie, but isn't Alice beginning to look a bit like a Shetland pony? Here let me take over. Alice, dearest, what say we cut the whole top, it's half gone anyway."

"How are Mr. Wentworth and his wife?" Anne Marie had moved out of the way, turned and now fidgeted with the lace table scarf on the dressing table, straightened the brushes and combs, arranged some creams and bottles of lotion, never acknowledging the two sets of eyes that followed her every movement.

"Oh Anne Marie! Never tell me you are still in love with Robert Wentworth."

"She *adores* him." Alice managed to pull away just in time from her sister's pinch. "She still runs from the room whenever he visits with father, or she blushes and stammers if she cannot escape in time. Robert is always very civil to her too. He's a perfectly splendid fellow, Anne. You are so silly."

"Sit still Alice! Heavens, I very nearly sliced your ear off just then and that would be horrifying; it would *completely* unbalance your coif. Anne, he is married, dear, and that pale little wife of his is about to make him a father. Even worse than that – he has no family connections, nothing really to commend him; and, did you hear that when his father passed it was found out there was *no money*! Imagine that, a distinguished old gentleman with *gaming debts*! Why, it's taken poor Mr. Wentworth four years to pay them off and begin again. And he didn't need to – Papa was ready to settle the accounts himself."

"I think that was quite splendid, I really do; I think he's quite splendid. He's very brave," Anne burst out suddenly, her face crimson.

"As do I, naturally. But, my dear, he's... poor." Kathy seemed to feel that was even worse than being married.

For a moment Alice watched as they stared at each other in the mirror. "There's another minor obstacle neither of you have mentioned yet, I mean besides his being married and completely unsuitable. Isn't he quite a few years older as well? You would be behaving as silly as Katherine with Sir John, don't you think? No offense meant, Kate."

"No offense taken, mouse." A snip too near her ear caused Alice to jump. "Oops. Sorry. I'm nearly finished, please sit still."

It was an unfortunate hairbrush incident moments later that concluded the grooming afternoon, taking all the girls by surprise. Kathy accidentally caught the brush within the child's thick tresses and none of them could dislodge it; a bit more cutting was needed. "I am sorry about that, Alice, I truly am. Really, you can barely tell it's been cut, especially if you don't show your left side too often. To get back to Robert, I heard Mama tell Papa that she believes he felt obligated to marry the chit. Very sad since the woman rarely comes to town to be with him and he's alone now more than ever before." Placing her hands over Alice's ears, Katherine leaned close enough to Anne Marie to whisper, "No one truly believes the child is even his." Katherine then stared meaningfully at Anne Marie, both peering at each other in the mirror.

"I don't wish to speak on it."

"Nor do I. I abhor gossip. Oh! Did you hear my brother Matt's had another run in with father? Aunt Katherine believes Papa and Matthew battle so often because they are much too much alike in temperament. She claims Papa was a wild child too, as wild when he was young as Matt is now, although I find that hard to fathom. Father is so conservative, really; rather old fashioned about affairs of the heart and lovers and mistresses and..."

"There. All finished, Alice." Anne Marie interrupted Katherine, deliberately.

When she looked up Alice sighed. "Mama's going to be very upset with you both."

"She won't notice, pet. Here keep this cap on your head. Like this, over your ears, no both. I think we need a bigger cap. Anne Marie, are Auntie Eliza and Uncle Wills attending Lady Catherine's ball?"

"No. George returns to Harrow for Michaelmas term and father wants us all to accompany him. It's silly, really, but the unvarnished truth is my poor old Papa is extremely sentimental. He is taking the idea of George entering Oxford next year very hard – well Papa *is* nearing six and forty; keeps saying how old we are all making him feel. He's sad that George will be grown up then you see, on his own. Anyway, we'll be arriving home much too late in the evening to be ready in time. Your mother and father aren't going are they? What! Never tell me! I don't believe you."

"Yes! I have even convinced Mama to have a fabulous new gown made for the occasion. Several new gowns are being fashioned, in fact, and all stylish ones, not that hideous style she usually orders; and, she's to have her hair done by Lady Catherine's personal attendant, and several pair of new shoes are already ordered, plus a lovely cape. Thank goodness she's finally begun to take stock of her appearance. After all, she is a Countess now – not some old soldier's wife. Countess Somerville. She hates when I remind her of that but it cannot be helped; at least she's attempting to belong, socially."

"I love your Mama just as she is." As she spoke Alice tugged on her hair, trying in vain to make the different sides' lengths uniform. "She's always so happy and she smells wonderful, like vanilla. And she's kind to everyone."

"Well, I like her well enough, of course. It's just that she's rather rustic. I wish she was rather more like your Mama."

"You cannot be serious! My Mama makes me very angry at times; she's not perfect, you know," Anne Marie pouted. "All she does is lecture me, day and night. She harps on what not to do and...and what not to wear and...and she's always giving me books to read and wanting me to learn Latin of all things. I don't know why she goes on and on about our minds being so important. Fellows don't care a fig about our minds. She says I am attempting to grow up much too fast and I should enjoy being a child! Can you imagine such a stupid thing to say, when I'm sorely *sick* of being a child. I want to know when I'll finally have a bosom worth noticing and she tells me it doesn't signify. Well, it does signify. I'm fifteen and I look no better than a ten year old boy."

"Yes, that's true enough."

"Alice!"

"I never said it was a bad looking ten year old boy you looked like, more like a lovely ten year old... Now what have I said wrong?"

Chapter Twenty-Two

Amanda stared into the beautiful cheval mirror before her.

A stranger with her face stared back.

"You look *magnifique,* madame. *Tres beau.*" The French seamstress that Aunt Catherine had retained to prepare an entire new wardrobe, turn Amanda out properly for the ball, was also studying the reflection. She could find no fault whatsoever with her handiwork, only with the grim looking woman wearing it.

"You don't think this décolletage a bit...low?"

"*Non!*" The seamstress's back stiffened; she blinked rapidly and huffed.

"Well, if this is truly what is fashionable..."

"*Excusez-moi! Madame,* I can assure you zat zis is ze most up to date, fashionable dress, ze hair is *beau, superbe,* ze shoes, ze gloves, they are all *splendide. Je ne comprends pas...*why ze figure of you, *madame,* was *creer* for zis gown! Ze *Comtesse* de Bourgh and *ma jeune dame ,* ze young *mademoiselle - Katerin,* she is your daughter, oui? You are zer *creation* as well as *mon.*"

That was exactly as she feared. Sighing, Amanda closed her eyes and wondered if any of it would make a difference in the end. All she truly wanted was to make her daughter Kathy proud of her and if this was what it took, if this was what the child really wanted, Amanda would try her level best to carry it off. She would outwardly adjust her appearance to fit society's accepted mode.

But, she felt ridiculous.

Her hair was a towering fright, her face painted, and her dress was acceptable but for one small detail – well, really, not so small. Her breasts! They were all but presented to the world on a platter, exposed for anyone's examination. She thought suddenly of the cows coming in from the pasture at her aunt's farm in Virginia. Tugging up the front was useless; there simply was not enough material there to save her from a future lung ailment. And, although she had seen the same style gown on other women, until now she had not truly appreciated how very draughty a room could feel.

Turning, she smiled weakly at the incensed seamstress. "Thank you for all your trouble, you may go now. Good bye." She turned to her maid, Willa. "Will you let my husband know I'll be down in a moment?"

Below stairs Fitzwilliam checked the hallway clock again, impatient to be started with this night, eager for it to be over with and done. At one point the foreign woman his aunt had forced upon Amanda bustled past him, muttering in a definitely Yorkshire accent of her true feelings regarding the birth origins of the British aristocracy. Soon one of the maids scurried down, announced to him that his wife was nearly ready, then promptly scurried back up the upstairs.

He continued to wait. Where the hell was she? They would be late getting there and that meant late in returning home which aggravated Fitzwilliam to no end. The older he became the more he enjoyed an early night and a good sleep. One maid after another was dispatched upstairs. Not one reappeared – it was as if the servants were being swallowed whole into the dark recesses of the second floor hallway. When his son Luke wandered past a bored Richard grabbed him about the neck and then father and son began to wrestle at the foot of the stairs, knocking into the hall table and chairs causing typical Fitzwilliam mayhem and destruction.

Laughing and whooping together as they were neither heard his wife finally descend the staircase. She called softly at first then cleared her throat. Holding his son in a headlock, both father and son turned in unison to face Amanda just as she reached the last step.

"Good god." Luke slapped his hand over his mouth and hoped neither parent had noticed his blasphemy.

Richard froze in his tracks. *Good god was right.* She had never looked like this before in all their years of marriage – so beautiful, so voluptuous, so sensual. He hated it. The bodice of the off the shoulder gown of dark green brocade was exquisite really, as was the entire gown, decorated with pearls and intricate beading; however, it was also a low cut, very tight bodice. It seemed to Richard that the stiff scalloped lace that trimmed the neckline was the only thing keeping her decent.

"Papa, let me go; I can't breathe."

"Oh, are you still here?" Fitzwilliam released his son's neck, but his attention was on his wife; his first, second and third reaction all territorial and very male. She was exhibiting a good deal too much of what he considered his and his alone.

"Well, Richard? Say something!" Amanda at first appeared very anxious by her husband's frown, his silence; however, that quickly gave way to simmering annoyance. Kathy appeared then at his side, beaming and clapping with delight, oblivious to her mother's growing anger, her father's frown or her brother's exaggerated gasps for air.

"Isn't she splendid looking, Papa? I do adore her hair that style."

Richard's gaze, however, had never reached that far, it could not get past the vast expanse of high puffed white bosom.

He scowled. "She'll put someone's eyes out with those."

Luke immediately began to giggle.

"Your Lordship..."

The formal voice immediately behind him startled Fitzwilliam and he turned quickly. *Blast,* when had the butler come up; or, had he been standing there the entire time, waiting patiently with their cloaks in hand? Amanda's cheeks turning a deep red seemed to indicate that he had.

"Well, what a thing to say!" Katherine pointed to her mother. "Do you know how hard she has had to work to look even this presentable? I for one am ever so proud of you Mama, I truly am. Remember, though, say as little as possible and smile, you have good teeth. And, heavens, no more than two dances with father; better yet, I've seen you both waltz, best not to dance at all. Oh, and *please* no hand holding. And you do remember you are not to remove your gloves? Good. Oh, and consider taking his lead when selecting any dining implements."

"Katherine Marie, that is enough! I think you and your brother had better leave us now, go to bed or do something. Amanda, forgive my outburst but I am a bit taken aback by your appearance, unaccustomed to seeing quite so much of you on display."

"Bear in mind she has nursed an obscene of number of babies. I truly believe she kept Andrew on the breast far too long this time. Perhaps, Mama, you could place your fan across your décolletage if it bothers Papa so, however it seems a horrid shame to hide such a lovely bodice. Oh dear, apparently you'll need a bigger fan..."

"Keep you mouth closed, girl."

"Whatever have I done wrong now, Papa?"

Avoiding all eye contact with their butler Amanda accepted her wrap and walked out the door in silence, leaving her husband and daughter standing in the hall.

"You really do look handsome, Mama." Katherine's feeble muttering was lost to the night.

"Kathy, you have as little tact as I do!"

"Well! Evidently, I am not appreciated in this family!" Kathy turned and stomped away.

Fitzwilliam snatched his hat from the butler. "And not a word, not a single, bloody word of my little remark is to be repeated downstairs."

The butler appeared to be properly offended. "I heard nothing, sir."

Slamming his beaver hat on his head and muttering loudly Fitzwilliam followed his wife out the door.

It was a long drive to the Rosing's Ball that evening. Fitzwilliam was irritated, both with his wife's cold silence and with himself for his silly comment, made before children and servants. He glanced her way occasionally but she sat in shadows, her dark cloak around her; only the glitter of the diamonds around her neck was proof of her existence.

"Where did you get that necklace? It looks very familiar."

In silence Amanda shifted her position presenting to him a bit more of her back.

"Amanda?"

She did not respond.

"I have asked you a civil question, Amanda, I expect a civil answer. From where is that necklace?"

Still she remained silent.

"At least give me the courtesy of acknowledging that you hear me!"

"It is one of the Fitzwilliam family's great heirlooms, Richard; a necklace that is mine by right as the wife of the current Earl. Aunt Catherine presented it to me, since you were either uninterested in doing so, or ignorant of its existence. She had grown tired of waiting for you to retrieve it from the bankers and assured me it would be perfect for this dress. If you would prefer I not wear it, I will remove it." Her hands went up to the clasp at the back of her neck.

"Stop this instant! I'd forgotten about the goddamn choker and that's the truth of it! I've rarely thought twice about any of those trinkets, never expected it to come to us – to you – as I never expected to become the Earl. Gaudy nonsense! The last I remember all this rubbish was in my brother Regis' possession and it's been years since I last saw any of if on my mother." His voice sounded callous even to his own ears. Closing his eyes in frustration he continued on in a deliberately softer tone. "It looks very nice on you. Catherine is correct, it is yours now, to do with as you wish. You look fine."

Her hands went back to rest in her lap and she turned her back on him once again.

"Bloody hell! Will you be giving me this icy treatment all evening?"

Again, she did not respond.

"This is damn unfair, Amanda, damn unfair! My remark was made in jest. Whenever did you become so bloody sensitive; I always make ridiculous remarks, always try to make a moment light. I meant you no harm, you know I love you! At least look at me. Very well, Amanda, two can play the silent game, I can be just as cold and unfeeling and heartless! Of all the fucking..."

"*Stop your cursing will you please! I am sick unto death of your language!*" That got his attention. It was possibly the first time in their marriage she'd actually shouted louder than he. "Yes, I do know you and you know me, and I love you also; but, at times, Richard," she closed her eyes for a moment and then continued, "oh at times I grow very tired of your humor, very weary of your so called 'witticisms'. In fact, there have been one or two moments in our marriage when I was not all that amused, when I would have preferred a kind remark, any sort of small encouragement, or compliment, instead of your usual juvenile derision! *There are even times, Mr. Fitzwilliam, when I'd like to bop you on your bloody head!*"

Hell must have just frozen over, Amanda had actually cursed. Fitzwilliam's eyes blinked rapidly, his world upended. "That was most unjust; most unfair of you, Madame. You have wounded me deeply."

Not knowing whether to laugh or cry, Amanda merely shook her head. When the coach came to a stop before Lady Catherine's beautiful old mansion she turned her back fully on her husband again and accepted the hand of the footman who assisted her from the carriage. Fitzwilliam watched her descend, his eyes narrowed slits. He did love her with his whole heart, more than life itself; but, he knew there was also no one else in the entire world that could make him so damn angry!

"You look absolutely adequate, my dear; doesn't she Richard? I have impeccable taste you know. Mademoiselle Lilly has dressed queens, empresses." Aunt Catherine scrupulously examined Amanda with her quizzing glass, the better to admire her creation. "This must have been quite the challenge for the poor woman. Richard, doesn't Amanda look fetching? Richard?" When her nephew said nothing, she arched an eyebrow towards him. "*I said,*" Catherine repeated loudly, "*that your wife looks attractive.* You may respond at any time you wish, but I pray it is soon. I am old and have several health issues."

"The dress is too low cut; she exposes herself too much."

"Well, I never...!" Catherine was aghast. "That statement was outrageous! You cannot presume to lecture to *me* – on *haute couture*! I'll have you know that I personally selected the design of this gown, the color – by the way Amanda, try not to say too much, you'll pull the evening off so much better that way. And stay out of direct light. And you may wish to keep those lovely long gloves on your hands; they are dreadful, simply dreadful. Your hands I mean, not the gloves. The gloves are divine..."

Amanda closed her eyes, her fragile and battered self confidence tottering about like a drunken sailor. When she opened them again she was shocked to see a furious Richard towering over his aunt. "Enough! I won't have another word said against her by you or by anyone else, do you hear me? She's perfect in my eyes, always was and always will be, and she certainly has no need of your instructions as to deportment or appearance."

Aunt Catherine was speechless, an unheard of occurrence; poor hell had just frozen over a second time.

A flood of emotion pressed into Amanda's heart and her eyes began to sting. Why had she doubted him, even for a moment? Here was the husband she loved and knew, her other half. She hesitantly glanced up at his face but he still appeared aloof, was still distant with her.

"I shall now escort you both inside. When you wish to leave, Lady Somerton, you may send word to me through a footman. Aunt Catherine, you will now take my other arm. Are you both ready? *Good!*"

Richard grabbed a drink from a passing tray, attempting to pleasantly greet all the people who crowded about him now that his presence had been announced; an Earl was invariably fawned over, praised. Men were actively seeking his attention, women preened. He smiled graciously at all and bowed, turned this way and that to acknowledge each speaker.

He had tried to avoid these types of people his entire life, found their society not only shallow but mind numbingly dull. Surprising, then, that he had grown to appreciate his duties at the House of Lords so much, not that anything of consequence was often accomplished there – just the reverse. But it was satisfying to stand on an equal footing with men who controlled the destiny of the realm. If he could influence just one vote for right in the entire time he was a member, well, he would consider his life *there* a success.

But not *here*...here he was standing in too tight shoes, in a stuffy, overcrowded room filled with perhaps the homeliest people he'd ever seen in his life.

And it was this subculture that he deplored, the 'ballroom' politics, back room deals, secret alliances. He preferred his fights open and bare knuckled, and that thought made him smile again.

Why had he agreed to this evening; how had he become entangled in this damn mess? Oh yes, now he remembered. It was his social climbing daughter and his Mad Cow Aunt. The 'mad cow' herself must have instantly sensed his thoughts; she often did. At that precise moment she scowled at him so he winked back at her, making her even angrier.

It was then he noticed the dancers, most especially his Amanda, twirling and smiling in the arms of another man. *She really is beautiful; even more so now than when we first married. I don't tell her nearly often enough, do I?* She was changing partners too often, looking much too tired. A man well known for taking liberties with other men's wives suddenly cut into her dance, he twirled her away in his arms, around and around, winking, smiling – leering at her exposed bosom...

"That does it! This ends now!" He began to make his way through the crowd more quickly. "Excuse me...excuse me...*out of my way!*"

Chapter Twenty-Three

The gentleman who had interrupted her dance was a 'Sir' of some sort. He was handsome in that peculiarly English sort of way, slender, pale skinned, elegant. A rather bold fellow he had introduced himself to her earlier in the evening and had been continually shadowing her ever since. What Amanda could not remember for the life of her was his exact title and whether or not he was above an Earl in importance, or below. She hoped above because with any luck that would aggravate her thick-skulled, overbearing and irritating husband tremendously.

She only wished she could remember the man's name. He was father to a young man with whom Kathy was enthralled at the moment, so it was important that Amanda make a good impression. It was really too bad about his breath, though, and he was rather careless with his hands, although he politely apologized each and every time.

One more 'misstep' and I will scratch out your eyes. Amanda wanted to say this but did not; instead she concentrated on not speaking at all and counting her steps while dancing. The room grew warmer and more crowded, and her feet throbbed. He was speaking so she smiled and nodded and tried to pay attention. As they passed each other during the Quadrille he would exclaim in stops and starts that he was a very important person and that it was her great good fortunate that he was currently unencumbered. Unencumbered with what was the question, the noise and the music were deafening.

Their dance finally over the gentleman led her off the floor to the far side of the room; however, with the crush of people now in attendance he explained there were no chairs available, no place to rest in the stifling room. He kindly inquired if she would like to join him out on the veranda to view Lady Catherine's fabulous rose garden.

Amanda nodded, relieved for any opportunity to enjoy the fresh, crisp, air of a lovely evening. Besides it might aggravate her husband and make him sick. She smiled brilliantly at that thought, leaving her new companion with a breathtakingly lovely, yet incorrect, impression.

The gentleman believed her to be deeply enamored of him, of his position, his wealth, his power. She spoke very little; perhaps she was slow-witted – the thought cheered him. She should be quite easy to seduce and the pleasure would be all his...

"Thank you for the use of your arm, sir. There is a bench no farther than these doors that may do, with a splendid view of the park." For some reason he chuckled at this pedestrian remark and led her out into the cool night air.

"You appear so proper on the outside, so prim; but, I sense that beneath all your finery you are a goer, Madame, a thoroughbred through and through. You are created as I am, specifically for the race." His nostrils flared and his eyes seemed to roll up into their sockets for one brief moment. "...such fine fetlocks," he murmured huskily.

"Pardon me? I don't comprehend your meaning, sir."

He laughed uproariously. "The *pahk*? My *ahm*, too *fahr*,' I say, you mimic that dreadful Boston Brahmin accent very well. '*Pahdon* me?'– adorable. Are you equally adept employing a Spanish accent? I wouldn't mind it if you were, as a matter of fact. I always felt French accents very seductive as well."

Amanda ignored him as she lowered herself to the bench. Bone tired after two hours of dancing, her feet were sore and the material on the heel of her expensive new slipper was torn, all of which was dispiriting. Suddenly he was sitting so near to her that she became alarmed. She tried to calm herself – after all they were perched upon a harmless little stone bench within view of several hundred of the *ton's* finest. Amanda reasoned she should have no fear of compromise.

Besides, nothing short of a gun muzzle to the head would convince her to reenter that ballroom until she cooled down.

He searched the grounds then stared longingly at a more secluded bench, one much deeper within the garden. "Would not the view of the...roses...be better *farther in,* away from the crowds?" Since he addressed half his remarks to her chest Amanda began to feel even less in charity with the fellow than she had before. In fact, she was becoming very annoyed with him.

By the manner in which you stare, sir, I believe you have too good a view as it is. She wanted to say this but she did not; instead she shook her head and fanned herself. "Pardon me, your Lordship, you are too, too, kind, but I shan't be capable of accommodating even one more step." This time she remembered to speak as Lady Catherine had instructed her, employing the lofty British accent which she often used at home when she desired to amuse her husband and children. He swiftly leaned over her, grabbed her hand and licked her open palm.

"My stars, what are you doing?! You stop that this instant." Amanda's eyes rounded with alarm. "Let go of me!"

"Mrs. Fitzwilliam, I hope you won't think me too bold, but I must confess to a most powerful attraction for you; most ardent if you understand my meaning. You are so delightfully womanly – delicate yet passionate. And, so very exquisitely..." Again his gaze drifted slowly down her body and he moaned "...formed. My lady wife doesn't understand me, never did really. She cares nothing for my needs or wants – and I have great needs, my Goddess, strong *throbbing* wants. She's left me, the wife I mean, returned to the country; I am totally alone here. I am very wealthy, did you know that? Filthy rich. Swimming in it. And quite lonely, did I mention that? Oh, I yearn for you, Mrs. Fitzwilliam, I need you, quite desperately, in my bed. I own a yacht." He began to nibble at her ear.

"*Pahdon* me?" Amanda squeaked, slipping right back into her Boston Brahmin. Nothing like this had ever happened to her before and she had crossed the ocean three times, twice with only a maid for company. The man was insane, obviously. She would just scream for help; but, no recognizable sound emerged, just a sputtering of saliva. His hands were moving quickly then, too quickly. One had slipped into her hair and grabbed hold, pulling her head back, the other went around her waist. He seized her against himself in an intimate and rib breaking embrace.

"Goddess, oh those lips...open your mouth for me...please... vixen, don't turn your face from me, I know you want this...your struggles only excite me more...ouch, how dare bite me you little bitch, so you prefer to play rough do you...!"

"Am I interrupting?" Both Amanda and the gentleman jumped at once.

"Richard, thank heavens!" Amanda gasped and her body slumped in relief.

"What in blazes...? How dare you! We desire privacy here, if you please, sir! Do you know who I am?" After squinting several moments into the glare of the open doorway the gentleman was finally able to identify the speaker. "Why, Somerton! Is that you? Oh, I say, old chap, frightfully sorry for the outburst; but, as you can see, I am a bit (*heh, heh, heh*) busy shall we say. Give us a moment, there's a good fellow." It was at this point her words registered into his fevered brain. "Richard?" He licked his lips for a moment. "Did you just now call Somerton, Richard, Mrs. Fitzwilliam? You did, didn't you? Yes, I thought you did. Sounds vaguely familiar. Richard! *Richard Fitzwilliam? Good God!*"

Fitzwilliam stood within the open door frame, his arms crossed over his chest. "Gratifying to have my identity so swiftly established. You do realize, Howard, the party activities are meant to take place inside of my aunt's home, not outside."

Howard's face grew deathly pale. He looked first at the Earl of Somerton then back to the woman beside him, the woman whose hair he still held.

"I strongly suggest you take your hands from her ladyship."

Howard whimpered once and his hands sprung away from her body as if they were on spring latches.

"You're very quiet, sir." Fitzwilliam strolled slowly forward. "Most unlike you, really, whereas a moment ago you couldn't shut up. In fact, I found your proclamations of desire quite entertaining. Or I would have, if they hadn't been directed to *my wife.*"

"Forgive me, your lordship. I hadn't realized." Howard attempted to stand. "This was most unfortunate, a most unfortunate misunderstanding, indeed, your lordship. Believe me, no offence was meant, no dishonor intended. I am well aware of your prowess at dueling, sir, and your magnificent war record, oh my yes, very commendable, truly; so, I hope you don't misconstrue my behavior here. I assure you I meant no disrespect..."

"Apologize to Lady Somerton and then leave us." Fitzwilliam had by now reached the bench and he did not look to be a happy man. Standing with his legs braced apart and his hands fisted on his hips, he glared intently at the panicking gentleman.

"Hmmm? Oh yes, most definitely. Please forgive me Lady Somerton. You see I didn't quite catch your name when we were initially introduced – the music being very loud – and we were standing so near to the viola that I was distracted and then when I asked, you said Fitzwilliam so I never..."

"You should go now, Howard." Fitzwilliam spoke softly. Too softly. Howard attempted twice more to move but his legs seemed to fail him.

"*Get out!*" The thunder of Fitzwilliam's yell reverberated in the still night. People passing by the doorway stopped, dancers slowed their weaving steps then came forward; all were watching in morbid fascination when they heard Fitzwilliam yell, "*And if I ever – ever – see you sniffing around my wife again you'll be pissing out of your bloody mouth! Literally! Do I make myself perfectly clear, Howard!?*"

Howard ran like hell into the laughing crowd.

Fitzwilliam turned toward his wife. "I can't leave you alone for one minute, can I?"

"I am not speaking to you."

"You know Amanda you really must use your title now when someone inquires about your identity. I understand your distaste for the English aristocracy but, well, you do live in this country and it does tend to uncomplicate things!"

She turned her back on him.   "I wonder who is shouting so loudly; all I hear is a great wind..."

"All right, that does it. You and I are going to have a little chat." He clasped her hand and pulled her to her feet, dragging her far out into Aunt Catherine's famous rose arbor, to one of those more private benches for which Howard had so yearned. She plopped down hard then vigorously employed her fan.

Fitzwilliam positioned himself before her. "Well? I await your apology."

"*My* apology? Ha! You can wait until corn grows from your ears then." After several tense moments she kicked his shin. "Why, why did you say such a crude thing in front of the children, in front of the butler? I know when you're teasing me and I know when you're upset. And please don't lie to me and say it had anything to do with this stupid dress, because I know it really did not."

"Oh yes it did!" He grunted angrily, resisting the unmanly urge to rub his shin, then he sighed and sat beside her. "It's not a stupid dress. It's actually a beautiful dress and you look beautiful in it. You really do. It's just not a dress you would ever have chosen for yourself. It's not you."

"Why ever not?"

"Well, for one thing it's a dark color."

"If you aren't going to speak honestly with me I'll go back inside!"

"I am being honest with you! You have not worn a dark color since you left that hideous situation you lived in with your mother-in-law. You hate dark colors with a passion."

"I'm a matron now; long in the tooth and in my dotage. Old women do wear dark colors."

"Well, that's a rarely witless remark from you I must say. For one thing a matron doesn't possess a bosom such as yours. Oh, do stop becoming angry at my every remark about your bosom. You're beautiful, Amanda, lovelier this day, and at this age, than when we first met. My dear, Sir Howard Pumphries was positively drooling over you, the vile little bastard. I should have ripped his bloody heart out."

"Oh, Richard, what a lovely thing to say."

"My God, you Americans truly are a bloodthirsty lot, aren't you?"

"Now you're just being flattering." No longer in the least bit angry she playfully nudged his shoulder with her own. "You look quite handsome yourself tonight. That waistcoat looks well on you."

"It does?" His chin hit his chest. "Really? Which one did he put on me?"

"My heavens it's a miracle you remember to wear your small clothes at times." She shook her head. "All right, so what else is wrong with my dress? Is it the neckline? You do realize that the *décolletage* on this dress is less extreme than many of the other gowns here tonight."

"I wouldn't know; I haven't looked at any other décolletage."

"Liar!"

"I am not! All right, Amanda, my problem with this dress is that you are allowing yourself to be manipulated by our daughter, because she has some ridiculous, cork brained notion that her acceptance into society depends entirely upon you and your

...*décolletage*! What a silly word that is anyway, I feel a fool just saying it."

"Well, where is the harm?"

"For one thing isn't that a great deal of responsibility for one bosom?"

"Forget my bosom for five minutes, would you please! I am her mother, Richard; I want to make her happy. She's at an age where looks and position are important."

"Whatever happened to my little colonial insurrectionist; 'Don't Tread On Me' and all that other gibberish? Do you seriously want our daughter to place importance on such shallow measures of worth? Don't you believe we should expect – no demand – better from her?"

"Young women have only one measure in life for success – marriage. The competition for husbands is brutal and Kathy is not as submissive a female as most gentlemen desire. She'll have a harder time of it, Richard; at least I fear she will. Oh, I realize this all appears trivial to you and perhaps a little desperate, but acceptance is most important to her right now. She's ashamed of me and that's probably normal at her age." Her hand went up to silence Richard's loyal protest.

"I understand how she feels because, for a while, I felt the same about my own mother. It seemed to me that she spoke too loudly and laughed too much. Oh, how I wanted to cringe when my father's wealthy and important patients would visit us. She would fawn over them, people who were really no better than us. I suppose she was uncertain of herself, could never learn to judge people for their character instead of their wealth...oh my stars, I've just talked myself out of this, haven't I?"

Fitzwilliam grinned. "That's the easiest argument I've ever won."

"That's the *only* argument you've ever won." Leaning forward she wetted her handkerchief on her tongue then briskly began to rub out the smudge her foot had left on his trousers. "You need to get new dress shoes, Richard. These must be at least ten years old."

"They are perfectly fine; nothing in the least wrong with them."

"Stand up and put your foot on this bench so I won't need to lean down. Will you look at this? I can clearly see the shape of your toes outlined on the leather tops!"

"Let's get back to the subject at hand, shall we? You wish Kathy to be proud of you, correct?"

She nodded.

"You are a smart, beautiful, compassionate woman, the daughter of a fine gentleman. I am convinced you are already a source of pride to her; at least you are if we've done our job correctly in raising her. You do not need to change, Amanda. Your daughter needs to mature, understand what is truly important in life. Give her time."

She sighed. "Well, I am much too tired to argue with you any more."

"And isn't that always welcome news."

"Furthermore, my feet hurt and I'm hungry. There, the smudge is gone." She patted his knee affectionately and stroked her hand down his calf, admiring the fine material. "Well, what do we do now?"

"Anymore of this leg rubbing and I'll be taking you behind those bushes and tossing your skirt over your head."

"My poor darling, you really do miss your days in the military, don't you?"

He grumbled and tried not to smile. "Very amusing. Now may I continue?"

Nodding she stood then kissed his cheek.

"I say we sneak away right this minute, hurry home..." Pulling her into his arms he kissed her forehead, "...throw some blankets on the floor before the fireplace in my study..." he kissed her nose, her temples, her eyes, "...and make love like rabbits." His mouth finally found hers and they shared a deep, thorough, loving kiss. "Afterwards, if we've been very quiet and not woken the children, we will steal into the kitchen for a late night raid of warm milk and cold chicken. How does that sound to you?"

She brushed her fingertips across his lips. "It sounds heavenly. I even anticipated you and did my monthly calculations. It's the perfect time for us. There is absolutely no danger, none whatsoever, of my conceiving this night, at this time of month."

Amanda was with child again before midnight.

Chapter Twenty-Four

"Fitz, wake up, it's almost time for callers; I wouldn't miss this for the world. Look lively man!" Darcy had awoken his cousin by first kicking the stool out from beneath his feet and then just kicking his feet. "Gad, you're worse than a baby – you've drool on your chin."

"What? What are you talking about, callers? What callers? What time is it?" Fitzwilliam pushed his cousin's handkerchief away then with bleary eyes looked up at the mantel clock. One in the afternoon and he was exhausted, had not gone to sleep until nearly five that morning. "Dammit, brat! I hardly slept at all last night. And what's this nonsense about callers? We never have callers – never even put up the knocker most days. Oh, hello, little Alice, I didn't see you there. Do not ever employ the type of foul language that I do. I am a wicked, impious man. I should be shunned from society."

Alice patted his cheek and giggled. "That's all right, Uncle Fitz. I never listen to you, truly I don't."

"That's my little darling."

"May I sit near you on this couch?"

"Of course, you sit wherever you wish. Just push the cats to the side; that's it." He stretched and yawned. "I've a taste for something sweet. I'll ring for cakes and tea, shall I? Sensible girl. I do like your cap — the girls been slashing at your hair again, have they? Wait a moment, what were you saying before, Darcy? Explain yourself."

"Your mind moves along about as swiftly as a plow horse in mud, doesn't it? Well, here's the thing, from what Elizabeth learned in a rather circuitous manner from Aunt Catherine this morning, you will soon be receiving quite a number of callers. Evidently, someone's ladies maid is sister to Catherine's cook — brilliant news network these servants have. Anyway, you and your dear wife are the rage of society and your appearance at Aunt C's last evening caused quite the sensation — everyone's talking about a particular incident involving a very disreputable gentleman I shall not name." Pressing his hands over Alice's tender ears Darcy mouthed, "Did you truly threaten to rip off his ...appendage?"

"Oh, that. *Bah,* only in the most circumspect manner, Darcy. As always, I was most respectful — merely told him he'd be pissing out of his mouth."

"Fitz, little ears..." Darcy moaned. "Alice, when the visitors arrive make your curtsey and then run up to the playroom."

"Oh, Papa, *please,*" she whined and drew out the final word of entreaty until it sounded like a snake was loose in the room. "Let me stay. I wanted to be with Uncle Fitz when he explains whatever happened last night. It sounds as if it was very exciting."

"Alice, hard as it is for me to agree with your father, he has the right of it. Let me just ring for that tea and then you go up and play." Accepting the handkerchief from his cousin he wiped his chin then drank the remnants of his cold morning coffee and grimaced at the taste. "Well, that's pretty beastly."

At that moment the door flew open and Katherine Marie twirled into the room, a foaming circlet of white ruffles set against the pale green muslin gown. She threw her arms around Darcy. "*Tante* William, I thought it was you! *Bonjour! Combien merveilleux de vous enseigner.* Wonderful to see you. Oh, isn't this a heavenly day? Cards have been arriving all morning, even flowers! *Bonjour, mon petite Alise!*"

"It's afternoon, not morning anymore, Kath. You should say *bon après-midi*– I think." Alice beamed at her cousin, enjoying Kathy's rare good mood. "And I believe you just said it was wonderful to teach us. And you called my father your aunt."

"Really? *Jamais l'esprit!* Never mind, French was never my best subject and I am in much too good a humor to worry about minor mistakes. I say, I like that cap you're wearing, just pull it down a little more on the left – no, my left. That's it. Where's Anne Marie? Where's Auntie Eliza? I certainly hope George is not here! I am very annoyed with him."

"Auntie Eliza is with your mother and Anne Marie will be here in a few moments, as soon as she finishes her dance lesson. And please don't tell me you and George have had another falling out! I will never understand the two of you." Darcy twirled his goddaughter around by her upraised hand. "My, you look very pretty today, and happy for a change." He kissed the top of her head. "We missed you last evening, George especially, for all your quarreling."

"I would think Meg Hiddleston would be enough company for him, the way she hangs on his every word. Yes, I heard he had invited that drab to see him off to school. The only thing Georgie could miss from me is a good swift kick up his..."

"Katherine!"

"*Désolé chère tante.*"

"*Désolé chère oncle*," corrected Alice.

"Pardon?"

"You just said 'pardon dear aunt' again, instead of 'uncle'."

"You are becoming *tres irritant*, Alice. *Mon pere* did you see Princess Esterhazy has sent you a gift? A man's jewelry box of all things! I have never seen the like, it is *beau chic*. We must have done very well last night."

"We?"

"All right – you and '*ma mere*'. Isn't it wonderful? I saw Aunt Catherine's carriage pull up just a moment ago so brace yourselves, *ha ha!* Stop this instant, Papa! Where are you going? I am certain she's come to gloat over her role in Mama's great success last evening. She looked lovely, Uncle Wills, she really did. Mama I mean, not Auntie Catherine. Papa, I asked, where are you going?"

"You said Catherine was here didn't you?" Fully awake now Fitzwilliam was struggling to rise from his chair.

Darcy sighed. "I thought we'd have more time. Oh well, Alice I believe we had better miss this show." He reached his hand out for his daughter.

It was too late. The door to Fitzwilliam's library flew open, the Fitzwilliam butler entering fast behind Lady Catherine, a terrified expression on his face.

"*How could you! In all of my days...well, it's unheard of, unthinkable, medieval! Such behavior is simply not condoned in civilized society! Merciful heavens! Threatening to steal from a peer of the realm! What, what could you have been thinking?* Oh, hello, Darcy. I trust you are feeling well. Lovely new hairstyle I see, very smart."

Darcy and Fitzwilliam stared quizzically, first at her and that at each other.

It was then that Catherine noticed Alice. "Good heavens, who are you? You look oddly familiar."

"I'm Alice, Auntie Catherine."

"Alice you claim, we shall see about that. Why do you wear that cap? Whatever is under there...upon my word, what has your mother done to your hair? Here, put that back on you poor, poor thing."

"I know I will hate myself for pursuing this; but, unsurprisingly enough I am having difficulty following your conversation, Catherine. That comment you made before, about my 'stealing from a peer'? Whoever said that?"

"Never tell me! How many men did you threaten to steal from last night? Good heavens, Richard! Am I to be hearing from the entire social register because of you?"

Fitzwilliam bit hard on his upper lip to prevent himself from shouting. "Just tell me to whom you refer to presently, if you please."

"Howard Pumphries of course!"

"Now we're getting somewhere – it's on the road to Bedlam but at least we're moving. All right, did Howard Pumphries actually claim I was going to rob him?"

"You know perfectly well what *you said*. It is well documented you were there for nearly all of your horrid attack upon his person and your scandalous words spread throughout the ballroom like a firestorm. You terrified him, Richard; made Sir Howard most agitated – unto the point of *perspiring*, vile man."

"Just tell me straight out woman! What did he claim I said to him?"

"Don't call me woman, as if I were some sort of Scandinavian fish seller. There were witnesses, Fitzwilliam, so you cannot deny it! He said that you

threatened to go after the Pumphries *Family Jewels'!*
I have never been thus humiliated in my entire life!
To envy another family's baubles, to cause a scene, in
public...well it has created havoc, pure havoc. And for
what, I ask? We have a treasure trove of gems at your
disposal! Did I not, myself, finally coerce your own
wife into wearing the priceless Fitzwilliam diamonds
last evening? And here you go and..."

Darcy immediately turned away and began rubbing
the back of his neck, intently studying the mantelpiece
structure. Fitzwilliam was less subtle. He threw back
his head and let out a hoot of laughter. "I don't believe
this, what an idiot that man is."

"May I ask what you could find so amusing in this
fiasco?"

Cupping his hands over Alice's ears so she wouldn't
hear the crude comment a second time he repeated
softly to Aunt Catherine exactly what he had told
Howard. Aunt Catherine fell backward onto the
settee. "Stop! Oh my ears...It's worse than I thought!
You're ruined! We are all ruined!"

"No. It cannot be possible." Kathy, who had been
listening in mute horror, now stared at her father in
disbelief. "This is a nightmare and I shall awaken if I
just pinch myself. Ouch. Oh no!" All her hopes and
dreams for a grand match were dead, her parents now
evidently a *ton* laughing stock. "You attacked
Geoffrey's father? My Geoffrey?" She was ruined. "You
insulted Sir Howard Pumphries – in front of
everyone."

"Kathy, let me explain."

Her mind raced ahead, certain all that was left to
her now was the convent. "*I* am ruined. Father how
could you...!" The girl ran from the room in tears.

Chapter Twenty-Five

Invitations received in the weeks following Lady Catherine's party were returned with polite regrets, personal calling cards were tossed into the fire, the knocker came down and was packed away. The Fitzwilliam parents returned to the quiet life they had always loved – alone with children, family, and close friends.

Two months after the disastrous 'Incident of the Family Jewels' as the disagreement with Howard Pumphries had become known among the *beau monde,* it was already long forgotten, replaced by other, and much worse, scandals. Harry and several friends had left for their post university grand tour, on his own now that he was twenty and soon to be formally betrothed to his darling Celeste, the twins Matthew and Mark were away at Harrow, along with George Darcy. Life was quiet, and getting quieter. Too quiet, Fitzwilliam worried at times. He hated quiet. Quiet never did bode well for him...

Fitzwilliam rose, anxious and tapping his knife against his glass in a vain attempt for attention. Amanda stilled his hand before the crystal shattered.

"Quiet!" The bickering and giggles came to a sudden to a halt.

"I have an important announcement to make which, I hope," he pointedly looked each child in the eye, "no, which I am certain, will be received as happy and joyous news to our family. Your mother is with child."

"Oh, no, not again!" Luke slumped in his chair.

"It had better not be another girl!" warned four and one-half year old Andrew at the same time. "We have more than enough – we've done our share!"

"You cannot be serious!" Katherine tossed her napkin on the table. "I don't believe this." Andrew took the opportunity of her distraction to steal her bread roll. She slapped at his hand but was too late and he snorted with laughter. "This whole family is a disgrace."

The seven year old twin girls, Mary Margaret and Mary Elizabeth, at first delighted with the news now began to pout and moan, taking their cue from the other children when they realized all were upset.

"Silence!" Fitzwilliam braced his hands on the table before him.

"I have all my pets caged in my room just as you ordered, Papa; no one has been bitten in ages and I will not put them out for *another* new baby! He'll have to find someplace else to sleep. Maybe with Luke; he has the big bedroom all to himself now." Andrew wiped the butter and jam from his mouth with one swipe of the back of his sleeve.

Luke slapped a hand to his forehead and shook his head. "I just thought of something horrid! She could have twins again, couldn't she? She's always having twins."

"We will be the source for all the jokes in London, if we aren't already!" Katherine abruptly stood, her chair nearly tipping over. "I will never, ever again be able to show my face. I hate you both!"

Luke, as all the others, had concerns only with his own interests. "That means we will miss visiting with Harry when he returns to Oxford from his tour, won't it? I knew it; and he was going to introduce me to the cricket players!" He was generally disinterested with anything unrelated to sports. "He was taking me sailing again too! I never get to sail. I never get to do what I want to do."

"Be quiet! All of you!" Fitzwilliam thundered.

Amanda, already pale, appeared ready to burst into tears.

"That does it! All of you out of my sight! I am sick to death of the lot of you! Go to your rooms! Now!" The explosion of irate protests to one of their father's rare punishments resulted in his window shattering, "*Leave!*"

A quarter hour later the couple sat alone, Fitzwilliam at the head of the deserted breakfast table, Amanda at his right, their morning meal untouched before them. He had no idea what to say to her. He was angry with his children, stunned by their selfish behavior.

"Well," he finally had downed his fourth cup of tea. "Shall I speak with the girls or with the boys?" The couple often would sit with the children after similar confrontations to answer questions, soothe hurt feelings, settle arguments. When he saw the look of despondency on Amanda's face his heart nearly broke. He placed a hand over hers. "Amanda, do not take on so. It will come out right in the end. They're basically good children. I think."

"Could you speak with them alone, just this once?"

An unbidden shiver ran up his spine, she looked so pale. "Are you feeling ill again?" He reached for her forehead but she pulled away.

"Not ill; just tired. Very, very tired."

"Have you been taking your heart powders?"

"Yes, Richard. I'm certain it's not my heart, merely my age. This is nothing really." She patted his hand. "I confess I never thought to go through this again."

"On that subject and before I speak with the children I have something to say."

"What is it?" She turned to face him.

"Amanda, this must be the last child. I know your religion means a great deal to you but you have experienced more and more difficulty with each delivery. Frankly, it terrifies me. If anything were to happen to you – my God, it doesn't bear thinking of! I would not want to live. Don't scoff at that, I am quite serious. The children would be well looked after – Darcy and I have a mutual agreement regarding our families. He and Elizabeth would see to them, take them in as their own; and we've certainly enough money for the children to live in luxury all of their lives, secure even for several generations. But, if you were to... die, I would follow quickly, either naturally or..."

"Richard! Shush. Nothing is going to happen; I only need to rest a bit. And you're right. Perhaps it's time I speak with my priest, for this truly must be our last child." She stood, took his arm and leaned into his embrace. "You worry too much, you know. All is well."

He held her close so she would not see his alarm. In all the years of their marriage she had been adamant about following the church's teachings. He knew now how very ill she must truly feel.

Chapter Twenty-Six

The bedroom door to her mother's rooms opened and Katherine came to her feet, recognizing the young maid who dashed out. It was Daisy, a girl Kathy's age, someone who she had spoken with often. Katherine stepped from the shadows and called out in a loud whisper. "Daisy!"

The poor girl started at the noise then ran to Kathy's side. "You gave me a fright."

"How is my mother? What is happening?"

"Oh, miss, I don't know as I should tell you."

"Please Daisy, please." Tears flooded Kathy's eyes.

"There, there, Lady Kathy, don't take on so. Oh, it's been real hard on her, real painful like. I don't think I could ever have a babe after this. And how her ladyship tries not to cry out! Why she near bit clear through her lip with the last pain! And there's blood down there, you know what I mean? She's tearin' up or something. I'm getting you upset; I'll say no more."

"No, please Daisy, I need to know. What does Dr. Anthony say?"

"Oh, Dr. Milagros is angry, at her and at everyone it seems. I never seen him like this – never. Not even when Master Andrew took those powders from his bag and gave them to the sick cat, may God rest his poor feline soul. Oh, I have to go – I'm supposed to see if

Mr. and Mrs. D are here yet. Your mum's been asking for Mrs. D." With that Daisy ran to the door then she turned back once again. "I'm never gettin' married. Never."

More frightened than ever, Katherine sank slowly down onto the settee and covered her face with her hands, returning into the shadows to wait.

Darcy's carriage approached the portico at Somerton House, the horses twitchy, eager for their well earned respite and a good feeding. He, Lizzy, and their two daughters had arrived in London the evening before and had been out shopping for gifts all morning; stopping by Aunt Catherine's in the early afternoon they heard the news. The servants' gossip his Aunt relied upon as gospel revealed Earl Fitzwilliam's wife had just that morning begun her labor, and as Elizabeth and Amanda had always been there for each other during these times, the little family set out immediately for the Fitzwilliam's home.

"I am glad Mama will be with Auntie Amanda," whispered Alice once the footman had handed the sisters down from the coach. She watched her father as he listened intently to the Fitzwilliam butler then he motioned to his driver, said something to him.

"It is too horrible to imagine." Anne Marie shuddered. "I dread the thought of childbirth." Although she was five years older than her sister, Anne Marie was much more delicate than Alice, was much more easily upset.

"I imagine Mr. Wentworth feels the same way now."

"What do you mean?"

"Well, I heard from Papa that Mr. Wentworth's wife died two months ago in childbirth, didn't you know that?"

"No! That poor man, how dreadful for him." Tears filled Anne Marie's eyes.

"Dreadful for him? Dreadful for her, rather. She must have died in agony; the child was stillborn." Alice shook her head sagely. "Papa said he's a broken man, was drowning his sorrow in work until he very nearly collapsed and Papa and Uncle Fitz had to sit him down and lecture him. And you know how adept those two are at lectures!"

Anne Marie wiped away her tears and sniffled. "What a horrible thing to have happened to him – I mean his wife and child dying, not the lecture...hold on a minute, why did Papa tell you all this and not me?!"

"He was probably afraid you'd cry."

"That's ridiculous. Well, maybe. *Oh my*," she suddenly sobbed.

"Do you still harbor a *tendre* for him? You do, don't you?"

"No longer, no. That was only a childish fancy, long ago forgotten." Anne Marie delicately blew her nose and composed herself. "Frankly, I don't know why any woman would wish to marry. The entire process seems so undignified – I mean the liberties that one must allow her husband – and then face childbirth as well? I have no desire to ever be courted."

Alice shrugged. "Well, the way I see it, women have been marrying and having babies almost continually since Adam and Eve, haven't they? And the practice continues, some women even having more than one child. Look at Mama. Heavens, look at Auntie Amanda herself for that matter. Eight babies already and this, her ninth! I mean, why do women go through childbirth so often if it is that unendurable, unless perhaps the rewards were greater than the shame or the risk? Of course, many women *do* die in childbirth, but that could only happen to her once..."

"Alice, you're making me ill."

"Why? What have I said?" But then Alice stopped speaking and glanced in the same direction as Anne Marie stared, at their parents, seeing the concern on her father's face as he spoke with their mother. After a moment the couple approached their daughters.

"Is something wrong? Mama, Papa."

Lizzy thought carefully before she spoke, unwilling to instill what would be, hopefully, needless anxiety into young minds, but also unable to lie. "There perhaps is a problem with the birth."

"Oh, no!" exclaimed Anne Marie. Such a simple statement and yet, following on the heels of their recent conversation, it somehow encapsulated all the apprehensions of motherhood for unmarried girls, all of the terrors of child bearing. The young women held hands and listened intently, their eyes bright with unshed tears.

"Now, now, don't borrow trouble, girls. Come along," Darcy stretched his arms out to shepherd his daughters back to the coach, a sympathetic smile softening his face. "Your Mama is needed by cousin Amanda and she could be here for quite a while so I thought I would take you home, then return here later for a spell. There's really no sense in you having to wait around. Besides, your governess is expecting you, I'm sure you have a great deal to tell her..."

Neither child moved, both yearning for more information. He could sense his daughters growing anxiety for one of their family. "The babe is giving a bit of trouble to his mother, rather like George did with *your* mother. You've both heard the funny story many times." In truth, the girls had heard the story once or twice and no longer found it quite as amusing as they had as children. The reality was that their father and mother had believed she would die in childbirth and it was only through Amanda's assistance that Lizzy had survived at all.

"We would both rather be here, with the rest of the family Papa." Anne Marie spoke, Alice nodding her agreement. "We can both rest in Kathy's room if needed."

As they passed through the front doors Alice tugged at her father's coat sleeve and whispered, "Papa, do you need to be Catholic to become a nun?"

When Darcy and his daughters entered the library, Alice's gaze, as always, first sought out her beloved Harry. She had not seen him in a lifetime, nearly three years, his studies at Oxford and her visits to London or Somerton never coinciding with family homecomings. He looked so different, no longer the gangly, skinny seventeen year old she had last seen. He was a man now, fully grown. His shoulders were wider, his body thicker, his arms and legs long and powerful looking. Her heart patted wildly in her teeny breast. Impossible as it was he had grown even more handsome, an earthbound angel in disguise.

"Uncle Wills!" Harry was leaning a hip on the table where George Darcy sat with someone; however, he stood when he saw the Darcy's enter. The sound of his voice, so much deeper, more masculine and mature than she ever remembered, left her breathless.

"Father." George rose and came quickly, along with Harry. "Father, it's good to see you." They shook hands and hugged. "Glad I came straight here instead of going to the house. When I heard about Auntie Amanda I knew you and mother would be arriving at some time so I thought I'd stay around, meet the new cousin. I shall ride home with you lot; I've sent my luggage on home already."

"It's grand to see you boys as well. Sorry I missed your football match at school last week, George. Couldn't be helped. Fitz and I have had our hands full readying Robert for the election."

"You've missed more than one match, father."

"I've seen more than I've missed, George. I do try, and I feel badly that I even missed one. Think how much worse it would have been if I had sought the election for myself. You're not that upset, surely. I'll be at the next, I promise."

George turned away, feeling childish for his momentary pouting and not wanting his father to see the hopeful light in his eyes. He directed his attention, instead, to his sisters. "Hello you two; good heavens, how perfectly dreadful you both look. Did you ride here outside the carriage or within? Why don't you go up to our old rooms and freshen up!"

"George," Darcy admonished, shaking his head. "Must you start in immediately teasing your sisters?"

"Who's teasing?"

"Anyone who wears his hair as wild and as long as you do has no room to comment upon another's appearance." Anne Marie flounced by her brother, as ready to fight as any other sibling. Alice had not, however, heard the mocking comments. Her gaze was on the young woman who had been sitting with her brother and Harry.

It was Celeste. It was always Celeste. Alice suddenly felt ugly and little and very silly for still holding a wish in her heart. She was only a child, trapped within a child's body. Not beautiful or womanly. Not. Celeste. She fought back the juvenile tears already near the surface and turned away.

For a moment Harry was stunned at Alice's apparent snub. She was such an agreeable, darling little thing, always had been. He loved her dearly and had been eager to see her again, wanting to hear her laughter, always feeling the need to know she was protected, to shelter her from the world. Still reed thin and plain as a duck, she had grown in the three years since he had seen her last, but not by much. She still had much too much hair; and, poor dear, her features – her mouth and eyes – seemed far too bold for such a small head.

None of that really mattered to him though, because she was his little Alice. It was her good opinion of him that he craved, and her company, even as young as she was. Before today her open admiration of him had filled him with warmth – he had come to expect her fussing, her loving gaze, as his due. This coldness toward him was something new and very unsettling.

"What? Oh, I'm sorry Uncle Wills. What did you ask?"

"I wondered if you've had any word about your mother?"

"Father says there is some trouble and Uncle Tony is having a difficult time reasoning with her, but that's nothing new; Mama and Uncle Tony always disagree about something." He turned to Alice and Anne Marie. "I barely recognized you two. Why is it that the Darcy side of the family has all the good looks? Come and give me a hug and a kiss."

Anne Marie ran into his arms for hugging, but Alice remained distant. He dearly wished she'd smile at him. The anxious day was weighing heavily on his heart as it was and Alice's natural optimism and cheerful comments could always make him laugh and feel better. One of the many reasons he loved her was that she brought happiness to all around her with her quick wit and joy of life. "Your brother is an ignorant ass," he whispered in her ear and sighed a bit with relief when he heard her giggles.

"Hello, Mr. Darcy." Celeste now approached, gently claiming Harry's arm. Darcy noticed something different about the couple, a knowing that had not been present before.

"Hello, Celeste, how good to see you again. You remember my daughters, Alice and Anne Marie?"

"Yes, of course." Celeste smiled kindly at the two girls. She and her soon to be fiancé had started to become rather intimate with each other, actually very intimate, so she felt womanly, and therefore more in charity with little girls who might desire him. She even felt a bit guilty these days for the unwarranted and strange jealousy of the child standing before her. Whatever could she have been concerned about? Little Alice Darcy was still an infant, odd looking and plain, and obviously – poor thing – so obviously in love with Harry. Celeste gave Harry's hand a little squeeze.

"Hello Anne Marie. Hello, Alice. You've both grown so that I hardly recognize you either."

Chapter Twenty-Seven

Katherine opened the door barely wide enough to peer through. Fearing her mother to be at the mercy of their usual staff of incompetent maids, her heart pounded at what she might see. The room itself was bright, the curtains having been pulled as far back as possible to reveal a very large, unfashionable room designed more for her parent's comfort than for style. Hadn't Kathy moaned to her mother just the previous day how dearly the entire house needed updating, the décor was that old and passé? Nothing befitted the home of an Earl and his Countess. Where was the Rococo, the Gothic styling? For goodness sake Mama still had a Grecian chaise by the window in her sitting room. "Really!" she had exclaimed, "...and vertically striped wallpaper, Mama. What were you thinking with that? Dreadful!"

Kathy shivered at her own words. What did any of it matter with her mother now suffering only a few feet from her and she could do nothing but watch and pray? She was powerless. What if her mother died? Kathy squeezed her eyes shut and gulped back the sob that would expose her, knowing her father would force her to wait downstairs with the others if he knew she was there, watching, waiting. She returned to a chair in the far corner and sat.

The clock striking eight awakened her. She was glad to see she had drifted off to sleep for only a quarter hour but now she heard her Uncle Anthony speaking, his voice raised. Perhaps that was what woke her. She tiptoed to the door and quietly opened it again. Anthony never allowed himself to appear upset or look disheveled, yet there he stood by the window, his shirtsleeves rolled up, his collar undone, shaking his finger in anger over something.

A movement in the cheval mirror, a reflection from the opposite side of the room, caught her eye. It was her father, come to stand beside the bed, his large hands scraping back hair that looked even wilder, if possible, than usual. When he leaned forward he was out of view in the mirror, so Katherine shifted her stance once again, just in time to see him bring something up to his lips to tenderly kiss.

It was her mother's hand.

Tears stung Kathy's eyes. That was just too sweet. Over the years she had rarely seen any sort of interaction between her parents without children around. It was strange to see them like this, exposed and vulnerable together; unguarded.

It is as if they were an actual man and woman...a couple...lovers even. Kathy stared on in fascination.

Her father sat on the chair beside the bed, pure worship for his wife in his gaze. He smoothed back the dampened hair from her forehead and she pressed her cheek into his hand, turning her face to kiss his palm. Tears shone brightly in their eyes, their foreheads touching then as they whispered to each other, kissing each other slowly and so very lovingly, almost passionately.

Katherine clasped her hands together beneath her chin, seeing them for once almost as a stranger would. Here was a world in which she had no place – she felt an interloper, but she could not look away because it was so lovely, a private moment of a devoted couple. A couple in love with each other.

A sudden gasp from her mother interrupted her reverie and caused a panic in the room. Her beautiful Mama began to writhe in agony; she grasped frantically for her husband's hand and bent forward as yet another rolling wave of pain engulfed her.

"Mama..." Kathy sobbed, and though she thought she had whispered the word it was said loud enough for Anthony to hear. He crossed quickly to the door.

"Niña," he said. "What are you doing here? You would do better to be downstairs with the others."

"I should like to see my mother – immediately. Stand aside if you please." Kathy could easily be just as haughty, could be just as intimidating, at ten and five as her Aunt Catherine was at sixty. *And how formidable will this one be at thirty?* Anthony bit back his grin as the child attempted to push him away.

"No, no, no, little one – *Dios mio* you are strong – your mother is not able to see you now. Go to your brothers, go speak with Harry. He will explain." Taking her elbow he forced her to turn around, guided her back into the sitting room and then closed the door behind them. However, she was a determined young woman, driven now with heart pounding panic and fear as she struggled.

"Release me this instant! I wish to speak with my Mama and I wish to speak with her now! Leave go of my elbow and stand away from that door! I'm warning you, I'll kick you, I swear I will! You *cannot* prevent me, *tio*! Let me by!" She was rapidly becoming hysterical, her voice quivering wildly as she raged on and on.

The door behind Anthony suddenly opened and her father stepped out. "Kathy! Lower your voice.

Anthony, I'll take care of this. Please go to my wife and tell her I'll be with her in a moment." Fitzwilliam took in the sight of his proud daughter – her eyes flashing a combination of fury and terror, her fists ready to do battle and clenched at her side, her feet prepared to dash past him at any opportunity.

Anthony chuckled. "Better you than me, Richard," he said then returned to Amanda.

While it was true that the drama of the past months had caused a rift between father and daughter nothing could dim the love. For all of her misspoken French and imperious attitude Fitzwilliam understood his daughter better than she understood herself. She was, by far, the most vulnerable of all his children and the most easily hurt. As second born so soon after the twin boys, and Luke coming quickly after her, she had always sought for an added measure of attention from her father, extra love from her mother; but, with so many children there never seemed enough time to satisfy her, enough love to console her.

"Kathy, you need to go downstairs with the others. Listen to me – look at me. No, you cannot go in there at the moment. I will come down and speak with all of you when I'm able, but I will not leave your mother now and you simply cannot go in." Weary almost beyond his endurance, Fitzwilliam's hand began to rub the back of his neck.

"What is that in your hand? A rosary? You can't have a rosary, Papa, you're not Catholic! Ooh, that's a sin, I'm almost certain of it! If anyone should say a rosary it will be me not you – give that to me! Papa, it won't count if you do it! How do you even have a rosary?"

"Kathy, enough! This was a gift to me from your mother at our wedding, it was her father's – will you please stop trying to snatch it away!" Finally capturing both her wrists in his hand, he hid the offending beads behind his back, out of her reach. "If you must know your mother gains comfort from praying her beads so I am saying them with her."

An overwhelming panic began to tighten its grip on her heart. "Oh dear *Jesu*; Papa, is she going to die?"

"No child, of course not! Why must you always go to these extremes, Kathy? All right, all right, things are very difficult for your mother at the moment. The baby is in a somewhat bad position and we are discussing what's best."

"I have heard the maids talking. They say that the baby may kill my Mama! That it won't come out, that she is in great pain and I myself have heard her cry out, several times."

Oh Lord, what to say to her. He had never consciously lied to his children, had always included them in any and all decisions that affected their futures; but, this was delving into matters a child her age should not need to hear.

"Sit down here, next to me, and listen. The baby is positioned strangely within your Mama – now do not be alarmed, it happens occasionally. In fact, it happened to Auntie Eliza, and generally things right themselves; but, as the hours pass your mother grows weaker. Anthony knows of several methods to adjust the babe but it *is* taking time because the child is... a bit larger than the rest of you were."

"But Mama has had so many children with no problem before. Why is this one being so difficult!?"

"Well, your Mama is older now and the older a woman becomes the more difficulty she has. Having the 'Marys' seven years ago was, frankly, well, rather hard on her heart."

"This is all your fault!" Kathy jumped to her feet. "How could you? Go take a mistress as other men do!" She began to shout and pound on his chest. "You leave my mother alone! Stop sleeping in the same bed as she – oh, that is just so disgusting and common! No one's parents sleep with each other night after night like that! Find someone else!"

"How dare you say such things to me?" For the first time in his daughter's short but very vocal life Fitzwilliam had to restrain himself from striking her. Grabbing her by her upper arm he physically dragged her across the hall into his own sitting room then spun her around to face him. Now safely away from his wife's hearing, Fitzwilliam's voice boomed out. "You've gone too far this time, child, grossly overstepped your bounds! How dare you! Take a mistress! Of all the...damnation, how do you even know of such things? Your mother and I made vows to each other, Katherine; pledges we both hold very sacred. I could never be untrue to your mother – never. This part of our marriage is private! It is between husband and wife and of the most personal nature there can be between a man and a woman! It is certainly of no concern to you!"

"But it is my concern!" she sobbed hysterically. *"My Mama is going to die!"*

Shaken by her words he pulled her roughly into his arms and held her as she wept. "Oh, Kathy, stop saying that. Please. I cannot bear it. You don't understand the whole of it; there are things I am unable to explain to you, but trust me," he sighed deeply, wanting to sob himself. "If there was a way to prevent your mother from becoming pregnant I would find it out. Her religion, you see...it seems to rule that part of our life and will not permit... well, there are boundaries as to what we are allowed and she has been very determined to stay within those boundaries. I try my best, Kathy... well it's rather tricky... I suspect the whole idea really, it's so unproven... you see we cannot use... that is to say I cannot remove... there are certain days... French people... I am somewhat unsure as to when to begin the day count actually...well, you know your mother loves her babies more than life itself and I would not put trickery past her at times..." He reined in his tongue before he let loose his own private aggravations. "I hope I've made all this clear to you."

Kathy had listened especially carefully during her father's brief and rather bizarre explanation of marital relations, this was very important after all; but, it was no use. Certain essential facts eluded her. Finding herself no more enlightened than she was before she began to sob once again, quieter perhaps, but just as heartfelt; for comfort she burrowed herself deep within his arms.

"Shush, little goose," he soothed.

She rested her head upon his chest allowing him to dry her eyes with his handkerchief. He kissed her forehead, thinking she looked more like his baby girl now than she had for years. "What will happen, Papa?" she asked quietly. "You won't allow her to die, will you? Please promise me, you won't let her die."

"No, I won't allow her to die." He hugged her tightly. "Our biggest problem at the moment is that your Uncle Anthony and your mother are at loggerheads with what to do, and they are both stubborn as mules. She refuses to let him attempt anything that may harm the child." He hesitated on how much information he should give the poor child. "Your mother wants him to perform a procedure to remove the babe from her stomach."

When she looked quizzically up at him he explained what that meant.

"No! No! You can't allow that! That will be agony for her – oh no, no, no, no!"

"Calm yourself! I would never allow her to be cut open dearest, believe me, and besides, I doubt Anthony would do it, no matter how much she begs and threatens. God forbid, but, if it does come to a choice, I have told Anthony already, away from your mother's hearing, that it is her life over the child's. She *will* hate me for the rest of my life, as I will probably hate myself; but, that decision is not open for discussion."

"Good! You fight her, Papa!" Katherine was back in command again, alternately swiping the tears from her eyes with the back of her hands and clutching at his shirt. "We need her here with us, you and I. I don't care about another stupid baby!"

"Kathy!" Shaking his head in exasperation, Fitzwilliam placed his finger on top of her lips.

The door opened and Amanda's maid peeked into the room, looking around quickly for Fitzwilliam. "Your lordship," she called softly but her whisper was urgent. He was up and gone at a run.

"Make certain Lady Katherine returns downstairs please."

A short while later Anthony was speaking quietly with the midwife, explaining to her what he required to be done next. Fitzwilliam stared blindly out the window and waited. The room had finally emptied of maids, and, for a time at least, there was quiet. Kathy had shocked him with her words but she had the right of it. He had failed to protect the person he loved most in the world and now what would happen to them all if...? The thought was too terrible to contemplate. But by God, if they could survive this child, there would never be another.

Amanda suddenly cried out.

"*Querida*, do not push as yet. Richard, come here please, quickly – I need you..."

Kathy stirred uncomfortably in her sleep, her limbs stiff from being curled up beneath her on the chair, an infant's cry in the distance barely registering. She yawned abruptly. She felt groggy and confused, refusing to open her eyes because her lids felt so very heavy and besides the dream she was slowly waking from had frightened her with people sounding like yapping dogs and servants crying. If she didn't open her eyes perhaps she could pretend she and her parents were back the way they once were, best of friends, chums forever. If she didn't awaken she could pretend her mother was right now in the old kitchen and they could bake a pie together, or bread. Mama had always yearned to teach her how to bake. Better yet, they could go out to her mother's garden. That would be nice.

However, no matter how hard she tried to pretend things were fine the tears were already streaming down her cheeks, unwanted reality seeping in. The shouting from her dream was growing more distinct, closer.

Another baby cry silenced everything.

Blinking her eyes open she saw her father come slowly into focus, his back to her. Uncle Wills stood beside him, bracing him, his arm all but holding her father upright. The other children – her sisters and brothers, her cousins – were clustered around, the girls in tears, the boys wide eyed and serious. They were all staring at something.

I am still dreaming. Yes, that's it, I must be. Slowly her father brought a bundle up to his lips to kiss. It was something small and wriggly; and, by the glassy look on everyone's faces, something wondrous. Harry leaned over to kiss the bundle as well, then he placed a comforting hand upon her father's cheek.

Harry was crying.

She had never seen Harry cry before.

The baby was alive! The thought stabbed into her brain. *The baby was alive!* If the baby was alive, then her mother was.....? Muffled sobs behind her made her spin around and she saw several of the maids, the footmen, the butler, even the cook huddled at the door and peeking in, tears streaming down their faces as well.

Katherine let out a blood curdling scream.

She tore from the room and across the oak and marble foyer; servants leapt from her path as she stormed up the staircase. Everyone around her was sobbing, but she did not stop to ask why, she just pushed and shoved them away – and all the while she was screaming...

"Mama! Mama!" It was all she could do to remember in which direction her parents' rooms lay. As she ran she stumbled often, scraping her knees, knocking over vases, she begged and pleaded with God. *Please my Lord, don't let her be dead, oh please God please God, not my Mama!* Gasping for breath she finally reached the bedroom door, stopping then only for a moment to brace herself for what she would find. She turned the knob and entered.

It was darkened within, quiet, still. The bed was empty, stripped of its sheets by maids who whispered as they replaced the linens. Where had they taken the body? Where was she? She spun around wildly.

Wiping away her tears with the pad of her hand she screamed her demand, *"Where is my mother!"*

Chapter Twenty-Eight

"Katherine?"

Katherine gasped. Her mother's ghost had heard her and was evidently reaching out from the great beyond. Kathy stopped breathing and closed her eyes, blocking out everything else to listen. *Speak to me, mother, I am here for you,* she sent the telepathic message to heaven because surely her mother was there with baby Jesus. *It's almost as if you are in the room with me; even now I feel your loving presence surrounding me...*

"Kathy. Close the door, child, and come in." One of Kathy's eyes popped opened. Oh no! Poor Uncle Wills – that was definitely Auntie Eliza's voice. Was there no justice in life! Sweet God in heaven, they were *both* dead now, together, forever bound in the great eternity.

Actually, it was very nice and completely, totally, proper for her mother's greatest friend to have committed suicide just to join her.

"Katherine Marie, are you all right?" Her mother's voice was more urgent now. "Are you ill, dear? Come to me; let me feel your forehead."

The spirit voice was emanating from a part of the room far to the right. Kathy peeked around the door, amazed to see her mother sitting rather awkwardly on a chair, her feet up, her hair limp looking and soaked with sweat. Auntie Eliza was draping a shawl around her shoulders. "Lizzy, it is warmer than July in here; do you *really* believe a shawl is necessary?"

"Be quiet and do as you're told." Auntie Eliza sounded exasperated. It suddenly dawned on Kathy that if the two old friends were arguing all was as usual and they were both alive.

Mama was alive.

Sobbing, she ran into the room, dove onto the floor at her mother's feet and wrapped her arms around her mother's waist. All coherent thought, all pretence, all disagreement, tension or recriminations were swept away by the unbelievable joy of finding the person whom you love most in the world *still in the world,* still living, when you had thought them dead.

"Kathy, do not bother your mother now, she's been through quite a bit today."

A tearful Amanda shook her head. "No, no, no. It's quite all right, Lizzy; not a bother, not a bother at all." She rocked her child tightly in her arms, soothingly; she kissed her head and silently gave thanks.

"Truly, she should be downstairs. In a short while, Katherine, we'll have your mother back in her bed so that she can be more comfortable, and then you may visit."

Amanda placed a stilling hand on Lizzy's arm. "Sshh. Elizabeth, let her stay, please. Don't you see? She's made her choice. '*We must celebrate and be glad,*'" Tears of joy ran down her cheeks as Amanda spoke the words from a favorite passage in the bible, the parable of the Prodigal Son. Her voice was breaking, "'*because this child of mine was dead and is alive again, she was lost and is found.*'"

After giving them a few moments Lizzie gently nudged the girl, drawing her back as far away from her mother as the child's death like grip would allow. "Kathy, at least release your mother for a moment, the bed is ready and she really should rest. Katherine? Can you hear me, dear? Your knuckles are going to split if you don't loosen that grip."

With Lizzy's help Amanda slowly stood, Kathy still maintaining her hold on her mother's waist with her eyes firmly pressed closed and her lips set in a hard straight line. A maid ran over to support Amanda's other arm and it was this way that the strange foursome made their way to the bed.

"This is all very odd," muttered Elizabeth.

As soon as Amanda settled into the bed Kathy began adjusting the pillows behind her head, helped her raise her legs up, covered her and tucked the sheets so firmly that they were like a binding across her mother's chest, as if she feared her mother would suddenly roll over and fall off the mattress.

"Are you all right, Mama? Are you comfortable?" Kathy asked over and over again.

"I'm really quite all right, I just feel very sore and very tired. Now, come and lay down next to me so that I can hold you." Kathy happily snuggled into her mother's arms. It was this picture that greeted Fitzwilliam when he entered the room.

"*Jesu*, is the chit all right! She ran through the house as if her shoes were on fire!"

Amanda smiled and yawned. "She thought I was dead. Isn't that sweet?"

"I shall never understand your logic, wife. Come in, children."

Harry entered first, holding his newest brother, Edward William. After him the rest of the children tumbled in, trying their best to behave but failing totally, all just about bursting with excitement.

"Have you seen him, Kathy?" the Mary's echoed each other's voices.

"He's a brute," laughed Luke. "He'll be wonderful at football. I'll want him on my team."

"You must see his feet, they're huge," added Andrew. "Can he stay in my room tonight?"

"Don't bring him here, I never want to set eyes on him; he's nothing but a trouble making monster – oh my, he really is lovely, mother! How precious." Kathy's gaze softened immediately. "He looks so much like father. Isn't he a handsome lad?"

"Did I not just say that very same thing? A tremendously handsome lad, no doubt of that." Fitzwilliam beamed at the fussing infant. "And a hungry lad as well. All right, you lot, everyone out and give your mother and her new babe some privacy."

It was some hours later and George Darcy hated that he was so concerned. He meandered about the house, looked into rooms, found nothing of interest anywhere then slipped outside. The relief was overwhelming when he found her. She was sitting alone beneath a large elm tree in the garden, her forehead resting on her knees, her arms locked around her legs.

"Kathy?"

When she didn't look up he sank down onto the ground beside her, "Kath, you feeling any better?"

She shook her head.

"I think your cat is about to give birth. You won't start screaming again, will you? Not without fair warning at least." If possible her shoulders slumped even lower. She turned her face and stuck out her tongue at him; he started to chuckle. "Bloody hell, what were you thinking? You scared the blazes out of us all."

"George Darcy, you are the last person in the world with whom I wish to speak at the present moment, so be a good laddie, and kindly go to blazes."

"Ah, I see. I'm in the presence of Miss High and Mighty again. Beef, it's only me here." He nudged her shoulder with his. "C'mon, lassie, give us a cheeky kiss."

"Will you ever stop thinking of me as some sort farm animal?"

He swallowed back a teasing remark when he saw the raw, almost vulnerable look in her eyes. "Stick out that tongue of yours again and I'll show you just what I think of you."

That certainly shocked her into silence. Doubt and hope warred within her, both giving way quickly to mistrust. "Don't tease me, George. Not today." A huge tear coursed down her cheek.

"Kathy, what is it? You're scaring me. What's happened?"

For a long while she didn't answer, then after a great sigh and a large gulp of air she cleared her throat. "Have you ever thought, Georgie... have you ever given any consideration to your parents' death?"

"Bloody hell!" Now he was shocked. "That was not the response I expected just now, not in the least. No, of course I haven't." Feeling annoyed and anxious he squirmed about for a moment. "Are you daft? Why ask something like that? You always do that, Kathy, you're always going on about some sort of calamity or death or some tragedy! If you ask me you spend a little too much time with our crazy old aunt. You'll be checking your pulse every five minutes soon, like Cousin Anne."

"I know." She stretched out her legs then folded her arms about her middle. "Well, I've just been sitting here, thinking that as we are growing older our parents grow older as well. Eventually the years will catch up with them...you know...they'll start to fail in health and require care and attention. The roles we play here, child and parent, will be reversed then, won't they? It would be as if we are the parents and they the children." A blade of grass she had been worrying was tossed to the side. "And then they'll pass away leaving us to play their roles with our children who will in turn watch us grow old and feeble. It seems a sad sort of cycle to me, that's all."

George studied her for a moment then turned his gaze to the same far horizon where she looked. "You never do entertain any simple thoughts do you? Well, frankly, I've never ventured down this very morbid avenue of thought before. Parents are just...parents...there all the time. *Everywhere.* They harangue us until we nearly lose our minds then one day, arbitrarily it seems, they decide we are capable of taking charge of ourselves." He shuddered. "Damnation. I hate this, thinking that my father or mother may die one day. I rather depend upon them, you know; I even like them both, quite a lot actually. Whew, this is lowering! Well, I shan't mind taking care of either one – or both when the time comes. I'll need an understanding wife of course, but my parents never need worry about their future. I would hate the thought of them struggling along on their own when they're very old."

Kathy sighed, nodding her agreement with him, and then the former adversaries were friends once again, content together in comforting silence for a time, the warm sunshine helping to soothe any fraught nerves of the day, the cool breeze stroking them gently, like kind hands. Katherine began to speak softly.

"I thought she had died. I was absolutely terrified. I thought that she had died before I could tell her how very much I love her and how truly proud of her I am. I've been horrid to her, George, a pig. I have said the most outrageously cruel things and she's never struck back at me. Never. She would just tell me she loved me, over and over." Kathy gulped back a threatening sob. "I am so very ashamed of myself. I even pretended last month that Auntie Eliza was my mother. I lied to someone and pointed your mother out instead of mine when he asked about her. Mama found out and...oh, it hurt her terribly. I thought my father would strike me dead that day. I wish he had."

"Don't say such a thing, Kath. Not ever. But why would you be ashamed of your mother? She's marvelous fun and always very cheerful. And she's really smashing looking – stop glowering at me, she is and you know it. She's kind and gentle too. Why, Kath?"

"I was afraid that a certain someone would hate me if he knew she was *foreign*, so I deliberately misled him."

"Who?"

"Peter Pumphries."

George stared at her in disbelief. "Peter the Arse?"

"Shush up, will you?" Quickly she looked around to see if any adults were in the vicinity to hear the coarse language children invariably use in their parents' absence. "Whyever do you and Matt and Mark call him that?"

"Because he couldn't wipe his bottom without a map – he'd need actual written instructions. He's very nearly addlepated."

She tried to appear affronted only to end up pressing her fingers to her mouth, stifling a laugh. "That is revolting. What a disgusting thing to say."

"And yet sadly true. Don't tell me you have a *tender* for that oaf? Aw, Kath, he's not half worthy of you. You can be such an imbecile at times."

She arched a brow. "There was a compliment somewhere in there, wasn't there?"

"I believe there was. Good lord, hard to believe, that." George suddenly turned to look at her. "Did he kiss you?" Her answer somehow meant the world to him.

"No! Made a rather feeble attempt once, however, so I kicked him in back of his knees. He went down like an elm. Said I was fortunate he condescended to even speak with me, seeing as my mother was part red skinned savage. So I kicked him again. I boxed his ears too."

Relief flooded his chest and his heart beat once more. "Good for you, old girl, well done. That's my Kath."

They lapsed into silence once again then, enjoying each other's presence and the crisp cool air, their hands resting side by side on the ground. After a while though, *somehow,* George's hand found its way to Kathy's – then slid across it – then gently enclosed it within his own. Her heart raced wildly, she turned to find George already watching her.

His gaze dropped from her eyes to her lips and the whole world stood still.

When their mouths finally met it was the gentlest of touches, a tender pat, a bare caress of a kiss; she was beaming outrageously when they separated – the only encouragement George needed.

Their second kiss followed instantly and deepened with new passion. Their mouths opened, tongues hesitantly began to explore. After several moments they separated once again and now George was beaming, outrageously.

It was the third kiss that sealed their fates. Their mouths slanted and opened wider, hungry now; fingers stroked faces, gripped hair, hands began to explore and fondle whatever crisp, clean muslin and wool they could find.

He pulled back first, finding his continued breathing becoming more and more difficult; he gazed intently into her eyes. "I've been waiting for you for such a while, Katherine Marie Fitzwilliam; such a long, long, while."

"You – waiting for me?" she sounded wondrous and a little breathless herself. "How very odd, since I've been thinking the same thing, that I've been waiting forever for you, George Bennet Darcy."

Chapter Twenty- Nine

Darcy and his son George glared at each other over what had, at one time, promised to be a delectable breakfast. When Elizabeth entered the room, later than usual that morning, she immediately sensed the tension.

"Whatever has happened?"

"You son has lost his mind, that's what has happened. Of all the dim witted, nonsensical..."

"I knew you'd take on like this, go against me! I knew you wouldn't understand!"

"Understand! What is there to understand? That you are a spoiled child?"

"Oh my..." Elizabeth looked first to her oldest daughter for enlightenment; however, Anne Marie's head was deeply bowed and her eyes averted. Her daughter Alice, on the other hand, watched with rapt excitement. She finally returned her gaze to her husband and son.

"I should appreciate very much if there were no more rash and angry statements made. Now, George, be still for a moment and let your father speak. William, what has happened?"

"George wants us to give him permission to marry! This young buck of ten and seven fancies that he's in love!"

"I beg your pardon. In love? But with whom?"

"Kathy Fitzwilliam."

"Don't you say her name like that; in fact don't you ever say her name again!"

"Oh be quiet and sit down. He keeps jumping up and down as if this was a rabbit's warren. Of all the absurd, ridiculous... has she spoken to her parents yet? Why in heavens name would you...?" Darcy paled suddenly with his next logical leap in thought. "Anne Marie, Alice, go to your rooms at once. Give your brother and mother and me some privacy here."

Anne Marie stood quickly, her eyes filling with tears; and, as she passed behind her brother she gave his shoulder a gentle squeeze of alliance.

Alice took this opportunity to secure the remaining sausage from her sister's half eaten breakfast then merely piled more food onto her own plate. "I can't go yet, Papa. I've not finished." She began to shovel food into her mouth at an alarming pace.

"Alice. Out."

"But I'm still very hungry, Papa. I am much too skinny, everyone says so. I may fall over in a dead faint if I don't... Oh, I never get to hear anything! You always keep me in the dark and I am so ignorant I don't even know what I am supposed to be missing! It's not fair!"

"Out!"

Alice pouted and grumbled as she stomped her way to the door, following her sister from the room.

Elizabeth placed a hand on Darcy's arm then took her seat. "Calm yourself, dear."

"Whatever is wrong with these children of ours — oh, for heavens sake! Alice! I know you're hiding behind the door, I can see your foot! Go! No, not you, George, you sit down. You and I need to speak... *Alice Go!"*

The door to the breakfast room finally slammed shut. "I never get to hear anything!" were the muffled final words they heard, fading into the distance.

"Where have we gone wrong with our eldest and our youngest child, can you tell me, Elizabeth? Thank heaven for our middle child, Anne Marie. At the very least I know I've nothing to fear from that quarter. She's a dutiful, respectful – George why are you smiling like that? What is the meaning of that smirk?"

"Not a thing, father. May I leave the table now?"

"No! Of course you may not leave the table! I want to know how long this...whatever it is...has been going on between you and Katherine Marie. I thought you two were like sister and brother, that you detested each other like any other normal siblings. How in the world did it go from that to lovers?"

"William! What a thing to say? Lovers; really, William. George? Oh good heavens, George, why aren't you challenging your father over that remark? George, say something, quickly."

"Why do I need to say anything? He knows all there is to know, so let my father explain the whole thing. He is the all powerful King of Pemberley, the man who defies the Duke of Devonshire and always has his way, the man who is grooming his favorite, his hand chosen, Mr. Robert 'Perfect' Wentworth, for the House of Commons. He has the world in his pocket and now he wants me! Well, he can't have me! I am my own man!"

"You can't even have a proper shave yet! I would never have spoken to my father thusly, with this sort of disrespect! You tell me right now, George Darcy, have you compromised that girl? Have you?"

"How dare you speak of the woman I love in that manner!"

"*Sit down!* Woman he loves – do you hear him? A callow youth such as himself proclaiming an undying love!"

"Both of you stop this instant. Nothing will be served with this shouting. Now, we will discuss this in a calm, rational manner, like adults. George, please dear, when did you discover your feelings for Kathy had changed? Was it recently?"

Glowering and sullen, George stared at his father with the same intense emotion experienced by generations of other adolescent young men before him; a resentment borne through the hunger for respect, a growing sexual frustration and the impotency to finally take command of their own lives.

"Kathy and I have always been close and our true feelings revealed themselves this year; well, all right, actually it was three weeks ago, after Teddy was born. I am willing to wait until she turns sixteen. That will be in two months."

"Very big of you."

"William, stop, please. This is a serious subject; we must remain calm and rational. George, you are to leave for university in a few days. Perhaps, when you've finished with your education, and if you both still feel the same, we can discuss a marriage."

"I will not be attending university either."

"*Are you insane!*" Elizabeth, a woman who had always yearned for a university education, leapt to her feet.

"I take it that we are no longer to remain calm and rational!" Darcy drove his fists into the table and stood, leaning over his son. "Bennet George, hear me and hear me well. You *will* go to university and you will be *properly educated.* I will not have some ignorant oaf taking over the responsibilities of

Pemberley. I will not turn over my family's legacy to an illiterate. In the future..."

"Pemberley, Pemberley – that's all I've ever heard from you my whole life. Well, did you ever consider that I may not *want* to take over Pemberley? No, I can see you never did, because you are so in love with that pile of...of bricks and dirt you think everyone else is – well I am not!" George pushed himself back from the table. "I've decided to join the cavalry, the 9th Light Dragoons. I can secure the rank of Captain for little more than three thousand pounds and that will provide me with a private room and an adequate monthly pay. It's all I want – it's all I've ever wanted and if you'd bothered to ask me just once you would have known. Kathy and I will be married and she'll come with me. We'll travel the world together."

Darcy plopped down onto his chair, stunned. "You really are insane. Just how do you propose securing this commission without *me*, George? I certainly shan't pay for such nonsense. Are you prepared to enlist along with the wife beaters and the horse thieves?"

"I have money set aside, a little anyway. I'll get the rest somewhere – Uncle Fitz! He will understand; he'll help us."

"You'll be lucky if 'Uncle Fitz' doesn't rip your head off!"

"George, *think* – Kathy's parents will never allow this." Elizabeth was bewildered and growing more and more alarmed by this first open rebellion among her children. Why, George had always been such a wonderful, thoughtful, loving child. What in heavens name had caused him to change so; why was he so desperately pulling away? She had seen it happen in other families, but never expected it to happen in her own. She looked pleadingly at her husband to make sense of it.

Her husband was only furious.

"Do you honestly believe my cousin stupid enough to allow his daughter to marry at sixteen; that his hopes and dreams for her future could ever – ever – entertain the notion of living in the squalor of following the drum? You're smarter than this! You would need to pay a good deal more than *five* thousand pounds for a commission that provided separate and private living quarters, especially ones decent enough for a respectable woman to live in; then there is food, clothing, necessities, medicine – forget servants. Kathy will need to be prepared to cook and clean, mend...and then children! The Fitzwilliam's are a prolific lot, George; she'll be with child before the door closes. And by God, you had better have been truthful with me. The two of you had better not have anticipated your marriage vows!"

"I have already given you my word on that yet now you impugn not only my honor but hers as well. How dare you! Blast both you and Pemberley! I am sick to death of this place and sick to death of this conversation. *And sick to death of you!*"

"*Well, at present, I am not very thrilled by the sight of you either!*"

George turned on his heel, stormed angrily from the room, and slammed the door in his wake.

A pale and shaken Lizzy turned to her husband, tears welling in her eyes. "He could not have meant what he said, could he?"

"That he is sick of the sight of me; that he hates Pemberley? I have no doubt he meant that in the heat of the moment as much as I meant whatever I said. Lizzy, I don't think I know my own son any longer." Darcy's hand trembled when he reached for his coffee so instead he placed his palms flat atop the table and closed his eyes. "Blast. I never thought to see this day. My own dear father must be laughing up in heaven right now; I remember fighting with him like this, being so angry at times that I wanted to put my fist through the walls."

"He mentioned Robert Wentworth. I always did fear that he would become resentful of the time and trust you place in that man, he never could understand what you were trying to accomplish, poor boy. Oh, William, he has no idea how many sacrifices you've made for him."

"He has no idea how many sacrifices we've both made, Lizzy. None of the children do; but that's as it should be. They have no reason to know – any sacrifices made were made for love of him, for love of all three of them; not for show, nor for gratitude. It still stings, however, doesn't it? I thought I could avoid damaging my family by refusing the Commons seat myself years ago, but it seems I was deluding myself."

"William, do not second guess your actions. You chose the best path for our family back then, I have absolutely no doubt of that. And, I begin to have a suspicion that conflict between parents and children is simply unavoidable. Perhaps, we've just been fortunate up till now."

"Lizzy, do you think he and Kathy have...?"

"No, I don't think so, they're so young; but who can say? And is it really so far fetched that they could be truly in love? Kathy would do very well for him. She has a fire in her I've always admired, feels true joy in merely being alive; and, they are great friends already, too – the best of friends really."

"Elizabeth. You cannot approve of them marrying at so young an age."

"No, of course not; but, love is irrational by its very nature and bewildering to the young and innocent."

"It's just as bewildering to the old and sated." They smiled briefly at each other but the humor faded quickly. "God, I only pray they still *are* innocent."

"He always was eager for you to see him as a man, with respect; with trust."

"Well, he certainly got my attention; however, respect and trust are still apparently waiting to be achieved. I'd best go up and speak with him, clear the air. Did you ever envision, Elizabeth, that being a parent would require so very much talking? It never seems to end.

"I'll have to go to Fitz about this, too. I don't look forward to that conversation in the least." Darcy stood to leave then stopped and turned. "By the way, do you know why George was smirking so when I said we had nothing to fear from Anne Marie? I thought that very odd as well. Do you know, Lizzy, I am beginning to believe we don't know half of what our children do."

Chapter Thirty

It was late morning and the house was quiet for once, his wife was shopping, he surmised with his daughters, his sons probably terrorizing their tutors somewhere in the house. Solitude such as this was indeed a rare gift to a father of nine and Fitzwilliam was determined to make the most of it. He sat before the wide opened window, relishing his pipe and watered down port, and carefully perused the agony column from the Morning Post. As he puffed away he would occasionally lean his chair back on its two legs to glance at the door to his library or he would listen for her footsteps. *Women! Bah!* Since he had that episode two years prior, a slight chest pain really – could have been a digestion problem – she had become completely irrational about his smoking, *and* his drinking. The idiot doctors had agreed with her and wasn't that always the case? It was so bloody aggravating when she was right.

"Pardon me, your lordship."

"Yes, Bates."

"Mister Fitzwilliam Darcy is here to see you, sir. Are you receiving visitors today?"

Old Mr. Bates insisted upon always announcing Darcy, even though the families were in and out of each other's homes a dozen times daily; and, no matter how many times Fitzwilliam had told the man he needn't announce his cousin, the butler stuck to his duty, refused to lower the standards of a better age. Most days Darcy would come and go through a side door without notice; evidently however, today was not one of those occasions. Fitzwilliam could see Darcy in the hallway, strolling to and fro, picking up the odd knick knack or studying portraits that lined the walls.

"Mister...? Whom exactly did you say it was?"

"Fitz, I am in no mood for this," Darcy muttered out loud while examining the silver imprint on an ancient plate.

"Mister Fitzwilliam Darcy, sir," repeated the butler, apparently unmoved by the tetchy figure drifting about the hall.

"Darcy you say. Well, well, well. Let me think on this...."

"And, why do I never remember to bring a gun with me?"

"Ah, yes – *Darcy*! Tall fellow, bit of a rag-mannered dandy, a coxcomb actually, if I remember rightly; fusses all the time about his neck scarves and his expensive boots. Do I really wish to encourage an association with him? What do you think, Bates?"

"About what, your lordship?"

"About my shoving this expensive boot up his..." Darcy's voice faded to a rough cough as he examined a particularly odd miniature of one of their mutual relatives.

"Shall we allow him entrance?"

"I am certain I shouldn't presume to offer an opinion, your lordship. This decision is yours entirely."

"Tell him I've brought along that rare bottle of French brandy he's been attempting to steal from my cellars." Darcy was now leaning against the doorframe, directly behind the butler. "Go ahead, tell him."

"He says he has brought liquid refreshments of a particular sort."

"Eureka! Show the rascal in."

As Darcy entered the room he laughed outright at his cousin, sitting like a bird perched upon a chair before the open window, waving pipe smoke outside. "How absolutely pathetic you are. You don't really believe Amanda doesn't know you're still smoking, do you?"

"Ha! She doesn't suspect a thing; I have this down to a fine science. I even wear the old banyon robe to prevent the tobacco smell from permeating my clothes."

Selecting one of the more comfortable nearby chairs, Darcy set it next to his cousin's, then reached into his pocket for his own pipe. He snatched Fitzwilliam's tobacco pouch from the table. "Give me that, it's evidence."

"Blackmail more likely."

"Shall I go now for the glasses, sir?" Bates still hovered at the door.

"Yes, yes, of course you should. Bring up some biscuits too while you're at it, Bates, and some pie. And cheese. Maybe a bit of cold beef. Cold chicken wouldn't be turned away either, just be certain to heat it all up." Smiling contentedly, Fitzwilliam blew the aromatic smoke out the window.

"What brings you here so early? We aren't expected at White's until eight at the earliest. I hope you're bringing a good deal of blunt because I am feeling particularly lucky today; need to win back some of what you won from me..."

"We have a problem, Fitz."

"Oh, I don't like the sound of that by half. What do you mean 'we'?" Fitzwilliam's gaze narrowed on his cousin in sudden concern. "Is Elizabeth all right?"

"Elizabeth's fine."

"You're not ill, are you? Come to think on it you do look a bit pecky around the gills. Well, that is to say *more* pecky around the gills than usual. Stomach acting up again?"

"No, I'm fine. We had a bit of an upset at home a while ago."

"You also? Damn me, we had a fine free for all here as well."

"Really?" Darcy was surprised at his friend's placid outlook. "Then you've heard?"

"Yes, of course I've heard. Nothing goes on within my family without my knowledge. That's the mark of a great father Darcy, strong communication with his young."

"Well. You surprise me, Fitz. I am all astonishment." Darcy stared out the window, the wind taken out of him at his cousin's acceptance of the situation. He wondered what to say next. "I never expected you to be so calm. Are you saying you approve?"

"I'm all for it; felt the same way when I was a lad his age, eager to confirm my virility, prove my manhood. Nothing like it really, to get a young stud's juices flowing. I couldn't wait to unsheathe my dagger, get into the meat of things as they say. His mother was none too pleased, but she soon saw the right of it. Of course, I shall assist as much as possible, make certain he becomes attached to the right people, oil the way for him myself and put in a good word..."

Darcy, whose eyes had become rounder and more horrified with each word, began to realize something was terribly amiss. "What in bloody hell are you talking about?"

Fitzwilliam scowled back – he detested being interrupted. "My, aren't we in a foul mood. I'm speaking of Harry, of course. I've purchased his commission for him, in spite of his mother's very vocal objections, but she saw the right of it eventually. Pretty cheap too – three thousand; but, that's what the boy wanted. It's a Captaincy with the 9th Light Dragoons. What did *you* think we were discussing?"

"So that's where he got the idea."

"Speak up, Darcy, or bring your chair closer, you're mumbling worse than a minister. On second thought, just speak up."

"What? Oh, I thought you were discussing George and Kathy running off to get married, his enlisting in the army and her becoming a camp follower, pounding her laundry along the riverbanks of Spain." Darcy waited patiently, watching in fascination as his cousin's initial confusion slowly cleared.

Fitzwilliam suddenly began to gag on his pipe smoke. "Are you foxed? Is this your sick idea of humor?"

"No, not mine. This is entirely George and Kathy's sick idea. Let me see, how did it play out? Oh yes, apparently they've fallen madly in love with each other within the last two weeks or so and wish to marry. George will be joining the 9th Light Dragoons as well – you'll be footing the bill by the way – and Kathy is ready and eager to follow the drum. They further believe that the army will provide them with suitable housing, servants, and perhaps even a nice carriage; if not, they are more than confident that they can live on air and army rations." Fitzwilliam stared back in mute shock. "I take it then that you were *not* in communication with your young about this."

Fitzwilliam stood slowly, sputtered something incoherent, and then sat down again.

Then he exploded.

"Of all the stupid...idiotic...this had better be a joke, Darcy, because if it is not...Bates get in here...Bates!...find Lady Kathy for me...immediately...what do you mean she's not in the house...where is she...out?...out where exactly...what do you mean you don't know...damn it to hell, where's my wife... what do you mean you don't know... does no one stay home anymore...tell me the moment she comes in... either one...mother of god I'll lock her up, I swear I will...!"

Darcy calmly poured out their drinks, waiting for his cousin to stop bellowing and stomping about the room. It did not take as long as he had feared.

"Darcy, what is all this? She's a child, she's fifteen years old. How can she possibly be in love – she still has dolls on her bed! Oh, forget the glass, hand over that bottle!"

"Sit down, Fitz."

"How long have you known about this?"

"I found out only today."

"Want to get married? Want to get married! They're just babies! She's ten and five!" Fitzwilliam was red faced and incensed and mumbling the same phrases over and over. He sat down roughly on his wobbly, spindly chair, then, all at once, he jumped back up to his feet, his face pale. "She's not..."

"No, Fitz. I don't believe it's gone that far."

Fitzwilliam sat down again and exhaled.

"How do you know for certain?"

"I asked George and he says not. Apparently, I offended his sense of honor by even suggesting that possibility."

"Well," Fitzwilliam closed his eyes with relief. "If George says nothing's happened between them, I will believe him."

How curious, Darcy thought, *that my cousin could readily believe my own son, when I still had doubts*; he felt somewhat guilty as Fitzwilliam continued speaking.

"I am very disappointed in my daughter, however, sneaking behind my back like this. All the while I thought she was finally becoming dutiful, ladylike – so demur. I say, I thought they hated each other; they did, didn't they? They fight like an old married..."

"Exactly so. Listen, Fitz, I think we should keep calm, perhaps sit down individually with the children and explain our objections to a marriage. They are really too young to know their minds yet and they will miss out on so much if they marry now. We need to rationally explain to them both the drawbacks of what they are contemplating."

"Right you are, right you are." Fitzwilliam took a long pull at the bottle. "Then I shall lock her in her room. I know, I can have that immense scullery maid of ours stand guard... "

"You do realize that if we command them to not see each other it will be seen as another challenge to them, to their independence. At times I think George would leap off a cliff if I just warned him not to venture too near the edge."

"I am not allowing her to marry, Darcy!"

"Of course not. I thought we'd suggest they wait a few years, until George finishes his schooling and returns from the usual post university tour of the continent. I would so hate for him to miss that experience. And Kathy will have had her season in society by then and her presentation at court. They will be older and perhaps even may find others.

However, if they still feel the same about each other, we will support that also."

"Or I could just tell Kathy that George has abandoned her and run off with a barmaid. She doesn't know I've found out about them. Why do you roll your eyes in that manner? She would believe me, Darcy; I can be very convincing when I choose to be."

"That's appallingly deceptive, even for you."

"I knew you'd like it."

"You can't do that, Fitzwilliam – you do realize that, don't you? Good, at times I'm not so certain."

"You agree we must separate them though, do you not? I mean literally – physically. They're so young how can this really be true love? They're just maturing and feeling their oats, confusing friendship for passion, I'll warrant."

"I suppose you're right. Well, there's a sentence I never actually thought I'd utter. I do so want George to enjoy this particular time of life – on his own for the first time, going off to university, meeting new people, perhaps getting into some slight trouble, learning the discipline of scholastics. He definitely must travel the continent with his friends, like we did, like most young gentlemen do. Thinking back on our tour, gad, I wouldn't have missed it for the world."

"Especially Venice. Do you remember Venice, brat?"

"Of course I remember Venice; and, I still have that bottle of cognac we purchased – the last one of us alive will toast the other and then get foxed out of his mind." Both men chuckled. "Damn, you're only young once; he'd regret missing all that in later years, I just know he would."

"I feel the same about Kathy. She's talked of nothing but her court presentation since she was an infant. Do you remember, her first words were not Mama or Papa – they were 'Your Royal Highnesses'?

She's planned her Presentation Ball to the last button and feather, her gown, her hair... and then there's all the parties she'd miss, all the excitement. Who knows, they may truly be suited for each other, but we'll need to insist they wait for a few years at least. I'll take my family up north to Somerton early this year. Distance, that's what's needed."

"And I'll let George know he's not receiving a half-penny from either me or you. If he doesn't continue on with his schooling he's out on his own, responsible for his own food, lodging, clothing..."

"Lord, they will hate us."

"Fitz, I'm beginning to believe that there is no way to raise children without that possibility. Thank goodness I have one sensible daughter."

Anne Marie Darcy moved quickly through the hallways and up the staircases of the Parliament offices, her maid, a few years older and much wiser, scurrying quickly behind.

"I don't like this. I don't like this one bit, miss."

"Shush, Sally. I am merely delivering some biscuits to the gentleman. I mean him no harm."

"I know what you mean him, miss, and you've brought him enough biscuits this week to sink a frigate. You make him very uncomfortable, you really do. It's not proper, is all I'm saying."

"Sally, how can you even think such a thing? You are at my side always. Mr. Wentworth and I have never been alone, I am a relative of his employer, I am the daughter of his mentor. Certainly I have a right to show compassion, friendship. It is my Christian duty."

The two were standing just outside the door of the offices of the Earl of Somerton, both nervous and arguing in loud whispers, attracting the unwanted attentions of gentlemen passing behind them.

"I'm saying there's friendly and then there's friendly. You are the cousin of his employer who is a peer of the realm, miss. Mr. Wentworth is not your equal and your showing up here so often puts him in a very delicate position."

A secretary for another peer stopped behind them and bowed, all the while his gaze intense upon Anne Marie. "I'll thank you to move along there, sir," snapped the maid loudly, and so he did. She continued without skipping a beat. "You're only fifteen years old, Miss Darcy! This is just not right."

"Mr. Wentworth enjoys our visits. He's told me so."

"And how could the poor man say otherwise?"

Anne Marie felt as if she would burst into tears at any moment. Feeling both anxious and embarrassed, she was frightened to be seen by John as forward, yet she was equally frightened that he would not see her at all. More men walked past, some too busy to notice, others lingering to smile. Sally Cummings, a stout, good hearted woman possessing the face of a bulldog, scowled at them all. Anne Marie reached out for her hand. "Are you saying, Sally, that he doesn't truly like me; that he's only being kind to me because of his job?" She didn't dare look her maid in the eye for fear the woman would see how hurt she was.

"No, miss; now don't take on so. What I'm saying is the opposite, that the man has *feelings* for you — very strong feelings. I've seen how he struggles with them. But they are feelings that he cannot act upon."

"But why ever not?"

Sally stomped her foot. "Because you are..."

Just then the door opened and John Wentworth saw before him two very surprised and blushing ladies — one a loyal servant he had come to admire and the other the most beautiful girl in the world, the girl who was much too young for him and too far above him in station.

And, her visits were quickly becoming both the high points and the low points of his life.

"I thought I heard someone out here. Miss Darcy, more biscuits? You are spoiling me. You'd both best come inside. I am nearly finished in here and then I'll escort you home – again."

1841
"The Adults"

Full physical and intellectual maturity
Legally able to engage in a contract,
marry and possess firearms
Caregiver to physically declining parents

"Backward, turn backward, O Time, in your flight,
Make me a child again just for tonight!"

Elizabeth(Akers) Allen.1832–1911

Chapter Thirty-One

"Penrod! Captain Harry Penrod! Ten-shun! Front 'n center, man." Snatches of drunken laughter could be heard from the tavern immediately below the brothel's second floor as two cheerfully inebriated soldiers staggered their way down the seedy hallway, listening at doorways for any sign of their friend.

"Harold, my precious? Is that you? Are you decent?" loudly whispered Captain Clyde Buntley at one door.

"Quiet, mon; listen. This may be him – the moaning sounds definitely upper crust and faintly Peak District," remarked Major James Durand at another.

After counting to three they kicked open the door, the two soldiers shouting "Surprise!" as they entered, only to be greeted by the screeches and curses of complete strangers. "Good heavens! Most humble apologies, Madame, sir, oh m'goodness another Madame, upon my word – terribly sorry, couldn't feel worse, really, couldn't feel worse if we tried." Backing from the room, as any gentleman would, Major Durand attempted to refrain from staring at the naked threesome before him.

Captain Buntley, however, was more drunk than his friend and therefore less attuned to the delicacy of the situation. He beamed at the women and blew them kisses to which they responded with giggles.

"Oh, you've sweet darlings there, sir, no question about that at all. I say, are they perhaps your great grandnieces?" The boot that sailed past nearly clipped the captain's head before he could duck to the left and close the door.

"Irritable people at times, these Northerners."

"Prickly, indeed."

"Shall we continue our quest?"

"Yes, I believe we shall."

They listened at several more doors, occasionally shaking their heads or raising a brow. "Harry, where are ye lad?" Durand called out.

A suspicious looking broom closet door was snatched opened, the room thoroughly inspected and then the door shut. "Ghastly 'commodations. Smallest beds I ever saw," Buntley slurred.

The half dressed Durand continued to stride down the hall, listening. "Harold, I certainly hope ye were attendin' to the Colonel's dressin' down we had last week, about succumbin' to the sins o'the flesh. Harold?"

"He's not here!... I've left! Now go away!" That shout was followed by a loud thud, a woman's shriek and then a noisy crash.

"Oh my, my, my. Sounds as if he's working without a net."

Sir Harold Augustus Penrod, and his two brothers in arms, had been in the small Spanish garrison town for a week awaiting their discharge orders, preparing to return home after serving Her Majesty Queen Victoria in India and Afghanistan for two very arduous, long years. They were only three of many decommissioned members of the Thirteenth Foot, the much honored regiment of the Battle of Jellalabad.

Jellalabad had been a remote British outpost, not much more than a wide road with a fort really, located about eighty miles east of Kabul. Be that as it may, beginning in January, 1842, fifteen hundred British and Indian soldiers defended this small town against attack by the five thousand man Afghan army of Akbar Khan, the siege continuing for five grueling, bloody, months. Outnumbered as they were none had really expected to live, the city occupants had long since lost hope, and all had nearly starved to death.

At the end of June a British counterattack eventually routed the Afghans. The city had been defended and the surviving soldiers of the Thirteenth were now the heroes of the empire, given ten gun salutes by every British garrison along the route of their long departure march through India. Queen Victoria herself directed they now carry the title "Prince Albert's Own."

However, all this adulation was lost on Harry and his friends. They were exhausted with fighting, thoroughly sick of killing. They wanted nothing more than to return to home and sanity, the grandeur they had thought war having long since evaporated, the problems they had thought to escape by volunteering for this punishing duty now ridiculously minor in comparison.

In the end they had fought side by side not for Queen and country, but for each other, for friends and fallen comrades; for survival – as all soldiers do. All three were now cashing in their commissions and eager to return to the lives they had fled years before. Buntley and Durand were returning to their homeland and estates in Scotland and Harry Penrod was returning to London, where he would need to deal with the loss and heartbreak that had kept him so long from the family he adored.

"Where the devil are your clothes?" Scrubbing a hand hard across his eyes Harry Penrod had finally focused his gaze on the gentlemen standing before his bed, both of whom were backlit by the glow of the hallway lamps, neither man wearing anything more than smallclothes and bay rum aftershave. And smiles.

"Dunno," Durand said, genuinely perplexed.

Buntley belched loudly. "'Scuse me, mudmimwa...midmiwas...ma'am." He bowed as best he could to the woman in Harry's bed. Producing a cheroot from behind his ear he winked at her. "D'you have a light, you divine little...?"

"That does it." Harry fumbled about on the table beside him for something to throw, grabbing a bottle. Scrambling further into the room Buntley took hold of the dresser to steady himself. "I'm ready, Harold – toss away."

"Oh bloody hell." Instead of throwing the bottle Harry began to laugh. "...if you're not both out of this room in five seconds it's a Military Tribunal and death at dawn for the pair of you."

Sensing the danger had passed Buntley looked up then saw something move before him. He poked a finger at the soldier reflected back at him within the dresser mirror and squinted hard at his likeness. "You look very familiar to me, sir. I believe we were in the same graduating class at Eton...class of 1830. How about 1826? 1831? It was one of those anyway, if I did, indeed, finish...can't remember. Not talking, eh? Harold will you introduce me to this incredibly handsome but rude fellow?"

Harry grunted a laugh and reached for his glass of liquor, lighting a cheroot for himself as well. Durand pinched the cheroot from his friend's mouth and grabbed the glass. "Sorry, laddie, but it's time for us to go home."

"Why, what time is it?"

"Tuesday."

"Huh? *Tuesday!* What happened to all the other days? There's supposed to be seven, I distinctly remember that from university." Harry swung his legs over the edge of his bed and stood, staggering and scratching both his head and other parts of his anatomy. He licked his dry lips. "My teeth are furry."

"Cover yourself! Oh, what a wee ghastly sight that is, ye poor lad."

Harry began to say something in his own defense then stopped suddenly. "Your trousers, that's it! Where the hell are your trousers? Oh God, I hope you weren't stupid enough to leave them back in your own rooms with those women! You both collected healthy final pays if I remember correctly; you do have that on you...somewhere – don't you?"

Suddenly sober the Captain and the Major both bolted from the room, tripping and crashing into furniture and walls on their way.

"Idiots." Harry grumbled. "Imbeciles."

Harry stuck his head under the courtyard water pump for several moments. "Let me drown here." It had been a trying two hour walk to reach their barracks with all three men occasionally taking time out to vomit along the way, but they had arrived on time, miraculously before midnight, with a full five minutes remaining of their final week long leave.

"Ye know, Penrod, I enjoy myself as well as the next mon but you – ye always go to extremes. You'll no' make thirty years if you continue livin' in this manner."

"Don't preach to me, Jimmy, please."

After lowering Buntley into his bed first the two other men then crawled into their own beds. The night was quiet and still. "George Darcy was one o'the few that could keep up with ye. I think he was even a wee bit worse, if that's possible. On the slippery slope ye both are, headin' straight to the devil himself."

Harry smiled in the dark. George's reputation for debauchery was legendary and generally unfounded. Harry wasn't certain why his best friend denied himself a bit of fun occasionally, always claiming he was off to wilder pursuits, but he would never be the one to betray him as basically an innocent. "You sound more the highlander as you sober, did you know that?"

"Ye mean that I sound less of a mindless fool."

"Either you go to sleep right now, or I'll shoot you — you make the choice."

After a brief quiet Durand began to speak again and Harry groaned. "I'm that worried about ye, son; you canna throw your life away like this. All right, the lassie broke yer heart and married another — but that was years ago, mon! And *you*, still carryin' the torch for her — well, no woman's worth it and well ye know it."

"Jimmy, I'm not carrying any torches nor nursing any heart break; I swear to you those wounds healed a long time ago."

"Then what pains ye so?"

Harry was silent for a long while before he spoke. "It something I cannot tell anyone, not even you old friend."

"Ach, you're soundin' sentimental now. Verra unmonly if ye don't mind me sayin'. Your biggest problem is ye think much too much, lad; ye brood. I've had me say and I'll say no more."

"I should be so fortunate..."

As usual, however, sleep eluded Harry; memories flooded back of his family, of his friends, of happier days...of *her*. God how dearly he missed them all, his brothers and sisters, his cousins; and, how heartsick he was to not have seen his parents more often, especially now that they were growing older and he was more mellowed by life. They had all visited him frequently, of course, but that was in the days before he volunteered for Afghanistan. He treasured those memories.

He had even returned to England upon occasion but was always tense because *she* was there and the idea of seeing *her* and not being able to hold *her*, to kiss *her* – well, it was just too disheartening.

Only a dozen times since her birth had he even been in her presence, each blessed moment, though, searing itself into his heart. No one knew about this love of his except for his father and, of course, Celeste – before her passing.

She was his heart and his soul, his breath, his pride and joy.

She was his daughter.

Chapter Thirty-Two

The three soldiers picked at their breakfast – the bits of runny eggs that clashed dreadfully in their stomachs with chunks of burnt ham. Buntley responded to the pounding knock on their door with a creative curse then disappeared for a moment into the hallway, murder in his eyes. When he reentered the room he held aloft two bundles – a small but full sack was in one hand, two lone letters in the other.

"You would not believe this but our mail has finally found us." He tossed one letter to Durand, retained the other single letter, and then tossed the sack at Harry.

Harry's sick countenance lifted instantly. "And here I thought they'd all forgotten me."

"You know, you don't half deserve the attentions of your family, Penrod. Evidently this sack has been following you, and growing, all the way from Afghanistan. Pity you're still here, really – I could be steaming open your correspondence. Well, step lively, lad, I want to hear all about your 'diamond of the first water' brothers and your Corinthian sisters; or, was it other way round?"

After placing his uneaten plate of food on the floor Harry upended the bag of letters onto the table and then rubbed his hands together.

"Hurry along, will you? What news is there from the Fitzwilliam mob?" It was considered a shared treat, receiving mail while far from home; most were thrilled to receive one or two letters in a month. Harry Penrod generally received over a dozen.

"First, my mother's..." Harry searched out and located his mother's letters. Opening them all at once he set them in order before him, the oldest to read first, grinning boyishly at the wafting vanilla scent, rather embarrassed by his own sentimentality. "Mama always did love to bake," he muttered roughly then began to quickly scan the pages. His friends waited, eager to hear the latest news of the group of brothers, sisters, cousins, uncles and aunts that formed the closely knit Darcy and Fitzwilliam families. They all wrote regularly to Harry, especially his brothers and cousins, some to brag, several to complain, a few as always to seek his counsel as the eldest child of the family. He had been their rock and refuge, their great confidante, for all their lives.

"Well, my father has recovered completely from his riding accident, thank heavens and my parents are battling yet again over his smoking and diet. She tosses out his tobacco pouches but he buys new supplies and hides them about the house 'like a squirrel with his nuts.' Dear God, my brother Luke is involved with an opera dancer! Oh Luke, how is that possible? Wasn't he just nine years old? Mother wants me to write him and beg him to stop seeing the woman who is apparently five years his senior – *well done*, Luke. I imagine there is a letter in here somewhere from Luke asking me to write mother to beg her to stop haranguing him." Buntley confirmed the presence of not one but three letters from the nineteen year old Oxford lothario.

Harry laughed and continued. "Oh, listen to this! Because my sister Kate caused such a scandal in town last winter, wearing men's trousers to the theater, Aunt Catherine has written her from her will – again. I imagine there is a letter from Aunt Catherine somewhere as well."

"Aye, here it is. I'll put that on the bottom."

"Any word from brothers Matthew and Mark, since we already ken that wee Luke's enjoyin' himself – that sounded rather biblical." Still laughing, Jimmy began to open his own letter from his father then sighed at its usual dry and formal tone, a monthly report intent on itemizing his shortcomings, giving no hint of humanity. He crumpled it and turned his attention back to Harry

"Now let's see, where was I? Matthew and father are still battling almost daily, no news there, constantly at odds over Matt's 'debauched' lifestyle – thank heavens the old man can't witness *my* lifestyle. Mark has been in France with George researching some sort of railway machinery for Uncle Wills and was joined by Matt – probably to escape father – but all have now returned home and my brothers are planning to do another grand trip with Luke in tow. Well that sounds like a bit of fun, perhaps I'll be able to join them.

"Mary Elizabeth and Mary Margaret have inherited the pet hospital from Andrew, collecting 'every injured animal and slithering sick snake' they can find. They've been given a small outbuilding to use as a veterinary for their nursing – that's very nice. Oh not again. Oh damn, Andrew has been sent home from Harrow and father is furious with him. Let's see what he did this time...he was found drunk and sleeping on top of the main building, hanging by his belt before the steeple. Bloody hell, he's only fourteen isn't he?

Or is he sixteen? Reckless fool." Harry swallowed, becoming nearly undone by the homesickness rising up within him. "I should be there, they all need me. I've missed so much."

"Cheer up! You'll be seein' them soon, laddie."

"What about the Darcy's?" asked Buntley. "Anything at all? Are you quite certain? There's usually one or two lilac scented missives from the divine Anne Marie. I tell you, Jimmy, she was the loveliest thing I have ever seen. Are you absolutely positive her marriage is a happy one, Harry? He's a bit older than she."

Without glancing up from his letter Harry slapped his friend across the back of his head.

"Ouch!"

"Yes the marriage is a happy one. Robert Wentworth is a capital fellow as well as a brilliant and popular member of the House of Commons. He's also very large and quite possessive of her so mind your thoughts."

"Very pretty young filly she was, Jim – thick, dark mane of hair and eyes the color of kidney pie..."

Harry slapped the back of Buntley's head once again.

"Ouch! Would you please not do that? You're giving me a headache."

"And I said, stop speaking about Anne Marie. I'm right here, you know. I can hear you whispering."

"Well, bloody hell, Penfoot, I am forbidden to lust over *her*, you glare each and every time I drool over your sister *Katherine,* you've outlawed even a modicum of curiosity for the *'Mary's'*! I need something; I live vicariously through you, you know this. Throw me anything. Wasn't there another Darcy sister somewhere? Diane or Ann or something simple like that."

"Alice." Harry grew suddenly ill at ease.

"Wonderful, you see that wasn't so hard; now we're getting someplace. Tell us about her. Is she as lovely as Anne Marie?"

"...oh, I don't know." Harry shrugged a shoulder and looked away. "How does one describe Alice? She's...well, she's singular looking, and, truthfully, that's the... simplest thing to say about her appearance."

His friends looked first at each other and then back at Harry. "I'm sorry now I asked." Buntley tried unsuccessfully to hide his grin.

Harry became very defensive. "Listen you two, she has a wonderful personality. No, stop laughing – she really does. She has a remarkably fine soul I tell you; and, she is extremely engaging, not in the least bit dull witted is little Alice. She's clever and funny and she has great character. And very nice skin."

"How are her teeth?"

"Excellent."

"Bloody hell, she must be hideous."

"She is not hideous, damn it. It was just that her features may have been a bit too large for her head, and her face was a definite square shape, not the more pleasing oval. Her eyes were nice though, with long lashes – an unusual grey color as well, perhaps a tad too close together and her brows were rather thick, well actually very thick. One of them drifted occasionally. Her eye drifted I mean, not her brow, so her parents had her wear an eye patch for a spell, to strengthen the weak eye. Unfortunate nose also – rather long and patrician for a child yet a tad broad in the middle. Poor thing always looked as if she had just brought a flute up to her lips. Odd colored hair that never took a curl...indentation on her chin... huge ears..."

When he looked up at his friends they appeared horrified. "They won't breed her will they?"

"I have not seen Alice for at least six years, any memories I have are of her as a mere child; I'm certain she's changed by now... if there is any justice in the world. Everyone looks a bit odd in those middle years, don't they? And she really was the sweetest little thing, followed me everywhere."

"Well, Harold, *that* pretty well completes the description of a boil on your arse."

"Quiet! Both of you, please let me read this letter from Anne Marie."

"Finally, the exquisite Anne Marie. Does she mention me at all?"

"Bloody hell, I don't believe it!"

"Well, if we are going to brawl over an innocent question like that..."

"What? Oh, not you. I can't believe what I am reading! Of all the double crossing, despicable, loathsome, repugnant..."

Durand sat up quickly. "It must be about George."

"Oh, it's about Darcy all right. The arrogant pup is getting leg shackled!"

"I dinna believe it! What sort of young lass would be that desperate?"

"*My sister!* Listen to this, Anne Marie writes that Kathy and George finally ceased arguing long enough to realize they are 'in love' and a wedding is being arranged by Aunt Catherine within the next few months. She wants to know if I'll be able to attend. I'll be damned! Her brother, the bastard – or should I say the late bastard since I will destroy him – will be writing to me to ask if I'll stand up with him!" Harry began to tear through his other letters. "There must be one here from George...wait until I get my hands on our young Mr. Darcy...and all those times he was asking after her I thought it was brotherly like concern! I'll rip his heart out if... ah, there it is. Hand it to me."

Tearing open the letter Harry began to read, becoming more and more overwrought with each line. Paling suddenly, he stopped. The wind rustling the leaves outside their quarters was the only sound heard in the room.

"Does he say if Anne Marie asks after me at all...?"

"Be quiet, Buntley!" snapped Durand. "Harry, what's happened, lad?"

Harry never responded to either friend, never even heard them. Instead he ran an unsteady hand through his hair and concentrated on breathing in and out. *Oh my God. Oh my God.* Appearing confused he stood then looked about the room. "I need to leave for home as quickly as possible. Jim, wasn't there a ship departing tomorrow? I'll have to speak with the Colonel, I must be on that. Where's my valise?"

"I'll find your valise, but there may be difficulty gettin' ye on that ship, laddie; maybe the next. Buntley go and find out the sailin' particulars for Harry. Now Harry, sit for a moment and tell me what's happened."

"It's my father. He's had a severe heart attack."

Chapter Thirty-Three

Harry arrived at the old family residence in London less than two weeks later, early on a Sunday morning. He drank in the sight of the refurbished two story frame mansion with its huge black doors, its new stone pillars, and its balconies like sentries on either side, their drapes pulled closed. The house had been added upon and added upon over the years until it was unrecognizable from its beginnings, now twice the size it had been in his youth, the neighborhood suddenly appearing fashionable with other newer homes going up as well. And, as usual, there was no knocker on the doors; but, he hadn't expected one. His parents hated courtesy callers and the *ton* had long ago given up on the Earl and his Countess.

Childhood memories came flooding back instantly. The home might now look different to him, the grounds grander, and the neighborhood more impressive; but, the people and the love within had remained constant, of that he was certain. He remembered football in the front yards, rides throughout Hyde Park and St. James, early morning pillow fights between the children with their parents joining in upon occasion. Even those numbingly dull Sunday masses were now treasured remembrances, and afterward the return home to a huge breakfast and laughter. For years Uncle Tony had arrived for tea every Friday and stayed through dinner, Aunt Catherine's almost daily appearances, her tirades, her sputtering in and out, surrounded by her ever present King Charles spaniels.

And, of course, the Darcy's. The two families were so close that the parents and children were almost interchangeable.

How he had missed his parents, his adored mother and his beloved stepfather, a man he admired above all other men. At this moment Harry had no idea the true state of that man's health. No one wishing to alarm him, later letters from the family had all given differing opinions as to the severity of the attack. When he finally found his father's lone note it had simply said, "...your mother is upset over nothing! She'll come around sooner or later."

As soon as Harry closed the gate behind him he heard the howling and barking; hounds of varying sizes with dubious pedigrees came circling around from the back. One dog in particular was racing before the others, a silly grin wiping away any real threat. "Buttons!" Harry shouted. It looked so like old Buttons that Harry's heart gave a leap. Then he remembered hearing of the family funeral three years before when the remains of that beloved family pet were laid to rest in one of the flower beds.

This must be a grandson or great grandson, however – the dog looked so similar. Immediately he jumped up on hind legs to lick Harry's face, as poor a watchdog as Buttons had been before him. Harry laughed and ruffled the dog's ears, greeting all the others as well, barking scamps who circled him begging for equal attention. "It is truly grand to see you," Harry whispered, at ease for the first time in three years. "Truly grand."

Yes. It was very, very good to be home.

Walking around to the back of the house the first sibling he encountered was his sister Beth. She was sitting on the ground holding a saucer of milk before her, coaxing a frightened and newly bandaged cat forward. "Harry..." she whispered, her eyes rounding and staring incredulously up into his smiling face. "It can't be. Is it really you?"

"Hello, monkey."

Initially she moved slowly, backing away from the battered animal who was now, finally, taking nourishment. Once she was well in the clear she flung her arms around her brother's neck and squealed. "Harry! Harry! Harry! How wonderful! Oh Harry, is it really you? I've missed you very much. Mama will be so glad; she was worried when you never answered our letters."

"I never received a note until the week we were to board the ship for home. How is father?" It was then that a face identical to the joyous one before him came into view around the side of the house.

"Bethy, I don't think this rabbit is especially hurt but I do worry for her paw... Harry." An immediately sobbing Meg ran straight into his arms. "Oh, Harry..."

"I knew you two couldn't be very far from each other." He scooped up Meg and twirled her around then all three held each other, hugging tightly. "God I've missed you both; but, my heavens how you've grown in two years, or is it three? You make me feel ancient just to look at you."

"But you *are* ancient, Harry," replied Meg, her teary smile infectious.

"Oh, thank you so much for that remark. Now you won't receive any gift."

"What gift? You have a gift for me? I was only teasing, Harry. You are my favorite brother, you know you are..."

"Never mind about that," said Beth. "Come inside quickly – things are very bad there." She reached out her hand.

Harry stopped and his breath caught. "How is he? How is father?"

"Terrible!"

"Meg, don't say that. God will hear you."

He looked from one sister to the other. "What do you mean, terrible. How terrible is he?"

"First, come inside and see to Teddy and Drew. They are already in trouble and now they are trying to kill each other."

"No, wait a moment. Tell me about father."

Just then he heard shouts from the inside doorway. Charging up the stairs two at a time he entered the hallway as seven year old Edward and sixteen year old Andrew were trying to kick the feet out from beneath each other. After initial whoops of greetings and rough hugs the three began to shove and wrestle, inevitably ending up rolling about on the floor, sending furniture skidding across the highly polished oak flooring of the back service entrance. A large table crashed to its final resting place.

"What in bloody hell is going on down there!?"

Harry stopped immediately at the sound of that familiar bellow, relief washing through him. His brothers took quick advantage of the distraction, pinning Harry face down, shoulder to the floor and the wrestling began anew.

Fitzwilliam stomped down the back staircase shortly before the butler and two footmen came running from another direction.

"Your lordship, forgive my laxity at keeping the noise level down for your nap. I was unaware of any fracas taking place."

"Damn it all, Bates, I was not sleeping – *and I do not nap* – so please stop fussing over me! It's only those hooligan sons of mine again. Throw a tarp over them, there's a good fellow." It was then he noticed a vaguely familiar form buried beneath the heap of arms and legs. "But who's the third one down there, on the bottom? Elizabeth, Margaret, stop squealing for a moment and tell me who it is your brothers are attempting to murder."

"Harry!" The girls shrieked in unison. Fitzwilliam crouched down for a closer look.

"Well, send me to perdition, but so it is. Let him up you ruffians!"

A laughing Harry extricated himself from the pile. Once standing he helped his father back to his feet, pulled the big man into his arms and unashamedly engulfed him in a strong embrace. Tears threatened the both of them. "Steady on," grumbled Fitzwilliam. "I don't remember giving you permission to be taller than I; or, am I standing in a hole?" Fitzwilliam's voice was hoarse at first but he laughed off his emotion, cupped the back of Harry's head and squeezed it affectionately. "Well, well, well, I'll be goddamned," he said quietly. The two men were, by then, holding each other at arms length, each studying the other very gravely.

"You've gotten fatter."

"I have not!" Fitzwilliam was both amused and highly insulted.

"Oh, yes you have."

"My body has merely begun to ready itself for the winter."

"Evidently it's going to be one horrific winter. I do like the beard though. How in the world did you manage to grow out a ginger one?"

"Ginger with plenty of white; in fact, I believe every white hair I have is from you. And look at you with that ferret on your lip. Your mother's not going to like a mustache on you, boyo, I hope you realize that. It makes you look your real age and gives away hers. Teasing aside you do look good son, you really do."

"How are you feeling, Papa? Mother's letters all sounded concerned."

"Bah! You're mother's a woman and therefore hysterical most of the time." He easily held off his laughing daughters who began to pound on his arms, expressing their displeasure in that unique Fitzwilliam family way.

"I told you he was terrible, Harry. He ate all the scones this morning before we even reached the table. He's a menace."

"In this house you must grab what you can – eat swiftly and leave nothing. It's the only reason I've not starved to death with these two around." That statement brought the girls forward protesting once again, with more indignant shouts and giggles.

"Have you seen your mother yet?"

"Not yet." Harry shook his head. "I arrived only moments ago and was immediately attacked. Where is she?"

"She's downstairs. You know she's always happiest in her kitchen with an apron on; the only countess I've ever known with flour imbedded permanently beneath her fingernails."

He had not seen her in over three years but the time had been very kind to her. She looked calm and happy, at home sitting there at the large kitchen worktable – sipping tea, discussing the week's dinner menus with the cook, examining shopping lists and deciding about linen replacements. At the other end of the table a roast was being prepared and oysters soaked in a large bowl. Scullery maids bustled about, chatting, washing dishes or sweeping the floor. An old dog snored in the open doorway.

Abruptly all became silent. Sensing a change in the room, Amanda looked up, staring and unbelieving. "Harry..." she whispered, momentarily frozen to the spot. Pushing back her stool she stood slowly, a hand over her pounding heart. "Harry..." she repeated, her voice hoarse, tears brightening her eyes. Taking one faltering step after another she moved around the table. Then suddenly, with her arms opened wide, she ran to him.

Harry immediately grabbed hold, buried his face in her neck and closed his eyes; he twirled her around, tightening his embrace. It was difficult for either to speak. "I've missed you," he whispered into her hair.

"Let me look at you." She pushed back far enough to study him, her tear filled gaze doing a thorough and motherly examination. "Harry, you have a mustache."

"Yes, I know. Do you like it?"

"Not especially, makes me feel old," she giggled and sobbed at once. "You've lost some weight also."

"Just a bit. But you look especially fine, Mama. How are you feeling?"

"Much better now you're home for a while, and safe." As her voice caught in her throat she sobbed and pulled him back into her embrace once again. It took a few more moments for her to regain control of her emotions and finally relax her grip.

"Now, let me go. I need to have a proper look. Are you all right? Does he have any injuries, Richard –

anything you detected that he would not have told us about?"

"No injuries other than those inflicted by his own brothers here."

"Excellent. We were so frightened for you during that horrible siege."

"I wrote and wrote letters but nothing was able to go out and then everyone's mail was lost in the fires at the end. I'm so sorry to have worried you."

"Thank goodness your father still has influential friends at the war department – well no longer actually; he nearly drove them all mad with his ruthless threats and bullying. He was wonderful. Believe me, by the time he was finished they made it a point to keep us informed, perhaps too much so at times... well, be that as it may, such honors you young men have received! Much deserved honors I might add. Oh, my darling child, I'm so very happy that you're home. Look everyone..." Amanda turned toward the sniffling maids and the weeping cook. "Look Lily, he's home."

"Yes, and so he is – Master Harry, it's that good to see ye."

Harry nodded a greeting to the servants that had crowded in and then hugged their old cook. "Miss Lily you look beautiful."

"Oh, go on with you!" The woman blushed and beamed then wiped her eyes on her apron.

"When must you go back?" At her question he turned once again to his mother.

"Well, that was the big decision I was pondering in those lost letters. I suppose the last siege made it easy for me, though – I have resigned my commission, finished with the army for good and all. I've done my turn for Queen and country and am home to stay, if you'll have me."

Pressing hands to her mouth Amanda could no longer restrain her emotion. "Oh, thank you, thank you sweet *Jesu*, my prayers have been answered." She hugged her son to herself again, finally giving in fully to her weeping.

Harry heard his father loudly blow his nose behind him. "Be careful son, she'll be quoting scripture next," Fitzwilliam grumbled as he wiped his eyes with his handkerchief.

"There, there, now. I'm fine you two, truly I am. See, I haven't a scratch on me. I tell you we even were able to eat well – stole five hundred sheep from the enemy and had lamb chops and mutton stew until we thought we'd burst." Her head rested against his heart so Harry stroked her hair, patted his father's arm, the roles of comfort and reassurance reversed for the first time.

The child was becoming parent.

"Now dry your eyes mother – look here, someone bring a glass of water for my father. When you're both able, you can tell me how everyone is."

Amanda wiped away her tears and laughed. "Well, let's see, you know that Matt and Mark have been traveling, Andrew is home temporarily from Harrow, however he's so close to finishing anyway, Richard, perhaps he won't need to return? Luke is back at Oxford..."

"Where is Kathy?"

"Oh! Harry! You've been gone so long you could not have heard the news! She's engaged – yes, to Georgie Darcy!"

"Well, as a matter of fact, I did receive a letter from Anne Marie mentioning something. A bit surprising, that, wasn't it? Were they courting for long? Were you aware of any infatuation between them?" If this sudden romance was one of George's odd whims, if he hurt his sister in any way, friend or no, kith or kin, he was a dead man.

"Yes; as a matter of fact we were aware a few years back that they cared for each other, they had even spoken of marriage then, but at fifteen and sixteen – well, they were much too young." Fitzwilliam rubbed his neck as he remembered. "The whole incident spoke more of youthful rebellion than anything else. That's when we spirited Kathy away to the country and Darcy carted George off to University. Both were angry with us at first but then I believe they had a falling out. Kathy took exception to what she saw as George acquiescing to his father's wishes too quickly, and you know Kathy. Her mood swings are impossible to fathom at the best of times. She then seemed to forget him entirely, ended up becoming infatuated with so many other young men that that then became another new worry."

"Oh, lord, yes I do remember being a bit concerned with her myself. The few fellows I met were dreadfully dull, though; none of them could match her spirit."

"I thought the matter behind us, I truly did. George finished University and Darcy purchased the commission for him. Then one day, it was nearly a year ago I believe, early winter, out of the blue George comes marching up to the house in Somerton and demands to speak with me. Gave me a true dressing down he did, said Darcy and I had interfered in his life once but we had better not interfere again. He then told me he and Kathy had lost precious years and were going to marry just as soon as he could find her and shake some sense into her.

"I explained to him, calm as a vicar of course, what his father and my reasoning had been, and that during those years he had received a brilliant education and had seen the world. And as for Kathy,

well she had been presented at court, had experienced
a very successful first season, refusing a great many
offers of marriage I might add, and, that she was
currently being courted by a very distinguished
Marquis...and then he very nearly went for my
throat."

"It was quite romantic."

"Do not be vexing, Amanda, it was not romantic in
the least! The boy was livid, shouted at me like
someone crazed, said he had heard all about the
bloody Marquis – excuse my language ladies – said we
had no control over our daughter at all! Now, Harry,
you know very well that George is like another child to
me, I love him like a son. I wanted to beat him
senseless. Next thing I know he's pulling Kathy out of
the house and dragging her through the garden and
all the while they were shouting at each other
something dreadful."

"He's very good for her, Richard. I believe he
restrains her from engaging in too many outrageous
escapades."

"Your mother forgets about the 'trousers at the
opera' episode last year or any number of antics she
indulges in with her brother Matt."

"Richard, the opera incident was for George's
benefit – don't you men understand anything? It was
what prompted George to seek her out again, he called
it 'the last straw' – isn't that adorable? And besides, it
wasn't that scandalous; she did wear a long frock coat,
very few people noticed and Matthew and Mark stood
with her the entire time. She knew George would be
there and she wanted to shock him into action."

"Well, it worked." Fitzwilliam added. "She's
absolutely exhausted me. From behaving like a sixty
year old dowager at ten and five she suddenly turned

hoyden on us in her dotage. I will be extremely happy when she's George's problem and not mine."

"Oh, and now who's being vexing? It will break your heart to lose her. George and Kathy are very much in love, Harry." His mother's smile showed how thrilled she was for her daughter. "The Darcy's have taken Kathy to visit with Jane and Charles in Bath but they'll return next week to begin the final preparations for the wedding which Aunt Catherine has asked to give. Your father and I were happy to make this lifelong dream of hers come true – oh stop rolling your eyes, Richard."

"Over two hundred invited for the Wedding Luncheon at last count, Amanda! Two hundred. I don't know more than a dozen people I care to meet on the street let alone have in my home! And I have no idea who is expected at the church. The old dragon thinks I'm made of money."

"Good lord." Harry began to laugh. "I thought weddings were meant to be private affairs, only for the immediate family."

"To Aunt Catherine, that is immediate family." Fitzwilliam grumbled and groused on. "Ridiculous waste of money, feeding all those politicians and toadies of Darcy's not to mention my mother's insane relatives whom I'd assumed were already dead or committed. We are spending a bloody fortune on a pack of strangers."

"Oh, be still." His wife flapped her hand in his direction. "At times you behave worse than our children."

"Amanda, please do be serious. You know perfectly well there is *nothing* worse than our children."

Chapter Thirty- Four

Harry was unable to sleep. It had been like that for him since the long siege in Afghanistan, since the battles and bloodshed. Too many emotions, too many memories of friends killed; too much remorse at his own part in the killing. So, he made his way quietly through the house, down to the kitchens. Seeing a light coming from beneath the pantry door he pushed it open slowly and saw exactly what he had suspected. He closed the door quietly.

"I believe he's in here, Mama!" Immediately he heard the crash of a chair followed by a string of curses. He could not hold back his laughter when, upon entering the room, he saw his father wildly waving smoke away from the vicinity of his face.

"Oh bloody hell, it's only you!" Fitzwilliam shook his head, picked up his stool and roughly shoved it back to the table. "You scared the shit out of me."

"It serves you right."

As Fitzwilliam watched his son enter the room he felt such great pride in him. The boy was muscular, broad shouldered, strapping. "Get away from the doorway will you, you're blocking the air flow." At twenty-eight Harry was in his full stride, *and no longer my little boy*, his father mused, rather regretfully. Harry was a man fully grown now.

"Did Mama bake today? I'm ravenous for her biscuits." Well, maybe that little boy *was* still in there, somewhere. "Why are you hiding in here smoking your pipe?"

"What pipe?"

"That pipe, the one you're holding beneath the table. And by the way you'd better bring it up or you'll burn the house down."

Fitzwilliam contemplated denial at first but then brought the forbidden pleasure back to his lips. "Don't tell your mother, there's a good lad. Don't want to go upsetting her."

"Then don't smoke."

"I rarely do this, Harry! Only on nights when I can't sleep, or over the holidays, or when I've had a difficult day or during months with one syllable..."

Harry walked into the next room, emerging moments later laden with bread, butter and cheese and a cold plate of chicken and ham. "No cakes but plenty of food. Are you interested?"

"Oh hell yes, this is capital!" Fitzwilliam rubbed his hands together. "Harry, I hate to ruin your illusions of your mother but she's turned vicious in her old age. She has been forcing me to eat *vegetation* before I am provided *meat* – plant life, Harold. I've been reduce to eating flora. She'll have me consuming the shrubbery soon and then can small insects be far behind? Hand over that cheese."

After Harry placed the food down he brought over plates and utensils from a cupboard. Taking Fitzwilliam's wine glass he took a sample sip then frowned at the weak taste. "Is this truly the best we can do?"

"And yet more indignities... She waters my wine too."

"I don't see how you can stand this. If I were her husband I'd simply lay down the law to her."

"That way lies madness, son." Fitzwilliam's grim brow waggle made Harry chuckle. Glancing over his shoulder his father reached into his shirt pocket, brought out some keys and tossed them over. "I have a stash of the better liquor locked away – hidden in the back of the pantry in a box marked 'war rations'. Fetch us a couple of first-rate wines."

Harry returned shortly with two bottles of the very finest and then the true feasting began. Sitting side by side the men ate, occasionally in companionable quiet but more often commenting on family, friends or life in the army, or laughing at the dogs that danced and barked about the kitchen chasing after bits of food tossed to them.

After a while Harry leaned back in his chair and sighed, closing his eyes. "God it's good to be home. I've missed this."

"Are you planning on finishing that chicken leg?"

Harry's eyes popped open. "Yes, I am and keep your bloody hands away from my bread."

They continued their meal in peace, finally relaxing together as men often do, with liquor, tobacco and silence.

For a while.

"Father?"

"Yes, son."

"Have you seen her?" Harry had asked the question at last, blowing the smoke from his cheroot into the air above his head. "I've had word they come into town now, that they even reside here during season."

Fitzwilliam was expecting the question. It was the same every visit, every letter. "Yes, it's true. He has purchased a house on Jermyn Street; and yes, I have seen her."

"It's been nearly four years." Harry looked at his father. "What does she look like?"

"She's going to be a beauty, Harry; looks very like Celeste, more and more so every day. I'd say she definitely has your eyes, however."

Harry swallowed and clenched his jaw, then took a drag from his smoke. "It's gratifying to know she has something of me." When she was first born Harry could visit in secret to hold his daughter. Those were precious memories to him, but painful and much too few. However, even that limited access had ended with Celeste's passing four years earlier in childbirth. His daughter had been but three years old the last time he saw her.

"Your mother and I have never spoken about this, does she know?"

"Not from me, no." Harry was not surprised that his father had not betrayed this confidence, even to his mother. "Have you ever heard gossip about the child?"

"No, I myself have never heard anyone questioning her paternity. You know the *haute ton*, however — even though there are dozens of children whose parentage is dubious, as long as no one is foolish enough to give voice to the obvious, everyone pretends ignorance."

"That's true. God knows how many half brothers and sisters have wed over the years."

"This must be hard on you, son. If it is any consolation at all I have heard it said Percy is a devoted father to her; she appears most happy, if a bit overprotected at times."

"That should be comforting to me, and perhaps, if I was a better man it would be — but frankly, it is not and I am not. All I can think is that my child is somewhere out in the world being cared for by a stranger." He shook his head and stared into his wine.

"It's almost more than I can bear at times." The only sound in the room was the old clock on the hearth mantel.

Harry stood and wandered over to the window. "She's like I was, you know. Ignorant of her true father..." Gripping the sill, he leaned forward, his burning head touching the cool glass, his eyes pressed shut. "Damn it. I should have remained in India."

Fitzwilliam placed his glass carefully on the table. He felt ridiculously hurt. "I'm your true father – perhaps not by blood; but, no blood relative could love you as their son as dearly as I do."

"Father, forgive me; that is not at all what I meant! You've been absolutely the best and I love you, you know that; and I know you love me. Why, without you – damn, I can't even imagine such a life. It's just that knowing my real father didn't care for me I wonder, at times, if I was to blame for his estrangement somehow – for his rejection of me and mother. I'd hate for my daughter to find out someday that she was another man's child and wonder the same. Oh what does it truly matter if I'm here or not?"

"How can you be so insensitive? Of course it matters! It matters to me, to your brothers and sisters, to your aunt and uncle, to your cousins; and, most importantly, it matters to your mother! Over the years you've found all manner of excuses not to return home to your mother because of this and your absence has wounded her deeply. Does that truly surprise you so? Did you believe she would stop needing you, worrying about you, merely because you were gone from her house? Harry, parents are parents forever! It does not end the day the child decides for himself that he's all grown up and moves on; the concern of a parent for that child never lessens!" Fitzwilliam suddenly stopped shouting. He felt old and tired, too tired for yet another battle with one of his headstrong children. "The pain you feel, the aching need within you for your child, is universal; but, it is too late now, she legally belongs to another. You played with fire, you and Celeste, and you must accept the consequences."

"She knew she was with child, father; Celeste knew. She could have stopped me from taking my commission. If I'd any idea of what was happening I never would have left – you know this. We would have married immediately. But, Celeste wanted her title and the prestige of being a Percy. How can I not but feel bitter? She left me with no voice in the matter, no chance. You may as well know I've made certain inquiries. I've decided to contact a solicitor and see if I have any rights."

"Are you mad? A father's first obligation is to ensure what is *best* for his child, not its destruction. You will ruin Christina's life if you pursue such folly. Why, she would be called a bastard, an outcast, if her true paternity became known, and it *would* become known. The *haute ton* is ruthless, it feeds on scandal."

Harry stared out the darkened window, furious with the truth of his father's words, with the knowledge that in the end he could really do nothing. Fitzwilliam shook his head and was suddenly weary, yearning now for a bit of rest after so much food and wine and emotion. "John Percy is a dull man, Harry, but a good one, and he appears an exemplary father. In the end we are all prisoners of our past, good or bad – there is no escaping that." Harry's back stiffened with every word his father uttered and Fitzwilliam knew that there was no use pushing the boy when he was like this, stubborn as he was.

Just like his mother.

"Oh, and there is something else you should know now, before you hear it from someone else. John Percy has been courting a young woman and from what I've been told he is absolutely besotted with the girl. There is a real possibility that he will make an offer of marriage to her father in the near future."

Harry's shoulders slumped in defeat. It was what he had dreaded the most, that Percy would marry and take his little girl away. "Do you know who she is?"

"Yes. Alice Darcy."

Harry could not have heard that correctly. "I beg your pardon?" He turned and stared at his father. "Alice Darcy?" The pressure in his chest eased up slightly. Alice Darcy? This could be a perfect solution to his problem – Sir John Percy marrying into the Darcy family, why it would the nearest thing to marrying into his own, the two clans were that close.

But Alice Darcy?

"I cannot believe this. Alice? Are you telling me the truth?"

Fitzwilliam chuckled. "Indeed I am, although I am not as certain of Alice's feelings for him. She may very well turn him down."

"Poor Little Alice turn down *a Percy*? The man is a direct descendent of one of the most historic families in England and incredibly rich to boot. What woman in her right mind would turn him down? She wouldn't...would she?"

"Poor 'Little' Alice can pick and choose whomever she desires, Harry. She has had dozens of suitors already and at least as many proposals. Percy could be just another love struck swain in hopeless pursuit."

Harry rested his hands on his hips. He was missing something here. "Are we speaking of the same Alice – Plain Little Alice Darcy? Not to be cruel but the Alice I remember would be fortunate for any offer of marriage, let alone one from Sir John Percy."

Fitzwilliam grinned. "Well, son, plain Little Alice Darcy is plain no longer."

Chapter Thirty-Five

"Papa?" Alice opened her father's library door, peeking inside when she received no response to her light knock. "Papa, are you asleep in here?" Her eyes scanned the room until they settled on the elegant gentleman in question. He was, as usual, hard at work and unheeding of his surroundings.

From the doorway she could take a moment to admire him. At over fifty years of age he was still one of the most handsome men she had ever seen, the slight graying of his temples merely adding another layer of elegance. It really was unfair that some men grew better looking with age and none were more handsome than her father. "Papa, the house is on fire – quickly, freshen your cravat."

Darcy looked up and immediately smiled, the sight of his youngest child lifting his spirits. As always she brought a burst of sunshine into his day.

"My goodness Alice, what a stunning bonnet you wear." He removed his *pince nez* and pinched the bridge of his nose. "Are you going out or coming in?"

"Just coming in." Untying the ribbons she slipped said hat off her head and presented it to her father for his inspection. "And a mere hour ago I was informed that this very bonnet is two years out of mode, so a lot you know. I am a fashion disaster according to Kathy

Fitzwilliam and her London seamstress so I just purchased a whole season's worth of new dresses. My heavens but you've been hard at it while we were shopping, haven't you."

"What are you going on about? I've only just... oh my word, is it truly that late? No wonder I'm famished."

"How has the British empire survived all these centuries without you? Father, really, no more working for the afternoon, I beg you. Rest on your laurels, you've enough of them, and that's a fact."

"All right, all right, I was finished anyway. Such a harridan you've become." They chatted and laughed as he began to gather his papers into neat piles before him. At this time of his life Darcy had found a rather surprising benefit to fatherhood — not only did he love his children with every fiber of his being, but he actually liked them as well. In fact, they were among a handful of people (a circle which seemed to grow smaller and smaller every year) whom he considered his dearest friends.

"Just out of curiosity, what nonsense were you working so industriously on today?"

He arched his imperial brow causing her to giggle, a reaction he thoroughly enjoyed and expected. It was a family facial gesture they all shared now. "As you well know John Wentworth is making his first important speech before Commons next week; thought I would help him out a bit by jotting down notes. Being as he is one of the youngest of the Whigs, as well as in the minority party, I'm as nervous as a mother cat tossing her kitten onto the Royal Ascot racecourse."

"Father, John has been Uncle Fitz's second spear in Parliament for ages, his family's expertise in government is third generation at the least, and he's a mesmerizing speaker. He will do splendidly; you've nothing with which to concern yourself. Oh! Your new frock coat and trousers for the wedding have arrived, very smart looking! Mama has had new dancing slippers made for you also, and – now don't scowl so! You know you love dancing as much as she does."

"I like your dress."

"Absolutely pathetic attempt at changing subjects. Try again."

"I read your latest story in the Ladies Gazette. Very stimulating."

She arched a uniquely Darcy-like brow back at him. "I was unaware you read the Ladies Gazette. Imagine my horror."

"Your mother is the subscriber, Alice; followed me around for hours slapping me on the head with her copy until I relented. Were you as alarmed as I by the drastic modification in necklines?"

"Be serious will you? What did you think of my story?"

"Your latest *nom de plume* is Archibald Awning."

"Well, it was that or Armand Azure. I'm running out of men's names beginning with 'A' – Barouche Barkley is next. Stop stalling."

"I enjoyed the tale very much, although I thought lightning striking down the evil Baronet just as he was about to strangle the helpless orphan a bit '*deus ex machina*' for my taste."

"They paid me two pounds more than the Standard ever did."

"In that case it was brilliant."

"Shall I read you my next story? It's called "The Evil Emir and the Hounds of Hell." They'll publish it next month."

"...and your dowry grows ever larger..."

Darcy listened proudly as his youngest child read aloud the next installment of her Ladies Gazette series and gratified her by laughing at all the right places; he truly did enjoy and admire her work and wit. And, as always, she amazed him. Somehow, he mused, sometime during the past five years Alice Darcy had been transformed. Not in her character, which had always been among the finest he had ever known, nor in her intellect or disposition, nor in her loving devotion to her family.

No. Somehow, somewhere, Alice Darcy had become a London beauty. Their awkward little goose with the big ears, the long nose and the huge intense eyes was now counted among the finest looking young women of this, her first season. Social arbiters had decreed her looks 'unique', her appearance 'exotic'. Of course, she had always been beautiful in her parents' eyes; he and Lizzy were totally prejudiced when it came to their children, always would be.

"'… and then the couple, newly feeling the emotions of great love, shared a great kiss.' The End. Did you hear any of that?"

"Of course I did. By the way, Avila is north of Madrid – in Spain; not in Portugal."

"You *were* listening! Was it all right?"

"It was first-rate. You really are very talented."

"Thank you, Papa." Alice beamed proudly and then appeared to sober at a sudden thought. "Oh, by the way, John Percy came into the book shop while Mama and I were there this morning."

"Ah." The John Percy 'problem'. Five weeks into the season and she had already snagged the town's premiere catch. "You know Lady Catherine has invited him to your brother's wedding."

"Hardly surprising. I believe she's notified all of Burke's Peerage by now."

Darcy folded his hands over his still trim stomach, leaned back, and laughed. "Poor old Fitz – and he was finally becoming accustomed to having all that money too. How many have been invited, do you know?"

"At least two hundred, and that's just to St. George's. Getting back to John, Papa... he asked again to see you, wondered if you'd be home tomorrow evening as he had something important he wished to discuss with you."

"I see." Darcy sat forward in his chair. "Well, we both know what that is, Alice."

"No we don't."

"Oh, of course we do. He's in love with you. You know this, your mother and I know this, and half of London knows this." Darcy moved his ink pot and papers absently about his desk as he thought what to say next. "This is his second request to speak with me; I can put him off no longer." He was aware that the man wanted to insinuate himself within the family, make an offer of marriage for Alice; but, Darcy was uncomfortable with the whole idea. In his opinion it was too soon, the man was rushing her. Besides, Darcy wasn't certain the match would be a good one, even with Percy's illustrious name and all his money. They were too opposite in their personalities, too conflicting in their approaches to life, Percy being rather dour and serious, Alice always open and joyful. But, if she truly cared for the man, he would not stand in her way.

"Father, you should that know, if – all right, lower that brow – when he makes his offer... I am leaning toward accepting him."

He tried to hide his dismay. He had more than half hoped his daughter would tease about it, laugh the notion off. Darcy cleared his throat. "I see." The silence between them grew almost oppressive.

"He's known to be quite the conservative, Alice. You are aware of that, aren't you? I tell you this because, well, you so love to laugh and to sing…to write. In Sir John's exalted sphere you might be regarded as something of a radical."

"He laughs, Papa. On occasion he even hums. And, he knows of the writing and although he doesn't seem to admire the idea, neither is he off put by it – not that I am aware of anyway. He's very kind to me, you know…and he genuinely seems to be a good parent. He loves his daughter, that's important, isn't it?"

"Well, yes, of course it is, but Alice there is so much more to marriage. Why hurry your decision; you're bound to meet a good many more young men during the next few months. And what about love? You have not mentioned love."

She smiled indulgently. "I've met almost all the eligible young men already and the ones I've turned down have gone directly onto other young women; so, I ask you, how deeply in love with me could they really have been? Love is a fantasy, Papa. I prefer to marry someone dependable."

"Love is a fantasy? I can assure you I fell deeply in love with your mother, and very quickly. Of course, it's true she didn't feel a reciprocal passion for me until she saw Pemberley…"

Alice laughed, relieving the tension she had begun to feel. Her mother's initial animosity toward her father was a subject that had fueled many humorous discussions within the family.

"Dearest, forgive me for being rather blunt; but, since I know your character is not one to chase fortune or fame…well, are you accepting Sir John because he was once married to Celeste?"

His daughter's laughter subsided. "I take exception to your implication." She shifted nervously, fearing her father was too close to the truth, that he would soon uncover the real reason for her interest in John Percy.

"Don't fly off the handle; just give the thought some consideration will you? The rivalry between you girls was always quite intense. Perhaps without realizing it you feel this is a way for you to finally be vindicated. You'd have her husband, her prestige... *and* her child."

Alice's face pinked up and she couldn't speak for a moment. "It has *nothing* to do with the child; I *never* gave any of that a thought."

"Let me suggest then, as your father, that you *do* think – give yourself more time before committing yourself to a betrothal. Remember, I am suggesting this, not demanding; although as your father I have the right." He chuckled when he saw her roll her eyes.

"Oh, all right, all right. I shall try and commit myself to deep thought before any permanent promises are made."

"I think that is an excellent idea. And, who knows, you may just fall in love with the man anyway."

"Oh, you and love again..." Her jibe was abruptly silenced by the sincere look in his eye. "I shouldn't tease you. You love Mama very much, don't you?"

He spoke without a moment's hesitation. "More than my own life."

Her heart squeezed painfully, she swallowed as if a wishbone were caught in her throat. "*You* are just a silly old romantic, Papa." And all of a sudden Alice felt perilously close to tears.

"This is true." Walking around the desk to her he held out a hand. "No more talk of suitors today, or of romance. I wish to see all the nonsense several hundred pounds can buy."

Chapter Thirty-Six

"Alice, how lovely you look!" Lizzy admired her daughter as they both stared into the cheval mirror before them. Never before had she seen such a dress; never before had her young daughter looked more beautiful. "Let me see the slippers." Lifting the hem of the beaded sheath gown Alice revealed beaded, satin slippers covered in an ivory material, the color and beading matching an overlay of shimmering beaded tulle that covered her satin gown, her cap sleeves and her elaborately worked small train. Tiny satin ribbons threaded the girl's rich dark tresses, at her ears and her neck sparkled clusters of diamonds. "I was skeptical when Mrs. Chauret described the design to me — it sounded so busy; but, this really is magnificent. You will outdo even your last success."

"Not with such a beautiful young Queen and such a handsome Prince in attendance. I doubt a soul will notice me tonight."

"We shall see. Well, here are your gloves; we'd better hurry. George and Kathy have already left but your father, Uncle Fitz and Auntie Amanda all await us downstairs."

"Where are Anne Marie and John? They haven't left yet, or have they?"

"Yes. I told them to go ahead with George and Kathy. We'll meet them all at the ball and enter together as one family."

It had been some time since Harry had worn civilian clothes and daytime dress for men was different now, more relaxed, thanks in part by the advent of a trim, handsome young prince. Favoring a much more masculine and understated mode of dressing, his influence had sent the bright colors, the fussing and pomp of the previous royal court out of favor. Now men wanted a lower collar, less stiff and pointy, with neck scarf tied in a bow.

However, evening wear was still regimented, every man dressing alike in a black tail coat, black knee pants, black silk stockings, black vest, starched white neck cloth and shirt, white kid gloves and patent leather pumps. The only variations allowed were shirt studs. Darcy and Fitzwilliam both wore small diamond studs. Harry wore gold.

"You haven't said how I look, Amanda," prompted her husband.

"You look as handsome as ever, Richard."

"That's not much of an answer though, is it?"

Amanda laughed, as he meant her to. "You look ravishingly handsome, dear, but not too much more so than Harry."

Harry just then had his finger sliding along the inside of his collar, struggling for some leeway. "I feel ridiculous."

Although he may have felt ridiculous he looked exceedingly fine, at least to his adoring mother. His black jacket of the finest cloth stretched across a very broad back, his starched shirt front presented a well formed chest, the low cut of his silk vest gave hint to his slim waist. His legs in black breeches and stockings were long and beautifully shaped; his feet and hands large, well formed.

"I see what you mean," grumbled the proud father in Fitzwilliam. Amanda stood up on her toes and kissed her husband's cheek.

Darcy entered the room just at that moment.

"I swear, it's still not safe to leave you two alone in a room." He strode to Amanda's side and gave her an affectionate kiss. "You look wonderful as always this evening."

"How nice that *someone* noticed."

"I said you looked nice. I'm certain I did. Well, I was thinking it anyway." Fitzwilliam shoved his hands inside his trouser pockets. "Darcy, Kathy has spoken of nothing but your trip to Bath and your visit with the Bingley's. Sounds like you all had a splendid time."

"Yes, we did. George..." Darcy sensed someone approaching him from behind so he turned. "What's this? Harry! I hadn't heard you were returned from India. Let me look at you!" He grabbed the young man by his shoulders, too stunned to mask his emotions, his sincere joy apparent for all to see. "Oh, you look splendid, boy; absolutely splendid!" They hugged briefly then manfully patted each other's backs.

"He's been home several days but I couldn't bear to share him with anyone yet." Amanda's tears of happiness were always near the surface.

"I can certainly appreciate that. Well, this deserves a toast of some sort." Darcy poured champagne and handed the glasses out. "Oh, I should warn you, Lady Catherine will be arriving at any moment, Fitz. Escape is still possible."

Before Darcy had even finished his statement Fitzwilliam had begun reaching for his gloves as if to leave. "Oh no you don't," Harry laughed. "Stay right where you are. I cannot wait to see Aunt Catherine again. I've missed her more than I missed any of you lot."

As if on cue the butler opened the door to a resplendent Lady Catherine de Bourgh, and to her equally resplendent, although pale, daughter, Anne. "Darcy, the most dreadful thing has just happened," she announced, gliding into the room.

"You needn't concern yourself, Aunt Catherine. We were expecting you."

Catherine's gaze narrowed on the lesser favored nephew of the two. "If I were not already angry with you I would say something scathing." She then allowed each of her nephew's exactly one kiss upon her cheek. "Bah. You barbarian, you've made me forgot what I was going to say." Turning to acknowledge Amanda's presence in the room Catherine hesitated, obviously searching her memory for the woman's name. It was nowhere there to be found. "Hello, niece," was the best she could offer. "Darcy, if that is champagne I shall have my first glass now, if you please. Anne shall have one also. It's very good for the chest.

"Ooh, I remember now. As I was saying, the most dreadful thing has... Harold! Harold Augustus is that you? Oh my heavens, come here at once and give your old aunt a kiss." Opening her arms she welcomed her grandnephew with a gentle hug then held him at arm's length to look at him. "Fitzwilliam, your son is here! You must have noticed his presence for some time, why was I not informed of his return? Harold, you look very handsome. Was he always this tall? Really? You are not already married I take it; excellent – Anne, sit up straight!" By then she had begun to push him gently toward her daughter Anne who was seated beside the closed doors, sniffling into a handkerchief and checking her pulse. "Have you met my daughter, Anne?"

"Yes, of course I have, Aunt Catherine." He laughed and bowed. "Hello, Anne, splendid to see you again." As Harry bent to kiss his cousin's hand, the doors to the sitting room were opened again, this time by Elizabeth. "I am so very sorry we're late, we had a slight problem attaching the train to Alice's gown. But, it was worth the trouble; see how lovely Alice's new dress looks." Harry stood promptly but his shout out of greeting to his favored little cousin immediately died on his lips.

In fact, his whole prior life seemed to slowly come to a stop and wait in silence for the briefest of moments. When his breathing started up once again, it seemed as if a new world had begun.

"Oh brilliant, Aunt Kate, you're here." Alice beamed with delight at the sight of her grand aunt. Taking Catherine's hands in hers she bent to press her cheek against the wizened dowager's. "You look wonderful tonight; I love your hair done in that fashion."

"Alicia!" Catherine held the girl's hands apart and Alice posed cheekily so her dress might be better admired. "You are a dream in that gown."

"Do you really think so, Aunt Kate? It's not too daring, is it? I've never worn anything so extravagantly flimsy before and I am freezing. There is very little material on top, you see; I keep pulling at it to no avail. Fashion, evidently, is chilly stuff..."

"Nonsense. You would prefer fustian, perhaps? No, this is perfect. Alicia, I swear child you have the most faultless figure I have ever seen − exquisite décolletage; and, I don't think it is daring in the least. You look just as I did at your age, although I was taller with a much more regal bearing." Her aunt had brought up her quizzing glass for closer inspection.

"Let me see you." Darcy turned his daughter around to face him, alarmed by the very mention of décolletage. *Good god,* he thought, *whenever did all this happen to her*? He beetled his brow. "Elizabeth, isn't this a bit revealing for a child her age?"

"*Papa...*" Alice whined, embarrassed with all the attention paid to her bosom.

"William, she is not a child in the least, she's a young woman now, and this dress is tame by comparison to others you will see tonight. No, I believe she looks perfect."

Amanda and Fitzwilliam added their praise until Alice's cheeks pinked with just the proper mixture of embarrassment and gratification.

Then suddenly the fine hair on her arms seemed to suddenly rise with unknown excitement. She looked around the room, from her Uncle Fitz to her father, both beaming like cats sprawled in the cream. "What is it?"

"Look who is returned to us, Alice." Amanda raised her hand to beckon someone forward from the side.

Her heart stilled, she closed her eyes knowing instinctively who was approaching now behind her.

"Harry." she whispered.

Then she turned.

Her tender memories of a young Harry faded in the blink of an eye when faced with the new, much more masculine reality of him – so much taller and broad shouldered, so very stunning with his tanned face and white teeth. His eyes sparkled, his mouth...oh, those beautiful lips that she had dreamed of kissing for so long.

"Harry, how, I mean when, I mean..." She was babbling. "I had no idea you were returned to us. No one said anything..."

"Isn't this a wonderful surprise?" Lizzy stepped forward and hugged Harry tightly, kissed him, cupped his face. When she finally spoke, her voice was filled with emotion. "Oh, my dear child, it really does my heart good to see you again."

"You look beautiful as always Auntie Eliza."

"I may burst into tears if I am not very careful; give me a moment. Will you be home for a while?"

"Not for just *a while*; actually, I've resigned my commission, afraid I'll be around on a permanent basis now." He turned to look at Alice and placed his hands on his hips. "And, if my mother hadn't mentioned the name I never would have known it was you. Alice Darcy!" He held out his arms. "Won't you greet me also?"

Although trembling with emotion on the inside, adulthood had brought at least a semblance of poise to Alice. "Of course, forgive me, Harry. I was just so surprised." The moment she went on tiptoe to kiss his cheek sparks ignited within her and she gasped. Amused, his gaze briefly locked onto hers.

"Oh, you can do better than that, Alice, can't you?" His hands pulled her toward him for a hug, his arms surrounded her. She could do nothing but hold on, if only to remain upright on wobbling knees, her eyes closing as she inhaled his familiar scent. In that brief embrace she felt his heart pounding against hers, felt his warm breath on her neck. He stepped back, cleared his throat and chuckled. "Well, not everything has changed. You're still too short for a decent cricket player."

She heard nothing, her senses still reeling from his touch.

"Well, I think we'd better be going." As Alice listened to her father speak, she wondered how he could sound so calm. Wasn't the room spinning wildly

out of control for the rest of them also? "It would not
do to arrive after Her Majesty and the Prince and then
need to beg for entrance."

Suddenly then everyone was bustling about. Darcy
helped Aunt Catherine to her feet as Amanda was
attempting a last minute smoothing of her husband's
always obstinate hair, Lizzy was locking arms with
her daughter and laughing merrily. Darcy tried to
forcefully demand order come forth from chaos as he
hurried them all through the door into the foyer.

"Harry, are you coming, son?" called Amanda over
her shoulder.

"Of course, Mama. I'm just retrieving my gloves – I
placed them here, somewhere. I'll be with you in a
moment." Quickly, Harry crossed out of sight toward
the sideboard and then stood staring blankly at the
wall, hoping no one had noticed his humiliating and
very physical reaction to *her*. He put a shaky hand to
his forehead and closed his eyes. Good lord but he was
in shock, completely disoriented, bewildered and
utterly dazed. He snatched the brandy decanter and
poured himself a drink, downing it in one gulp.

"Well, bloody hell," he muttered.

Chapter Thirty-Seven

The ballroom of the Duke of Devon's London home was ablaze with candles; Jewels glittered blindingly among these the most favored of England's renowned *haute ton*. All were waiting in great anticipation for young Queen Victoria and her beloved husband, Prince Albert, to arrive for their first social appearance together since the birth of their son and Royal heir, Albert Edward. There would be no dancing until the Royal couples' appearance but there was still an abundance of excitement. Groups of titled and aristocratic families mingled with other groups of titled and aristocratic families, and they waited.

Harry noticed none of it – he had to gain control of himself, he had to think. Standing apart from his family he laughed, greeted old friends, shook the hands of men with whom he had attended school, many now married and fathers. Military officers he had known over the years approached him warmly, old acquaintances were renewed.

Yet, even as he mingled with others, his thoughts were constantly elsewhere.

What sort of changeling is she he wondered, and not particularly happily. The shock of that first sight of her would remain with him always, burned into his mind and memory, now and forever.

Plain Little Alice - Ha!

'All delicious cheekbones and enchanting eyes' – hadn't that been his mother's loving description of Alice earlier in the evening when on their way to Pemberley House? Damn, what else had she said? He had paid her no heed, discounting any further comments as those of a doting godmother. The reality of Alice was stunning, and a rude awakening, rather like a lit match to your boot or cow dung in your saddle bags.

Whatever happened to the odd little duckling that had been 'all facial spots and large ears'? Bloody hell, it was not only her amazing grey eyes with their elegant dark brows and long lashes, or her luminous complexion, or her dramatic bone structure. It was also that glorious auburn hair, masses of dark silk-like tresses, the lips – moist, pink and full, luscious; the swan like neck, the shoulders white as doves' breasts, the bosom – *good lord the bosom* – very full, very firm and very high. And, had he actually become sexually aroused when having pulled her into his arms for a hug his fingers briefly touched the top swell of that equally well rounded bottom?

Mortifying...

Harry cleared his throat then downed another glass of wine, nodding absently as the conversations continued on around him – but, all the while he was catching glimpses of her in the crowd, of the men surrounding her, flirting with her. He grew more and more aggravated.

Appalling behavior...

She was smiling at every buffoon, every ass that approached; she was like some seasoned coquette, taking pleasure in every witless remark. Every time he heard her laughter his body tightened in response.

Look at her, would you? I mean, really...

She was even now touching some rakehell on the arm – this behavior of hers was insupportable. A lady never touched a gentleman, especially an old, leering, bastard such as that...that...who in bloody hell was that anyway? *Oh.*

It was the Archbishop of York.

I must be losing my mind.

A gentleman approached Alice now, as she spoke with the illustrious cleric; a man a bit more sophisticated than the boys who still hovered nearby, staring and whispering. This man he knew.

Harry approached his mother and pulled at her elbow. "Isn't that Sir John Percy over there, speaking with Alice?"

After glancing in the direction her son indicated Amanda hesitated before answering. She had seen an angry look flash across his face. "Yes. Do you remember him?" she asked.

"Indeed I do. He hasn't aged well, has he – appears to have mislaid the entire central strip of his hair."

"Don't be unkind, dear; he could be part of the family soon. I have heard from a most reliable source – all right, Auntie Eliza, but don't breathe a word – that a betrothal between them is being considered. If all goes as planned it could be announced as early as Christmastime."

"Christmas?"

"Yes. The wedding would be next summer or early autumn I suspect."

"Really? That's rather a long engagement isn't it? Not a very eager bridegroom." *Or has no need to be eager.* That unexpected thought made Harry's blood boil.

"Harry, shush! Nothing's been decided; I'm merely relating to you the speculations between two husband hunting Mamas. It would be quite the triumph for her... Harry! Please cease looking at him in that way, will you? I don't want you making a scene here. What's past is past."

He smiled and kissed her forehead. "Of course, mother."

"Oh Harry, I understand, dear, if you still harbor a bit of resentment over Celeste marrying the man; but, the fact is, she was ready for marriage and you simply were not. You were too eager to see the world – don't you recall, son? You were bursting for adventure and, oh, how you both would argue over *that!* And then for that girl to die so young! She had everything to live for – a loving husband, a beautiful daughter. How ironic if Alice, of all people, were to marry Percy now. Remember how those two would hiss and claw at each other? It was as if Celeste somehow felt threatened by a child nine years her junior. Frankly, I thought that rather petty of the girl. Alice was always a darling, always sweet, and how she adored you... Oh, Harry, I hope I am not upsetting you with my ramblings."

"Not at all." Now that he was calmer, he was thinking more rationally. When his father had mentioned this coupling Harry had thought it highly unlikely – but that was before he had seen Alice! Now he knew the sense of it; a beautiful young girl could easily attract an important man. This had happened with Sir John Percy before, had it not? Evidently, Alice Darcy was as ambitious as Celeste had been, chasing money and title. He felt his ardor for her cool a bit.

And, wasn't *this* the perfect solution to his problem! If Alice Darcy married Percy – became mother to Celeste' daughter, *his* daughter – the child would be welcomed openly as a part of his immediate family. He could be 'cousin' Harry to the child and allowed unlimited access; he would see her whenever he chose.

Unless Sir John decided to marry another…

He hoped not, that would make his situation impossible. No, no, no; he would make it his business this marriage take place, if it was at all within his power. Hopefully, Alice was still the adoring, obedient child of old and he could use that. He was not proud of the idea but he knew he could convince her to marry Percy, take advantage of her adoration of him.

He would 'court' them both, accompany them all the way to the altar if need be.

He only hoped he would survive it…

Chapter Thirty-Eight

The ballroom was gradually coming to order, the footmen now standing almost shoulder to shoulder against the walls, the crowd being encouraged, in truth begged, to move to the opposite sides of the immense ballroom and open a path through which the Royal Couple could pass.

Suddenly the excited murmur increased to a heated buzz. Queen Victoria and Prince Albert had indeed just arrived, would be entering momentarily; the orchestra began the traditional Trumpet Voluntary and people wedged in the back began jostling for a more advantageous position within the elongated ballroom. It was all sparkling chaos. The Darcy and Fitzwilliam families were large enough in numbers, and important enough in stature, to have secured a position in the front row at mid-point, and all the time they waited they were chatting and laughing among themselves, continuing their happy reunion.

Standing beside her brother George, Alice passed a gloved hand nervously across her hair, smoothing any stray wisps, her stomach fluttering in anticipation. She suddenly reached around him and tapped her father's arm. "Papa, John Percy has asked me for the first dance." To be heard over the deafening racket she needed to nearly shout, "...but I explained to him that might cause unnecessary speculation, so I secured another partner; could you send word down the line, remind Luke. If he grumbles at all tell him I can *unarrange* that carriage ride next week for him with Mary Bexton as easily as I *arranged* the thing. That will aid his conveniently 'spotty' memory."

Darcy nodded and turned to relay the message to Fitzwilliam who was standing on the other side of an oblivious Lady Catherine. Fitzwilliam tapped his finger beside his nose. "Right, say no more," he said then turned, whispered to his wife Amanda who spoke with their son Matthew, who in turn whispered to his brother Mark. Mark was horrified; he grabbed Luke by the shoulder. "Why on earth is Alice insisting you dance with Lady Margaret Beaton? That beast is nearly forty if she's a day. Even you can do better than that."

"Oh bloody hell..." Moaning, Luke wrinkled up his nose, leaned forward and cast a narrow eyed look of disapproval toward Alice. When he caught her eye he shook his head vigorously.

She scowled back at him.

"Well of all the...what right has Alice giving me the old fish eye back? First she blackmails me into dancing the first dance with her – causing me to *not* ask that lovely redheaded daughter of Lord Hemp – and now she wants me to dance with Margaret Beaton? If she wants Margaret 'Bloody' Beaton to dance so badly let her ask her herself. Honestly, Alice can be so demanding at times."

By the distressed look on Alice's face Harry surmised that whatever the original message was, it had been mishandled; perhaps he could turn this to his advantage. He jostled down the line of waiting dignitaries, stopping behind her; but, before he could say a word an excited hush enveloped the room. After three taps of his baton the conductor raised his arms for a timpani drum roll which was followed momentarily by quiet.

Then the music for "God Save the Queen" began.

Her Majesty Queen Victoria, and Albert, Prince Consort, appeared at the top of the staircase and instantly a rush of whispers swept through the entire gathering, with dry eyes being few and far between. Everyone had turned to face them, all had begun to sing. *"God save our gracious Queen, long live our noble Queen, God save our Queen."*

Victoria smiled warmly. Everyone was moved by the sight of this fresh faced young woman, and how could they not? Here was the living symbol of their homeland, Sovereign Queen as well as a loving wife, and a new mother. The world seemed to have changed overnight taking away with it the indolence and decadence of the Courts of George IV and William IV; before them now stood wholesome youth and the bright future of England.

When the anthem ended the applause began, swelling as the Royal couple slowly descended the staircase.

"The gel as her figure back already. Well done!" Even Aunt Catherine was beaming.

The Royal Couple began to make their greetings, slowly passing the long line of waiting dignitaries, stopping occasionally to say a word to one special person, smiling recognition to another, nodding acknowledgement to all. Everyone bowed and curtseyed to the couple as they passed. Occasionally someone too far back to see properly would even shout out a greeting. The entire crowd was enraptured.

When the Queen reached where Lady Catherine de Bourgh stood she smiled and began to speak; however, the doyenne was determined to complete a formal court bow, a traditional St. James Bow, to her sovereign, something she had been unable to accomplish without toppling over since the reign of George III. Victoria immediately raised her hand to stay her. "Lady Catherine, you need not bow quite so low to us any longer and how very good it is to see you again."

"Oh Your Majesty forgive me, my age has robbed me of the ability to give you proper obeisance."

"You have given proper obeisance to many monarchs before; let us say your account is paid in full."

"May I express my felicitations to you, and say how pleased we all are that you have produced an heir so soon. You must have tried very hard."

Although still quite young Victoria was an accomplished diplomat already, accustomed to all manner of people and odd comments; without blushing or stammering over Catherine's remark she moved the conversation forward. "I see you have your nephews with you." The Queen smiled warmly at the beautiful young men and women standing on either side of their respective parents. She first acknowledged Fitzwilliam and Amanda and their huge brood. "You have a lovely family, Lord Somerton, Lady Somerton."

Fitzwilliam and his wife bowed and curtseyed, both beaming with pride. "Thank you, Your Majesty."

Queen Victoria then turned toward Darcy and Lizzy. "You have a very charming family as well, Mr. Darcy, Mrs. Darcy." The Queen motioned toward Alice, who curtsied. "She's very lovely, is she not Albert?" The Prince nodded his agreement politely. "What is your name?"

"Miss Alice Darcy, your Majesty."

"You were recently presented, were you not?"

"Yes, I was, ma'am."

"Very sweet." And before Alice could register another thought the couple had continued on. Having been singled out by the queen she felt absurdly close to sobbing.

"That was a magnificent *coup d'état*, Alice." Surprised, she turned to see Harry standing behind her. As she looked up she felt helplessly at sea with it all, with the entire evening, emotional and unguarded – her infatuation for him could not be concealed at that moment if she tried. His mouth went dry and his heart constricted, then it began to pound. He actually needed to consciously stop himself from reaching for her, hugging her to him.

"I am still shaking," she mumbled in awe.

He gave himself a mental slap. "Um...What was that message you just sent down to Luke? I'm afraid it got rather jumbled."

"Oh, nothing important. I forget, really." Her mind was mush, feelings were overwhelming her and Harry stood too near. It was becoming all too much.

"Alice wanted to avoid giving the appearance of preference to a gentleman here for the all important 'first dance', so she coerced Luke into taking her out. However," Alice's face flushed with embarrassment as her father explained over music that had already loudly begun. "...it appears Luke's now asking Lord Beaton's widow to dance for some reason. How strange. Anyway, Harry, why don't you take Alice into the first dance? Unless you've already..."

"No, I have asked no one else. I would be honored, Uncle Wills."

"Is anyone going to consult me about this?" Her heart pounded with both indignation and excitement. How would she ever survive dancing with Harry

Penrod, being held in his arms? How would she bear another moment *not* in his arms?

"Alice? I won't embarrass you, I promise. I dance much better now than I did when you were five years and I ten and five – and you won't need to stand on my feet this time." His gaze on her was gentle and loving. He seemed to be searching her face, her hair, capturing her image, every freckle, every lash. He settled finally on her lips and the room became suddenly still. "I won't hurt you, Alice," he whispered, his eyes looking dark beneath half closed lids.

Alice was speechless.

He placed her hand atop his arm then turned to smile at Darcy. "I'll take grand care of her, Uncle Wills, keep the hounds at bay as it were, for as long as she wishes." When he looked back into Alice's clear grey eyes, heaven help him, his heart began pounding even harder in his chest. He must be mad, he thought. This was a most grievous mistake, most foolhardy, and he knew it – but, he could not stop himself. He was that desperate to hold her in his arms, just for a moment.

"Thank you, son." Darcy had already turned toward his wife and they processed with the others onto the dance floor, everyone now waiting as the Queen and the Prince came forward to take their place in the center.

"Shall *we* begin, Alice?" He stared at her in such a way that the simple question seemed suddenly to have many meanings.

"Oh, yes, Harry."

A baton was tapped, then silence. Chopin in B minor and the music of a waltz began. Victoria and Albert took their first twirling steps alone but soon the general dancing commenced, two hundred couples spinning and weaving together, a choreography of perfection, a magnificent swirl of satin, diamonds, feathers and lace, all illuminated by a thousand candles.

And, as they circled along with the others, Harry remembered when Alice had been a bundle of silk and ribbons before, held in his nervous young arms, after her christening at St. Paul's Cathedral. Then he remembered a bouncy toddler, giggling and squealing, her face smeared with peach juice, her chubby fingers reaching up for him to wipe clean. He had helped teach her how to swim and ride a pony, had cleaned off bloody knees, dried tears from her eyes.

First he had loved her as a baby, then as a sort of pesky little sister – what was she now to him? The emotions that heated his blood and filled him with intense desire were neither fatherly nor brotherly.

He remembered a birthmark she had on her tiny bottom when an infant, one Kathy and Anne Marie had decided resembled a frog, and he grinned wickedly. "I wonder what it looks like now, Little Alice." His voice was deep and raspy.

She had been watching him, sighing dreamily; when he spoke, her gaze drifted from his lovely eyes to his mouth.

"What did you say?"

Seeming in a dream himself Harry realized he wanted nothing more than to kiss her, right there, right then, before Queen and God and everyone, throw her over his shoulder, escape and never look back. His desire for her was nearly overwhelming him.

"I say, pardon me? May I cut in?"

Harry stopped. Confused and livid at whoever was intruding into their private world he spun around, wanting to confront the trespasser. It was Sir John Percy. Then it all came back to him. The man who had taken Celeste from him – the man he had hated for a

while, then envied, then pitied, and who now seemed
sad and forlorn, nervous and weak.

The man raising my daughter.

The man whose favor Harry had to win.

"Pardon me. I wondered if I could...I mean I was
hoping I could cut in, please. Alice, don't be cross with
me." Sir John blinked up into the eyes of the taller,
younger, much larger gentleman and swallowed.
"You're her cousin, Sir Harold Penrod, are you not?
It's a pleasure to meet you, sir. I read all about your
heroism." They shook hands. "I thought I recognized
you from newssheet drawings. Forgive me, but, I
hoped perhaps I could cut in here, just for a moment. I
know Alice wished to avoid the inevitable gossip. You
see we are (ahem) courting, in a fashion; and, well,
now that you've danced with her for a few minutes –
nothing more respectable than dancing with a well
regarded male relative, what – and, before the other
young bucks begin to crowd in..."

"No – absolutely – quite right." Harry backed away
from Alice and bowed. "Of course, Sir John..."

"Harry?" When Alice looked back into Harry's eyes
the passion she had seen there was gone, as if she had
imagined it; he appeared completely indifferent to her
now. She had been deluding herself, still a childish
fool, a dreamer and always would be, for Harry.

"Enjoy yourselves, Sir John, Miss Alice. I'm off to
the gaming rooms." A warm smile twitched at the
corners of Harry's mouth as he bowed and turned
away.

"What a splendid chap." Sir John cleared his throat.
"His size is a bit off putting at first but he really is
most pleasant. I believe he was acquainted with my
late wife. Well, Alice, shall we?" And before she could
object Alice and John were swallowed up into the

twirling mob, anonymous among the hundreds of other couples turning in unison.

Chapter Thirty-Nine

"Will this night ever end? I've never been so bored in my life." Luke had always hated inactivity such as this; he leaned his forearms on the upper gallery banister and watched the hundreds of couples below primly socialize. It was midnight and he had danced a total of three times – once with the very odd Margaret Beaton, a sacrifice asked of him by his cousin Alice, although why he hadn't a clue, then once with his mother and once with his Auntie Eliza. His obligations in that area were, blessedly, discharged; and, he had been anxious to depart since dinner had been served, two hours before. There was no real reason to remain.

"Why can't we sneak off to a pub or a boxing match or something, anything other than watching all these ancient nabobs look down their noses at each other?"

Matthew slumped into the chair behind his brother and closed his eyes. "Formal balls are always mind numbingly dull, made more so this evening with the Royal Couple's attendance. Everyone's on their best behavior, hence the boredom."

"There's a match tonight over at the Dog and Duck – Patterson will be fighting, and Bill O'Brien is representing Cheapside. It may still be going on. Oh look, the Archbishop is dancing with Aunt

Catherine...seems to be some sort of struggle going on as to who will lead... "

"Nothing to wager on there." Hands in his pockets, Mark strolled forward to lean a hip against the banister and have his own look. "She'll have him pinned in a minute, best flat hand wrestler I ever saw. To return to your question Luke as to leaving – it's not done until Her Majesty and the Prince have gone and I hear she's having a wonderful time." He turned back toward his brother Matt. "I say she is awfully pretty, isn't she?"

"Yes, she really is. Motherhood and Prince Albert seem to suit her. If only there were some young women here not in on the marriage hunt! Max Robins has taken a mistress I hear, a widow. That's what I need – an eager woman."

"You mean a desperate woman." Kathy and Alice had approached without the boys noticing.

"Well, that would certainly help, yes," he smiled. "Did I mention that you both look extremely healthy tonight? Don't roll your eyes, Kathy, that's the best compliment I can come up with as your brother. Where're George and Harry?"

"They've been in the gaming rooms since dinner ended – here they are now, coming up the staircase toward us even as we speak. It's high time you two emerged. How'd you both do?"

"I broke even but it was Harry who impressed us all."

"George you are such a trial at times." Harry stopped beside Mark and Luke at the banister and peered down with them to watch the lackluster couples below.

"Won big did he?"

"No. Lost two hundred pounds." George nudged Harry and grinned. "Worst luck I've ever seen. But actually to be fair, it wasn't just bad luck was it? You really are the most appalling card player I've ever seen, always were – no skill whatsoever. I'm not even certain you recognize there are four suits; *and*, you have the attention span of a very small pillow."

"Who are you again?" Harry's gaze swept across his forlorn looking cluster of cousins. "Well, this is certainly a glum looking, if well dressed, group. Why is no one downstairs dancing?" His perusal rested briefly on Alice but she was distracted and distant. She looked away, still angry with him he supposed for allowing Percy to cut into their dance, but it was all for the best. Harry had no intention of standing in the way of *that* marriage. Not in the least. And he refused to think about how excruciatingly difficult it had been to walk away from her, to hand her over to another man, especially that man. His jaw clenched at the thought and he found himself suddenly cross with everyone and everything.

"Luke's bored. What shall we do about that?" Matthew laced his fingers together behind his head and looked from face to face. "Come on, let's have some ideas – but, whatever we do we'll need to remain up here. The Mamas downstairs were hounding him – it's that floppy hair of his; drives their daughters wild."

"Isn't there a library on this level? We could see if they've any scientific journals there, read a bit." Mark's academic suggestion was met with moaning protests and calls for the vengeance of God.

"Good lord, it was just a suggestion." Mark groused.

Then Kathy grinned. "I have an idea. Why don't we play sardines? This house is perfect for it, don't you think, and it's laid out a bit like Somerton. There should be plenty of places in which to hide just off this gallery alone, in fact I believe this whole wing is open for the public. We could be lost for hours and hours and no one would suspect." She looked toward her fiancé George from beneath lowered lashes, reaching out for his hand.

"Well, all right." Matthew pulled himself up out of the chair. "Anything to stave off death by ennui – just make certain you two don't go off on your own for too long. I've got my eye on you, Darcy. There will be hell to pay if my sister were to do something stupid. Well, more stupid than usual."

Kathy shook her head. "You're an idiot."

"I love you too."

The second floor was indeed immense with a number of different galleries, endless halls leading this way and that, mysterious rooms, hidden alcoves and out of sight balconies. They decided to limit themselves to only the public rooms that adjoined directly to that particular gallery where they stood. Alice was selected as the first to hide and so the others closed their eyes and counted.

After several false starts she found an unobtrusive room which she entered silently. It was dark within, the only light coming from a doorway opening onto a very small balcony, so she ran there and undid the drapery ties, confident that the curtains would conceal her. *There*, she sighed wistfully, *finally I'm alone*; then, leaning her back against the door frame, she settled in to think of the evening's events and wait for the others to find her.

All night she had danced with the same men who always surrounded her, young bucks and old, eager to impress with talk of their lineage or their wealth. Only twice had she danced with John Percy, the most dances socially acceptable to any couple, but he had brought her endless refreshments, had come to her side after each set ended, publicly making his claim on her, ensuring the exclusion of any others. This was all Harry's doing and the very thought brought tears to her eyes. How often had she dreamed of the day he would return to her and find her so impossibly beautiful that he would immediately drop to his knees and pledge his undying love?

Reality was so different. Instead of being enamored of her he had handed his obligation off to the first man who came forward, thinking no more of her now than he had when she was twelve years old and so pathetically in love with him.

She brushed a tear from her cheek.

"What's this?" The voice was a husky whisper only, but she would recognize it anywhere. "Crying, sweet? Did you fear no one would find you?" His tone held a gentle tease.

"Harry." It was more whimper than statement. "How did you? Find me that is – I thought I had the perfect hiding spot."

"You do, goose, but you forget I know you too well."

She arched a skeptical eyebrow at him.

"Well, that and I saw your very pretty slippers peeking from beneath the curtain. Are you still angry with me?"

"I never said I was angry with you, Harry."

Now he appeared skeptical.

"Well, I was a bit disappointed with your haste to hand me over to Sir John. Why did you do it, Harry? John was the man I had hoped to avoid for that dance, everyone here gossips so, and you knew that. Or did you?"

"I had an idea that it was he, but why play that sort of game Alice, why wait?"

"You really don't know, do you?"

"No, I don't. He wants to marry you doesn't he, and you're seriously considering it?"

She nodded, her eyes downcast.

"I say snatch him up then; he adores you. I am certain you're aware he's a most premiere catch, has everything a young girl like you could want – a historic family, prestige, great wealth. No need to play coy any longer, child, you've hooked him right and proper. Now you need merely reel him into the boat and beat him senseless."

"Is that truly your opinion of me? Do you think me that shallow?" Just then they heard laughing voices outside the door.

"Come on, this is nowhere to hide; I know of someplace better and we need to talk." With that Harry pulled her across the room and pushed open a hidden door that led into a servant's hallway cluttered with carts, odd chairs and brooms. When closed the door was flush with the wall and hardly noticeable from the outside.

"How did you know this was here?"

"I've been to this home before, for parties, you know. Was that your foot? Sorry." It was very nearly pitch dark with the door closed.

"Just how many women have you dragged in here, Harry Penrod?"

"Sh! Someone's entering the room."

They heard the door to the adjacent room open. "Harry, are you in here?" Matthew stood in the doorway squinting into the dim light. "Come on, Harry, where are you?" Alice began to say something but Harry covered her mouth with his hand; with the other he pulled her to him, pressed her head gently to his shoulder and whispered to be still. They stood like that, waiting in the dark, her forehead resting beneath his chin, her mouth soft and wet against his palm. Harry's resolve to remain aloof from her began evaporating swiftly.

His nose began to nuzzle her temple.

"Is Alice in here?" It was Mark now entering the room.

"I don't know. Alice are you here? She doesn't answer — she's a great Sardine player that way." Matthew had lit one of the candles and was staring at a display case. "Look at these pistols will you? They are bloody gorgeous. Must have cost a fortune."

Alice looked up at Harry causing his hand to slip from her mouth. They could barely make each other out, but the heat of their bodies and the pace of their breathing kept increasing. He could feel her breasts shifting against his chest, smelled the scented powder from her bath. Gently he pressed his lips to her forehead, to her eyes, to her cheek, her neck, her ear...

When she turned her face into his palm and kissed his hand Harry began to lose control. His body pushed hers back until she hit the wall behind her.

"What the bloody hell was that?' asked Mark.

"Dunno, servants more than likely, moving furniture. Did you see this saber? It looks a bit like father's old sword."

He was ravenous for her lips. His head slanted and his mouth came down hard, his tongue sliding deep inside, his arms encircling her like a vice. While he feasted he felt himself grow hard against her stomach and he immediately abandoned her lips to nip at her shoulders. His hands stroked them, caressed her back, her waist. Reaching for her bottom he cupped those round, firm, little cheeks and squeezed tenderly, pressed them together, lifted her deliberately to fit snugly against him. His mouth again took hers, his tongue invaded ruthlessly.

Half laughing and half groaning he whispered into her ear. "Alice, darling, am I dreaming this?" His hands cupped her breasts and fondled them, molded them. He kissed the tears from her eyes. He bent and pressed his face deep into her cleavage.

Alice was in shock. *This was Harry.* She was with Harry and he was doing wonderful things to her, giving her sensations and feelings she'd never known existed. Equally on fire as he, and having absolutely no idea what to do, she suddenly grabbed hold of his own round, firm, bottom and squeezed with all her might.

He bit back a yelp and immediately pulled her hands away. "Don't – please, Alice. I am losing control here."

"Sorry," she whispered, desperately. "Seemed like the thing to do." The ridge pressing between them became somehow larger and their mouths collided once again.

"Remember Da's old pistol, from the army? It's a wonder he shot anything at all with that. This room isn't off the kitchens is it? Sounds as if someone's eating soup..."

"Speaking of Da, have you told him yet that you're leaving for America?" Mark studied an ancient painting over the fireplace of a small child sitting upon a pony. "This is nice."

"Looks like the old Duke as a child, dressed in a frock, doesn't it? Hope it's a lad and not a lass anyway – wouldn't want to be caught with a woman who looked like that. What did you ask me? Oh, right. No, I haven't told Da. He's so angry with me most days that I don't think he'll find it a great hardship for us to be apart for a few months. Have you decided? Are you coming with me or not?"

Mark shrugged his shoulders but couldn't bring himself to look at his brother. "I'd like to, Matt, you know that. It's just that...well..."

"It's that woman, right? Bloody hell, all problems seem to begin and end with a woman, don't they? Well, suit yourself Markie, it's your loss." Matthew's disappointed bravado could fool anyone but his twin.

"If it wasn't for her you know I'd love nothing better than to see America with you; we'd have a grand adventure, that's for certain. I just don't seem to have any sense anymore; she's consuming me, Matt."

Alice's hands glided swiftly up the front of Harry's chest then slid into his hair. She pulled his head down, pressed her lips harder against his. His mouth was devouring her, his tongue probing and licking and driving into her with an urgency that made her heart pound. As he turned his head, slanted his mouth again against hers, his hand skimmed down the outside of her thigh – he pulled her leg up, his hand cupping the back of her knee for a moment, then he pushed back hem of her gown and slid his hand beneath.

She was undone, wild; she rubbed against him, she grabbed for his arms, his shoulders.

"The servants here sound awfully clumsy, don't they? Let's try the next hallway – I saw a billiard room there." The door opened and Harry's brothers left, closing the door behind them, the sound somehow reaching into the mush that was now Harry's brain. He turned his face away long enough to gasp for air but Alice whimpered and pulled at him.

"Alice wait." Harry pushed away. "Have mercy, girl, let me get my head straight, please." Inhaling deeply he stepped far back from her and bent over at the waist, hands on knees. He knew he was seconds from humiliating himself. After a moment he straightened, opened the door a crack then turned to speak with her. His heart stilled.

She looked aroused, flushed, thoroughly kissed and sexy as hell. She launched herself forward again. "Stop! You remain right where you are!" Pressing a hand across his mouth he shook his head. "Dear lord, you've bewitched me, that's exactly what you've done, Alice Darcy. I'm too old for this nonsense; I must regain some semblance of propriety here." But in reality he feared it was much too late, years too late. He was obsessed with her, he wanted to grab her and plunge deep inside her; his body ached for her.

"I love you, Harry," she gasped. "I love you so much. I love you more than anyone or anything in this world." The enormity of what she kept repeating gradually hit him. He turned his head away and she feared at that moment she had lost him.

"Don't turn from me, Harry, please."

He looked back at her and smiled. "Love me, Alice, more than anything?" His hand went to her cheek. "You don't really believe that, do you?"

"It's true. I've loved you forever, Harry."

He took deep breaths and as he attempted to calm himself he patted her hair into place and straightened the shoulders of her gown. "Well, if that is indeed the truth, I believe I'd better exercise greater control of this situation." Taking hold of her wrist he led her from the servant's hallway and into the visitor room once again, closing the door behind them. He took some time before he spoke. "We've been missing too long, and this is no place for any proper discussion of your future. I'll come to your house tomorrow. Your father will be home, will he not?"

Alice was in shock at first, but now she understood. He didn't trust himself anymore; and, truth be told, she didn't trust herself much either. He was correct, they would have to do this the proper way, make their arrangements.

The dream of her young life was suddenly only hours away from becoming her reality. And, once he had spoken with her father, there could be more intimacy between them without guilt, more time to be alone without society's recriminations. Sneaking kisses behind closed doors was for sporting girls, not respectable young ladies.

"I understand, Harry."

"Do you really, Alice? Excellent. No! Don't you come one step closer to me, you siren! Not until I've spoken with your father."

She nodded, happy at last. "Whatever you say, Harry." Tomorrow she would be Harry's and the world would know it. After all the years she had loved him, her moment had finally arrived.

Chapter Forty

The following day, Alice Darcy glided into the breakfast room to join her family for their first meal, although it was well past noon. They had not returned home until four in the morning and all had slept late. Radiantly happy she moved smoothly behind the chair of her brother George and bent to kiss the top of his head. "Good afternoon, dearest brother."

"Must you shout?" His face was an odd hue.

"Too much of a good thing, George?" asked his mother.

"I have no idea to what you are referring, but please, mother, if you have a care for me at all, don't clink that spoon quite so vigorously."

Lizzy's chuckle caused her son to wince once again.

Alice went to her father and kissed his forehead. "Good afternoon, my darling Papa. Is this not the most gloriously beautiful day?" In fact, it was foggy as pea soup outside and the dampness was making Darcy's knees ache. Curious, he put his paper down and stared at her. Then he noticed her dress.

"What are you wearing, Alice? Are you going out?" Instead of her usual comfortable jumper and slippers she had on one of her new daring outfits, a pink confection with white lace at her puffed cap sleeves and around the scooped neckline, her hair was piled high upon her head in an intricate and elegant manner, little curls bobbing about at her temples. "...and what in the world have you done with your hair?" His daughter's hair was her least favorite morning chore, the length and weight of it more bother than anything. Generally it was pulled back from her face and tied with a ribbon at the neck, or braided and carelessly coiled. Rarely did she bother to fuss with curls when at home.

"Don't listen to those two, Alice." Lizzy offered her cheek for Alice's kiss. "My child, you look lovely today. I am gratified that one member of my family was sensible last evening and did not expose themselves to ridicule."

A blush came to Alice's cheeks and she turned her face away.

After a moment of studiously scrutinizing her daughter, Lizzy put down her fork. "Are you expecting a visitor today?"

Alice often had suspected mothers were mind readers, her Mama's comment now solid verification. "No. No visitors." She strolled to the buffet, picked up a plate and placed a single coddled egg on it, along with one or two pieces of fruit and cheese. Returning to her customary place at the table she sat.

"If that's all you're going to eat then you must be ill." Darcy peered at her from above the newspaper. "You usually tuck away ten times that amount, easily. In fact, most days you could devour the provisions of an entire boys' public school."

"Well, goodness, is everything I do so worthy of comment?" She sought immediately to change the subject, divert suspicion. "Georgie, why are you home and not at your place on Curzon Street with the twins?"

"Actually, I'm no longer living there, left the leasing details for Matt and Mark to sort out since Kathy and my home is ready to occupy. I've been bringing my things there – Alice can't you just pick the food apart with your fingers? It's only fruit and that knife is a bit noisy. Thank you – I have been moving my things to the new house slowly but the bed doesn't arrive until later today. In fact, Matt, Mark and Luke are meeting me there tonight for supper – no women allowed I'm afraid. We're going to rough it as Matt says. By the way Mother, that reminds me, can you tell cook to fix up something that I can serve. Nothing fancy, five or six removes should do very nicely."

"The Spartans could have learned a thing or two from you boys..." Darcy mumbled from behind his newssheet.

"I heard that. I said we were roughing it, not barbarians."

"I refuse to burden our servants with extra work." Lizzy held up her hand to deflect his imminent pleading. "You may, however, ask cook *yourself,* but it's entirely up to her whether or not to agree – I want you to make that perfectly clear to her. She's not indentured you know; and, you will compensate her royally for any service she provides."

"You've become a labor leader suddenly. Who are you and what have you done with our mother?"

"Never mind that. Where will you be eating your daily meals until your own staff is in place?"

He smiled as adorably as he could at his mother. "I thought I would just eat here. There's always too much turmoil at the Fitzwilliam's dinner table; spoils my digestion. Perhaps I could bring my laundry by as well. Oh, and my sewing. I've one or two shirts that need mending." George yawned and stretched his arms. "I tell you it's truly wonderful to be out on my own."

Darcy began to chuckle.

"Well, this will always be your home...," as she spoke Lizzy kept a concerned eye on her daughter – something was unsettling about her this morning. "... but you may not burden our servants. When is your staff coming on?" At his guilt ridden stare his mother's back straightened. "You are *not* taking our staff, George!"

"It's only for a short while, Mama. Kathy has that part organized wonderfully only I have no idea when or who or what."

"All right, all right. Perhaps you can ask one or two of the servants if they'd like to assist you for the interim – you and Hudson were always close, I'm certain he wishes to remain with you as well, yes that's what I thought – but, the rest are only on loan, just until your new staff arrives, and you will pay them all extra for this, *and* it must be cleared with Mr. Winters."

"What time are the boys due for your dinner tonight?" Alice was becoming uneasy. Awake all morning she had been waiting for Harry to arrive and speak with her father, now the afternoon was well underway.

"They're coming by at around eight I think. We will eat like swine, play cards, belch...typical manly behavior." He turned to his father. "You are invited as well, Papa, of course." George adored his father and had not meant to exclude him from the dinner, but very often conversations among young men would be scandalous to their parents. Parents knew so little about love and sex.

Especially sex.

"Splendid, George, I should love to attend." He laughed outright at his son's horrified expression. "That was a jest, George; I have no desire to hear boys lie about their conquests. Although you do realize I *was* young once – around the time of the Flood, I know but still, Fitzwilliam and I were both a bit wild at one time. I'd have many a hair raising story to add, I can tell you..." Darcy stopped speaking when he saw the skepticism in his son's eyes. "... however, I will spare you that."

"You are good and kind, Father, and thank you on behalf of your son and nephews for not providing us with what I am certain are splendidly lurid details of your debauched youth." George pushed back his chair, winced at the noise, and stood. "Well, if you'll all excuse me, I think I'll go back to bed for a while and pray for death, or at least for my head to fall off – whichever is first."

Lizzy glared at him. "That's not at all amusing, George."

"Sorry, ma'am, and please stop slamming your napkin around."

A quarter hour later Mr. Winters entered the room. "Yes, Winters," said Darcy.

"Sir Harold Penrod is here to speak with you, sir. I've put him in the day room off your library, sir."

"Heavens, Winters, Sir Harry is family, not visitor. Tell him to join us in here."

"I mentioned that to him, sir, but he was very specific as to where he wished to speak with you."

"Oh, I see." Darcy folded his paper after a moment and rose. "I hope nothing is amiss at Fitz's home." He stood quickly and left the room.

Alice could barely contain herself. Leaving her nearly untouched food she rushed to the window, straining to see if Harry had brought the carriage. Perhaps they could go out for the afternoon, be alone for a while.

"Alice?" Lizzy's intuition never failed and her alarm was growing.

"Mmm? Yes, Mummy?" There was no carriage, but she recognized Harry's magnificent stallion, Cobbler, being held by a footman in front of the house. Such a disappointment, that. Well, perhaps he couldn't stay long this morning.

"What is it, Alice? You may as well tell me now child."

Alice twirled, joy glistening in her bright eyes. "Oh, Mummy, he loves me. Harry loves me. He's here to ask Papa for my hand. He loves me, Mummy."

Lizzy froze; fear for her child seemed to stop her heart. "Are you speaking of *our* Harry, Alice? Harry Penrod?"

"Yes! Yes, of course I am! What other Harry do we know? Harry loves me and he's asking Papa for my hand even now. I am so very nervous," she held out her hands. "Look, see how I'm trembling. Oh, Mummy, I love him so very much."

"Yes, dearest, I know you've always been fond of him. Did he actually *say* that he loved you, Alice? Did he *say* he was going to ask your father for your hand, use those actual words?"

Alice became exasperated with her mother's slow wits; however, she retained admirable control of her temper and smiled indulgently. "No, Mummy, he *showed* me he loved me! He left me no room for doubt – believe me in this."

There, *that* had shocked her mother into silence.

"What do you mean, he *showed* you?" Lizzy began to stand, her heart now pounding.

"He kissed me, are you satisfied? Last night – at the ball – he kissed me with all the passion of a man deeply in love and then told me he needed to speak with father. Yes! He loves me, Mummy."

"Oh, Alice. A man's kiss can mean so little at times; perhaps the result of too much wine or merely being alone with a beautiful woman, the mood romantic and the opportunity convenient..."

"Harry would never play that sort of game with *me*! Why do you never see my side of things? You just don't want me to be happy."

"Alice, that is simply not true. I merely want you to wait a while, see what your father has to say – heavens, see what Harry has to say first. He may feel obliged for giving you the wrong impression last night, for having been carried away. The poor man has been away for years and now, with one kiss..."

"So you are saying the only way he would offer for me would be out of obligation."

"No! Alice, you are deliberately misconstruing my words!"

"He was very ardent, mother, we both were. There! I cannot make it any clearer to you that our feelings are of mutual passion and devotion. Oh, what's the use; you'd never understand such ardor in a thousand years. I refuse to speak with you any further about this. I will go to my room and wait for Father's summons, and then you'll see you were wrong, mother, wrong! Harry loves me. He loves me!" Alice ran from the room in tears.

Chapter Forty-One

It had been over an hour and Alice *assumed* Harry and her father were still behind closed doors, although she had been locked in her room the whole time. Initially, when she had run from her mother, she had stopped to listen at the door; heard them laughing within, could smell the cigar smoke, had even seen the butler enter with a bottle of brandy, yet neither man had asked her to enter, nor had they even called for her mother. Alice brushed aside her growing fears and came down the stairs to listen again at the door. All was quiet now. Knocking softly she realized her hands were shaking.

"Come in."

She looked about the room. "Where is he?"

"Where is...? Oh, Harry? He left a while ago. Do you see my pipe? I'm certain it was here a moment – ah, there it is. Yes, he was in a bit of a rush, said to give you and your mother his regards. Seems he's an engagement for the theater late this evening and wanted to pick up flowers for the young lady; such a thoughtful fellow. Did he tell you he's leaving to visit his relatives in Boston? Yes. He's sailing shortly after George and Kathy's wedding, and Matt is to go also. Since I'm to see Fitz at White's tonight he was hoping I could broach the subject of their taking Luke with them, see how much of an uproar it would cause. My goodness but that makes me nostalgic for the times Fitz and I used to have. The Fitzwilliam lads going to America! Makes one shudder; serves the colonies right though... Alice, what is it?"

Darcy had been rambling on and on, returning a number of books to their rightful shelf positions, his back to his daughter. When he turned he saw how deathly pale she had become. Her back was pressed up against the wall and her hands covered her heart as if she were in pain. "Alice!"

"He said nothing else?"

Darcy was at her side in a moment. He reached for her arm but Alice held him off, waved off his concerns. "Did he not say anything else, Papa?"

"Well, he was pleased at how smitten Sir John Percy is with you; in fact, he was quite animated on what a magnificent match *that* would be for you. I suppose he's right, I can't tell anymore. I told him whatever made you happy was fine with your mother and me. I think you'd better sit down. I'll pour you a brandy."

"No." She shook her head. "No, thank you, Papa."

Darcy watched as tears overflowed her eyes to stream down her cheeks, and he cursed himself for a fool. How had he not foreseen this? He knew his daughter, he knew of her lifelong attachment to the boy, her schoolgirl fantasies. She had been waiting so long for his return, and now this. "Oh, my poor Alice. He wished you all the happiness in the world, and particularly mentioned you'd be a wonderful mother for Sir John's daughter, Christine; seemed particularly eager she be included in future family gatherings should you marry John. That's perfectly understandable, really, since she is all that is left..."

"...of Celeste." Alice finished the sentence for her father. All that was left of *him and Celeste,* she corrected in her thoughts. "I should have known," she whispered. "It was the child; it was all about the child." The little girl looked so like Harry that Alice was amazed there had never been gossip. *His child.* The prospect of being stepmother to Harry's daughter had been the main reason for her decision to marry Sir John. The moment Percy had introduced her to Christine, Alice had known the truth and had loved her almost as her own.

"You are frightening me. Come and sit, I insist upon it, Alice. Do you have a headache?" He led her to a chair and as she sat he placed his hands gently upon her shoulders. She was trembling. "You're cold, is that it? Are you feverish? No, then you'd be hot. What can I do, Alice? Damn it to hell speak to me, what can I do?" Crouching before her Darcy took out his handkerchief and began to dab at her tears.

"I'm all right, Papa. Truly I am. Just give me a moment." Alice took the handkerchief from him and pressed it hard against her eyes, but her sobs only grew worse. After a few tense moments she finally spoke. "Do you think you could find Mama for me?"

Chapter Forty-Two

The next weeks were given over completely to wedding preparations. Apparently the entire city of London was abuzz regarding the upcoming nuptials of Bennet George Darcy and The Lady Katherine Marie Fitzwilliam, the ceremony to be held Wednesday, the eighth of September, 1841, St. George's Cathedral, Mayfair. Many had their parts to play – vendors, clerics, sisters, brothers, cousins, four parents, several aunts, a few uncles – and all this activity was being orchestrated by none other than the Grande Dame herself, Lady Catherine de Bourgh, who was in daily, if not hourly, contact with the rector.

The Rector had come to accept the entire experience as both a trial by fire and as a true test of his faith.

During those weeks, Harry and Alice saw very little of each other. He was busy restoring the house in which he now resided, a home built by his great grandfather and populated by a succession of Penrods ever since; the home he had inherited along with the family title of baronet. Penwood was a small but proud property which stood mere blocks from both the Darcy's London home, Pemberley House, and the Fitzwilliam London home, Crossgate. With the help and guidance of his mother, and sisters Beth and Margaret, new furniture was arriving almost daily, old furniture was being reupholstered and refinished, new draperies measured and stitched, prior servants sought out, new servants interviewed.

Occasionally Harry would see Alice at the opera or at the ballet seated always in the Percy's opulent box, the marriage between the couple a foregone conclusion in society's eyes. Only a formal announcement was now needed. Each time he would tell himself he must go there and ingratiate himself, make amends for his abysmal behavior. He would need to regain her favor if only for his daughter's sake; but, he never could quite control his emotions long enough to approach them. Instead he would remain rooted in his seat – seething – then be angry with himself for seething – watching her smile at Percy, or laugh at a witty remark from Percy, or place her hand on Percy's arm. The man obviously had much more strength of character than Harry since he never appeared to react to her touch, whereas Harry was pretty well certain he'd have been dragging her off into the shadows every five minutes.

He saw them at musicales also, and twice at Gunter's but he just could not approach them. Instead he would leave immediately and spend the next few days stewing in torturous thoughts of what they probably did together when alone. Not even the now certainty of seeing his daughter in the future could calm the jealous rage rising within him.

Alice was busy in her own right. She had decided to forego much of the little season's activities to spend quiet time with John Percy. His daughter still in the country, the couple took advantage of this time to be alone together, to become better acquainted and to smooth out the differences that were becoming worrisome to them both.

Sir John found he was not exactly shocked, but rather somewhat alarmed with Alice's 'blue stocking' tendencies. Specifically what bothered was her peculiar interest in Roman history, her ability to read in both Latin and Greek (neither of which he was proficient in), her political awareness (she and the entire Fitzwilliam family, including the Darcy's, were Whigs, unfortunately); and, of course there was her writing, especially her writing for publication in the Ladies Gazette. He hoped that was a sort of feminine diversion only, perhaps even a vanity, possibly an affectation; and, he was willing to come to some sort of compromise if necessary.

As long as she stopped.

For her part Alice appreciated John's kindness to her, but *not* his spiritual reflections that could ramble on for several minutes...if not hours...if not lifetimes. Then there were his frequent naps, often while she was still speaking. He never took any ungentlemanly advantage of their time together, never pulled her onto his lap, nor did he lead her into darkened rooms for kisses. *Thankfully.* She had absolutely no desire to be treated as wantonly by her John as she had been by Harry, nor would she ever again risk losing her heart. That had been an appalling lesson, cruelly learned.

She was glad that Harry had fallen from the pedestal she had put him on so long ago. He was no longer the hero of her childhood, her knight in shining armor. No, far from it. In fact, in her opinion he had developed clay feet the size of Wales. She cared for him and always would, she even understood his motives, but she would never forgive him. *Never.* She would be a dutiful wife to Sir John, and an adoring mother to Harry's daughter, but she would never be *any* man's 'plaything', before or after marriage.

That nonsensical dream of love had forever flown.

Chapter Forty-Three

"There you are." Darcy's irritation at his cousin could sometimes know no bounds. As always, the man was late, would probably be late for their children's wedding the following day. He would more than likely miss his own funeral... and, if he did somehow attend the funeral, he would surely be poorly dressed. "Is your valet blind? What the devil colors are you wearing?"

Fitzwilliam's beard pressed onto his neck cloth as he looked down. "Haven't a clue. What's this? Looks greenish – oh, wait, that could be a relish." He sat down heavily and then signaled for his usual glass of port. "Have you been waiting a long time?"

"Yes, I've been waiting a long time! We were to meet here over an hour ago."

"Don't be churlish! I've had a hideous day, you have no idea what my home is like right this minute. Everything is a mess, everyone is on edge. I swear half the time the girls are screaming at each other and then they fuss with each other's hair. Females. Incomprehensible. I understand why Kathy's nerves are a bit stretched what with Aunt Catherine screeching in her ear, showing up at all hours, making outrageous demands; but, can you please tell me why Anne Marie is so weepy eyed?"

"She's with child."

"Quite right, I'd forgotten. Well in that case she's behaving very well and she looks radiant. Say no more. Ah! My port – thank you, Bartholomew." The two old friends then sipped their drinks, both appreciating a moment of rare and blessed quiet in their day. Here at White's they could freely smoke, an activity forbidden Fitzwilliam due arguably to a possible heart ailment his wife insisted he suffered from; and momentarily to Darcy for fear of smelly draperies and burnt carpets before the Wedding Ball that evening. Darcy lit his pipe then tossed the contraband tobacco pouch to his cousin. They puffed away in silence for several moments.

Fitzwilliam eventually spoke first. "Well thanks for nothing, Darcy, this tastes like shit."

"Bring your own damn tobacco next time you bloody ingrate. All right, all right; it was the only humidor I could find. Elizabeth and Mrs. Winters have moved everything about; my sanctuary, my home, is at sixes and sevens due to this evening's rout. How is yours?"

"The same, if not worse. Amanda's convinced herself there is dirt lurking somewhere and she has made it her death wish to expose it for what it is, preferably before Aunt Catherine's mammoth Wedding Breakfast tomorrow – we are expecting thousands apparently if the grocer's bill is any indication. I truly wish the children had just run off to Gretna Green. I even offered to drive the carriage for them, but *no* – I tell you it's their mothers alone who desire this type of romantic extravaganza. The whole thing has descended into madness."

"And, I fear it will all repeat itself soon. John Percy and Alice have finally decided on an Easter wedding. I shall put the announcement in the Times the week before Christmas."

"You don't look particularly pleased, Darcy – this is good news; all of your children married, out of the house. I would certainly be celebrating."

"I'm uneasy over the entire thing. I had hoped Alice would wait a bit and enjoy her first season. Oh, we always assumed Percy would offer for her; however, she and I had discussed her getting to know him better before making her decision, and then suddenly she tells me it's a *fait accompli*, she's promised to marry the man. It's not like her really, she's not changeable. And, another thing that concerns, is they have no mutual interests, no friends in common – she has yet to invite a single acquaintance of theirs over nor have they visited with anyone. The two of them sit home each evening behaving for all the world as if *they* were the chaperones instead of us. It's hideous. He reads Fordyce aloud – ghastly business, that – while Alice knits. I want to shake them both. No, something is terribly wrong. I don't believe they suit each other in the least."

"Do you wish me to speak with her?"

"I don't think it would help really. I fear her problem is one she'll need to sort out for herself."

"Odd that you should be so troubled with your daughter; I am having difficulties with my boys as well. Since the twins have taken over the lodgings on Curzon Street they've been involved with one incident after another, and when I say 'they' I mean Matthew. He plays a dangerous game with his women and his drinking to excess, visiting those gaming hells. We never behaved like that, did we? Oh stop rolling your eyes at me."

"I shudder to imagine if they've done half the things we did."

"Well, that's true enough."

"Fitz, have you spoken with Harry recently?" Darcy's sudden question surprised his cousin.

"What? No. And for the first time he concerns me more than Matthew. He's not been home to see his mother for weeks and from what I've gleaned through the servant underground he drinks himself into a stupor nearly every night at the clubs or alone at home."

"Have you been spying on him?"

"Of course; he's still our child no matter that he's taller than I. Besides, I prefer the term 'concerned watchfulness'. He's been to Mrs. Cleary's."

"Good lord, is she still in the business?" The well known Madame had been a courtesan when Darcy and Fitzwilliam were young bucks.

"I hear she's now off her back and up on her feet, in a manner of speaking. She owns the whole damn place. When I think of the rates she charged; well, I am fairly certain she could easily afford the purchase with my custom alone. Hell, she could have acquired Balmoral Castle with my custom alone and I believe I've lost my train of thought here. Do you get as easily distracted as I, Darcy? I was saying to Amanda the other day..."

"Oh heaven help me, find a point in there somewhere would you please?"

"Be quiet. Where was I? Harry you say? Oh yes – Harry. From what I gather he marched into Mrs. Cleary's establishment, paced around for a quarter hour, then stormed out – argued the whole time with Ned Hyde-Pickering's son about army food. I sent around a note to him yesterday, asked him to be home for me this afternoon. As soon as I leave here I'm going there directly."

"As a matter of fact Harry appeared a bit unsettled the last time I spoke with him."

"When was that?"

"He came to the house a few weeks ago, the day after the Duke of Devon's ball for the Queen. He has concerns about you, as we all do just not for the same reasons. Apparently the boys are going to America and he would like me to keep my eye out for any changes to your health, and they want Luke to join them. Did you know about the trip?"

"He told me all, confessed during my sly yet brilliant interrogation of him."

"You found his travel packet, didn't you?"

"Yes, it was resting on the table beside my luncheon plate along with a letter from his great uncle, Horatio Sayer. I very nearly ate the damn thing I was so starved. I did eat the entire platter of sliced ham as he explained their itinerary. My, the price of pork's gone up this year, hasn't it? Anyway, where was I? Oh, yes – America. I'm very glad they'll be meeting their American relatives at last; this uncle writes often asking us all to visit. In fact, Amanda and I are thinking of joining them there next month. She's wanted to return to Boston for so long and would dearly love to see her uncle herself before he passes..."

Darcy squeezed his eyes shut. "Try to focus on our conversation here, Fitz, for just a few moments longer. The thing is, although Harry said he was excited about leaving, his enthusiasm for the trip appeared forced to me. I sensed an undercurrent of emotion in him – annoyance, irritation; something. He paced the room and kept rubbing his forehead, all the while smiling and telling me how fortunate it was that everything had turned out well for all concerned, for John and Anne Marie, for George and Kathy, especially for Alice and Percy. Another thing I found strange was his insistence over Percy's daughter being welcomed into the family. Is something going on here,

Fitz? I find it extraordinary that Harry is so concerned for another man's child, especially a man who stole his betrothed away from him while he was away in service to his country."

"Don't be melodramatic, brat. Harry wasn't really ready for marriage and family back then – he wanted to see the world. Celeste was eager to marry."

"Well, the thing is, after he left the house Alice came in, expecting to speak with him. She became quite upset when I told her he was going away, appeared devastated really, especially when I mentioned his encouraging the match between her and Percy and his joy with the idea of having Celeste's child in the family." When Fitzwilliam shifted rather nervously in his chair Darcy leaned forward to clasp his cousin's forearm. "What *is* going on here?"

"Perhaps it was the knowledge that the child she will raise is Celeste's. She was always a bit envious of Harry and Celeste, you know that."

"That makes no sense. She knew Celeste was the mother yet she was especially looking forward to becoming stepmother to the girl. In fact, I begin to sense that the child was a greater incentive to her accepting John than any affection for *him*. No, something is missing in this; I believe I know what it is and I don't like it."

Fitzwilliam began to understand as well. Blast him, Harry was toying with too many lives and jeopardizing too many hearts. "Let me speak with Harry, Darcy. I would need his permission to tell you certain facts..."

Darcy grabbed his wrist. "If it involves *my* child's happiness you will tell me now."

Fitzwilliam wrenched free. "Well, it just so happens that it also involves *my* child's happiness and I will *not* speak on this subject without discussing it with him first!" The two men glared at each other for long, tense, moments. "Do I make myself clear, Darcy?"

"If you are going to Harry's now I should come along." Darcy rose from his chair, angry and anxious.

"Don't push me on this, Darcy," Fitzwilliam said ominously, standing as well. "I will deal with my son in my own manner."

"Very well, do it then! And, I will know from you tonight how it affects my daughter, or I will speak with Harry myself tomorrow – wedding or not!"

Chapter Forty-Four

Fitzwilliam banged on his son Harry's door until it was finally opened by a scruffy looking little man craning his neck back in order to take in the much taller and larger figure of Fitzwilliam. "What do you want?" the butler snapped.

"What do you mean, 'What do I want?' Let me in – it's raining out here."

"His lordship is not home to visitors today. Go away."

"Well of all the – I'm not a visitor, I'm his father!" With those words Fitzwilliam easily shoved the door inward forcing the fellow to fall back. "Where is he?" Fitzwilliam brought a scarf out to dry his rain drenched face and neck then began to unbutton his cloak.

"You wait here, and don't drip on anything; I'll see if his lordship is in to you."

"*You* wait here you pompous little oaf!" Then, over the shouted protestations of the spirited butler, Fitzwilliam went stomping down the hallway, depositing his dripping cloak and hat, gloves and scarf on various chairs along the way.

"You can't do this! Wait a minute, you've no business in here – this is a private home not a public house!"

"Shut up or I'll step on you! Harry!" Fitzwilliam bellowed, "Where in bloody hell are you?"

Racing ahead to the end of the hall the servant braced himself across a closed doorway. "If you know what's good for you, you'll leave now, before I am forced to inflict bodily harm." This bravado was undercut almost instantly by the man closing his eyes tight and flinching.

"You'd need a stepladder." As he spoke Fitzwilliam picked the butler up and set him aside. "I'm his father you idiot, not a cutpurse."

"*You* say! How do I know..." The door was then suddenly opened.

"Papa! Damn, how stupid I am; I forgot you were coming today. It's all right, Bricks."

"Are you certain, sir? He looks a right ruffian to me."

"Harry, is this monkey intended to protect you? You'd do better getting a pup from Aunt Catherine's spaniels! What the devil's going on here?" Fitzwilliam then saw a figure in the darkened corner begin to move forward into the light of a window. He recognized immediately it was his son, Matthew, badly bruised and bloodied.

"Dear God, what has happened to you?" Matthew's face was all in shades of black, yellow and blue; bloody cuts could be seen above his lip and around his eye, the latter so badly swollen that it was nearly shut. A strip of cloth secured Matt's left arm stiffly against his rib cage, and, to top it all off, the lad was limping.

Harry spoke first, knowing his brother would have difficulty in doing so, both physically and emotionally. "Matthew was involved in a slight scuffle."

"*Slight!* Damn, he looks as if he jumped in front of a carriage!" Heartsick with worry Fitzwilliam instead erupted. "What the hell sort of trouble have you gotten yourself into now?!"

Matthew gasped with the pain of a fractured jaw when he first tried to speak. Tears welled in his eyes. "You should see...the other fellow," he finally mumbled.

"*Other fellow*! Oh sweet *Jesu,* do you think this humorous?   I despair of you, Matthew, I truly do. We've given you everything – a good home, the finest education...and this is how you repay us, with worry, with disappointment, with sarcasm."

"Father, please stop. This truly was not Matt's fault."

"It's a waste of... your breath, Harry!" Matthew struggled to speak while retaining a shred of his dignity. "He d-d-doesn't care a whit."

"Don't you try to turn me into the villain here, boy, and don't you dare go home to your mother looking like this. She worries herself sick over you as it is!"

"I'll go any... damn place I want – you are not...you are not the master... of me, you never were! Ow."

"Will you both quiet yourselves?" Before Harry could finish Matthew had pushed past them both and was opening the door.

"Matthew, do not walk out on me! I demand answers. Tell me what has happened!"

"You already have... me tried and...and convicted so what... do you care about facts! Let me...let me...let me leave now, please. I fear... I'm going to...be sick."

Matthew then stumbled from the room, slamming the door shut behind him.

"You don't know how many times he's come home like this, Harry. I am terrified one day he'll be called out, or he'll call someone out. What am I to do with him? Damn me if I could still take a hand to his bottom I would."

"Sit down. Calm yourself before you have another heart attack." Harry poured two glasses of port handing one to Fitzwilliam. "And don't even consider hitting him; he's strong as an ox and a grand boxer – the best. Besides he would never hit you back and that would only make you feel worse. And this, for once, was not his fault."

"A likely story." Fitzwilliam tossed back his drink and almost crushed the glass with his bare hand.

"He was mistaken for Mark."

"Mark? I don't believe it. Mark is the responsible one of my children, the only responsible one. Unless – was Matthew passing himself off as Mark to fool some woman? It wouldn't be the first time."

"Not exactly. All right, here it is. He was at Preston's Gaming Hall earlier this morning – now settle down, let me finish before you go off half-cocked again. The husband of a certain young woman mistook him for Mark. Interesting aside – apparently, Mark runs a bit deeper and darker game than any of us suspected. Be that as it may, the husband and two others were waiting outside and, thinking he was Mark, attacked him. Three against one, but from all accounts Matthew gave as good as he got, or better."

"Don't defend him! He's been involved in one scrape after another since he was ten and five." Hands raking his hair Fitzwilliam paced to the windows and back several times before he was calm enough to speak again. "I take it that is why that little bantam rooster at the door is refusing visitors." He patted his coat pockets to no avail. "Where's my pipe?"

"I did request he keep a look out for unsavory characters. Apparently he has a discerning eye."

"Very humorous, Harry...damn it to hell, I've misplaced my pipe again. Why could Matthew not tell me what you just have? Why does he fight me straight away?" Fitzwilliam began rummaging about Harry's desk. "Give me a cheroot, anything."

"No, you're not to smoke. To begin with you never did give him the chance, did you? You never gave him the benefit of the doubt. And, I'll tell you something else. Because he is your son and heir, the one upon whose shoulders rests the entire Fitzwilliam family fate, name and title, he's anxious. He fears he'll fail you, doesn't feel he's half the man you are. Don't scoff. Father, he's always trying to impress you, or hadn't you noticed? He adores you. Your good opinion of him means *everything.*"

Fitzwilliam's brows beetled in disbelief. "He surely hides that well enough."

"You *know* he loves you. We all do. But he *especially* has a terror of looking the fool in front of you and somehow that leads him to do foolish things. I think he wants to prove to you how independent he is."

"Well, he has done that." Fitzwilliam finally found some tobacco and papers in a humidor on the floor. "Eureka!"

"Give that to me – now." Harry snatched the humidor away.

"No respect..." grumbled Fitzwilliam. "By the way, who are these bastards? I'd like to have at it with them myself, the cowards. Three to one you say, and he acquitted himself well?" He tried hard not to look pleased. "He is a grand fighter, that's the truth. How dare those bastards attack my boy! I can still hold my own you know – I'll just see how tough they really are..."

"Settle down, soldier; wait a bit before you storm the castle, all right? Besides, we have a wedding tomorrow or had you forgotten? Matt's staying here tonight – thinks to keep Mark from discovering the truth. Supposedly Mark is not even aware the girl was married, though I doubt that. You know Matthew really is a wonderful brother and a very good man, if still a bit young and wild."

"He's not *that* young, Harry." Fitzwilliam shook his head. "Oh, I know he's a good man and I love him enormously; I'd just like to kill him is all."

"Cut line, father. You're not even that angry anymore, I can tell."

"He doesn't know that. All right, I'd better go up and speak with him. Evidently the doctor has seen to him already? No long term ill effects? Good. Then I shall *insist* he attend the Darcy's party tonight for Kathy and George. That alone will certainly guarantee his *not* attending and lend him any excuse he needs to stay away and rest, although how he'll hide that swollen lip and eye from his mother tomorrow I haven't a clue."

"I don't think he's thought that far ahead yet."

"Oh, I nearly forgot – there was a specific reason I came to see you."

"Damn, I was hoping you'd forgotten me. All right, what have I done?"

"You've been avoiding home, that's what. Your mother misses you and worries. I believe she has given you adequate time to set up your household, entertain your friends and burn holes in your carpets. This house is no longer new to you; you should visit her more often. It's such a little effort for you and it would mean everything in the world to her."

"I know and you're right. There's been something on my mind these past weeks but that's no excuse to hurt mother. I shall be at the party this evening, and I promise to make it up to her."

"That's all I wanted to hear. By the way, you know that John Percy will be there tonight. Will that be uncomfortable for you?"

Harry turned toward the fireplace. Shrugging a careless shoulder he lit a cheroot and kept his voice level. "I thought as much. Perhaps Mark and I can hide out in the old nursery with Luke and Andrew, play the pianoforte for a while and get drunk up there."

"I need to ask you something." Fitzwilliam scratched his neck. "Did you by any chance encourage Alice to go ahead with this betrothal to Percy? Her abrupt decision took Darcy somewhat by surprise and he has reservations about the match, wonders at her eagerness to be a mother to Celeste's child. Truthfully, I believe Darcy suspects, and I am fairly certain Alice knows, that you are the girl's father. She always was a bit in love with you, you know."

"No. I have never told another soul, save you, about Christine." Harry took a draw on his smoke. "And as for her being in love with me – no longer, I'm afraid." He stared intently into the fire. "Shall I tell you a story? Several weeks back, at the Duke of Devon's party – you remember that party, I'm sure – Alice and I, well frankly we shared a rather passionate encounter."

Fitzwilliam jumped to his feet. "You what?"

"You heard me well enough I think. I'm not proud of what I did, must have been carried away by her beauty or too much wine, I don't know what came over me frankly. Then she said she loved me, had always loved me. I was stunned. It was not what I wanted, you see – not what I had planned in the least. Uncertain of what to do or what to say to discourage her affections I came up with a brilliant plan. It was a plan I knew would work, born as it was from my own experience. I deliberately led her to believe I would offer for her. I told her I would speak with her father the very next day; and then, later that night, I approached Percy, told him she was eager to pursue a commitment with him, that she wanted to marry."

Harry flicked his cheroot into the fireplace. "The following day I did go to the Darcy's requesting to speak with Uncle Wills. I imagine Alice waited a long while to be summoned, poor darling. When she finally realized what had actually happened...well, I imagine it was quite mortifying for her. Believe me, nothing cools ardor faster than humiliation, I learned that firsthand from none other than Celeste herself. So you see, with the most economic of gestures I accomplished my two goals – ending Alice's attachment to me and ensuring my daughter's future."

"And to think I believed Matthew to be a disappointment. How could you do something so despicable?"

"Oh, it wasn't accomplished without a bit of personal bloodletting father, believe me. But, *my* child will be where she belongs, in *my* family, and I shall be able to see her any time I wish. I have to believe the end will justify the means."

The crackling in the fireplace was the only sound for a long moment.

"I hope this was worth losing a bit of your soul then, Harry."

"Father, I don't need you to make me feel any worse. I feel wretched enough already."

"Well." Fitzwilliam shook his head in disbelief. "If you want my opinion..."

"Thank you, but no."

"...you're no better than a procurer."

Suddenly feeling white hot rage Harry kept his voice deliberately calm. "I beg your pardon? What did you just say?"

"What's the matter, you're hearing left you? I said you're no better than a pimp, Harry. That got you're attention, didn't it? Can't speak any plainer than that." Fitzwilliam stood squarely before his son. "What else do you call a man who uses a woman's body for his own gain? That's a pimp, son."

"How dare speak of Alice that way!"

"Ah, interesting. I see you don't deny the name for yourself but you defend Alice. Well, you misunderstand me there; Alice is the one pure heart in this whole mess. I am fairly certain now that she knows Christine is yours, as anyone who loves you would. And, even though you have used her and tossed her aside, she more than likely feels this marriage to be the only way she'll ever have any part of you to love. Your child. Now it makes sense to me. And would you like to know what the true irony is?"

Harry slammed his fist down on the fireplace mantel. "No! I keep saying no and you merely go on and on! You talk entirely too much, Father!"

"*You're* in love with *her*, Harry. Yes, you poor idiot, you've probably always loved her. I'm beginning to believe that nonsense about matches being made in heaven, because surely you two have been oddly attached in some way all your lives. In fact, you are so in love with Alice that the knowledge she will be bedded by another man, that she will have children with another man, that she will eventually grow to respect and honor another man – well, it will drive you mad."

"All right, Father, you've had your say." Harry could feel the bitterness, the rage, surging throughout every part of his body, growing and expanding like wildfire. "I think you'd better go up to Matthew now."

But Fitzwilliam ignored him and continued on, his voice growing a little louder with each word, "Me? Well, I would lose my mind – the woman I love being pawed and groped. Darcy tells me that Percy is wild for her you know, quite eager to be wed. The wedding date's been pushed forward. Yes, springtime now. Truthfully, they are probably as good as married already..."

"Enough! I believe you have said quite enough!" Harry strode across the room, his fists clenching and unclenching, his face red with fury. He reached for the bell pull and the elfish butler burst into the room. "Show Lord Somerton up to Baron Fitzwilliam's room – immediately." He then turned to his father. "Tell mother I'll be late this evening." Without another word Harry turned and briskly left the room, slamming the door behind him.

The room was deathly quiet.

"Well, well, well – I'll be goddammed." Fitzwilliam shook his head and grinned, then chuckled outright. The butler stared at him with narrowed eyes, suspicious still.

"You know, I like you," Fitzwilliam said cheerfully. "You'd make a wonderful lawn decoration. Now – show me to my other son's room pleasantly and I'll try not to toss you out the window."

Chapter Forty-Five

"John, your shoes! Why in heavens name have you worn those old boots and not your dancing pumps?" But even as she spoke Alice could think of several reasons. John disliked dancing, therefore lent no significance to it; and, rightly so since he had no sense of rhythm and no real appreciation of music. His only interest was old coins. And birds. *Sketching birds holding old coins would be his idea of heaven.* Alice's gaze drifted over John's pinched in face, his sunken eyes, and long scrawny neck. *In fact, he rather looks like a bird, doesn't he?* Her thoughts were becoming less and less charitable as their wedding announcement approached.

"John, did you hear me?"

John stared at his feet as if they had betrayed him. "Well of course I heard you, Alice, I am formulating my thoughts." He sighed. "Now I shall have to begin again. Give me a moment...ah yes, I remember. I reasoned thusly — one customarily sees dozens of single young gentlemen at the odd ball eager to dance, wanting to dance, especially with a beautiful young woman such as you; and, it is equally true that eighty-seven percent — no perhaps that's a tad too high. I should say seventy-six percent — oh dear me, that's much too low. I shall compromise and say then that approximately eighty-two percent of them are much better dancers than I. Give or take. I should only be in your way and there *is* that thirteen percent chance that I may break your toe and then you will be crippled, unable to attend your brother's wedding. All things considered I thought I'd just slip into your father's library during the party and look up some items I'm researching in his catalogues. Maybe take a nap."

"Well." Alice blinked her eyes rapidly to stave off the drowsiness that often overwhelmed her when he spoke. "I see." The sad fact was that she was actually thankful...at times she much preferred he not be with her. "I believe you're absolutely correct, John, and what a noble sacrifice. You don't even need to stay late, you know; or, remain at all for that matter. Go home early and get a good night's rest."

"Thank you for your consideration on this. As you know when I stay awake past eight in the evening I have such a difficult time in the morning; my stomach becomes quite upset which, in turn, affects my bowels. But I daresay you shall find all that out for yourself soon enough. These are the sort of learned intimacies that truly fill a marriage." He kissed her forehead and then settled into a corner chair to close his eyes and await the guests.

Within five minutes he fell fast asleep; and Alice, to her growing shame, was grateful.

The windows of the old Pemberley mansion, the house that was the pride of St. James Square, were ablaze with lights and the front walk was crowded with curious on-lookers; the great square clogged with carriages. Harry arrived late to the ball at the Darcy's home that evening. Struggling to make his way inside he was greeted by both friends and relatives, kissed by women he barely knew. He had left his companion, Lady Lydia Carstairs, at her home directly after the opera, ignoring her entreaties to remain, sorry he had contacted her again after so many years away. He was not up to pretending an affection for a woman who was noted to be agreeable only for gifts – the larger the gift, the more agreeable. She would find another companion she shrieked when tossing a boot at his head. He escaped shortly before the candle stand in her hand hit the door.

"There you are," squealed Mary Margaret. At ten and six years of age she was ecstatic beyond belief to be at her very first ball with her hair piled high in a precarious configuration and her dress floor length for the first time. "Can you believe this crush? It is *the* rout of the season – everyone, but everyone, is in attendance. One of Her Majesty's younger cousins danced with Kathy and Papa said Mama looks so beautiful that he dare not leave her side for a moment and Mary Elizabeth sipped some of the forbidden fruit punch which made her sick to her stomach and she vomited and Andrew danced with me! So did Mark! And Georgie as well! I love dancing."

The young girl took but a moment's breath before launching into monologue number two. "Oh! And Matthew is here – he looks absolutely horrid, everyone says so but I think he looks marvelous – like a pirate. He told mother he was thrown from his horse but the word is that someone no one ever heard of before named Sir Levenby or Lewfenkey – probably a gypsy – mistook him for Mark and had him beaten by fifty huge seaman from that new country – what is it called – oh yes, Brazil – the coward not daring to face either Matthew or Mark alone, man to man...to man. Mark didn't even know the stupid girl was married, or so he claims but Mark never lies so that's that and he's distraught but it's not his fault, really, all things considered."

"Take another breath before you faint."

Meg nodded vigorously, gasped, and then continued. "We all know the whole story, Harry, except mother and father of course, but evidently, Mark was unaware of her true identity, she used someone else's name – I don't think that was rather fair, do you? Mark thought they had to keep their romance a secret because she said her father was a Vicar! Can you imagine that? He is so brilliant in science and mathematics and so gullible with women and that is hard to fathom considering Matthew needs to peel women off and they are identical so there you see. I knew the first time I saw her she was a scheming little person. Well when Mattie informed Mark tonight that she was married Mark was quite shocked and they had a terrible row but that was earlier and now they've made up however Matthew had already tricked Mark and went to the gaming house in his place fearing that there would be trouble."

"How in the world do you do that? I would pass out straight away. Breathe again please. My head is throbbing; I don't want to carry you from the room."

"Yes, yes, all right."

"You should be hawking newssheets down on the river bank – such lung capacity. There, your color is returning; give me the rest of the news. Is Luke in trouble at school? I haven't had a chance to speak with him in private. Did anyone discover he was one of the group that removed all the doors from the privies and arranged them atop the chapel roof?"

"No, he's in the clear for now, but did you know Andrew nearly had his arm torn off at Harrow during a football game? Yes he did! Oh, stop looking at me like that; I never exaggerate, I've told you that a million times! He is in agony, poor darling, trying not to move it too much, keeps it pressed to his side whenever Mama and Papa are around. They don't know by the way, so don't mention a thing."

Harry nodded and grabbed a glass of champagne from a passing waiter. "Take a sip," he told his sister. "Just one sip you greedy thing." As casually as he could, he asked the question uppermost in his mind. "What of Alice? Is she here?"

Mary Margaret's quick mind flashed along her catalogue of impressions from earlier in the evening. "Ooh, yes, and didn't she cause quite the stir. She danced with a widowed royal Duke. I can't remember which one but every girl was green with jealousy; he seemed quite taken with her, asked her to dance a third time but she declined him! And then she danced with Milo Burnett and Freddie Churchill. Then of course Uncle Wills danced a minuet with her – heavens I hate that stuffy dance, can't believe they still offer that – then Byron Oglethorpe danced with her twice, both Bunny Persall and Jeff..."

"More than sufficient information – stop. Why is she not dancing now?"

"Now? Oh, it is too late now; all the ladies in the wedding party have returned to our house to prepare for tomorrow. John Percy escorted Alice to the house ages ago and Anne Marie left with John just before you arrived. I am certain we'll all be awake and chatting the entire night..."

"Wait a moment – Alice left *ages ago*...with John Percy...alone? *In his carriage?* Is Uncle Wills aware of this?"

"Yes, of course. They are betrothed you know, though it's not been announced as yet, but still she does have the betrothal ring, a Percy heirloom, so their behavior is perfectly acceptable, besides it's common knowledge that they've set a wedding date, Alice and John I mean, and that they are so very much in love. And are they not the most beautiful couple, perfect really. Well, *she* is at least and who really notices the groom? *Hahaha.* I think it's ever so romantic. Don't you, Harry?"

"Don't I what?"

"Think it romantic! Something is wrong with your neck, it's turned all red."

"I'll tell you what I think, I think Uncle Wills is being entirely too lenient with her, but he always was. She is a spoiled and willful hoyden who is being allowed to run fast and loose without the restrictions she so obviously requires, and I think Sir John Bloody Percy had better take her in hand once they're married!"

"Lower your voice would you! People are beginning to stare! Hello, how nice to see you again, Lady Philomena. Lovely gown; I've always loved that dress, each and every time you wear it – oh dear, sorry, didn't mean to offend." Mary Margaret turned her back on the eavesdropping Countess who had, by then, stomped away in a huff. "Whatever is the matter with you? And what can you mean, speaking like that about Alice?"

"Well, first of all it sounds as if she danced with nearly every ambulatory male here."

"It isn't her fault they pursue her like a pack of drooling dogs. My word would you look at how tight your jaw clenches and did you know you have a large blue vein on the side of your temple? Her behavior was totally proper, Harry. Between dances she remained a fixed presence by Sir John's side – well, across the room from him really – but still, she watched him constantly. Actually, now that I think of it I believe he was dozing on and off."

"How convenient for her..."

"Ooh, that blue vein is getting larger; that can't be healthy. Be that as it may, the few moments Percy was awake he could barely pry his gaze from her. People in love just have that particular way of watching each other, say, across a crowded ballroom. You know, like this..." With that Mary Margaret struck a pose she considered to be very seductive; she fluttered her lashes, pouted her lips, placed one delicate finger to her cheek.

"You look ridiculous."

"I need to practice more. To continue, from what Kathy said, Alice and John leaving alone was planned beforehand, so they could take their time reaching our house this evening, *if* you know what I mean – well, good heavens, your jaw is going to crack if you keep grinding your teeth like that. How odd. Where was I? Ooh, yes, Kathy said Alice told her maid who told Eve Longstreet's footman who told Emma Bakers third cousin's cook..."

"Could you hurry this up please, Meg!"

"Harold Penrod! If you can't speak civilly to me I won't tell you that Anne Marie believes Alice and John may just up and elope, and quite soon too. Yes, I thought you'd be surprised. I heard Andrew say it more than likely since John's probably gone 'without' far too long; although 'without' what I haven't a clue, he's richer than anyone we know. But it is so romantic...Harry? Harry, whatever is wrong?"

"Apologize to mother for me. I'm leaving; I've another appointment and I'm late." Harry felt he would lose his mind if he remained one more minute. He always seemed to be storming *from* rooms lately – or *into* rooms. Whatever was wrong with him better end soon because his father had been right about one thing. He felt he was going mad. With a glowering look to those around him that effectively discouraged any commentary he spun on his heel and left.

"That was rather rude." Smoothing back the ringlets that framed her face, a suddenly famished Mary Margaret turned toward the dining room.

Chapter Forty-Six

It was finally the morning of the long awaited wedding, a cool, early autumn crispness to the air. Outside of the carriage that transported father and daughter to the church the world was continuing on as usual; vendors shouting out their wares, horses trotting to and fro, people hurrying on with their daily lives.

Inside the carriage, however, it was quiet. There were secret conflicts being felt by its two inhabitants, clashing emotions of joy and sadness.

During the ride to the church Fitzwilliam had struggled to control his emotions, managing only an uncharacteristic quiet. The bitter fact was his little girl soon would forever belong to another man and there was nothing he could, or would, do to stop her. *This is the way of life* he thought. A child is yours to raise, cherish and protect, but only for a very short while. They then leave you to raise their own children, travel their own paths. His darling Katherine was no exception. She was now ready to begin her own life.

She is going to leave me...

Having watched his emotions play across his face for several minutes Kathy reached for her father's hand. He had been studiously avoiding any eye contact but now he turned and gave her a watery wink.

"I love you, Papa," she whispered, tearfully. "Never forget that."

"I love you as well. You are precious to me, child."

Alone in the carriage together they had just left their home and were heading north to the cathedral, the rest of the family awaiting them there.

There is so little time left and it passes too swiftly...

His child's hand brought with it a thousand memories – pirate patches and dollies and whispered confidences. He squeezed his eyes shut against those unmanly tears, inhaled deeply against the pain in his chest and swallowed down the lump in his throat. Having not cried in front of another living soul since his son Edward was born he certainly would not do so here and now.

"It's all right if you cry, Papa. Your secret would be safe with me."

"Don't be nonsensical. Men don't cry. We are not so easily given over to emotion as you women are."

She sobbed out a sudden laugh. "You are such a bloody poor liar..." His surprised bark of laughter was a relief to them both. "Well? How do I look?" she asked.

"You look hideous; let's return home and forget this whole silly business. Oh blast; here, we can share my handkerchief."

"You know you will always be my first love, Papa. There is *no one* in the world who could replace you and I could never really leave you. And, just think, soon there will be little Darcy's running about for you and Uncle Wills to spoil."

Fitzwilliam narrowed his gaze at her. "How soon?"

"*Papa!* At least one day more than nine months, I can assure you." She and George had long before decided to wait until marriage for that sort of intimacy. They knew they were in a minority among their friends, both still virgins, unheard of in an age when the rest of the world seemed obsessed with the physical aspects of love. She and George wanted the act to be special, to be remembered forever between them as cherished. She blushed so adorably that her father kissed her forehead and laughed. They began to reminisce then, relive happy memories of birthdays and Christmas, father and daughter excursions. Too soon St. George's Cathedral came into view.

"Here we are, sweet; are you nervous?"

"Not in the least, surprisingly; I'm more excited than anything. I've loved George for such a long time that I suppose I take this all as to be expected. I've no doubts."

"Good. That's what I've always wanted for you. That's how I felt about your mother – no doubts, although I had only known her but a handful of weeks before we were wed. When you have found the right person you somehow know."

"I always thought that very romantic of you, Papa."

"Tell your mother that. She insists I've not a romantic bone in my body."

"Oh, I don't know. Having had eight children together I suspect she must find you very romantic occasionally."

"Alice! That was indelicate of you to point out. Accurate, but indelicate."

Darcy had settled his family in the first box pew with the Fitzwilliam family then went in search of his son. He found him standing alone in a small room, staring out the window at the brilliant autumn morning. "George, there you are. How are you feeling? Nervous?"

As soon as George turned to face him Darcy knew all was well; he was relaxed and happy, a sense of exhilaration about him. "Not a bit. I'm so glad you came back, Father. Is Mama seated?"

"Yes. Alice and John are there as well, as are Anne Marie and her husband. You look splendid, son."

"Thank you, father, I feel splendid. Has she arrived?" He did not need to specify who he most wanted to see.

"I believe just; I could hear the buzzing escalate as I came back here. The church is packed to the rafters with aristocrats and your Aunt Catherine is swooning with joy. Even cousin Anne is smiling."

"I wish Harry would arrive soon. I'm worried about him; he never did turn up at the party last evening."

"I just saw him." Darcy nodded. "He looks a bit peaky but at least he's mobile. He was on his way back here but I motioned for him to wait, to give you and me a moment alone before the wedding."

"Why?" George's happy expression went suddenly serious. "Is everything all right?"

"Absolutely." Darcy cleared his throat. "Yes, absolutely. I...I just wanted to tell you how very grateful I am to you... you know, the way you've taken so much from my shoulders with regard to Pemberley. But, it's not only that, you know... I hope, well that is...I don't always express my emotions very clearly... you know how dearly your mother... how much I..."

When George began to chuckle at his father's mumblings Darcy laughed as well. "I'm terrible at expressing sentiments aren't I? Give me a decent crop report to explain any day. Oh, you needn't grin so. What I wanted to say is – well, here's the thing. George, you've been a joy, a complete delight to me as a son. I respect you immensely – your integrity, your strength; the cloth of your character is of the very finest. You've grown into a man I am proud to call my friend." Darcy had finally expressed all that he had felt for his boy over the years. He reached out his hand. "I love you, son."

George was nearly overwhelmed; he cleared his throat but his voice still sounded rough. "I love you, Papa. You have no idea how much your good opinion means to me." With that the young man pulled his father to him, enfolding him into an emotional embrace that involved some tears, a great deal of back slapping and eventually ended in laughter.

"I trust neither of us will speak of this again," Darcy dabbed a handkerchief to his eyes.

"I won't tell a soul." Harry was standing in the doorway, smiling. "And, I hope you're both ready because, George, a very beautiful bride awaits you."

Darcy gave his son's shoulder one final squeeze then started back into the church. When he passed Harry he stopped to whisper. "You and I will talk today, my friend. I should like some answers."

Fitzwilliam and his daughter waited, hidden away in the bride's side vestibule, as the choir within the church droned on and on, hymn after hymn, canticle after canticle.

He felt restless, she impatient. They grinned at each other occasionally when the sounds of a particular hubbub within the church reached their ears. At least two hundred people were taking their seats, exchanging their seats, protesting their seats. They turned pages, whispered loud greetings, coughed. It all added to the building excitement and it all seemed to be taking forever.

"You know I really do like that veil and flower wreath 'whatsit' on your head. Very pretty. Different, isn't it, from a sensible bonnet, but not unpleasantly so. Of course you realize I have no fashion sense whatsoever. If I approve it must be disastrous..."

"Why, thank you, Papa. I think. *Oh!*" Suddenly her hand tightened on his arm as two of the vicar's assistants opened the doors and beckoned to them. "There is our music." The huge choir had finally risen to sing *Ubi Caritas et Amor* – 'Where there is Charity and Love'. Kathy turned to her father and beamed. "It is our time," she announced excitedly and then the finality of the moment beset him. His central role in her life was at an end.

"Are you ready, Papa? Shall we shall walk this long aisle together?" She squeezed his arm for luck. "Good. Now remember, right foot first, then left..." she muttered, "...and please, be bloody careful."

The immense doors to the main church opened and the congregation as one turned to stare.

Chapter Forty-Seven

The entire Peninsular War had been a night at Vauxhall Gardens compared to what faced Fitzwilliam in that church when the doors opened. Millions upon millions of eyes were staring at *him* and not Kathy – he was certain of it. Obviously something was hideously wrong. Had he buttoned his breeches? Combed his hair? Washed his face? Was saliva dripping from his mouth? There was no way to discreetly check now but he was fairly certain Amanda would have noticed if he was still bare chested and hadn't pulled on a shirt.

He felt a tug at his arm but he waved that off as an annoyance. "Not now, Kathy," he whispered. Even though his thoughts were a bit murky he was fairly certain he was supposed to be doing something at the moment. Seconds later she was speaking to him again, the imp, but he was unable to really make out any specific words. "In a moment, dear." He patted her hand resting upon his arm. *Darling child.*

Then, from nowhere, he had the sudden sensation of falling forward, so, to stop himself from landing flat on his face with his momentum, he finally began to move.

Perhaps it was due to his daughter *pulling* at him, just a bit, *dragging* possibly a more accurate word.

Years later he would still be marveling at Kathy's composure that day, her poise as they processed down that unbelievably long center aisle.

Before him was 'The Altar', his ultimate Xanadu.

Harry glanced at his dear friend George as they waited at the altar. The man looked revoltingly calm and blissfully happy while Harry felt miserable. His head ached, he hadn't slept all night, and he hadn't eaten.

George nudged him and winked. "You look dreadful, Harry. I hope she was worth it."

"Pardon? I can't hear a thing with that organ pounding away above us – it could raise the dead. Dear lord, now the choir's singing again."

"Be still, the doors are opening. Bloody hell, this is it, Harry."

Both men turned toward the back of the church, along with the rest of the congregation. Kathy and her father soon came into view stopping at the beginning of the aisle, ready to begin their long walk. Everyone was on their feet now, not one person facing the men; all attention was focused on the exquisite bride.

"The old man looks a bit stunned, doesn't he; like a fox run to ground. What in hell could they be discussing at a time like this? Are they never going to – ah, here we go. Well, this is your final chance to make a run for it, George. If he doesn't slip and fall in those new boots of his your leg shackle will soon be here. Certain you want to go through with this?"

"Harry, stop being an ass. I love her. One moment more without Kathy by my side would be the end of me. I mean that. To be with her every day for the rest of my life, to have children with her, to grow old with her – there is nothing more sacred in the world to me. Have you never felt that way about a woman, Harry?

Harry?" When his friend didn't respond George glanced back and saw that Harry's eyes were moist, his attention off in another direction entirely. Curious, George followed his cousin's gaze to see what had put such a look of yearning there and was stunned to see the source.

Harry was staring at George's own baby sister, Alice.

"Dearly beloved, we are gathered together here in the sight of God, and in the face of this congregation, to join together this Man and this Woman in holy Matrimony; which is an honorable estate, instituted of God in the time of man's innocency, signifying unto us the mystical union that is betwixt Christ and his Church; which holy estate Christ adorned and beautified with his presence, and first miracle that he wrought, in Cana of Galilee; and is commended of Saint Paul to be honorable among all men: and therefore is not by any to be enterprised, nor taken in hand, unadvisedly, lightly, or wantonly, to satisfy men's carnal lusts and appetites, like brute beasts that have no understanding; but reverently, discreetly, advisedly, soberly, and in the fear of God; duly considering the causes for which Matrimony was ordained.

"First, It was ordained for the procreation of children, to be brought up in the fear and nurture of the Lord, and to the praise of his holy Name.

Secondly, it was ordained for a remedy against sin, and to avoid fornication; that such persons as have not the gift of continency might marry, and keep themselves undefiled members of Christ's body.

Thirdly, it was ordained for the mutual society, help, and comfort, that the one ought to have of the other, both in prosperity and adversity. Into which holy estate these two persons present come now to be joined. Therefore if any man can show any just cause, why they may not lawfully be joined together, let him now speak, or else hereafter for ever hold his peace."

Alice placed a hand upon her mother's shoulder as all watched the moving ceremony; and, with her back turned to Sir John, she prayed her growing sense of panic was not overly apparent. *Procreation of children? With John Percy?* A definite shiver of distaste ran through her. He'd rarely even kissed her lips, but then she'd never wanted him to; not in this lifetime, nor in the next. What in heaven's name had she been thinking? Lying beside this man in a marital bed would feel like a sin.

She bit her lip, hoping she would not start to cry. It was no use really. There was only one man who could ever possess both her body and her heart as well, and it was not John Percy. He was kind and loyal but the facts were there nonetheless – how would she ever exist in a loveless marriage? How would she ever surrender her body to a man when it belonged to another?

"Wilt thou have this Woman to thy wedded Wife, to live together after God's ordinance in the holy estate of Matrimony? Wilt thou love her, comfort her, honor, and keep her in sickness and in health; and, forsaking all other, keep thee only unto her, so long as ye both shall live?"

"I will."

"Wilt thou have this Man to thy wedded Husband, to live together after God's ordinance in the holy estate of Matrimony? Wilt thou obey him, and serve him, love, honor, and keep him in sickness and in health; and, forsaking all other, keep thee only unto him, so long as ye both shall live?"

"I will."

"Who giveth this Woman to be married to this Man?"

Fitzwilliam placed Katherine's hand within George's then stepped back. One step. Two steps. It was finally over. Turning, he joined Amanda in the pew, grasped her hand tightly within his and released the breath he had been unwittingly holding.

"I am so very proud of you today, Richard," she whispered in his ear. "And I love you dearly. Well done."

Chapter Forty-Eight

Alice remained in the family pew long after the service had ended while others of her family awaited George and Kathy's emergence from the Vestry. They were all chattering away, laughing, kissing, hugging, and for a few moments she was alone with her thoughts, forgotten in the excitement and joy of the day.

"I hear congratulations are in order. Well, you must be very pleased, Alice. You've done it, girl; captured the ultimate marriage prize. Well done, you. Sorry I won't be able to attend the ceremony, however. My brothers and I are off to America next week."

Alice stared up at Harry, astonished that she could both hate and love another person so much. She spared him no smile, no warmth, barely blinked as she stood. If only he weren't so beautiful to her still... Her chin went up and she scowled. "Good bye, Harry."

"Ah, she speaks."

Alice squared her shoulders as if for battle.

"If I'd known you'd be this vibrant and delightful, this charming, I would have brought your wedding gift with me."

"That would be entirely inappropriate, as is your mockery."

"Inappropriate, yes I suppose it is. You look well, Alice. I take it that Sir John is providing... *all* your wants now. He must be very enthusiastic with his attentions."

Her face pinked. "I am not so green a girl as to not recognize your meaning; and, so I wonder, Harry — how many ways do you wish to insult me in one lifetime?" When she realized her words had carried beyond them to the hearing of others she lowered her voice. "Leave me be, Harry. I want nothing more to do with you. In the future, if for some reason you feel you must contact me, do so only through George. However, I cannot foresee any real need for you and I to speak ever again."

"Alice, don't say that." He spoke low and leaned over her, his hands resting on the pew front. Alice had to turn away, his mouth so close to her forehead she could feel his breath. "We have a special history together, you and I — a bond. Now, I realize you're upset with me, I appreciate that. But, in time, well, perhaps we can meet in privacy; talk." His voice lowered even further. "You are a passionate woman, Alice. I am a passionate man. It is not unheard of in our social circle for understandings to exist between such men and women." He placed his hands gently upon hers. "There are many who enjoy discreet unions outside of their marriage, Alice; in fact, most of those unions are happier than the marriages themselves."

She smiled at him sweetly and his heart quickened. "If I had a gun, Harry, I believe I could shoot you where you stand. You disgust me; you make me want to bathe." She pulled her hands from his. "Listen to me carefully. Whatever I may have felt for you in the past is over and forgotten as of this minute. Do you understand my meaning?"

"Is that so?" Harry's blood began boiling with sudden and irrational anger.   He had achieved all he wanted. Everything was proceeding perfectly; his plans accomplished beyond his wildest expectations. So why was he so shaken? Why was he so enraged?

"Answer me! Do you understand my meaning?"

"Oh yes, Alice. I understand you perfectly well." He began to turn but hesitated. "Seeing as how we'll never speak again you wouldn't begrudge me one last kiss, would you, *cousin*?" Before she could protest he grabbed her by her upper arms and pulled her toward him, his mouth descending upon her, his lips hard and unyielding. Although harsh at first the kiss softened quickly, his grip loosening to a caring gentleness, the depth of their true feelings for each other overwhelming any anger. Once the kiss ended they stood forehead pressed to forehead for a moment, hands holding hands; a needed and steadying pause as their breathing calmed, a forever parting being held off until the very last moment possible...

"Good bye, Little Alice," he finally whispered against her cheek.

"Are you in need of this?" Still shaking from the confrontation with Harry, Alice had sought out a remote area of the church to sit and calm her nerves when a handkerchief was dangled before her. Looking up she saw her fiancé's mild countenance and felt immediately guilty. He was such a very kind man, why could she not love him? His eyebrow arched to emphasize his question.

"Goodness yes, John." Taking the white cloth from him she daintily dabbed away the tears that filled her eyes then blew her nose with a moist and lusty honk. Having just begun to sit John slowed his downward motion considerably then settled into the cushion and looked away.

"Feel free to keep the, uh, cloth, Alice," he muttered.

"Thank you, John. I shall have it laundered and returned to you tomorrow."

"Listen to that, will you?" A rowdy cheering from outside the cathedral signified that Kathy and George were most likely now climbing into their carriage and waving to one and all, perhaps Kathy was tossing her bouquet, perhaps George throwing coins in the air for the children. It brought her mind back to thoughts of her own upcoming wedding.

"John..." Alice began, but John was not attending her; he was checking his pocket watch.

"Well done. You know they are precisely on time. I do so admire that about your father, Alice. He is a most gifted organizer."

"John, I believe we need to speak."

"I say, Alice, do I look pale to you today? I thought I looked a bit wan this morning."

"Yes, you do; but you always do."

"No need to be quite so blunt..."

"Well, you did ask."

"It's not my fault that I have such a low tolerance to sunlight..."

"I know, John; I know."

"Perhaps I should cease rinsing my face with lemon water for a time; a day or two without wouldn't hurt."

They lapsed into silence and for the first time in a long while John looked at Alice – really noticed her. He bent over a bit to study her face.

"You seem upset, my dear. Are those dark circles beneath your eyes?"

"It's nothing of significance; I'm merely tired."

"Rest is very important, Alice. You should take naps during the afternoon as I do." He cleared his throat, picked at an errant piece of lint on his coat sleeve then stared up at the ceiling. "I saw you speaking with Penrod before, I believe I even saw him kiss you. Actually, for a moment he appeared rather brutish to me. I very nearly came over; but, then he's rather a large fellow, isn't he? Wouldn't do to get him riled up unless it's absolutely necessary. I hope that's not what's upset you, my dear. I'm certain the kiss meant nothing to him, after all men think differently than women about these things. Besides, people are always rather boisterous at weddings, strong spirits are the devils right and left hand. I hesitate to say this – but, I also heard that your cousins were sneaking into a room behind the vestry to drink champagne that they had hidden there. Not really proper, but, well, they are 'Fitzwilliams' after all (*haha*). Any number of little escapades may occur with those scamps. If you wish, I shall have a word with the rogue but I would rather not. More than like it's all a misunderstanding."

Alice looked away and the tears just would not stop, even as she kept trying to discreetly dab at them. "Yes, I'm sure that's exactly what it was, just a grand misunderstanding."

Oh dear, she's crying. John shifted nervously in his seat, never knowing what to do when a woman cried, but then, what man ever did? A sudden thought popped into his head, an uncharacteristic flash of intuition. Apprehensive, nervous, John checked his watch again, this time without really looking at it. He cleared his throat to ask a question – a question whose answer he wasn't certain he really wished to hear. "I say, Alice, you don't imagine you have a *tendre* for that scoundrel, do you? His family's always been close to yours, I know, and I realize you're fond of him –

however, I always believed it to be more of a sisterly attachment." She stared at her hands lying useless in her lap and said nothing. Tears were streaming down her cheeks.

"Ah. I see." They sat in silence for a few minutes more. John had one more question to ask, although he already knew the answer. "Alice, I need to know if your feelings for Penrod are romantic feelings, or are they just familial. You may have confused the two feelings you know, so I ask that you think deeply upon this. I can understand your loving him, as a brother – you have a tender heart and, after all, you've known the man your entire life. Is that it? Do you love him as a brother only, Alice?"

She pressed her hands over her face and tried very hard not to dissolve into wracking sobs. It was a moment before she could voice what they both knew. "I am so sorry."

"I see." Emotions overwhelmed him. John's heart was pounding in his chest, remembering the hours he had listened to Celeste cry over Penrod, compare *him* to Penrod, curse him for not *being* Penrod. There were times he had actually hated the name Penrod. He would not willingly return to those days, please God, not now, after all these years – he dreaded the thought.

"I should like you to be perfectly honest with me, Alice. I will not rebuke you or cast you aside, but I must hear you say this. Do you love him?"

Alice bit her lip as she swept the handkerchief across her eyes. She had never lied to anyone before and she could not lie now. "Yes," she whispered through a hiccupping sob. "I think you are a fine gentleman though, John. I do care for you."

John winced at her very polite words. Oh dear. He sighed. "However, you are not in love with me, is that it?"

"No, I am not in love you."

"Ah."

"Are you truly in love with me, John?"

"Oh, well, I am a simple man, Alice, and never given to flights of fancy. You are a damn fine looking woman, I'm fond of you and you're from a splendid family. Christine adores you. That's really all I need."

"John, don't you think that's really rather sad."

"It's enough for me."

"But, it's not enough for me."

"Alice – how can I put this delicately? You're not really silly enough to believe in romantic love, are you? Because if that's what you're waiting for, I can assure you that it doesn't exist."

"But you are wrong, John; it must exist, since love has broken my heart."

"Ah." He stared straight ahead, the little color in his cheeks fading rapidly. "Well, you've quite wounded me here; however, I don't feel broken. Possibly it's merely my conceit then that's taken the lance and not my heart – I couldn't say for certain at the moment." He swallowed hard; his eyes blinked back some moisture. Strange, that. Alice wanted to comfort and hold him, soothe his wounded pride, but she remained where she was, her head down.

"Perhaps there should be something more, I don't know. I suppose we should cry off then; no sense in having a marriage that will make us both miserable is there?"

"I am so sorry, John. I wanted to be a good wife to you, truly I did."

"Christine will be dreadfully disappointed. She so wants a woman's guidance in her life; and, then too,

I've always admired your family, you know. They are a bit of a wild group but always of good cheer, always loyal to each other. I hoped she could experience that sort of closeness. I have few young relatives, we rarely communicate and Celeste's family is all gone."

Alice smiled. John had never said he would be disappointed; he worried for his daughter only, the one true love of his life. He really was a fine father. "You and I are great friends, John; there is no reason to let that die. I should very much like to still play a part in your daughter's life, for as long as you'll allow me."

"Yes. We'd both like that, I think. We would both like that very much." He smiled thinly. "You're a good girl, Alice. Yes, we *are* great friends, aren't we? Shall I speak with your father then?"

"Yes, I think you should."

Alice suddenly realized that John was sniffling, his eyes moist. "Do you want your handkerchief back?"

"Ah – no." He eyeballed the wadded up piece of cloth in her hand and appeared horrified at the thought. "Please tell your father I'll come by tomorrow and speak with him. I'll not attend the wedding breakfast today, if you don't mind. There'd be a lot of questions and I shouldn't want to spoil the other's happiness. Perhaps I'll go home and have a nice soak in a hot tub, then I've some new coins I must catalogue. Take care of yourself, dear and I shall see you tomorrow."

How much time had passed she had no idea. Having closed her eyes in silent prayer she had fallen asleep, exhaustion simply overwhelming her. When she again opened them she was surprised to find herself alone, the church completely empty, her father's cloak for some reason across her knees. "Oh, good heavens! What's happened? Oh, those little animals! They've left without me!" Alice hurried to their pew and searched among the discarded programs and hymn books for her reticule and gloves. How could they have forgotten her here? Irritation gave way to alarm when she heard footsteps. They were echoing throughout the church, reverberating up the main aisle, growing louder and louder. Her brain was still a bit foggy. Was she alone in an abandoned building with a stranger? About to turn and run she heard her name called.

"Alice, is that you lurking about in the back shadows?" It was her father's voice, filling her with the same giddy relief as it did when she was a child and frightened of the dark.

"Here I am, Papa." She walked quickly forward then, to the center of the aisle. There was no one else in the world, save her mother, with whom she wanted to be at that moment.

"So you finally awoke. There was a momentary downpour delaying people who were leaving for the breakfast. I saw your eyes were closed, thought I would leave you rest a bit. I know you've had troubled sleeping recently. However, the rain has ceased so it's now time to go."

"In a moment, if you please. I wanted to examine the...the Last Supper painting behind the altar." In reality her eyes were burning and still puffy from her cry. A connection had been severed today and it saddened her deeply, the pain of hurting a good man like John was still with her. "Did you know these windows are Flemish glass?"

By the time her father reached the end of the aisle her back was to him and she was wandering back and forth, studying the famous painting, the canopy over the pulpit, the 'double-decker' reading desk to the left of the altar. When she felt herself suitably composed she turned to face him.

"Whatever has happened?" her father asked immediately and came toward her, placing his hands upon her shoulders. She should have known he would see through her. Her eyes mirrored her moods, just as her mother's did.

"It's not good, I'm afraid." She smiled but the tears began again. "John and I have ended our betrothal. Hopefully any damage I've done today was only to his pride and not his heart. I think so anyway, I hope so at any rate. Forgive me, father."

Darcy, who had been watching her intently, pushed a strand of hair from her cheek. "Forgive you? For what may I ask? I am only glad you ended it sensibly and before any permanence was affixed. And I'm not that surprised." He pulled her into his arms to hold her.

"And why is that?" In spite of the fact that her father had, as usual, been proven right, she snuggled into the safe harbor of his embrace. It was most irritating the way her parents could read her mind.

"Well, my goodness, listen to how annoyed you sound! Your mood swings are Homeric at times, Alice – even for a woman. All right, I shall tell you. It has something to do with your mother's theory about a happy marriage. She believes that most people desire a partner who possesses qualities of character they wish for themselves, but feel they lack somehow. Yes, I know, it's still a bit foggy to me too.

"Well, I thought of that when you first said you'd marry John. I never believed that you desired for yourself those qualities John possessed that *should* be admired. His seriousness, his methodical mind, his almost constant need for sleep..."

Before she could control it, a chuckle bubbled up. "What a thing to say."

"He's a good man, don't mistake me; but, he deserves someone who will fill his life with happiness, not regret; and, so do you my dear. Now, tidy yourself up, we must away or we'll be late for the breakfast. And, with all the Fitzwilliam's in attendance today sufficient food for the rest of us could be problematical."

"All right." Alice sighed and slowly began to pull on her gloves, retied her bonnet.

Darcy watched her closely. He had never seen his daughter look so despondent before and he suspected the cause was more than a broken engagement to a man she didn't really love. "Alice. Why did you agree to the betrothal in the first place, if you didn't care for the man?"

Startled by his sudden comment, she looked away. There was nowhere to run from this, nowhere to hide. "I did it because I felt it didn't matter to whom I was married since I can never have the man I truly love."

"Harry Penrod."

Alice was not so surprised that her father had guessed. The whole family had known of her feelings for so many years. However, she was stunned by her father's next question. "He was willing to sacrifice your future so that he could have easier access to his child – that was it, wasn't it? And yet you still love him."

"You knew about Christine? Did Uncle Fitz tell you?"

"I knew, but not from Fitz; he's never said a word. The man is a raving lunatic, but he can be trusted with a confidence. No, John Percy told me this morning before we left the house. He wanted to be assured of Harry's character since his child would have been associating with the families – now don't become angry with *him*. His concern was mainly for his daughter, as it should be. Apparently, John is very anxious that his daughter be cared for, in case some calamity should befall him; he wanted to be assured that she would be safe, and loved."

"I'm not angry with him, merely surprised. He never said a word to me about knowing the truth. Well, he was right to be suspicious as it turns out, wasn't he, and what right do I have to be upset? Oh, such a coil this has become. Harry will be furious with me, of that I'm certain; after all, I'm hampering his carefully crafted plan aren't I? But, just let him say anything, I'll give our Mr. Penrod an earful that will turn the air blue! In fact I hope he does confront me!"

"Harry? You don't really believe he'll be that angry, Alice, do you?" A niggling of concern began to churn up Darcy's stomach. "Harry was devious, of course, but in his soul he's a gentleman, serious, gracious, quiet..."

"Harry Penrod?" She looked at her father with near pity. "It continually amazes how little you parents know of us children. Harry is an unbending, stubborn, single minded man with a temper that rivals Uncle Fitz's. I have thwarted his plans, father. Of course he will be angry – he'll be furious! I can hardly wait."

Chapter Forty-Nine

A few coaches still lined the square outside, drivers picking up their masters to bring to the Fitzwilliam home for the wedding breakfast. Alice drew her father to the side, her eyes filling with tears again. The idea of the wedding festivities ahead was suddenly abhorrent to her; she dreaded facing family friends and relatives on her own, answering their questions. "Papa, I have a terrible headache. Would it possibly be all right if I just went home? You could express my deepest regrets to George and Kathy for me, but let's not spoil their day, please."

Seeing her so troubled grieved Darcy; he immediately agreed. "Of course, Alice; if you're certain you'll be all right. I'll explain to your mother what's happened and give your apologies to the others." He kissed her forehead, both with love and to feel for fever. There was none physically, but her heart was obviously in pain. "You go home and rest and your mother and I will be there as soon as possible."

"No need to rush on my account; stay and enjoy yourselves. I just need some time alone before the family discovers the truth and descends upon me."

Darcy motioned for his coachman. "Dram, take Miss Alice home, would you please? I'll ride along with Mark and Andrew to the Breakfast. They have room for one more in that carriage, I'm certain." He kissed his daughter's forehead again and handed her into the coach.

Home at last Alice gave way to her tears, luxuriated in them – wallowed in them. She removed her lovely gown and washed her face, her maid brushed out her hair. She then paced her room barefoot, wearing only her favorite old robe. Gone was all the finery and ribbons, all the pretence. She was stripped of all the allurements of a great London beauty, preferring to be plain Little Alice once again, wishing to go back in time to the days when her life was not so complicated – before men. Soon though she grew weary of her own misery and crawled into bed. She slept immediately and deeply, awakening an unknown while later with a start for some reason, the house eerily quiet.

A loud crash from somewhere in the house broke the stillness. Alice leapt from the bed, grabbed her robe and hastily tied the sash, opening her bedroom door to listen since she could never hear anything when the extra thick, mahogany doors her Father had insisted upon installing throughout the house were closed. She peeked into her sitting room, walked to that door, opened it a crack and listened again. Nothing at first, then there was shouting coming from the stairs and the sound of heavy footsteps.

"Alice Darcy!" An angry shout came from the hall. "Alice Darcy show yourself!"

"Harry?" She barely got the word out when he was there, pushing her door open.

"Where is he?"

"What is the meaning of this? How dare you come barging into my sitting room in this manner!"

"How should I come barging into your sitting room? How does Sir Bloody John Percy come barging into your sitting room?" Harry began a tear around the room, yanking aside draperies, looking behind the settee and chairs, opening and then slamming her many wardrobe doors. "The front door is locked tight; he won't escape me." Alice stepped back from him, staring on in astonishment as he began to advance toward her.

"You've gone mad. I suspected it would happen one day, but not so soon. I'd hoped you could at least reach your forties." She turned to run, thinking to escape into her bedroom but he caught her by the wrist. She wriggled wildly, but he was too strong as he pulled her hard against his chest.

"Where is he?" Harry demanded once again.

"Who?" She struggled against his grip.

Her hair was mussed and wild looking and he could see she was naked as the robe she wore parted slightly. His heart was pounding.

"That bastard! Where is he?" He shouted again. *"I'll kill him!"*

"Harry, stop this – let me go!" She wriggled and fought then finally kicked his leg.

"Ow! Why did you do that?" He released her immediately and grabbed for his shin. "That hurt."

"You must be joking! You barge into my room and grab me, all the while screaming about some man being here! Again I ask you, what man?!"

"John Percy! I know he's here, Alice; I can see you've just come from bed! Cover yourself damn it! Have you no sense of decency? *And where in bloody hell is he?"*

When she looked down she saw that her robe had, indeed, gapped open, the tie almost coming undone. Pulling the dressing gown tighter she secured the sash then pointed to the door. "I must ask you to leave. It is the height of unsuitability for you to be here, alone with me like this!"

"Ha! As if anyone would think twice about me being alone with you in here! I've slept in here or don't you remember? Yes I did! I hid here when I was too drunk to go home and didn't wish my parents to see me – you didn't complain *then*, did you, *Miss Darcy*!"

"I was six years old, you baboon!" Shoulders back and chin up she had very nearly out shouted him. "And your sister Kathy was here, and Anne Marie – look at this, I've broken a nail now. And we braided your hair that night, while you slept." A smile twitched at her mouth. "That was during your 'long hair poet' phase, I believe. The 'Lord Byron' years."

"Oh be quiet..." Harry was making a complete examination of her bedroom, her parlor, her retiring room; he had checked beneath her bed, behind the chairs, the draperies to her balcony – there was nothing.

He was perplexed.

"He didn't leap from the window, did he? Gad, he must be more stupid than I thought, we're two stories high. I suppose he hit the veranda roof then slid into those bushes there."

"Harry, he was never here! Oh, please just go." She could hear yelling outside and then suddenly there was a deafening clanging sound coming from somewhere in the house. Everything was in chaos, her head was splitting. If she screamed for help no one would hear. "You know, I suddenly feel I'm about to vomit."

He turned her to face him.

"Are you with child?" he shouted above the din.

A shrieking Alice attacked him with her claws extended.

Chapter Fifty

"Alice?" Darcy shouted, thinking he heard his daughter's raised voice coming from within the house as he and Fitzwilliam came running up the front steps. Immediately he grabbed the knob, pushing hard against the door with his shoulder – but, it didn't budge. It was locked tight. Darcy stepped back and stared in astonishment. "Well, that's very odd," he began. "Winters doesn't usually keep..."

And that is when Darcy's latest toy, the most recent innovation in home security, an electro magnetic door alarm, engaged.

"Oh my God, what is that?" Fitzwilliam's hands flattened over his ears. *"Is someone skinning cats in there?"*

"Oh, quit making such a scene! I'll have you know that is the newest advance in home protection from *New York*, an alarm that alerts the staff if someone attempts to break in. It's activated at night – however, there are a few glitches, it doesn't always disengage properly. I never know when..."

"I can't hear a damn thing you're saying! There's some sort of alarm going off!"

"All right, all right! Stand aside. Damn, which of these is the proper house key, do you remember?"

"Why don't you use one of those keys? Don't bother to answer me; I can't hear a thing – I believe I've gone deaf from that fucking alarm!"

It was no use, not one key worked; Darcy angrily threw them all to the side and began shouting and pounding on the door. His magnificent entrance to Pemberley was impenetrable, as it was meant to be.

Then suddenly, miraculously, all was quiet – the alarm within having died of natural causes, or having been shot. Darcy called out his butler's name several more times before Winters finally answered, "I'm on my way, sir." Darcy groaned. It would take a while for his aged butler's customarily slow walk across the marble foyer to answer the door. "Won't be but a moment."

Another crash and loud cursing was heard from upstairs. "Alice, is that you?" Darcy yelled, staring up at the second floor once again.

"Of course it's her you idiot. Vendors across the street can hear it's her." Fitzwilliam tapped his foot impatiently as they waited. "All of Mayfair can hear it's her. The problem is *she* can't hear *us* over all that caterwauling!"

"I have just about had it with you! I don't know why I allowed you to come here with me!"

"Allowed me! You dragged me from my horse – I would've been here ten minutes sooner than this!"

"Be still. I can't hear what's going on up there."

"I'm here, sir. I had to silence that alarm before the neighbor sent for a runner again," Winters shouted from inside. "It's been going off periodically all morning. Very vexing." The butler mumbled as he began the confusing and intricate process of unlocking the door. "I don't know why the door is locked, sir. So sorry. Although I had thought I heard someone come in a bit ago; however, by the time I arrived the door was closed, and..." The arthritic fingers were slow to grip the handle.

"For heavens sake pension the poor old chap off, Darcy; let him rest in the country, at Pemberley. He's not a serf you know."

"I *have* tried to retire him but he nearly burst into tears the last time I brought it up! Ah, here he is..." The door was just opening when Darcy and Fitzwilliam pushed passed the elderly man and ran up the stairs.

"I know about you and Percy, Alice, and I am quite disappointed in you. Shocked, in fact. I forbid this from going any further!"

"*You* forbid it? *You*? You, who are without a doubt the most pig headed, insufferable, imbecilic idiot I have ever known – and I say this with full knowledge that we share several relatives in common who would give you a good, honest contest for that title – *you* forbid it!" Her voice suddenly broke in a sob. "Oh, Harry, how could you?" The sob soon manifested into a full blown wail. "Do my feelings mean that little to you? Do *I* mean that little to you?"

"Stop crying!" demanded Harry. "I can't think when you cry like this!"

"It's the only way I know how to cry," she wailed anew.

"She's crying, Fitzwilliam. It's faint but I swear I can hear her weeping." Darcy and Fitzwilliam had finally reached the top landing and were both gasping for breath.

"He won't hurt her Darcy, I know he won't. This is all just a misunderstanding."

"*What* is a misunderstanding? No one has explained anything to me yet!"

"The boy's in love with her!"

"In love? Well, he has a fine way of showing it, shouting at her."

When they reached Alice's sitting room Darcy tried unsuccessfully to turn the knob then shoved the door with his shoulder. "It's locked," he growled, pressing his ear to the door. Oddly enough, he could hear less of what was going on inside that room now than when they had stood outside. For a moment, Darcy was peculiarly pleased with the solid craftsmanship of the thing.

He rapped twice. "Alice, open this door if you please. Alice? Alice, I will count to ten and if..."

"Darcy, stand aside." Fitzwilliam nudged his cousin, replacing the man's polite door rap with a pounding fist. "Harold! I know you're in there. Come out at once. Do you hear me? Harold! Come out or I'll beat you senseless!"

When Fitzwilliam turned he saw Darcy staring in disbelief. "Beat him senseless? Really Fitzwilliam? The man is nearly thirty years your junior and has the muscles of a blacksmith. He'd kill you. Now sit down, you look as if your eyes are going to explode."

"I could best him," Fitzwilliam already out of breath began to cough. "Bloody hell, I believe I *will* sit down for just a moment. I wish we'd eaten before leaving the breakfast, I'm feeling rather pecky with all this exertion. That braised pork looked exceptional today. I dearly love those coddled eggs as well, cook makes them just the way I like with buttered toast tips." Taking a handkerchief from his pocket he wiped the sweat from his brow. "It's stifling as hell up here. Why did you never install windows at the ends of these hallways, brat? At least we'd have some sort of cross ventilation."

"Oddly enough, Fitz, I had not foreseen this particular incident occurring in our future." Darcy pressed his ear to the door once again. "They *are* shouting, but it's very faint." A hint of color touched his cheeks. "They must be in her bedroom. Damn me. Alice! Alice Darcy you come out this moment! I am still your father, you must obey me!"

"I still don't quite understand what happened – one moment he was teasing his brother Luke then the next moment he was sailing out the door like a man gone mad. You were standing there, Darcy. What did you say to upset him?"

"*Me!* Well, of all the cheek! I'll have you know that your son is a bit of a hot head, if you haven't realized that already. He forced my daughter to..."

"Forced! My son! How dare you! My Harry is a gentleman! He has no need to force a woman for any reason. They adore him, swoon in his presence. I should call you out for that!"

"*You can't do that though, can you, so stop saying it!* It never made any sense whatsoever. I'm your second and you're mine. You can't *duel* with your own second. Now, what else can we try to get this door open?"

"Alice, please stop crying. It's just that thinking of you lying with that man..." He had gripped her arms and was staring intently into her baffled eyes.

"Pardon me?" Her sobs sputtered to a stop. "Harry, what are you talking about?"

"I've heard all the lurid details from your father – about how passionate you and Percy are with each other!"

"*My* father told you that?"

"Well, not directly. He told my father," Harry nodded as he spoke, supplying his own verification, "... and my father was pretty shocked."

"I don't believe it." She pressed her hands over her blushing cheeks. "You're all mad as monkeys."

"We're men, Alice."

"Precisely what I said!"

He glared at her. "What I mean to say is that as men we must uphold the honor of our families."

"Harry," Alice began, touched that he had come thinking to defend her perfectly intact honor. "I am not John's lover, not now and not ever. In fact, I have something to tell you, something you won't like at all. John and I have parted ways."

Harry went very still. "What did you say?"

"The betrothal is over."

"You've broken it off with him?"

"Yes. I'm very sorry, Harry. I know you wanted me to marry him but I cannot, I just don't love him. I realized it was impossible...I couldn't enter into marriage with one man when my heart wanted another."

Almost before she could finish speaking he had pulled her tightly into his arms. "Alice," he whispered his mouth so close to hers. "Alice, tell me it's not too late – tell me I haven't destroyed us completely. Alice..."

He repeated her name over and over as he kissed her mouth, her ears, her neck. His hands slid up into her hair, holding her still so that she couldn't escape even if she wanted. "I love you. I love you so much." Returning his lips to her mouth, he kissed her deeply, passionately, ending it all off with a gentle squeeze on her bottom that made her heart pound and her knees weaken. "Say it to me, Alice. Tell me you love me still. Please."

She stared, dazed and happy, up into the face she had known forever. "I love you, Harry. I have always loved you; and, I will go on loving you until the day I die."

"I hate you!" Fitzwilliam shook his fist at the obdurate portal. He turned to his cousin. "All right, on the count of three, Darcy – together we can do this; we'll slam our shoulders into this door and knock the bastard down." Both had removed their jackets and rolled up their sleeves. "Are you ready?"

Darcy nodded.

"One, two, three..." The two men rammed their shoulders into the door.

"*Oh my God!*" Fitzwilliam shrieked, holding onto his shoulder. "*Bloody hell!* I think I've broken something."

Darcy ignored his cousin's ravings. He planted his fists upon his hips, furious with himself, with his own body's limitations and frustrated with fear, his breathing labored.

"Mr. Darcy?" It was a hesitant Mrs. Winters, his London housekeeper and the old butler's wife of fifty years. "Whatever is going on, sir? Why, I could hear you both from a block away; the servants are returning from their holiday and hiding down below, many are crying! What has happened?"

"Excellent. Mrs. Winters, send someone immediately to my blacksmith to fetch crowbars and hammers. Meanwhile, have Mr. Winters gather all of the footmen up here." He turned to study the door further. "We'll need at least four men to knock this down, perhaps more. What do you think, Fitz? Fitz?"

Fitzwilliam was sprawled across hallway floor, rubbing his shoulder; his eyes were slits of incandescent fury. "Give me an ax and I'll take care of the bloody thing myself!"

"If all you wanted was to open the door, sir, well...couldn't I just bring the key?"

Fitzwilliam was still in agony, still holding onto his shoulder – however, he did manage a very commendable swing, the first of which Darcy was just able to duck.

He kissed the tip of her nose then slowly went down on one knee. Alice began to lower herself to one knee as well. "No. No, sweeting...no." He stood and gently pulled her upright. "I believe this bit is mine alone."

Comprehending finally what he was about Alice squealed with joy. She began to bounce in place and to laugh and sob at once. "Oh my heavens, Harry, oh my goodness! I do so wish we had witnesses for this."

"Be still. Do you have a cushion or something – oh, that's lovely, thank you." After Alice had yanked several pillows from her bed and tossed them on the floor before him, he knelt on one knee and took her hand, once again. "Alice Darcy, I love you more than anyone or anything else in this world. You are my morning star, my evening rest, my heart and my soul. Alice Darcy, will you marry me?"

Unable to produce a sound she nodded her answer.

"Are you certain?" he asked, his heart pounding with joy in his chest.

"Yes, Harry, oh yes!" She finally blurted out.

"Thank the lord." With a whoop she leapt into his arms and they tumbled backward onto the pillows, laughing and rolling to and fro on the floor, only slowing down when his heated gaze took in her shining eyes, her moist lips. He could feel her warm body pressed against him, recalling suddenly that she was undressed beneath the thin cotton robe.

His arousal was instantaneous.

He rolled over once more until she was beneath him then pressed his lips to her lips, open mouthed and hungry for her. A passion as she had never known before responded to him immediately and they were lost.

Chapter Fifty-One

"Do you hear something?" She stiffened, her back already arched. "Harry?"

"Pardon...what...?" He was confused for a moment, his mind a cloud of lust and disoriented.

"I thought I heard...! That sounds like Uncle Fitz — that *is* Uncle Fitz, swearing! *Oh no! My father*! Harry, hurry! Button your pants! Find my nightrobe!"

By the time Mrs. Winters had returned with the key to Alice's dressing room a handful of servants had gathered in the hallway. Darcy and Fitzwilliam burst into the outer room just as Harry and Alice emerged from her bedroom. The four stood staring at each other in astonished silence while Mrs. Winters, evaluating the situation much faster than the two fathers, turned to the curious onlookers and motioned them outside, closing the door softly behind her as she left.

The first thing Darcy noticed was his daughter's hair in wild disarray, then he saw that her robe was pulled out of alignment and her lips appeared to be swollen and thoroughly kissed.

The first thing Fitzwilliam noticed with regard to his son Harry was the boy's apparent struggle to pull his shirt over trousers which were still bulging.

"Bloody hell," Fitz grunted.

"Fitzwilliam?"

"Darcy..."

"Alice?"

"Father."

"Harry?"

"Papa."

"Uncle Wills."

"Uncle Fitz."

Both fathers began shouting in unison. "What is going on here...?" "We want explanations...!"

"Let me speak first, please," Harry's shout carried over their shouts. The two fathers immediately fell quiet.

"Thank you." Harry lifted Alice's hand in his. "Uncle Wills, I request the honor of your daughter's hand in marriage. I think you both should know that Alice and I wish to be married as quickly as possible."

"I should think you bloody well better!" barked Fitzwilliam.

"Uncle Fitz, nothing has happened, not really." Alice somehow looked both guilty and insulted at once.

"Not quite at any rate," muttered Harry.

"Alice?" Darcy looked questioningly at his youngest. "Is this what you truly want, child?"

"Yes, father. Oh, yes. I love him very much." She smiled up into Harry's adoring gaze.

"Uncle Wills, I love her even more. I adore her, worship her, her eyes, her mouth, her..."

"Enough – please no more details. If this is truly what she wants, that's all that matters to me. I am happy for you both. What about you, Fitz? What do you say?"

"I think they'll do well for each other. They're both insane."

"Then we have your blessings?" asked Harry, his arms wrapping around her waist, bringing her back up against him,

"Yes, I suppose you have mine. What about you, Darcy?"

She was glowing, this child of his, and radiating happiness like never before. "Yes, of course, I give you both my blessings."

The four then came together and everyone began to hug and kiss. Happy tears betrayed manly faces.

Alice was still laughing when she suddenly noticed her father was favoring his shoulder. "Father, are you all right? Oh no, how did you tear your shirt?"

"I'm fine, just the victim of another idiotic Fitzwilliam plan." He looked meaningfully toward Fitzwilliam who glared back.

"Let me have a look at that. I'll have your valet bring you another shirt; Mary can sew this tear before it gets worse."

Harry studied his own father's face. "You're looking a bit rough. And why are you limping? It's those boots again isn't it? I'll have to get you to a decent cobbler; I have just the man that can help."

"Excellent, Harry, thank you. You don't suppose I could get some eggs, do you, son? I like coddled."

"Yes. I know. Did you eat this morning? Oh, Father, you should have eaten before you came here – you always get wobbly without a proper breakfast." Harry rang for a servant and while he waited he watched Alice see to their fathers' comfort. She poured some water for both then she spoke with the servant who arrived and specified what foods could be served that would not upset older digestions. Tea had also been brought in and she was now pouring.

They were tending to their fathers as if they were the parents now, and Harry smiled supposing that that was just the natural progression of life.

"What puts that smile on your face, Harry Penrod?" Alice came to his side as they watched the valet bring a new shirt for Darcy and take away the old, the other servants setting up a small table before the fireplace then bringing in and serving the biscuits and eggs, ham and toast.

For their part Darcy and Fitzwilliam – lifelong best friends, loving cousins and brutal competitors – were grousing at each other and laughing, often at the same time.

He loved those two men fiercely, with all of his heart; and, he loved his lovely Little Alice more than life itself.

"Harry, did you hear me? What are you grinning about?"

"Oh, nothing much, only that I absolutely adore you." He kissed her temple then wrapped her in his arms and whispered in her ear, "...and that birthmark on your bottom – it really does look like a frog, you know."

Epilogue

1842

Darcy waited in his slippers and robe outside the Pemberley nursery. It was one in the morning; the house was quiet, still. He checked his pocket watch and wondered, not for the first time, why a man would really need to carry a pocket watch around with him in his robe. Perhaps Lizzy was right (yet again). Perhaps he was a bit too intense. Perhaps he should begin thinking of relaxing a bit, leave the day to day worries to his son.

He heard the sound of boots clacking down the hallway, coming from the east wing, and winced at the noise. That racket could wake the entire household, let alone the very important gentleman he was about to visit. Fitzwilliam came into view.

"Could you please be a little quieter?" Darcy hissed. "Why in hell are you wearing boots anyway? Don't you own slippers?"

"Yes, I own slippers, brat!" Fitzwilliam hissed back. "They are beneath my bed, at Somerton. We left in such a hurry yesterday, in the middle of the night I might add, that I had to pack my own valise and I forgot! Amanda was shouting from the carriage for me to hurry five minutes after your footman arrived."

As Fitzwilliam approached Darcy stood, his hand on the nursery door handle. "Did you bring the bottle?"

Fitzwilliam smiled. "Definitely. Oddly enough I forgot the slippers, but I remembered the cognac." They entered the room.

A sleepy nurse stood as sentry before the large white cradle. Generations of Fitzwilliam children had lain in that cradle. Darcy had, as had his father before him, and his three children after him; Richard had occupied the ancient bed as well, as had all of his children... "You may go, Nurse," Darcy calmly dismissed her. "We shall call you back when we are finished."

She looked at them both strangely. "Oh, I don't think my Master would appreciate me leavin' the tyke – and at this time of the mornin'. This is all very odd."

"Nurse, between my cousin and I we have twelve children. I don't believe we shall do any harm here. I'll explain it all to my son if he should awaken and come in."

"...well, I still don't like this..."

"Get out!" Fitzwilliam hissed and the woman ran from the room.

Darcy looked at his cousin then cocked his brow at him "Was that really necessary?"

"Yes, it was if we wanted to get rid of her; I'd like to get some sleep tonight. And put your brow down. It's going to stay that way one of these days."

He was the most beautiful child ever born to woman and the two grandfathers stared with wonder at the pink cheeks and porcelain skin, the tulip mouth. He was so small, so vulnerable.

"Who does he look like do you think? Did you notice he has a very pronounced chin – not unlike my own?" Richard stood on one side of the huge Fitzwilliam cradle while Darcy stood on the other.

"He also has a pinched head still, another feature of yours. Thankfully, he'll grow out of that one. I think he has George's eyes, don't you? He certainly has his feet – look at these." Darcy pulled back the tiny yellow blanket and gently palmed the little foot. "He has Kathy's nose, though, and her lung capacity. Heavens he can scream."

Fitzwilliam laughed, ran his knuckle gently long the baby's cheek. "He's absolutely perfect, you know. A tiny god and we're all here worshipping in wonder."

"Makes one feel a little immortal to see your child's child; it's almost as if you can see into eternity."

"Makes me just feel old to tell you the truth. Darcy, did you ever imagine we'd be this old?"

Darcy grinned and shook his head. "Never. Pour out the cognac."

"Right you are." Fitzwilliam picked up the old bottle and poured out two drinks, handing one to Darcy and picking up the other for himself. "A fine idea of yours, this."

When the two cousins had been young hell raisers, just out of university and making their grand tour of Europe, they purchased the most expensive bottle of Cognac they could find in all of France. The idea was that they would save the bottle for their old age, the survivor toasting the first of them to die, and getting good and foxed in the bargain.

"Well, this is better – to toast life, not death – to toast our first grandchild. Oh what will he see in his lifetime, Fitzwilliam? If only we could be there with him. What sort of world will he grow into?"

"I pray it's a world of harmony and good will; but, humankind being as it is, that's highly doubtful."

"Well, let's have our toast then. "To our first grandchild – Fitzwilliam Darcy, II!"

They clinked glasses and looked down at the little child between them.

Darcy spoke first. "To his having a long and healthy life, to his finding rewarding work, to his marrying as good a woman as his grandmothers are."

"To a future without any wars that need him."

"To our grandson – Fitzwilliam Darcy II."

The End

.